The Day She Died

Kat K

First published in 2025by Blossom Spring Publishing
The Day She Died Copyright © 2025 Kat K
ISBN 978-1-917938-16-7
E: admin@blossomspringpublishing.com
W: www.blossomspringpublishing.com

Chapter 1

The coffee had gotten cold.

Sara May Jensen stared at the empty document on her bright computer screen. It was waiting to be filled with distinguished words that would eventually charm the trousers off the unsuspecting reader. But no matter how hard she wished, the words wouldn't write themselves. She sighed in defeat, stepped away from the computer for the ninth time that day, and poured the cold coffee into the kitchen sink. Instead of returning to her desk and giving it another try, she plopped down on the old, worn-out sofa she had bought for six quid at a flea market eight years earlier. From there, she had a good view out the living room window. The sun shone and warmed everything in sight like a loving mother cradling her newborn. She knew she should be soaking up the sunshine; it would soon become an ancient myth when the merciless Nordic winter unleashed its wrath upon all things still living on this godforsaken island in the north. She just needed the strength to get up and go outside.

She didn't know when things had started to decline so quickly. She was thirty-one, and apart from some minor achievements, she hadn't accomplished much. She lacked focus and determination. She wasn't where she had always imagined herself being at this age, and it was beginning to affect her mental health. She'd never been an outstanding student, but she never worried about it because she had decided on her destiny long before the boredom of studying got the best of her. It shouldn't have mattered that she dropped out of high school, let alone graduated from some fancy university. It shouldn't have mattered because she believed she had a secret talent. She was the undiscovered superstar of the literary world. All she had to do was wait for the right moment, and then the story that would change everything would write itself. Consequently, someone would discover her masterpiece by sheer luck and offer her a lucrative book deal. After that, life would be filled with chocolates and roses, wrapped in the eternal glory of fame and fortune.

Time had passed, but not much had changed. No husband, no children. No university degrees, no career. Nobody had suddenly offered her the golden contract. Life was merely a series of tempting dreams and an ego too big for her own good. The TV interviews, radio appearances, podcasts, and endless invitations to the most glamorous parties should have been flooding her inbox by now, as if on a lavish conveyor belt. Her name was meant to be on everyone's lips. As soon as the right story emerged, people would become obsessed with it. But like any story, it had to be engaging. The beginning was easy. She had sat down countless times and started typing, driven by the allure of everlasting fame. The ending was even easier. It was bathed in the beckoning success that would follow. Yet somewhere in the middle, her mind started to drift. The interest disappeared as if it had never existed, and before she realised, she was back on the old, battered sofa, staring out the living room window.

With nothing to show for each passing year, she'd started doubting herself increasingly. She questioned whether she truly was what she believed herself to be. Was she an author or just someone wishing to be one? She had never published anything. She had never even finished anything. She wasn't short on ideas, only the ability to get them out of her head and onto paper. Numerous videos online hadn't taught her much. Self-help classes hadn't either. She´d even gone so far as to pay for a ridiculous lecture on positive thinking, where she spent two long hours in a dark hall listening to a twenty-three-year-old influencer, who seemed to have life all figured out, preach about how positive thoughts and good vibes could turn the miserable losers in the audience from failed deadbeats to successful CEO's only if they thought positively and paid enough money.

She tied her unwashed hair into a messy bun and grabbed her phone from the coffee table. Wearing her favourite grease-stained vest and ripped denim jeans, she lay on the sofa like an expired tin of beans and immersed herself in other people's digital lives. That was her heroin. She knew it didn't do her any good, yet she couldn't look away. How could everybody be so goddamned perfect? Alice, her old co-worker, was back home from her third trip abroad with the gang, her husband, and four kids, all looking annoyingly tanned and gorgeous. And there was Ethan, her old high school classmate, who had graduated with a doctorate in medicine from a Swedish university, standing next to the blonde bimbo he'd married. Engagement and pregnancy announcements flooded her newsfeed with countless posts about how great life was. Not to mention all the pictures of the perfect little Instagram homes taking over the market. It seemed you couldn't count it as a home unless it was deprived of anything remotely indicating that someone actually lived there. It was like the nation had suddenly suffered a collective breakdown and exchanged their actual homes for showrooms in IKEA.

She stared at the mountain of dirty dishes in her kitchen sink, which had been piling up for about a week. Not washing up until she had no dishes or cutlery left had become an unpleasant routine that she managed much better than writing five pages a day. The laundry pile in the bedroom had been there for about a month, and the bananas on the kitchen counter never stood a chance. Her flat was so filthy that there wasn't enough detergent in the country to save it. She'd been renting it at a fair price for the last four years and had grown to love it. It was comfortable and, some might say, even a little charming in its own gross way. It was one of four flats in an old wooden house on the outskirts of Iceland's capital, Reykjavik. Eccentric loners occupied the other three flats; she didn't care enough about them to get to know them properly. Susan, the old lady above her, was the worst kind of curtain twitcher, always sticking her nose into other people's business. She was the self-appointed guardian of morality and common courtesy, never running out of things that offended her. She shamelessly judged her young neighbour's sinful lifestyle and questionable choices more than once, especially if she dared to bring home a dubious gentleman of the night after too many pints at the pub.

You need Jesus! she commonly scolded from the floor above. Over time, Sara May learned to ignore it, which usually caused the old hag to back off. Things only escalated if Magnus, the old geezer in the flat across from Susan, got involved. The two argued until one of them gave way and slammed their front door shut, giving Sara May a moment to escape. She checked her watch. It was nearly four in the afternoon. As expected, the shouting in the hallway began again. Accusations flew back and forth with no clear end or real purpose behind them. Sara May wondered why Cooper, the young stoner living in the flat opposite hers, hadn't said anything or at least taken a side in this pointless argument. Maybe he was just too spaced out to care. The man had the brains of a tree stump; that was all she knew about him. Finally, she stood up from the sofa and stretched her arms and legs. Every bone in her body cracked like a glowstick. The fact that they didn't actually glow afterwards was one of life's cruel jokes. She had an hour to get ready and head off to work. With her back aching and her feet hurting, she was tempted to wallow in this pathetic self-pity and call in sick. Maybe yoga wasn't such a bad idea.

She buttoned up her cream-coloured jacket and braced herself to face the freezing September cold. The weather was lovely—frosty but calm. The stars spread across the evening sky like a net stretched over the entire city. But as beautiful as this scenery was, she had forgotten the one thing that characterised the capital during this dark time of year: the grey, slushy snow covered nearly every square foot of the city, terrorising innocent pedestrians. She hated this raw, nasty version of what would otherwise be a beautiful aspect of the Nordic winter and often dreamed of the Swiss Alps' heavenly, white, powdery snow. But until such a dream materialised, she would have to make do with this dreadful excuse for snow. Venturing out of one's home during this time of year was an act of incredible bravery. The relentless frost would bite into every cheek that dared to show itself outside, and the icy pavements, camouflaged with muddy snow, showed no mercy.

The walk through the muddy mess had led her to the high street in the city, which, as usual, was teeming with all sorts of people. Confused tourists tried to use Google Translate to understand the complicated street signs and restaurant names around them. There were also some locals rushing to get somewhere. She never understood why Icelanders were always in a rush, always so busy pretending to be busy. And, of course, groups of teenagers stayed out past their curfew, defying their parents' rules and taking advantage of whatever Friday night offered them. She remembered those days fondly. It had been a long time since she strolled down the high street. She didn't particularly enjoy shopping, as shops were usually crowded with noisy people, and she didn't care much for the hustle and bustle of city life. But it beat living in the cramped old town where she grew up. Just thinking about that place gave her the creeps. She was just as lonely in the city as she had been in her childhood town; it was just different. Being lonely in a city full of people was remarkably easy, yet she only had herself to blame for it. She never showed any interest in getting to know people. At best, she was described as an oddball. Over time, she convinced herself that being solitary was how all true artists operated. Writers, in particular. They were eccentrics, different from the rest, like a dusty old abstract painting that couldn't bear to see the light of day. True artists were like domestic cats, lost in the haze of cigarette smoke, consumed by their own brilliance. They didn't need human contact; it would only disturb their creative flow. By telling herself this, she managed to justify her dislike of social interactions. It was how she managed to survive her miserable existence every day.

Chapter 2

"Sara May, we need more cutlery!" Mr. Grant's baritone voice roared angrily through the entire kitchen.

"I'm on it!" she shouted back.

She threw a handful of dirty knives and forks into the ever-growing pile in the sink, rinsed it down, and tried to be as quick as possible without breaking anything. She couldn't afford to break any more dishes; Mr. Grant's patience towards her was already stretched to the limit. He'd only hired her because his daughter Paige had, at some point, decided that the two of them were best friends, and she had convinced her father that Sara May was a great employee. In the two years since then, Sara May had far from lived up to the promised expectations, and after breaking four plates in one month, her bright future as a kitchen porter depended solely on his kindness.

"Sara May, is the cutlery ready?" Paige asked impatiently.

"Here, take this," Sara May replied, handing her friend a bundle of newly washed knives and forks.

"Dad is so stressed. I hate it when he gets like this."

"He bloody knew it'd be busy tonight, but nobody told me! I'm on my last leg here!"

"If he starts getting nasty, don't take it to heart. You know how he is."

"Sara May, the cutlery!" Mr. Grant howled once again, sounding even more threatening than before.

Paige shuffled more cutlery onto her tray and hurried back into the main hall. Sara May stared at the pile of dirty plates and glasses beside the sink, which looked even more like Everest than the one she had just finished washing. Usually, there were two of them in the kitchen, but Tommy seemed to suffer from a mysterious illness that constantly affected him on Fridays and Saturdays, causing him to call in sick. Nobody knew exactly what was wrong with him, but the symptoms strongly suggested a severe hangover combined with an intolerance to too much pressure. Usually, she ignored it. Mr. Grant threatened to fire him every week, so trying to get him to follow up was a waste of time and effort. But she couldn't help but curse out the scrawny little bastard on nights like these. Why couldn't the lazy, slow-witted idiot just turn up and do his job like everyone else? Mitchell, the head chef, wasn't much help either. He just stood about picking his nose while his sous-chefs sweated their guts out, preparing food in the steamy kitchen that looked more like a sauna at this point.

Finally, the clock struck ten, and Mr. Grant flipped the Open sign to Closed. Those who had neither the will nor the strength to stay a moment longer hurried out faster than rockets on New Year's. The rest closed up and cleaned the place until it was spotless. Mr. Grant habitually was the last to leave, like a proud captain of a sinking ship. His habit had ensured the success of his restaurant for the past forty-five years. The place had long become a familiar part of city dwellers' lives, who occasionally treated themselves to finer things. Mr. Grant and his wife, Sylvia, had built a strong reputation on the island's restaurant scene over those years. They were known to be hardworking, honest, and kind, always ensuring their customers had the most rewarding experience. They now owned seven restaurants nationwide. Sylvia mostly managed them, as Mr. Grant preferred to focus all his energy on his flagship in the city centre, which he had run successfully from the start, earning a loyal customer base that grew each day.

"You all did well tonight. Sara May, sorry about the yelling."

"No worries, I'm used to it." Mr. Grant gave her a quick smile before continuing.

"It's going to be just as crazy tomorrow. We are expecting a group of approximately thirty tourists participating in the *Golden Circle* package, and they would like to add a food-tasting experience to their itinerary. So, we need to set the bar high; we don't want these people thinking we eat nothing but damn sheep heads and rotten sharks like some bloody savages!"

The staff chuckled softly. There was no way to tell if Mr. Grant was joking; the man held the Guinness World Record for speaking flatly, surpassing even the world's most skilled poker players.

"Mitchell, we're going to add a few items to the menu; I'll send you the list of ingredients later. Sara May, I'll drag Tommy here by the balls if he thinks he can skip out on another night. Paige, are the waiters all set for tomorrow? Paige nodded. "Good. Then I'll see you all here tomorrow night at five, ready to go! Thanks, everyone!"

"Sara May, are you going home?" asked Paige as the crowd dispersed.

"That was the plan, yes," she replied, putting on her coat.

"I was thinking of going down to Mackie's for a pint. You in?"

"Yeah, I deserve a cold one after tonight."

Paige smiled. Lately, it had become increasingly difficult to persuade Sara May to go out for a night on the town. Things had started to go downhill after they celebrated their thirtieth birthday, which hit them like a ton of bricks. Sara May had begun to prefer spending evenings at home, watching the telly instead of heading out for cocktails and gossip. She tried to justify it as a necessary isolation to enhance her creative mind. Something, she claimed, was essential for an artist of her calibre, even though she had never published anything in her life. The two friends hurried into the night. The city was buzzing with life this Saturday evening. Nothing quite compared to a nation eager for parties, longing to down a pint or two after a stressful week at work. There was something so charming about the nightlife on this tiny island. Those were the nights when pub-goers' deepest, darkest secrets would emerge after a few too many drinks. People took their feet off the brakes and let loose in manic joy that could end in many ways, giving Icelandic nightlife its appeal despite the occasional puddles of vomit.

Near midnight, the duo sat in a small candle-lit tavern in Reykjavik's city centre. At their age, the two friends appreciated the atmosphere of this tiny, well-hidden pub. The soothing jazz music was loud enough to be heard but quiet enough to be enjoyed, and the candles lit up the place with a calm, subdued glow, creating a warm and peaceful ambience. This was a place for those who didn't fancy loud techno music or elbow their way through crowds of sweaty strangers jumping around on a sticky dancefloor. This was a place for those who preferred sitting at a table, enjoying the relaxing tones of jazz while sipping on fine wine, in good company, and discussing poetry long into the night. Paige and Sara May felt they had reached an age where it seemed far more suitable to sit down for a drink or two in a quiet pub than to engage in a wet kiss with tomorrow's nameless regret. Sara May also believed it was more fitting for her image as a serious artist to be seen at such a classy establishment rather than a filthy nightclub.

"Man, it feels good to sit down. My legs are killing me!" Paige said as she rubbed her sore feet.

"You and me both. I'm telling you, if Tommy doesn't show up tomorrow, I'll ensure he never reproduces! Paige laughed.

"Maybe it's for the best. I don't think society can handle another Tommy running around."

Sara May smiled and took a sip of her pint. She hated to admit it, but she'd missed hanging out with Paige. She hadn't been trying to make new friends since moving to the city at eighteen, so the variety of possible drinking buddies was limited. But somehow, Paige had stuck with her from the very beginning, and for that, she was grateful. They enjoyed the same silly things, like binge-watching mindless reality TV shows on Sundays or staying up late debating whether a dessert stomach was an actual thing. Paige was simply the best, and Sara May couldn't imagine life without her. Sure, they could argue, sometimes so fiercely that even the Valkyries of Valhalla stayed away. But they always managed to make up in the end. Usually, all it took was driving around the city, eating ice cream, and blasting their favourite music loud enough for everyone to hear. That was their therapy.

"Have you given any thought to finding another job?" Paige asked.

"Yes and no." Sara May replied, running her fingers across the pint in her hand. "The kitchen is fine for now. Working nights is good for me because it allows me to write during the day."

"Come on! The kitchen is holding you back! You sleep until noon; when you wake up, you scroll through

Facebook and stare out the window. What kind of a life is that?"

"Jeez, thanks. You make me sound like a depressed drifter," Sara May replied, lowering her brows in frustration.

"Did you wear the white vest today? The one with the stain you can't get out?" Sara May scoffed.

"Yeah, so? It's my favourite T-shirt. Many artists have clothes they never take off; it's part of their creativity."

"When was the last time you wrote something? Come on, Sara May, stop kidding yourself; you're thirty-one years old! If you don't start planning for the future, you'll miss it, honestly."

"Who are you to preach, miss? "I work at my parents' restaurant." I know I'm no J.K. Rowling, but it's all I got! I don't have any plan B! And I judge myself for it plenty enough; you don't have to add to it!"

"I'm just saying it like it is. But it doesn't have to be that way!"

"You know what, I don't need this." Sara May quickly stood up from the table and put on her jacket.

"Oh, come on. I didn't mean it like that!" Paige begged, to no avail. Sara May stormed out the door, stomping her feet to ensure the entire tavern knew how insulted she was.

Paige sighed. This wasn't the first time they had argued over this topic. She should've known better. It was only getting more difficult as time went on, watching her best friend throw away her promising future just because she clung so tightly to a hopeless dream of becoming a famous writer. It was a foolish dream that belonged in the bin, and it hurt Paige deeply to see her friend bypass all the opportunities available to her so she could continue flirting with the illusion that she was about to make it. Sara May was incredibly talented, but could never put her talents to good use. She sighed once more and finished her pint.

Sara May hurried to the nearest bus stop. This lousy, below-the-belt jab from Paige had upset her even though she knew she was right. She'd been stuck in a rut for the last five years, if not longer, and she only seemed to sink deeper into the mud with each passing day. She was aware of all this and didn't like being reminded of it. On top of all this, she was carrying huge guilt for abandoning her best friend on a perfect night out, which she knew they both needed. Once again, she'd messed things up — not for the first time, and certainly not the last. She could feel tears welling up in her eyes as she quickened her pace. This had been a long and miserable day, no different from any other. She hated how often she found herself overwhelmed by feelings. Everything seemed to upset her, and when it did, she started overthinking until she was on the floor, crying hysterically.

This bottomless pit of emotions and thoughts was a mix of self-pity and self-loathing that she faced daily. It never led to anything good, but it was all she possessed. She struggled to manage it all, especially the feelings that seemed to flood her without warning every day. They suddenly burst through, overpowering her senses and her grasp on reality. This endless abyss of overwhelmingly complex emotions was about to send this seemingly ordinary Saturday evening down a terrifying path. Had she just taken a moment to observe her surroundings, she would have seen the car coming straight for her. She would have noticed the headlights. She would have heard the horn. Not even the shouts of those around her caught her attention. The only thing that pulled her out of her disastrous world of self-disgust was the searing pain that suddenly struck her out of nowhere, throwing her into the air, from where she then crashed to the ground hard, about twenty feet from the scene of the accident. She couldn't hear anything. She couldn't see anything. She only felt. She felt the paralysing pain shooting through her like a lightning bolt. She felt the fear that she had once again messed up, this time for good. Then, everything went black.

Chapter 3

Sara May slowly opened her eyes and looked around. At first, everything was foggy. When her eyes adjusted, she could see the outlines of tall buildings around her. They were all uniformly bright white with countless narrow windows, drained of all colour. It was as if she were standing in the middle of a foreign city created by someone who had given up halfway through. The buildings stood in a straight line, and in front of them were impeccably clean pavements decorated with white trees and benches, perfectly spaced apart. Between the two lines of buildings and pavements was a concrete road, unlike anything she had ever seen. There were no potholes, no speed bumps—nothing. It was just a silky smooth, light greyish street with no cars or traffic lights. She could only see two large, empty white trams moving back and forth down the street. Confused, she couldn't figure out where they came from or where they were headed. She looked around. Everything was so clean—no gum on the pavements or graffiti on the walls.

She checked herself. Aside from a minor headache, she felt nothing. Odd, she thought. Getting hit by a car and being thrown high into the air should have caused her excruciating pain. What was happening? Was she dreaming? Everything around her was shrouded in a pale white mist, devoid of colour. No matter how hard she tried, she couldn't pinpoint her location. Had she been hit so hard that they had to take her to a hospital abroad? When had she woken up and stepped outside? She couldn't remember. Was she all alone in a foreign city? She searched her pockets. Where was her phone? Did the hospital staff take it? Countless questions flooded her mind, but no answers came. Against her better judgement, she took a step forward but quickly realised she had no sense of movement. She couldn't feel herself moving at all, even though she was sure she was indeed walking.

None of this made any sense. At first, she didn't see any people either. But when she focused, she began to notice faint outlines that resembled human figures. *Strange*. Just like with the trams, she didn't know where they had come from or where they were heading. They all seemed to wear the same attire — milky-white robes that reminded her of the outfits commonly worn by men in the Middle East. Thin, cream-coloured ropes were tightly wrapped around their waists, probably to make this peculiar clothing more comfortable. She looked at their feet. They all wore white sandals, exposing their toes. She soon sensed that these people all had destinations. Some turned to the right, others to the left. Some headed south, while others moved north.

Slowly but surely, she realised she didn't perceive this place the same way as these strange people. It was as if a thin veil had been drawn between her and them. She could see through it, but she couldn't touch it. Those people seemed very much alive, yet at the same time, they felt so distant. As if they were just a figment of her imagination, she could hear their laughter, see their smiles, and even feel their happiness. But she couldn't get closer to them. She looked down at her hands. They were there, as white as ever. She'd never been one to get a tan. As a child, she convinced herself she was born to Irish parents and adopted by an Icelandic family. But although her hands were indeed white, they weren't as transparent as those of the people who walked all around her but didn't seem to notice her. She tried walking again, but with no success. She could feel herself move, but nothing around her changed. She looked for a way to tell time, but there was none—only some strange infinity. She didn't feel any pain. She wasn't hungry or thirsty. She felt nothing except the lightness of her being. If she managed to get moving, she would probably float into the mist-like air surrounding this strange place. So, maybe it was best not to move at all.

Suddenly, she saw a woman approach her. Despite being dressed just like everyone else, there was something different about her. She seemed more real, more of flesh and blood than the others. As she drew nearer, more details became visible. Her long, silky brown hair flowed freely down her back, swaying with each of her graceful movements. Her petite face was so delicate that not a single pore was visible. Her light pinkish lips complemented her hazel-brown eyes, reminding Sara May of two pieces of delicious Swiss chocolate. Her nose was slim, and her hands appeared as soft as cotton. Her slender waist added to her enchanting beauty, as if someone had applied a filter to this angelic creature, who seemed oblivious to her pure perfection. All around her was a warm, inviting light, bright at first but gradually fading as she drew closer.

"You are not supposed to be here, Sara May," the woman said softly but firmly.

"What do you mean?" Sara May replied hesitantly.

"You are not supposed to be here. You have to go back."

"I don't know where I am or how I got here. I don't know how to get back."

The woman smiled and extended her hand. Sara May

was sceptical, but suddenly, she felt an overwhelming urge to trust her. She took the woman's hand, and the surroundings changed instantly. Instead of tall white buildings and people dressed in white, there was nothing but a blue sky above and a flowery field below their feet, stretching as far as the eye could see. Sara May looked around, baffled. She had no memory of travelling to this place. She looked down and noticed she was barefoot. Surrounded by multi-coloured flowers so bright it was as if the sun shone from within each petal. The clear blue sky above resembled a loving mother's embrace protecting her offspring.

"You are not supposed to be here, Sara May," the woman repeated.

"I don't understand," Sara May replied. She was getting frustrated with these cryptic answers.

"It's not your time yet. You have a job to do," the woman revealed.

"What job?"

"Don't worry, my dear. We will be watching you."

"We who? Who are you?"

The woman smiled silently and moved closer to Sara May, who wanted to run away but couldn't move. Calmly, the woman placed her hand on her left shoulder. At that moment, Sara May felt as though she had been pushed down with immense force, like a train crashing into her at full speed. It made everything feel heavy and painful all at once. Then, once again, everything turned black.

Chapter 4

Sara May slowly opened her eyes and gasped. She felt the air fill her lungs, pulling her back to reality within seconds. Her body was heavy and stiff. Every nerve was aflame with searing pain, like they were being repeatedly pricked by a thousand needles. She sensed life rushing through her veins faster than ever before. Was this all just a dream? Or a nightmare, perhaps? Why was she so sweaty? She looked around but couldn't move. It was then she realised she was tied to a hospital bed with multiple cords and coloured wires all tangled together. They connected to monitors that emitted the most irritating sound. Beep, beep, beep. It was driving her mad! The lines on one of the screens moved rhythmically up and down, the numbers fluctuating, giving people a glimmer of hope that she wasn't completely dead yet. But for Sara May, this was nothing but a reminder that she'd been denied access to paradise.

"Are you finally awake?" a familiar voice asked.

Mum? What are you doing here? Sara May thought, still feeling too weak to speak.

"Oh, thank God! One more night in this Godforsaken dump, and I would've had myself committed to an insane asylum! And this is supposed to be the nation's capital! Shameful!" Aunt Marie jeered, filled with disgust as she looked out the window, overlooking the messy industrial area beside the hospital.

Aunt Marie was a woman of high social standing. A true bon vivant, she attracted attention wherever she went. Her demeanour was that of a dashing aristocratic lady who had long ago conquered the world and lived for nothing but the finest things. She was a true fashionista who enjoyed the finer aspects of life and was never seen wearing anything but the most stylish outfits, accessible only to those of the highest level of society. Through minor plastic surgeries and daily application of wrinkle cream, Aunt Marie didn't look a day over twenty-five. Or at least, that was what she convinced herself of, and no one dared to tell her otherwise.

Despite behaving like the blue-blooded noble she believed herself to be, Aunt Marie had chosen to live up north, close to her mother and sister. She made her fortune by marrying and divorcing naïve businessmen who were blinded by her beauty and allowed her malicious temptress to trick them into doomed marriages without any prenup. This enabled her to build her dream mansion, which now towered over the small town where she grew up, and gave her a chance to show off her tremendous wealth to all the envious people in town, as she so dismissively called them. Aunt Marie's lavish lifestyle did not go unnoticed. Just spending a few days in Reykjavik was more than she could handle. This pathetic attempt by a city to imitate the great metropolises of New York and Milan was, at best, laughable. No woman with an ounce of self-respect and heels in her Prada purse, just in case, would dare spend more than a weekend in this vile cesspit.

"Oh, Maggie, for Heaven's sake, call the nurse! The girl is awake; let's not dwell on it more than we already have!"

Maggie did as she was told. It had taken her years to free herself from her older sister's strong hold, and sometimes she still retreated. Sara May remained silent, unsure of what was happening. Why were her mum and aunt there? They hadn't visited her since she moved to the city thirteen years ago. She knew from experience this wasn't good. After a short while, a young, lively nurse with light hair tied in a bun answered the call. After performing all the necessary tests to confirm Sara May was alive and breathing, she turned to her and shone a light into her eyes to check her reflexes. When the light was about to permanently blind her, the nurse switched it off and put it back in her pocket.

"It looks like you're just about ready to go home. How are you feeling?" she asked, smiling from ear to ear.

"Who are you?" Sara May asked in confusion. The nurse laughed.

"My name is Erin. I have been one of the nurses caring for you for the last two weeks. Sara May was stunned.

"Two weeks? What the hell happened?"

"You got hit by a car. Pretty badly, actually. However, you appear to have escaped any serious injuries, as far as we can tell. You were put into a medically induced coma to avoid any swelling to the brain, and you responded well to the treatment you were given. I'd say your recovery has been nothing short of a miracle."

"That's wonderful! When can we take her home?" Aunt Marie asked, impatiently hovering around Erin. Unfazed by the pompous dowager's efforts to intimidate her with her closeness, Erin smiled reassuringly, which irritated Aunt Marie even more.

"The doctor would like to keep her here for a few more days just to make sure she doesn't relapse now that she's awake."

"A few more days? Are you kidding me? Don't you people have to clear the beds for some poor decaying bastards?"

"For God's sake, Marie!" Maggie frowned with embarrassment.

"It's so we can ensure she won't collapse once she's home. We only want the best for our patients," Erin replied thoughtfully. She was obviously used to dealing with people of all calibre.

"I swear, this is a conspiracy! You people are trying to kill me, forcing me to stay in this rat-infested swamp!" Aunt Marie yelled and stormed out of the room.

This was way too much for a condescending matron whose only crime was being incompatible with foulness and filth. As she rushed out of the room, accompanied by Nurse Erin, who had to attend to another call, Sara May couldn't help but feel sorry for the young woman who was only trying to be helpful. Trying to nurse everyone back to health while being poorly paid, overworked, and underappreciated couldn't be easy. Sara May looked at Maggie. At first, there was only silence. Despite her head being filled with endless questions, she wasn't eager to ask her mum any of them. She could never get the full truth out of her for some reason, so why bother? Just as she was about to lighten the mood with some small talk, another nurse entered the room. Her long, silky brown hair fell freely down her back, and her light pinkish lips complemented her hazel-brown eyes, which resembled two pieces of Swiss chocolate. Sara May didn't dare speak. A familiar feeling washed over her. She had seen this woman before. And then it hit her, knocking the breath out of her lungs. She could feel her nerves freeze; every atom in her body froze at that exact moment. It was her! The woman she had dreamt of!

"You!" Sara May whispered.

The woman smiled but didn't reply. She sauntered to

her bed, rearranged the pillows, and fluffed the duvet. Sara May didn't take her eyes off her. She wanted to grab her and ask her all the questions she couldn't ask her mother, but something held her back. It was as if she had been bolted to the bed and her voice stolen. The mysterious woman made the bed more comfortable before returning to the door. Just as she was leaving, she turned around and spoke softly with a perfect smile still plastered on her flawless face.

"Don't worry, my dear. We'll be watching you." And just like that, she was gone. Sara May sat paralysed with fear. The hairs stood up on the back of her neck, and she had difficulty breathing.

"Mum. Who was that?" she asked, her voice trembling.

"Who?" Maggie replied, slightly confused.

"The woman who was just here!"

"Erin? She's a nurse here, I think."

"Not her! The woman who was just here fixing my pillows and duvet."

"What are you talking about? Do I need to call for help?"

The golf ball in Sara May's throat rapidly expanded, making it difficult for her to swallow. Her skin prickled, and the chaotic flood of thoughts in her mind only intensified her fears. What was happening? Who was that mysterious woman?

Chapter 5

The rain pounded against the car windows on all sides. The tyres hit every pothole they could find, as if they were trying to turn this terrible rollercoaster ride into a hellish journey. Drugged and dazed, Sara May drooled onto the small pillow she'd been given to take home from the hospital. She held on tightly and tried to make herself as small as possible in the backseat. She was still struggling to control all the complex thoughts racing through her troubled mind. Therefore, she couldn't quite grasp the seriousness of the situation that had begun to unfold that morning. She didn't remember having checked out of the hospital, nor did she recall allowing her mother and aunt to take her home to Northtown.

Northtown. The name that could make even the toughest men curl up in the fetal position and cry. Northtown, where she'd spent her childhood, was in a small valley on the northeast side of Iceland—a shabby old slum, in her opinion. Eight hundred people's attempt at a town was all it was. She watched as the dull landscape rushed past. It consisted of mountains and rivers intertwining with occasional hardened lava from ancient eruptions. Nothing special. *What do tourists see in this?* she wondered. Northtown. She hadn't been there since she left in a hurry the day after her eighteenth birthday. She vaguely remembered throwing some clothes into her suitcase and rushing out to catch the first bus out of town, vowing never to return as long as she lived. And now she was being dragged back home against her will. But what choice did she have? She had to recover from the accident, and Paige was too busy to give her friend the twenty-four-hour care she needed. She'd been lucky, though. Aside from a nasty blow to the head and several bruises, she hadn't broken any bones. But it was the head injury the doctors were most worried about.

That was the reason they kept her in a coma for two weeks. That was why she was now being forced back to her hometown, powerless against the dynamic duo before her. They had both agreed that, if anything happened, it was the safest option to have her rest under their watchful eyes. Maggie had signed all the necessary papers, and, as she was the next of kin, the hospital staff saw no reason to protest this one-sided decision. Hating her old hometown wasn't enough of a reason. *Maybe I should have just started kicking and screaming; perhaps they would have committed me to the psychiatric ward*, Sara May thought to herself as she battled both nausea and a severe headache. Anything would have been better than what she knew awaited her in just a few hours.

The hours flew by, and before she could say a word, Aunt Marie's black 2023 Bentley Bentayga drove into the valley that cradled Northtown, a small suburban town hidden between two large mountains. It wasn't much to look at and usually didn't attract anyone's attention except from those who had decided to move there for reasons unknown to Sara May. Archaic and gloomy, it mainly served the farmers scattered around the valley. The tiny town centre consisted of a nursery, a primary school, a small community shop, a post office, a bank, a bakery, a pub, and several other small businesses that didn't stand out. Surrounding the centre were the neighbourhoods, dull and almost pitiful little clusters of houses built between the sixties and seventies. They acted like a frame around this feeble attempt at a town, giving it a somewhat alluring poise. It always reminded Sara May of a small American town in the 1930s. Kids ran barefoot during spring, and the town drunks had their seats at the local pub every day without fail. Life didn't change much in this tiny hamlet on the Nordic Island in the mid-Atlantic Ocean, and that's how people liked it. Those who grew up there wanted to stay because that was all they had ever known. Those who moved there of their own free will did so because they sought a quiet life with no demands or hassle. Nobody moved to Northtown seeking adventure and wealth.

"Aren't you excited to finally be home? How long has it been?" Maggie asked in a way that was too enthusiastic for her daughter's liking.

"Thirteen years," Sara May muttered into her pillow.

"Thirteen years? My gosh, has it been that long? Just think how excited everyone will be to see you again!"

Sara May rolled her half-closed eyes and paid no further attention to the two women sitting at the front. She had no hopes of seeing a torch-lit parade or a party in her honour. She doubted anyone had truly missed her. They probably wouldn't have even noticed that she'd left. As she looked out the window, she could see familiar surroundings. There was the deserted old cabin she often snuck into as a child with her two best friends, Chris and Eric. Stories about the place being haunted had been told in town for years, which worked as a magnet for curious little souls. They'd never encountered anything, though. There was also Old Gilbert's barn, which he'd always planned to fix but never got around to. Now, it just stood there, not amounting to much anymore.

Aunt Marie's luxury car finally hit the streets of Northtown. It had stopped raining, but the greyish, almost murky sky loomed over the town like a threat. *Fitting,* she thought to herself. The sun didn't fancy casting its beam on this place very often, especially not during cold winters. It probably didn't deserve it, anyway. As the car drove through, memories flooded like a burst dam. The tiny shop she´d frequently stolen sweets from was still there, as was her old primary school, where she´d spent more time in the principal's office than in the actual classrooms. And, of course, there was Aunt Marie's ridiculous leisure mansion. Her status symbol, her crown jewel, reminded the poor peasants below of the luxury that was her life, not theirs. Absurd really. It didn't fit in with all the low-key wooden houses in town. Aunt Marie didn't stop at her mansion. She had no desire to turn her palace into a hospital for her poor, injured niece. She wasn't that grand.

Finally, the car stopped in front of Sara May's childhood home. Reluctantly, she got out and looked around. She wasn't sure how she had ended up in this situation. Had she been so consumed by her misery and unhappiness that the universe decided to punish her for it? Someone had to take responsibility for this madness because there was no way in hell she was here by choice. Not much had changed since she moved away thirteen years ago. The house had recently been repainted in the same milky white colour as before, and the old rhubarb bush had grown considerably! Apart from that, it was mostly the same. The swing her father had hung from the thickest branch of the old oak tree was still there. And the white picket fence matched the alabaster-painted window shutters. The whole scene looked like it was straight out of a 1950s American home magazine. To anyone else, this was picture-perfect. But to Sara May, it was a never-ending reminder of bad memories she had spent years trying to forget.

"Sara May, your bags are in the boot! I've tidied up your old room!" Maggie yelled from inside the house.

Sara May came to her senses and hurried to bring her bags inside. She wasn't going to risk another shower while standing outside. It was even worse inside. Not a single chair had been moved. It was almost as if the house were frozen in time. The walls were mostly bare. There weren't many happy family photos or anything to show happier times. She was sure there had been joyful moments, but it was nearly taboo to talk about them after the divorce. She placed her bags in her old childhood room. The purple walls were still covered in posters of whoever she worshipped at the time, and every shelf was stacked with expired makeup and old CDs of popular bands from the early 2000s—a bitter reminder of times when hopes and dreams were still worth aspiring to. Suddenly, Maggie stuck her head inside.

"Sara May, I'm going to the Bread Box. You want anything?"

"No, thanks."

"You have to eat something. Remember what the doctors told you." Sara May rolled her eyes and sighed.

"Fine. Bring me….I don't know….a bagel with cheese or something."

"Why don't you just come with me and pick something out for yourself?"

Maggie turned around and walked away, oblivious to the fact that her daughter was in no mood for her mother's shenanigans. She let out a loud exhale and followed her outside. She had no interest in going out in public, even though she had just been discharged from the hospital, but she knew her mum wouldn't stop pestering her until she agreed to go with her. Aunt Marie had gone home at the earliest opportunity. The ghastly hardship she´d endured, having to stay in Reykjavik for a few days, required healing through drinking and online shopping. When outside, Sara May walked a few steps behind her mother to avoid pointless small talk about the weather and the latest town gossip. The two of them had never had enough in common to have a serious conversation, and still slightly drowsy from the long car journey, she wished to be left alone. On the other hand, Maggie was in excellent spirits, determined not to let her daughter's apparent distaste for life ruin her day. She knew full well when she signed the papers at the hospital that Sara May would protest heavily once she regained her senses. But every small achievement was worth celebrating. Being able to get her outside was a step closer to victory.

During her walk, Sara May paid close attention to every little detail around her. Every leaf and rock in this place was imprinted in her memory. She hadn't expected the town to change much in the last thirteen years, but this was ridiculous! It was almost like time had packed up and left this fossilised place. Even the old Bread Box bakery was still there, just as it had been for forty years. Locals had given it the name after a dramatic vote in which Paula, the pastor's wife, and her militant followers had vigorously spread rumours about those planning to vote against their idea of calling the bakery Sweet Cakes. Paula even went so far as to accuse the mayor and his wife of plotting a conspiracy against her. Sara May shook her head. Northtown's disputes had always been something of their own category.

"Hello, Maggie! Welcome home! I was beginning to think you'd decided to settle there in the South!" Bill Baker, one of the two owners of the Bread Box, loudly joked as Maggie and Sara May walked in.

"Don't be ridiculous!" Maggie scoffed, lowering her brows slightly, feeling playfully insulted. Bill let out a laugh.

"How's Sara May?" he asked, his signature smile still in place.

"You can ask her yourself," Maggie proudly replied and stepped aside, exposing a very vulnerable Sara May.

"Well, I'll be damned! If it isn't little Miss Mischief! My, you've grown! Still the same little devil as before?" he asked, beaming with surprise.

"Oh, stop it now, Bill. One can only hope the girl has grown up a little since then," his wife, Laura, facetiously replied as she stepped forward with a tray full of freshly baked bread for hungry customers.

Bill and Laura Baker had owned and run the Bread Box before Sara May was born. They met when they were only twenty years old and fell madly in love, so much so that they hadn't spent a day apart for over forty years. And that's the way they liked it. They were a comically close-knit couple who had worked together to create the best bakery in the entire country. They were known for their wholesome reputation and had, over time, earned both the respect and admiration of the locals, most of whom had become regulars at this cosy little bakery in the heart of Northtown. Bill and Laura were also known for their helpfulness. They were there whenever anyone needed anything, day or night. Not a single person in town disliked them. Their cheerfulness and warmth had turned the Bread Box into a heavenly-smelling community centre that welcomed everybody. However, neither the freshly baked goods nor the happy couple had repeatedly landed Sara May on their doorstep. It was their son, Eric. He was a year older than her and had been her best childhood friend. He had been her partner in crime, standing by her during her most notorious catastrophes. She had never gotten into trouble without him. At some point, Chris, Sara May's classmate at school, had been allowed to join the two, and together, the three of them had formed the most infamous trio Northtown had ever seen.

Every prank and act of misconduct in town in the late 90s had been linked to them, though minor enough for the police to dismiss it with a chuckle. Most people secretly enjoyed those lively little troublemakers, but a few huffed and puffed at their every move, shamelessly using them to illustrate how poor parenting and too much television had fostered a rebellious youth. Those innocent antics were among Sara May's most cherished childhood memories.

"Never thought I'd be seeing you again, kitten." Sara May was pulled back to reality when suddenly she heard a full-bodied male voice coming from behind the counter. Only two boys had ever called her that, knowing the only way to dare her to do something was to call her out on her bluff and point out her cowardice. That'd always pissed her off so much she ended up doing the stupidest things to prove she most certainly was not a coward!

"Eric, you remember the little wildcat, don't you?" Bill asked with the biggest grin on his face. Eric smiled.

"Yeah, I think I do."

Sara May was speechless. In all the years since she

hurriedly left town, she had never really thought about what had happened to her two best friends, Chris and Eric. She had just assumed they had grown up, left town at the first opportunity, and become some big shots somewhere, maybe even overseas. She saw no point in dwelling on the past because she never imagined herself returning there. Yet here she was, in the old Bread Box, her face redder than a tomato, standing across from a man who must have been voted Mister Universe more than once. This couldn't be little Eric! This man looked like a sculptor had crafted him! He resembled a finely carved statue of a Greek god that someone had stolen from a museum.

Chapter 6

Sara May escaped Bill and Laura's trip down memory lane by excusing herself and walking home alone without her mother. She couldn't understand why they felt the need to revisit all her childhood mischiefs to amuse the crowd at the Bread Box. Eric had finally stopped it, but it was too late. It was almost as if he had enjoyed reminiscing, which she found puzzling. She may have been the mastermind behind their antics, but he was just as guilty as she was. Dwelling on the past should have been as awkward for him as it was for her! She tightened her jacket and marched down the street towards home. She kept her gaze low, hoping no one would notice her. She didn't want to look around either because every corner held unpleasant memories; every step brought an unwelcome reminder of a life she'd rather forget.

It hadn't always been like this. There were also some wonderful times. She'd been surrounded by her family and friends, schoolmates, neighbours, and others who'd loved and cared for her as a child. She remembered racing between houses in the neighbourhood, being greeted and sometimes fed by multiple housewives as if she were their own, just like every other child in town. Northtown had always been a very family-oriented community, with its unofficial motto: *It takes a village to raise a child.* That was true in every sense of the word, and she could recall just how safe and loved she'd always felt growing up. Even the town drunks who wandered around during the day and slept on benches at night had been lovable goofballs who'd been exceptionally kind to the children in Northtown. She couldn't deny that this had been the perfect place to grow up.

But then, everything changed. Two days before her 10th birthday, she had been woken by her parents' loud argument on the ground floor. She had sneaked out of her room and hidden just above the stairs, in a spot where they couldn't see her, but she could still hear every word. There they were, her beloved mum and dad, fighting like never before. Something she had never seen before, and it scared her. She remembered her father saying he couldn't continue living in a lie; he had had enough. He stormed out of the house and slammed the door behind him so hard that the photo of the three of them on holiday in France fell to the floor and shattered into a million pieces.

This had been the last time she saw him—the man she always admired and loved so deeply. They'd been the best of friends, or so she believed. That day destroyed everything and forever shaped how she formed friendships and entered relationships. It changed her. She became guarded, unwilling to let anyone too close. In her mind, everyone who entered her life would eventually leave, and she didn't want to risk it. She'd never truly understood what her father meant by "living a lie." She had often pondered these words and ultimately concluded that he was just fed up with being a married man and wanted out. He was tired of pretending to be the perfect husband and acting as if his marriage was in top shape. Her mother must have felt the same because she couldn't recall seeing her make any effort to pursue him. She simply let him go. This, in turn, made Sara May extremely angry and bitter towards her parents. She hated her father for leaving her without saying goodbye, for walking away so quickly and without an ounce of remorse. She hated her mother for not going after him; she hadn't even tried. A long and difficult chapter in her life began that day. It was the reason she resented this town so much.

The following eight years had been terrible. She had become very withdrawn and struggled to connect with the same people she loved as a child. Her mood swings were all over the place, and she felt both lonely and scared. Everything had turned cold and hostile. People whispered among themselves, and the gossip spread from house to house like a tray full of unconfirmed rumours for neighbours to feast on. There had been a lot of gossiping behind curtains in every kitchen in Northtown. Despite being one of the main characters, she tried to steer clear of those vile stories, as she was sure she would otherwise lose her mind. The last thing she needed was for people to question her sanity on top of everything else. It was bad enough to be known as the rowdy, rebellious teen who was completely out of control. That was the description she heard most often. The worst part was the chatter about how she must find out the truth. She had no interest in knowing what went on between her parents before everything fell apart seemingly out of nowhere. As far as she was concerned, the marriage was over, and dwelling on what caused it wouldn't fix anything.

The day after her 18th birthday, she packed her bags and caught the first bus out of Northtown, never looking back. Nothing would stop her from leaving this old, obnoxious country life behind and starting fresh in the capital city where nobody knew her name or story. She seamlessly blended into the faceless crowd. She wanted to be the unwritten page, the writer she had always dreamed of becoming — the author of her own story, told in her own words. No dysfunctional parents or gossip-hungry curtain twitchers would decide her fate. The first few years had been tough, but with a lot of hard work and determination, she had managed to save enough money to rent a small ground-floor flat in the suburbs of Reykjavik. Most people wouldn't even have considered this old, empty lot that had been vacant for months. But for Sara May, it was an outstanding achievement, a sign of victory and long-awaited freedom. From then on, she worked hard to stay afloat and even climbed a step or two on the social ladder. Northtown was dead and gone. This was why she was furious about being forced to return.

"Sara May! Sara May!" a deep male voice suddenly shouted her name from a distance. She stopped in her tracks, shut her eyes, and prayed. "Please don't."

"I thought you were running away again," the familiar voice said, now much closer. Realising her prayers had not been effective, Sara May turned around.

"Hi, Eric."

"You can at least say goodbye this time," he smirked.

"I was just on my way home. I'm supposed to be resting."

"I was about to head to the Brewer. Care to join me?"

"No, I really should go home and rest. I had a little accident, and the doctors said I should take it easy."

"Come on, kitten. Are you gonna let that stop you?" he teased with a smile that didn't quite reach his eyes.

Sara May stood firm, trying not to be mad at him for using that old tactic on her. He seemed to have grown some balls; she couldn't remember him being so stubborn. The angel sat on her left shoulder and the demon on her right, fighting over her common sense. *Of course, you should go home and lie down to avoid possible brain damage, the* angel whispered. But the demon had a point. The man was so incredibly handsome, it would be an awful shame not to go with him for a drink or two. A clean-cut version of a male model with a rough exterior that reminded her of a hard-working man with bad intentions. This had to be some sorcery; he'd been a pimple-covered nerd with braces the last time she saw him.

"Fine. One drink. But only if you promise to walk me home; I don't wanna get drunk and drown in a muddy puddle; that'd be humiliating," she finally replied. Eric laughed.

"I promise."

Together, they headed to the oldest pub in town, The Brewer. A place that had belonged to the same family for decades and was run by Simon and Suzy Lewis, a married couple and parents of identical twin boys, Jack and Jake, who looked so much alike it was as if one had been run through a copying machine to produce the other. But despite their identical looks, their personalities were as different as night and day. Rumour had it that their parents clearly favoured one over the other. Jack was only two minutes older than his twin brother, Jake, but that was enough for Simon and Suzy to believe he was the rightful heir to the family business, and so they felt it was their duty to hold him to the highest standards. Besides the fact that the so-called empire was nothing but one lousy pub in a small town, Simon and Suzy Lewis harboured big ambitions for their older son.

As a result, Jake had been sidelined. The couple had always treated him like a spare part that had just tagged along, similar to the IKEA screws nobody knew where to place, ultimately ending up in a closed drawer, never to be seen again. Sara May had always sympathised with Jake. She wasn't sure if he was daft or if he'd just retreated into his own world because of the way his parents treated him. She had occasionally thought about him and wondered how he was getting on. Jake wasn't easy to get to know, and most people had given up trying. The pair finally reached the Brewer. Eric chose a charming little wooden table next to a window and sat down with two pints, one of which he pushed towards Sara May.

"What do I owe you?" she asked.

"A promise that you'll say goodbye next time you go," he replied with a cheeky grin.

"Did I cause permanent damage when I left?"

"You were my best friend. And one day, you were just gone. What was I supposed to think?"

She took a sip of her beer, avoiding eye contact. She had no satisfying answer to his question. The truth was, she'd always felt guilty about how she'd handled things. She knew it was her fault, but pride stopped her from admitting it. She couldn't change the past, so why bother trying?

"I had to go, Eric. You, of all people, should know that. I just couldn't stay here any longer."

"I know. But you could have at least notified me. I didn't get a chance to hug you. I didn't even know where you'd gone."

"I'm sorry. But I can't change what happened, so I don't know what you want me to say."

"Just let me know next time, will ya?"

"Alright, I will."

Eric smiled. He knew her well enough to know she wasn't telling him everything she wanted to say, but he didn't want to press her. That would only cause her to run away like a frightened deer. He was no better himself. He wasn't ready to admit that he'd never forgotten her, and his feelings for her ran deeper than he thought possible. So, it was probably best to keep it to himself. It wasn't confirmed if she'd stay this time or leave again in the middle of the night.

"So, what's up with you? Any wife or kids?" Sara May asked as she took another sip.

"No, nothing like that," Eric reluctantly admitted.

"Are you serious? A good-looking bloke like you? What gives?" Eric chortled.

"I don't know about that."

"Have you seen yourself, Eric? The last time I saw you, you were about to go live in a cave because you felt like a troll! Your words, not mine. And now you look like you were made in a lab!" Eric couldn't resist a laugh.

"Thank you for the compliment," he said, sipping his drink.

"So, why no wife? Are you gay?"

"No, not gay either. I just haven't been looking for anything serious. I've been helping old Gilbert on the farm; he's much more fragile than he used to be, so he can't do it alone anymore. I've also been helping at the Bread Box, making life a little easier for Mum and Dad. I just haven't had any time for romance, I guess."

"Shame. I bet Tracy's still waiting for the proposal you promised her in second grade. Eric smirked, clearly amused, as he put down his pint.

"No, she gave up on me a long time ago. She's married to Bobby Scott. They live on a farm just outside of town. Three kids, fourteen horses, fifty sheep. I don't think she's missing me all that much."

"Bobby Scott? I would have bet money on him being a drug lord in Colombia by now! He was always so weird."

"He's still weird; he married Tracy." Sara May let out a laugh. "So, what about you?" Eric continued.

"Oh, living the dream. A single and childless kitchen porter, and before I nearly killed myself crossing the street, I was living in a one-bedroom flat surrounded by some very questionable neighbours. You know, the typical Cinderella story."

"Wow. I would have guessed you were a married mother of five, running your own business and living the sweet life."

Sara May forced out an awkward smile and took another sip. Those last words had hit her like a ton of bricks. She knew she had been deceiving herself for far too long. She didn't need a reminder of it. Hearing she wasn't where she had envisioned herself pierced her more than a steak knife to the heart. The worst part was that she only had herself to blame. She lacked discipline and strength.

I got time, was the mantra she had told herself repeatedly—her everyday falsity. *I can start this later,* she had thought to herself and then spent the next two hours on the sofa, scrolling through social media on her phone or staring out the window. She wasted hours she should have used to nourish her goals and her dreams. Time was the fuel that her ambition needed and her dreams demanded. But again and again, she had wasted that time on something that got her nowhere in life, and that was her own doing. It was a tumour on her soul that was eating her up inside, but she would rather die than admit it.

Chapter 7

Exhausted but happier than she had been in a long time, Sara May strolled home after a good night out. She had stayed much longer than she initially planned, but she didn't regret it. She hadn't realised how much she needed a pint and a pleasant chat with an old friend. Reminiscing about their childhood mischiefs, it felt like no time had passed, and it was an absolute joy. Eric had also shared a lot about the lives of the people of Northtown. Some revelations had been a surprise, while others were expected. She wasn't shocked to hear that their old high school geography teacher had eventually suffered a breakdown and now lived out her days in an institution in Reykjavik, skimming through worn-out geography books and pointing out which birds flew south for the winter. What was more surprising was that Malcolm, her old primary school classmate, had moved to Denmark, where he met a girl and was now a happily married father of two half-Danish children.

Things changed in the blink of an eye in the age of technology. She had enjoyed listening to every piece of information Eric could give her. She'd even started to understand why the old hags in town craved their daily dose of gossip so much. It was oddly exhilarating and quite addictive. She smiled to herself. She hadn't drunk too much, only two pints, so she was well-equipped to face the hurricane that awaited her behind the closed front door at her mother's house. It was close to midnight, but she knew her mum was fully awake and ready to argue. She saw the lights turn on when she approached her mother's house. She took a deep breath and sauntered inside, careful not to fuel her mother's already seething anger.

"Where the hell have you been?" Maggie yelled the moment she heard the door open.

"I went to the Brewer with Eric."

"Sara May, you promised me you would stay here and take it easy!"

"I know, I'm sorry."

"Sorry, will not save your ass this time, young lady! Go to your room and stay there until the doctors give you the all-clear to go gallivanting all over town!"

"Mum, I'm thirty-one years old! I never agreed to come here, so you can bet I'll be out of this house whenever I damn well please!"

"You're risking brain damage! This isn't the time to be stupidly stubborn!"

Sara May pursed her lips and stormed into her bedroom. Maggie didn't see the point in continuing this argument, as this wasn't the first time they had clashed. She'd learned from experience, or so she thought. Her wishful thinking had led her to believe the rift between them had been somewhat repaired over the years. Realising it hadn't was a bit of a blow. They were still butting heads, and it didn't look like it would change anytime soon. Maggie sighed and turned off the lights, then headed to bed. She was too exhausted to care anymore.

Sara May tossed and turned in her old teenage bed, struggling to settle down. She missed her large, king-sized bed in her flat in Reykjavik. It was her most expensive purchase, but it had long since proven its worth. How pathetic was that? Those were the years when she was meant to take out a second mortgage on the house and borrow money to buy a new car. She was supposed to be budgeting for school expenses and her children's hobbies, and finding ways to pay for food and electricity. Those were the years when she was meant to be arguing with her husband over whose turn it was to pick up the kids, the years she was supposed to cook healthy meals for her family, but ended up ordering takeout and feeding the youngest dry Cheerios. Instead, she was lying awake in her old teenage bedroom, single and frustrated, missing a bed she'd bought at a flea market and stuffed into the messy place she called home.

Fighting with her mother hadn't helped. She wasn't sure why life had suddenly taken a serious turn. She must have done something terrible to make the universe think she wasn't deserving of all those nice things everyone else took pride in. She pulled the duvet over her head and tried to fall asleep again. Usually, it took her about an hour, sometimes two. First, she needed to review everything that had gone wrong in her life. Paige was right. Everyone was right. She was too focused on the negative sides of life and wasted too much energy blaming others instead of tackling her own issues head-on. She sighed and turned to face the wall. Whether it was the environment or just the exhaustion after the accident, it wasn't long before she drifted into a deep sleep.

Slowly, she opened her eyes. She felt tired and disoriented. Her surroundings felt familiar—a distorted version of Northtown. There was the Brewer and her old primary school, the Bread Box, and her mother's house. She noticed a few locals walking around in a daze. Suddenly, the atmosphere shifted, and she found herself standing in a strange, black-painted flat in the dead of night. She saw a young woman she didn't recognise. This mysterious woman had thick, wavy blonde hair that fell to her shoulders and a perfectly small face, with plump, slightly pinkish lips just below her tiny, inconspicuous nose. She radiated beauty and perfection. The young woman looked around with fear. She was wearing a colourful, slightly scruffy jumper and light blue denim trousers, looking like a model from a 90s teen magazine. Sara May didn't try to approach her. The woman looked lost, as if she had no idea where she was or where she was headed.

All of a sudden, a man dressed all in black passed Sara May, furiously stomping his feet as he went by. She didn't see his face, but felt she knew his body structure. He was tall, dark-haired, and bulky with broad shoulders. With clenched fists and seething with anger, he stormed towards the scared young woman and started brutally assaulting her in the middle of the flat. Sara May ran towards them to help her, but quickly realised she wasn't moving. Her feet seemed to be chained to the ground. She started yelling and screaming in hopes of diverting the attacker's attention, but to no avail. Her voice had deserted her. She tried waving her arms around, only to discover they were non-existent. She was as helpless as the poor young woman that the aggressive monster was abusing right in front of her eyes, and there was nothing she could do about it.

Suddenly, someone snapped their fingers in the distance, and the young woman collapsed to the ground, vanishing into thin air. Sara May looked at the man in black and saw that he was now fixated on her. His face was as dark as his clothing. Where there should have been eyes, a nose, and a mouth, there was nothing but a gaping black hole of hatred and violence. The man suddenly started running towards her at a fast pace. She howled with fear, then realised she was awake, sitting upright in her bed. It had been a nightmare. The sweat was dripping from her forehead, and her heart was pounding so fast it felt like a heart attack. Suddenly, the bedroom door flung open, and her terrified mother rushed in. She'd heard her daughter screaming.

"What? What's happening?" Maggie yelped, terrified that something serious had occurred.

"Nothing; it was just a nightmare," Sara May calmly replied, running her hand through her wet hair. Maggie sighed with relief despite being annoyed by the abrupt awakening.

"You don't wanna listen to the doctors; you don't wanna listen to me. Sure, do whatever the hell you want," she mumbled as she closed the bedroom door and walked away.

Sara May wiped the sweat from her face and briefly looked around the room. What was that all about? She hadn't had a nightmare since she was a little girl, shortly after her parents' divorce. Those had been similar, if she wasn't mistaken. A young woman, a male figure in dark clothing, and violence. Her mother had eventually given up and taken her to see a psychologist. He just brushed it under the carpet, saying, *'Children often dream according to their vivid imagination.* Sara May was too young to decipher the deeper meaning behind her nightmares, so nothing came of it. Eventually, the nightmares stopped, and Maggie had just written it off as her daughter's coping mechanism after the divorce. Sara May buried her face with her hands. Why did she have a nightmare so soon after returning to Northtown? Was the town having those effects on her? *I wouldn't be surprised,* she thought and shook her head. Then she lay down again, too drained to think about it any longer.

Chapter 8

"Sara May, it's nearly eleven o'clock! Get up, for goodness' sake!"

Maggie's voice cut through the air like a butcher's knife until it finally reached Sara May's fragile ears. Severely annoyed, she growled into her pillow. She hadn't had much sleep because of the night terror, and when she finally managed to fall asleep, she was tossing and turning. Overall, this had been an awful night, so she felt it was her right to sleep as long as she pleased. It irritated her that her mother treated her like a teenager, but that was probably how she saw her. After all, Sara May had only been eighteen the last time they faced each other. That moment was branded on Maggie's brain, which, in turn, found it hard to see her daughter differently. Sara May grudgingly got out of bed after one more shouting and two more warnings. "There ought to be a law against forcing people out of bed," she mumbled. Dismayed, she stomped into the kitchen and started looking for something to eat, finally settling on a box of cereal and a jug of milk. The old kitchen chairs were so brittle that it was a wonder they hadn't fallen apart years ago. Why her mother hadn't given her kitchen a makeover years ago was beyond anyone's understanding.

"Finally! I thought you'd just about died up there," Maggie fussed.

"And you just can't fathom why I moved away," Sara May snidely replied.

"Please, I'm in no mood for your crankiness, so give it a rest." I need you to do me a favour."

"You woke me up military style; why the hell should I

do you any favours?"

"Because I'm your mother, and while you live in my house, you follow my rules and do as I say!"

"I don't live in your house! I have a place in the city!"

"And when you're well enough, you're free to bolt back there, but until then, I suggest you stop complaining and do as you're told! I need you to go shopping for a few things for your nan, and while you're at it, stop by the Bread Box and pick up a few items," Maggie commanded, handing Sara May a list.

"Why can't you do it? I haven't seen the woman in thirteen years!" Sara May protested.

"That's why I'm asking. I have to cover a shift at the care home. We are short-staffed, and your Aunt Marie is visiting a man she met in Venice a year ago."

"Mum, I didn't even know Nan was still alive!" Sara May tried to object, but Maggie stood firm.

"Don't be silly; she'll be thrilled to see you!"

Without giving her a chance to reply, Maggie hurried out of the kitchen, already late for the shift she had foolishly agreed to cover. Sara May had lost her appetite. She stared into the half-empty bowl and let the anger within consume her. Ever since she was forced back, her mum had been shouting at her and bossing her around like a possessed rat, constantly contradicting herself. First, she'd demanded that she rest to avoid possible brain damage, and now she was turning her into a messenger for a woman she hadn't seen for years and had honestly thought was six feet under by now. She sighed and stood up from her breakfast, dragging her feet deliberately. Seeing her estranged grandmother was not high on her list of things to look forward to.

Grandma Gladys was a stern old witch whom most

locals seriously disliked. And for a good reason. As long as Sara May could remember, the old hag had always kept to herself and had never shown any interest in mingling with the townsfolk. She had regularly hissed at children who dared to venture too close to her house and despised anyone who tried to reach out to her. Her relationship with Sara May, her only granddaughter, was no better, and she never understood why. She couldn't remember ever having offended her in any way. Maggie had always told her not to take it personally; Grandma Gladys was just a bit eccentric. But it was hard, especially since she'd always felt the old woman should have treated her differently from other children, given that she was the only one blood-related to her. So, she couldn't help but feel personally attacked. And now she was supposed to run errands for her? What kind of madness was that?

She felt as if she had completely lost control of her life, and the more she tried to steady herself, the more she resembled a cow on an ice rink. What an absolute joke! She threw her bowl of cereal into the sink, biting her bottom lip to stop the tears from welling up. She wasn't about to let her mother make her cry! Instead, she decided to shake it off, hold her head high, and take back control of her life, no matter what! She was an adult woman! They couldn't keep her in this dreadful town forever.

Later that morning, she wandered through the aisles of the small food market, ticking off every item on the list she managed to find. Her old childhood home wasn't the only thing that hadn't changed in decades. This tiny store, her former workplace, hadn't even moved a single shelf.

Everything was exactly where it had always been, like time couldn't be bothered with this pathetic attempt at a supermarket. Luckily, she seemed to have changed enough, as few people appeared to recognise her, and for that, she was grateful. She had no interest in pointless small talk; she just wanted to finish this ridiculous mission and be done with it. She pushed the trolley to the register and waited patiently for her turn, checking her phone impatiently. Why hadn't Eric called yet? She'd given him her number; he said he would call.

"Oh, if it isn't little Sara May Jensen?" she suddenly heard a friendly old woman cheer behind her. She looked up from her phone and saw a little, white-haired old lady standing before her. She looked so old and fragile that she could easily be mistaken for an artefact from the National History Museum.

"Yep, it's me," Sara May awkwardly replied.

"I thought so. You're just the spitting image of…" the old woman continued before being unexpectedly interrupted.

The middle-aged woman behind the till loudly cleared her throat and subtly shook her head as if reprimanding the old lady. In response, the old lady excused herself and carried on shopping as if nothing had happened. Sara May was utterly baffled, to the point that she didn't think to demand answers. The old lady walked away, and the woman behind the till acted as if her strange behaviour was nothing out of the ordinary. Sara May finished packing her items into a bag, paid, and hurried out of the store. Once outside, she turned around, only to see the woman behind the till staring at her. She quickly looked away when she realised she was being watched. *What the hell was that all about?* she wondered, feeling uneasy as she left. Why had the woman at the till rebuked the old lady for innocently pointing out that Sara May resembled her mother? It wasn't as if she hadn't heard it before. At best, the old woman had become confused; they could have easily corrected her. She thought about it so intently that she didn't notice she had suddenly stopped in front of the bakery. The bell above the door signalled every new customer's arrival to Bill and Laura, and this time, it was Laura who greeted Sara May with open arms and a warm smile, as always.

"Hello, dear. What can I get you today?" she asked.

"I'm supposed to be buying some pastry for Grandma Gladys," Sara May replied, handing over Maggie's list. Laura refused.

"I don't need it. Old lady Gladys hasn't changed her ways for the last twenty years. I highly doubt she'll start now."

Sara May smiled and patiently waited as Laura returned to gather Grandma Gladys's items. She hadn't seen her Nan in ages, but somehow, Laura's description seemed very accurate. She paid little attention to the other customers while she waited. They mostly sat at the small tables strategically placed by the large windows facing east, allowing people to arrive early in the morning and enjoy their breakfast bagels while watching the sunrise.

"Isn't this Maggie's daughter?" a woman whispered to another.

"Oh, my word, it is!" another woman replied quietly.

"I swear, she looks just like Helena."

Having already engaged in a strange conversation that morning, Sara May decided to turn around. The two women had clearly been talking about her because, just like the woman behind the till at the food market, the two gossipers quickly looked away and pretended not to recognise her the moment she looked at them. If Laura hadn't called out to her at that very moment, she would have said something.

"Here you go, my darling. That should be everything. Eric usually takes this to her, but I'm sure she'll be delighted to have her only grandchild visit her after all these years," said Laura, handing her a bag of goodies.

Sara May thanked Laura and leapt out of the bakery. She could feel the two women's eyes burn a hole in the back of her neck. It was evident that the gossip was still very much alive and thriving in Northtown. Had she looked back, she would have seen the two witches chattering away, most likely feasting on this latest carcass. It'd now been two uncomfortable and unexplained incidents within one hour. That was far from normal. She remembered hearing all kinds of whispers and jabbering around her as a child, but she had never bothered memorising any of it because there was no truth to it. That's what Maggie had always told her.

"Don't worry about it, love. They're just bored," she'd always say.

"They're just jealous!" Aunt Marie had firmly stated.

Jealous of what she never knew. But being young and impressionable, she had just taken these words at face value. Her mum had to be right. Not much happened in this pitiful slum, so people ate whatever piece of meat was thrown at them. Events like a messy divorce provided plenty of gossip, enough for everyone. Filling in the gaps had never been a problem around here. So, she'd learned to ignore the hissing forked snake tongues over time. Eventually, though, it became so bad that she was forced to run away. She had no choice. But this she couldn't ignore. Who was Helena? She'd never heard that name before, let alone in connection with herself. What did they mean when they said she looked just like her? Did it have something to do with what the old lady at the food market said? No, it couldn't be. She tried to shake off the uneasy feeling that had wrapped around every nerve in her body. Something wasn't right. Something was carefully hidden in this small town, and Sara May's homecoming had shaken it so forcefully that people couldn't contain themselves.

Chapter 9

"Grandma Gladys? Are you home? "

No answer. Sara May slowly opened the front door and let herself in. She hadn't visited her Nan often enough to know whether her home had always been so messy and weird or if it was something that came with old age. The air was hazy with dust and smelled of old cigarettes and oaky whisky. The dark, forest-green walls were covered in crooked paintings and shelves filled with colourful glass bottles and strange statues. Old, musty books and half-dead plants were scattered throughout the house, blending in with some ragged furniture well past its prime. A scratched-up old sofa sat beneath a dirty living room window, and two wooden bookcases flanked the creepiest fireplace she'd ever seen. She wasn't sure if she'd entered her grandmother's house or a witch's lair that someone forgot to burn in Salem. She'd never seen anything like this, and it terrified her.

"Grandma Gladys?" she called out again, her voice slightly trembling. "I got your pastry!" she added to lure the old ogress out of her cave.

It worked. Grandma Gladys couldn't resist the tempting smell of the freshly baked pastry. Cranky and frail, the long-lived countess of Creepy Town crawled out of her nest, ambling towards her granddaughter as if trying to be both sceptical and dignified at the same time. Sara May wanted to run away as fast as she could. Had she for a moment thought her Nan was this traditional old lady who knitted socks and baked bread buns, she was sorely mistaken. There she was—the age-old queen of the mystical, the high priestess of all grouchy vultures that had ever lived. Standing across from Sara May, with her thick, messy grey hair, wearing a long dress that matched the green-coloured walls, and sporting numerous oversized rings and bracelets, Sara May wasn't sure how she managed to stay upright. She was a little hunched over, probably due to wearing all that flashy jewellery, but other than that, she seemed relatively healthy. Her giant glasses, resting firmly on her slightly curved nose, made her eyes look enormous. Grandma Gladys tightened her grip on her snake-like cane and stared suspiciously at Sara May.

"Who are you? Where's Eric?" she jeered.

"Nan, it's me. Sara May. Laura sent me," Sara May replied, holding the bag of pastries as proof.

Grandma Gladys squinted and huffed. She liked routine, and with Eric bringing her pastries twice a week, she avoided meeting more people than she cared for. Nobody had informed her of this sudden change, and she didn't like it one bit. However, the girl was standing in her living room, so she couldn't do much about it. She instructed Sara May to take the bag into the kitchen. She did as she was told, even though she wasn't entirely sure which way was up and which way was down in this oddly shaped cottage. The kitchen was no better than the living room, filled with strange items scattered everywhere, gathering cobwebs and dust. This couldn't be good for anyone's health. Following her Nan's stern, military-style instructions, Sara May put the pastry away.

"Who did you say you were?" the old ogress asked in a miffed tone.

"Sara May, Nan. Maggie's daughter." The witch heaved.

"That you are."

Something about this answer rubbed Sara May the wrong way, bringing back that same feeling she had before. There was something more behind these words. She'd never been close enough to her Nan to wonder if she knew more than she let on. The fact was that some people knew more about her parents' divorce than others because of how they talked. Her Nan had to be one of them. As a teenager, she was never interested in asking because she was trying to escape it all. But being back in her old hometown all these years later had not only ripped off the bandage but also sparked her curiosity. She needed answers to all the questions she'd had as a teen. Perhaps being older and somewhat wiser would help her better understand what really went on between her parents that led to the divorce. As she kept stacking the pastries away, Grandma Gladys continued being a spiteful old battle-axe.

"Put the bread in the bread box; don't just let it stand there on the counter!" she shouted. Sara May did as she was told.

"Nan, can I ask you something?"

"Depends on what it is," she hissed.

"Have you heard anything from Dad since he left?"

"Hah! As if anyone's interested in hearing from that pathetic old deadbeat. A poor excuse for a man, that's what he is!"

"I thought maybe he'd been asking about me."

"No. He hasn't. And if you had an ounce of common sense, you would understand what a blessing that is!" the old shrew seethed before she turned around and prepared to leave the kitchen.

"Who's Helena?" Sara May suddenly asked.

Quicker than a blink, Grandma Gladys came to a sudden halt. It was as if all life had been sucked out of the old woman's wrinkled face. She hadn't heard that name in over thirty years. It was the name that would eventually push her away from everyone she'd ever loved. The name was responsible for the turn her life had taken. The name that had caused her to live like a hermit, hating every living thing around her. How the hell did this gaunt-looking girl know about Helena? Who'd been blabbing? It was apparent that the events thirty-one years ago were still the buzz of the town. That bonfire hadn't burnt out. Slowly but surely, Grandma Gladys turned around and looked her granddaughter straight in the eyes, something Sara May had tried to avoid since entering the house. Something about this old shrew scared her beyond belief. Her eyes threw daggers at her, and she could feel herself being stabbed with a thousand little needles all over. She'd noticed that her Nan hadn't wanted to look at her much, but she hadn't been bothered since she wasn't keen on a staring contest. But now, there was no escape. Her Nan's eyes held her hostage and sent shivers down her spine. She'd said something wrong, and she knew it. Cold sweat dripped down her forehead, causing her to want to run for her life.

"What did you say?" Grandma Gladys hissed through her clenched teeth.

"Who's Helena? I overheard two women at the Bread Box talking about her; one of them said I look like her."

"They were mistaken!" Grandma Gladys fumed.

"I'm sure they were, but I'm still wondering who…"

"It's none of your business! Never mention that name again in my presence! You have no business being here if you're going to dig up some old dirt and throw it at me! How dare you?"

"I'm sorry. I didn't mean to upset you. I'll go." Sara May shivered with fear.

Slowly, she backed towards the kitchen entrance without taking her eyes off the furious old woman. She'd read enough crime novels to know you never turn your back on dangerous villains. As far as she was concerned, the old hag was likely to grab her biggest kitchen knife and kill her on the spot. Grandma Gladys was in no mood for an emotional goodbye. Her heart was pounding, and she could feel the intense anger inside her bubbling like lava about to spew. Some nerve that girl had! Coming to her house to drop such a nuclear bomb! This was an ambush, no more, no less! She must have suspected something; there was no way she'd lived this long and not had any clue, which was why this was such a sensitive topic. The more she thought about it, the more convinced she became that Sara May knew something and had only dropped by to gather more information. Well, she wouldn't get it here! This was a story Gladys Jensen would take to her grave if she had to!

Sara May hurried away from the house of evil as quickly as she could. The crumbled-down cottage was unlike any other home in town, and now she knew why. This was where the evil witch from every story lived — the one who tried to eat Hansel and Gretel, the one who wanted to poison Snow White. This was her dwelling. And now she had unleashed her famously furious temper on her own granddaughter, whose only crime was mentioning the name of a woman who was a giant taboo around here. Sara May's curiosity was at an all-time high. Who was Helena? And why was nobody allowed to say her name out loud?

Chapter 10

At nearly seven o'clock, Sara May dragged her feet through the front door. She had been at The Cocoa Bean, a small café on Northtown's high street, pondering all that had happened recently. Why had her nan reacted so harshly to a seemingly innocent question? She had eventually concluded that the old lady was becoming senile, which was causing her low-key, violent outbursts. After sitting in the café for nearly three hours, the staff politely asked her to leave as it was nearing closing time. She thanked them for their service and headed home.

"Mum, I'm home! Sorry, I'm late; I was at the Cocoa Bean!"

No reply. She called out again, but the house was so silent that one could hear a leaf fall from a tree outside. She walked into the kitchen, almost expecting her mum to be slumped over the table, fast asleep, like she had many times before, especially after the divorce. But the kitchen was as empty as a selfish man's heart. A note had been left on the table beneath a tipped-over glass.

I was asked to cover another night shift. There are some leftovers in the fridge. Love, Mum.

Sara May crumpled the note and threw it into the rubbish bin. The leftovers were tasty, but didn't compare to a steaming hot pizza on a Friday night. After searching through the limited selection of fast-food places in town, she settled on Pizza-Lot. She hadn't heard of it before, so it had to be new. That was a sign of quality in Northtown, as most of the older places had been around since the Viking Age and had long since lowered their hygiene and quality standards. Therefore, anything new was likely to be better. New meant fresh; it meant values. All things she was in favour of. After speaking to a slightly daft teenager, she lounged on her mother's light-brown sofa and waited for her delivery. What a time to be alive. Food was delivered to the door, and endless entertainment options were available on the TV – a luxury fit for royalty. After about twenty minutes of waiting, she heard a knock on the door and jumped up to answer.

"Chris?" she gasped, staring wide-eyed at the man standing in front of her.

"So, the rumours are true. The vicious wildcat is back. Hi, kitten," Chris replied with a grin, handing a stunned Sara May her pizza.

"What are you doing delivering pizzas? I thought you'd be the CEO of a giant corporation by now!"

"I'm halfway there. I own the Pizza-lot. And when I saw the order's address, I just had to come see for myself because your mum never orders from us."

"The owner? Then I reckon you must have time to come in for a chat."

Chris agreed and followed Sara May into the kitchen. She could hardly believe her other childhood best friend was standing before her. Like with Eric, she hadn't seen Chris for thirteen years, and her guilt towards him was no less. Those two boys had been her partners in crime, her best friends, and she'd left them without any explanation, causing her a fair amount of anxiety over the years. But now, Chris was sitting in front of her as if no time had passed. Chris Decker, so grown up, so handsome and fit, she wondered if he also owned a gym. Perhaps they were working out together, he and Eric. She couldn't keep her eyes off him. It was almost unbelievable how well they had both turned out. She felt like an embarrassing mishap compared to him. A fresh-faced forest goblin who hadn't gone to the gym since being filled with false confidence shortly after her thirtieth birthday. That lasted for about a week before a new doughnut shop opened close to her home. Who could resist that?

"So, who did you kill? Why have you returned to this horrible, ugly slum that you never wanted to see again? Your words, not mine," Chris teased.

"It's a long story," Sara May sighed.

"I got time."

"Short version. I had an accident, and Mum forced me to stay with her while I recovered."

"So, you'll be gone again when I wake up?"

"I'm sorry. I should've told you guys before I left. Do you still keep in touch?" Chris exhaled loudly, and Sara May felt an instant shift in his mood.

"Not exactly. But that's a story for another time."

"Very well. So, you own the Pizza-Lot," Sara May replied, desperate to divert the conversation away from the awkward path it was heading down."

"Yeah. I also work shifts at the Brewer as a bouncer occasionally."

"Hasn't Jack taken over that place yet?"

"No, and I doubt he ever will. He's obnoxiously rotten; he thinks he can become the next prime minister, imagine that. And Simon and Suzy support it!"

"You're kidding!"

"Wish I were. He's their golden calf, their ticket to royalty. You know how they are. Grabbing every opportunity to seem bigger than they are."

"Why do you work for them?" Chris shook his head as he tore apart another slice.

"It's just a few extra quid. I see Jake occasionally; that's nice," he replied and took a bite.

"How is he?" Chris shrugged.

"Same as usual. Doesn't talk much and keeps to himself. I can't blame him; he's been damaged by how his parents treated him. I give him some leftover pizza if I can spare it. I feel sorry for him."

Sara May absorbed everything Chris told her. It was shocking to hear how some people's lives had changed dramatically over the last thirteen years, while others had barely changed at all. Simon and Suzy Lewis were well-liked by some, but others strongly disliked them, mainly because they openly favoured one son over the other. Most people felt sorry for Jake, much to his parents' dismay, as they saw him as a stain on their otherwise flawless reputation. The couple dreamed of a respectable place among the country's elite; that was no secret. Rumours claimed they had tried many times to get on the guest list for various parties held for the nation's chosen ones, since those gatherings were known for hosting unofficial deals and signing contracts, often sealed with handshakes and cigars. They found that more appealing than staying in Northtown forever. This was also why they despised Aunt Marie, for she had always been able to waltz through those galas as if she were getting paid for it. That seemed to be enough reason to hate her guts.

After an hour of chatting, Chris stood up and prepared to leave, thanking Sara May for the pizza before he went his merry way. As she watched him go, she couldn't help but think, 'What if?' She'd always known that Chris had a crush on her when they were younger. Had she not left, and by doing so broken his heart, who knew what might have been? She closed the door and finished washing up after the much-appreciated meal. It was almost nine o'clock, and she was starting to feel tired. If only she could get a fraction of the energy that drove children into madness every day, oh, how sweet life would be! She tried to finish watching the programme she'd started while waiting for the pizza, but her eyelids had other plans, forcing her to turn off the telly and drag her feet to bed. She was too exhausted to worry about a possible nightmare. That was a problem for later that night.

Chapter 11

Sara May woke suddenly, panicking and sweating through her pyjamas. The same nightmare had occurred. The black-clad monster had rushed past her to reach the blonde lady and then mercilessly beat her until she slumped down and vanished. Sara May had watched the entire ordeal without being able to do anything to help. After the young woman disappeared, the black-clad figure of a man turned to her and started running at lightning speed towards her, so fast she couldn't make out the few facial features he had. She woke up just as he was about to grab her. Now, she sat upright in bed in the shadowy room, wrapped in a sweat-soaked duvet, trying to calm her rapidly beating heart. Damn it! She was in no mood to start washing her sheets in the middle of the night.

She got out of bed and walked through the eerily pitch-black house. The pillows and blanket on the living room sofa would have to do for the rest of the night. She strolled down the stairs and through the hallway until she entered the kitchen. Sweating like an out-of-shape marathon runner called for ice-cold remedies, and despite still being extremely drowsy, she managed to find her way to the fridge without any major mishaps. The moonlight and the mildly warm refrigerator light served as the perfect flashlight as she drank a bottle of water. Half-asleep, she returned the empty bottle to the fridge and closed it. And that's when she saw it. The sight made her heart leap out of her chest, and every fibre of her being recoiled. There she was! Standing next to the kitchen sink like a statue. The woman from her nightmares! The same wavy-blonde hair, the same light-blue denim, and that colourful, scrawny jumper that seemed to be from the mid-90s. She stood there, practically glowing, bathed in the moonlight shining through the window behind her. Sara May let out a blood-curdling scream.

She had never thought of herself as a proficient gymnast before. She always envied those flexible Olympic athletes who twisted and leapt in unusual ways, sideways and backwards. But judging by her frantic movements after screaming her lungs out, she could have easily won a gold medal at the Olympics. After running terrified into the living room at eighty miles per hour, nearly tipping over the sofa in sheer panic, she had planted herself firmly in one corner of the room. Slowly, she turned around. She had heard of people walking in their sleep; perhaps that was all this was. She was still asleep! She had to be! This was nothing but a continuation of her never-ending nightmare. If she pressed herself against the wall, the scary man in black clothes couldn't run past her. It was impossible. But if he appeared from somewhere else, she was trapped in a corner, and he could quickly reach her. Her mind was racing. She was done for!

"Please. Don't scream. I mean you no harm," the blonde woman pleaded weakly.

"Who are you? What do you want?" Sara May stammered, still facing the wall.

"I don't know who I am," the woman replied.

"This is a nightmare, this is a nightmare," Sara May repeated to herself, firmly keeping her eyes shut.

She'd heard of the usual effects of a head injury: dizziness, poor vision, and memory loss. But never in her life had she heard of people who'd been struck on the head and, as a result, started seeing figures from their nightmares just walking around as if they were normal people. She had to be hallucinating. Maybe Chris had hired a comedian who, as a prank, had sprinkled her pizza with funny shrooms. Maybe calling Chris to see how he was doing wasn't the worst idea. Slowly, she opened her eyes again. The woman stood behind the sofa, sending shivers down Sara May's spine. Terrified that this horror would escalate, she stood as still as possible.

"I come in peace," the woman reassured her.

"I don't care if you come in peace or start a nuclear war! You're not supposed to be here! You don't exist!" Slightly offended by that last comment, the woman lowered her brows and placed both hands on her hips.

"I'm sorry, but I'm just as real as you are. I'll have you know!"

"No! No, you're not! You're the woman I've been having nightmares about. There's nothing real about that! You're not real!"

"I had to show you what happened to me. Otherwise, you can't help me."

Sara May stared at the woman in disbelief. Help her? With what? She didn't even know this person, and she sure as hell hadn't figured out what was happening in her nightmares. The only thing she was sure of was that this nightmare had robbed her of a good night's sleep for three nights in a row, and it was beginning to take its toll. Perhaps this was all due to a lack of sleep. The doctors had warned her about that, which was why her mother had kidnapped her—to make sure she rested. This couldn't be happening. After what felt like an eternity, she slowly moved closer to the woman, shaking like a leaf. The slightest movement from this ghostly figure, and she would bolt, leaving a human-sized hole in the front door. Her voice was trembling.

"I don't know who you are or what you want. But I can't help you."

"Yes, you can. They said you could."

"They? Who are they?"

"I was here. I know it. But he hurt me. He's an evil man."

The woman made no sense, and Sara May struggled to keep up with her. But something about the apparition's timidly shivering voice urged her to listen more closely. Perhaps it was an illusion brought on by sleep deprivation or hallucinogenic mushrooms. But something, or someone, whispered in her ear that she needed to pay attention. She recalled the words of the mysterious woman in the white city. *You have a job to do,* she had said. Could this petite, blonde woman be the key to that job? She took a deep breath. If true, she would require all the courage she could summon, something she had been short on lately.

"If you want me to help you, you have to tell me more. Who's evil?" The woman, almost looking alive at this point, stared at the floor before whispering.

"He hurt me. They haven't found me. I rest nowhere," she replied, sounding confused.

"What do you mean? Who hurt you?" Sara May firmly asked.

Her voice grew louder, and as she let go of the last word, the woman suddenly vanished into thin air. Sara May jumped back and quickly scanned the living room with her eyes, but saw no one. Her feet felt rooted to the ground. Just as well. She'd be mad to look for that strange creature. She feared she might suddenly appear and scare the living daylights out of her. Slowly, she started backing towards the stairs until she felt safe enough to run upstairs. She sprinted to her bedroom and jumped back into bed, pulling her duvet over her head.

Shaking uncontrollably in a state of panic, she was close to hyperventilating and longed to cry. She'd been afraid of the dark her entire life without knowing why. The only explanation she could think of was that the dark contained everything she feared. She was terrified of what the dark was hiding from her. The night wasn't just something she had to endure to see a new day. The cold, coal-black Nordic nights followed no rules except their own. What good was it to be brave against something she couldn't see and to armour herself against something she couldn't feel or touch? How could such a fight ever be fair? Her irrational fear had caused many arguments between her parents. Her dad had tried to help her as best he could but never managed to make the dark disappear entirely. Meanwhile, her mother had always believed it was just drama, that there was absolutely nothing wrong with their daughter, and that she shouldn't receive any special attention. It was nothing more than childhood anxiety she would grow out of.

After a while, she finally gained enough confidence to stick her head out. Still trembling, she moved one foot out of bed, then the other, until she was steady enough to walk to her mother's study, taking it one step at a time. There, she dropped down in front of the computer, and soon, the bright light from the screen lit up the room. The blonde-haired woman's words kept her awake, wrapping around every nerve in her body. The woman had said the man was evil, and they had never found her. Could it be that someone in Northtown had done the unthinkable and committed a murder? Why had she never heard about it before? She searched the internet, but despite countless mouse clicks, she found nothing. No news articles, no statements. Not even a sentence in the local paper. How could this be?

She felt the room turn colder. This was too real to be caused by a head injury. No matter how much she tried to convince herself she was imagining the whole thing, the feeling of it being real wouldn't leave her. Something was happening, and she had to find out what. If only to end the nightmares. Her eyelids grew heavier, and she struggled to keep her focus. She was determined to uncover the secrets this town was hiding, even if it was the last thing she did.

Chapter 12

The alarm went off, and the phone vibrated in her pocket, waking Sara May abruptly. She had fallen asleep in front of the computer and was seconds away from drooling on the keyboard. She stood up and stretched, only to hear every bone in her body crack like a freaking glowstick. It clearly wasn't a good idea to fall asleep sitting down. People over thirty should never attempt such a stunt. She glanced at the clock. It was nearly five a.m. She was running out of time! Her mother would be home from her night shift within an hour, so she had to get out fast. She didn't want to explain to her mother that she'd started seeing a strange woman in the kitchen in the middle of the night. She grabbed her light brown jacket, wrapped it tightly around herself, and hurried into the darkness of the night, lit only faintly by a few dim streetlights on either side of the road. She had to push aside her fears this time. After walking steadily for about fifteen minutes, she reached her destination and knocked firmly on the door. A little while later, the lights flickered on, and a sleepy Eric appeared, wearing black boxer shorts and a thin navy-blue bathrobe that did little to hide his rock-solid abs. She was caught off guard, and with her jaw dropping halfway to the ground, she took a moment to admire this masterpiece. He looked so good! Scruffy, half-naked, and in desperate need of a clean shave.

"Sara May? What are you doing here? What time is it?"

"Five. I'm sorry I woke you up," she replied sheepishly, still hypnotised by his perfectly proportioned body.

"Five? "Is everything alright?" he asked, his concern evident.

"Yes, and no. Can I come in?"

Hesitant, Eric eventually dropped his arm, which had been holding the door, and gestured for her to enter. She felt slightly embarrassed, not considering that few people were awake at this hour. Perhaps it was a problem limited to those hallucinating from lack of sleep. Eric led her into the kitchen and began making coffee. He secretly wished it were something much stronger that would wake him up; the caffeine would have to do. Yawning, he sat across from Sara May and pushed one cup towards her. The coffee smelled divine. Eric, however, did not waste time smelling it. His body was crying out for caffeine right now! The first sip gave him the strength to open his eyes.

"Forgive me for asking, but what are you doing here so early?"

"Do you trust me?" Sara May replied.

"That depends on whether the caffeine will kick in soon," he sighed and took another sip. He did not sign up for this shit.

"I know this is gonna sound crazy, but you know me. I would never say something like this unless I had a good reason to."

"I knew you thirteen years ago. We were just kids."

"Can I at least tell you why I am here before you write me off?" she huffed. Exhaling loudly, he leaned back and gestured to her to continue. He still hadn't fully decided whether he was interested in listening. In the worst-case scenario, he would fall asleep mid-story and be branded as a bad host.

"Have you ever heard someone talk about a murder being committed here?" Sara May quietly asked.

"Murder? Here in Northtown? Not that I can recall. Why?"

"Well, I've had the same nightmare since I returned to

Northtown. And tonight…" Sara May hesitated before continuing. "…tonight, the nightmare became a little bit too real." Eric looked sceptical, narrowing his brows.

"What do you mean?"

"The woman from my nightmare was standing right in front of me. She was asking me for help. She said that the evil man had hurt her and that her body had never been found. She wanted me to help her find her body."

"What are you talking about? What evil man?"

"I don't know. And she didn't know either. She vanished before I could ask her more questions." Eric rolled his eyes not so subtly before leaning in closer.

"Sara May…" She interrupted him.

"I know this sounds crazy. But there's something not right here; I know it. Something's going on in this town that nobody's talking about!"

"Probably because it didn't happen," Eric replied as he got up to get himself a refill.

"Please, Eric. You're the only one I can turn to."

"Why? Because we were friends? You left! And you never said goodbye. I just woke up one morning, and you were gone!" Eric replied, raising his voice higher than he had intended.

Sara May leaned back in her chair and bit her bottom lip to prevent the tears from escaping. She knew she had hurt him badly the day she left, but she had never allowed herself to dwell on it because the guilt was too overwhelming. She'd hoped he'd gotten over it by now because if anyone could help her solve this mystery, it was him. Instead, he had turned her down. He ran his hand through his messy hair, then let it fall over his face, followed by a loud sigh as his head dropped. He knew he had to choose his words carefully.

"I don't know what you want me to say. I've never heard of someone committing a murder here in Northtown, and I don't remember hearing anything about it on the news. You've had a nasty head injury...." Sara May cut him off.

"It's not that!" she shouted.

"It may be real to you, but trust me, you won't convince anyone if you spread this shit around like it's a fact!" Eric yelled back.

"Just forget it!" Sara May snapped and stormed out of the kitchen.

"Sara May, come on. I didn't mean it like that!"

Those final words didn't reach her as she hurried out and slammed the front door behind her. Eric let out a deep breath to steady his nerves as he pinched the bridge of his nose. This woman had always been a wild horse; it was one of the things he loved most about her. Untameable, constantly forging her own path. He should've known this town was too small for her free spirit, that she'd eventually break away and leave. He was angry with himself for letting his inability to forgive prevent them from rebuilding their friendship. What the hell was he thinking? He was a grown man. He shouldn't keep the wound open like that. Sara May was unique; he'd always known that. "That ghastly excuse of a girl" is how locals most often described her. Thorny, a waste of good looks. She had shocked many respectable people with her antics that didn't suit the lady many felt she ought to be. And clearly, she hadn't changed one bit. So why had he then treated her like some crazy creature who had lost her mind after one blow to the head? Upset with himself, he poured the rest of the coffee into the sink. It had gone cold, anyway.

Sara May hurried back to her mother's house. This time, she let the tears flow freely, overwhelmed by terrible guilt and intense frustration. She'd gone to see Eric, hoping for some support; instead, he'd shattered what little self-esteem she had left. He might as well have called her a nutcase! Chris and Eric had been her only two friends then—her partners in crime, her two favourite guys who always stood by her, no matter what. Eric had been her fiercest protector; there had always been some strange, unexplained energy between them. That's why she'd been so sure she'd find the shelter she sought with him and be met with the understanding she craved so badly. But he'd turned away from her. How could she apologise to him when he refused to stand by her when she most needed him? She'd never felt so alone as she wiped the tears away with her left sleeve. She'd been forced out of her home in the city and taken back to this pathetic slum, all against her will. Paige was nowhere to be seen, and Eric had no interest in her. It was clear this was a battle she had to win on her own. And the more she thought about it, the angrier she became. How dare he? No, this war was hers to fight and hers alone. This modern Joan of Arc would be the talk of the town when this was all over!

"Mum! "I'm home!" she called out so loudly that the whole house echoed. Desperately tired, Maggie dragged her feet into the foyer to greet her daughter.

"I didn't know you left," Maggie yawned.

"I went over to see Eric. Can I ask you something?"

"Oh, can't it wait? I just got home from a long shift."

"Who's Helena?"

Suddenly, Maggie's face lost all colour. Her breathing grew heavy, her mouth dried out, and her body became stiff. Helena. The name she hadn't dared to say aloud for over thirty years. Partly, she had hoped she would never have to. A flood of memories burst like a broken dam, leaving her speechless. She had prepared herself for the day it might come up. But Sara May had never shown any interest in her parents' past. She never asked any questions, and when she moved to the capital, Maggie thought the matter was closed forever. But now, her daughter stood before her and casually mentioned this name as if it meant nothing, as if it held no significance. Oh, if only she knew.

"Where did you hear that name?" Maggie cautiously asked. She wasn't sure how to handle this sudden turn of events.

"I heard two ladies talk at the Bread Box. They said I looked so much like Helena. But Nan threw a fit when I mentioned her, and I want to know why."

Maggie felt the knot in her stomach tighten, threatening to rise up her throat and cut off her breath completely. Her heart pounded faster than a honey bee's wings, and her forehead and palms suddenly became sweaty. She knew she'd have to choose her words carefully. Now was not the time to stumble and fall. Her ex-husband John had been right all along. They should have told their daughter about Helena long ago—the ugly family secret. But Maggie had always refused, acting on the firm belief that she was protecting Sara May. Now, she was on her own. No husband to hold her hand and guide her through this mess she'd created with her stubbornness. What the hell was she supposed to do?

"Oh, honey. I am too tired. It was a long and difficult shift. We'll talk later, okay?" was all she could think of saying, cowardly backing out of this.

She gently tapped her disappointed daughter on the cheek. The story behind this seemingly ordinary name was so weighty that it required preparation, and right now, she had no energy to face that fight. She gradually walked away from Sara May, who was left behind, feeling betrayed and hurt. Someone wasn't telling her the whole story, and the fuzzier the answers, the angrier she became.

Chapter 13

"Honey, I don't know if I have anything for you to wear. You're so bony; I wouldn't feed you to my dogs if I had any," Aunt Marie called out from the other room. Ever so considerate.

"Well, Mum wants me to go to this service, and Nan will gut me open with a pitchfork if I dare go to God's House looking like trash. That offends him, apparently," Sara May replied, rolling her eyes at the thought. Aunt Marie shrugged as she walked over to the living room.

"He's forgiven worse things. Try this," she replied, handing her niece a plain, beige-looking dress before heading back to her master bedroom next door.

Sara May slipped into the dress and looked at herself in the mirror. She was horrified by what she saw. She'd never been much for dresses, especially not for special occasions. All this heterodoxy never sat right with her, something that her grand socialite Aunt Marie had spent many hours fussing over. *"A woman is always at her best when dressed to impress! Professional, determined, and seductive!"* she'd say. Words that sounded foreign to her niece, who thought of her job as a kitchen porter, where she'd spent countless hours scrubbing dirty pots and pans. It wasn't very glorious and certainly not something to wear a gown for. Her life wasn't exactly a fairytale. And now, all of a sudden, she was supposed to prance around like Pollyanna to be in the good graces of the God upstairs. As if.

"Aunt Marie, can I ask you something?" Sara May cautiously called out, cringing at herself in the mirror.

"Anything, darling, as long as it's brief and not about my love life. I'm having a little dry spell and don't need the reminder." Sara May smiled. Her aunt certainly had her moments.

"Who is Helena?" she then asked.

And just like that, the stormy clouds gathered, and the air grew thicker than in a smoky backroom. Sara May felt her body go numb. She could hear her aunt's feet pounding as she stormed back into the room, probably preparing herself for a war. She stopped a few feet from her niece, gathering herself like the true lady she was. She took a deep breath, composing herself before sharply rebuking Sara May for asking such a thing!

"Where did you hear that name?" Aunt Marie asked as calmly as she could

"Some ladies at the Bread Box said I looked just like her." Aunt Marie grunted.

"Can't those dann blabbermouths start chewing on something else? There can't be much more of this carcass to feast on! Who were these filthy, flea-covered swamp rats? "Did Paula send them?" Aunt Marie asked in a demanding tone. She'd always hated the pastor's wife. She found her to be a pretentious piece of work.

"I don't know; I didn't recognise them." Aunt Marie turned away from her niece, huffing and puffing with disgust.

"I'm sure they were! They've never learned to zip those ugly blowholes on their flabby faces! They're nothing but filthy gossipers; that's what they are!" she hissed through her teeth.

"Who's Helena?" Sara May repeated herself. This time, more firmly.

"Was! She was a dirty harlot, and that's all I'll say, or the church may catch on fire! Now, hurry up, or we'll be late!"

Sara May didn't dare disobey her aunt when she looked like she was about to explode! She had never seen her so angry. Marie Beatrice Jensen was known for her poised demeanour, which had annoyed all the grand dames in town for decades. They hated yapping about the controversial noblewoman of Northtown without getting any reaction from her. Aunt Marie had learned over the years to always keep her head held high and ignore the snide tongues. Armed with this attitude, she managed to land herself no fewer than four wealthy husbands who had no defence against the fascinating, slightly dangerous temptress. But now, her niece had managed to break through that wall, and then some! Waves had formed on the placid lake. Sara May had never feared for her life as much as she did now.

Although brief, the car ride to the church was uncomfortable and far too long. Aunt Marie said nothing the entire way there, and Sara May wasn't sure she would ever look at her again. This was proving to be a near-fatal blow. So, instead of trying to disturb her aunt's mood again, she just stared out the window. The sun had made a rare appearance on this otherwise dull Sunday, casting a warming glow over the plain surroundings. The church of Northtown was located a short distance outside the town itself. It was a small, wooden church painted a light grey with a white roof—a typical Nordic church surrounded by once-green bushes and leafless trees that had once sported a lush, lime-coloured foliage. The old timber benches inside didn't seem capable of fitting more than a few churchgoers, yet the place was packed, to Sara May's amazement. The interior smelled of old, wet wood; the colourful décor included a few paintings of Jesus and angel statues. She had hated this place since childhood.

She had been bored to tears every Sunday when dragged to service with her mum, nan, and Aunt Marie because they never let her behave like a child. She hadn't even been allowed to dangle her feet without her mother scolding her. It had never been a place for an energetic little girl who only wanted to embrace nature's freedom, climb trees, and get her dress dirty.

Aunt Marie parked the car, and as soon as Sara May stepped out, a wave of uncomfortable memories washed over her. The church looked much the same; the wood had become slightly damp, giving off a musty smell, and it desperately needed a fresh coat of paint. But it still held its charm, in a kind of sacred way. A crowd had gathered outside, but Aunt Marie was not in the mood to mingle. She ignored everyone and stormed towards the church to find her mother and sister, with Sara May following close behind, her head bowed to avoid attention. She'd noticed Bill and Laura Baker from the Bread Box, Simon and Suzy Lewis from the Brewer, and their twins, Jack and Jake. As usual, Jack was the life of the party, but Jake kept his distance, avoiding eye contact. And there was Eric, helping old Gilbert out of his car. Damn it! She quickly turned away. She still hadn't forgiven him for not taking her seriously when she needed him. She hurried inside and sat beside her mother in the front row. Neither her nan nor Aunt Marie acknowledged her, and Maggie stayed quiet, deeply embarrassed by the whole thing.

After everyone had taken their seats, the crowd eagerly waited for their pastor's arrival. Suddenly, the church doors swung open, revealing a larger-than-life figure of a man dressed in a black robe with a white collar at the neck, who strode in. Pastor Evans. A tall, husky man, slightly wrinkled, with thin grey hair neatly brushed back and a poorly groomed beard covering half his round face. He confidently walked to the pulpit, basking in the admiration and reverence his followers showered upon him. He stood there for the next hour, preaching in his deep, gravelly voice about the importance of Christian values, love, and kindness. Sara May did her best to stay focused, but this time, it wasn't the mundane material that disturbed her. It was the fact that the sun was shining outside, brightening the whole church, yet around Pastor Evans, the surroundings seemed dark and frankly frightening. He stood there like a devilish creature from a low-budget horror film. Was she losing her mind?

Pastor Evans was the same age as Aunt Marie and had been one of her closest friends growing up. Although their friendship had soured over the years, she'd remained loyal to the church; however, she'd never wanted to discuss what had come between her and the pastor. She wasn't a woman who wasted her words. Pastor Evans had always been a towering figure in Northtown. With his dedicated wife Paula's help, he had built a reputation akin to a demigod in the eyes of many. People from all walks of life visited his house seeking solutions to their problems, and he was never one to turn them away, regardless of the time of day. Because of this, very few locals had anything negative to say about him, and although people knew that his wife ran a gossip factory with her trusted little army of informers, nobody dared speak ill of the pair.

Sara May looked around the church. Eric was sitting a few benches behind, on the other side of the aisle, next to old Gilbert. Their eyes briefly met, but she quickly looked away. She wasn't interested in getting caught up in a staring contest with the man her head was angry at, but her lady parts lusted for. Again, she tried to focus on Pastor Evans's preaching, but with no luck. The same eerie black mist surrounded him, and she began feeling uneasy. There was no escape; she would have to endure it. She looked outside the window in a somewhat desperate attempt at distraction, hoping the sun would ease her torment. Then she noticed the strange woman from her nightmare, this time standing between two bare-branched trees, looking frightful.

"I do not rest," she whispered. Despite sitting several feet away, Sara May could hear her clearly, but before she could reply, the woman faded away as if she had never been there, leaving Sara May baffled and unnerved. After what seemed like an eternity, the service finally came to an end. She quickly stood up, hoping to slip away unnoticed. She didn't get her wish.

"So, the rumours are true! Little Miss Jensen's back in town!" Pastor Evans called out for everyone to hear. Sara May's head dropped with a heavy sigh as she turned around to greet the pastor with a forced smile.

"Yeah, guess I am."

"Good to see you again, kid. You've grown a bit since last time."

Feeling uncomfortable, she kept wishing the wooden floor would quietly swallow her whole. She'd never liked Pastor Evans or his wife, Paula, but she never understood why. They'd never been anything but lovely to her. There was just something about them — a negative energy of some sort — that seemed to follow them around, and it always gave her a chilling feeling that wrapped around every bone in her body. Aunt Marie had left as soon as she could, so Sara May would have to rely on her mother and Nan for a lift home. She knew from experience it would take a while because Pastor Evans was one of the few people Grandma Gladys actually liked. So, she would always try to chat with him if she was lucky enough to get his attention, while her daughter, well-liked by the locals, had to speak to everyone attending. Thus, it was easy for Sara May to slip away unnoticed, or so she thought. Just as she exited the door, she heard her name being called. She closed her eyes and quietly cursed her failed escape attempt.

"Sara May!" he called again. She reluctantly turned around to see Eric jogging toward her.

"What?" she angrily replied.

"I just wanted to apologise for how I acted the other day. I was tired; it was very early morning, and I wasn't expecting a visit. She crossed her arms, giving him the strongest death stare she could muster.

"I thought you, of all people, would back me up on this."

"I do. But surely you must hear how crazy this sounds!" Fighting the urge to punch him, she took a deep breath and turned to walk away from him. Eric quickly grabbed her upper arm.

"Come on, don't be like that." She swiftly yanked her arm back, furious at how boldly he'd acted.

"Let go of me, or I swear I'll scream!" she commanded, expecting her aggression to scare him off. But he didn't flinch. Instead, he moved closer, activating her fight-or-flight mode.

"Talk to Nana Lou. She can help you," he advised her, his voice softer than she'd expected from someone who had just been threatened.

"Is she still alive?" she asked, stunned at what she had just heard.

"Eighty-six and never better. Talk to her. You know she can help you."

She wasn't sure if he was pulling her leg, so instead of fully agreeing to his plea, she nodded and walked away. The crowd had gathered outside the church, as Pastor Evans's Sunday services provided a good opportunity to catch up. Sara May kept her head bowed until she was safely past them. When she looked up, she spotted a familiar face. Seeing Chris standing by his car and watching people stream out of the church made her heart skip a beat. His face lit up when he saw her, and after a brief chat, she accepted his offer of a lift home. Relieved that she didn't have to endure endless chit-chat about her life and the weather, she didn't notice the harsh looks Chris and Eric exchanged before Chris closed the car door behind her, then got in himself and drove away.

Chapter 14

Maggie had arrived home unusually late that day. She'd driven her mother home from church, and on the way, they discussed how best to handle the situation with Sara May. Grandma Gladys refused to participate and thought it best for Maggie to sweep it under the rug again. She seemed sure it would die down eventually, but Maggie wasn't convinced. She knew her daughter well. She knew that if Sara May set her mind on something, no matter how irrational, she would follow through. Remembering many impulsive and often temperamental decisions Sara May made during her teenage years—eventually driving her out of Northtown and to the capital without a backup plan—Maggie knew not to underestimate her. So, the question was how to approach this because wishing it away was no longer an option. She took a deep breath and unlocked her front door. Going against her mother's advice, she thought it was best to just get it over with. Perhaps it would help heal some of the wounds that had plagued her for years. She'd allowed them to remain infected for the last three decades, causing more harm than she realised. Slowly, she pushed the front door open and stepped inside.

"I'm home!" she called out.

"I'm in the kitchen," Sara May replied loudly.

Slowly, she entered the kitchen to find her daughter preparing a sandwich. The Sunday service had exhausted her, and she longed for some marmalade toast and chocolate milk. Waiting patiently for the bread to pop up from the toaster, she watched her mother sit down, but didn't feel like talking to her. Maggie knew it would be best to approach Sara May on her own terms, so she stayed silent too. For a while, only deafening silence remained. At last, Sara May finished her marmalade masterpiece and sat down opposite her mother. Maggie exhaled. It was time.

"You asked about Helena," she said, visibly uncomfortable.

"Yes. I wanna know who she is. Or was," Sara May replied.

"*Was* might be the right word, I guess." Maggie rubbed her palms together nervously. "You need to understand that this is difficult for me to discuss. And to be completely honest with you, I don't know where to start," she admitted.

"I just want an answer to this one simple question." Maggie sighed.

"This isn't a simple question, honey."

Sara May watched as her mother grew increasingly anxious, rubbing her knuckles vigorously. Why, though? Surely, talking about a seemingly ordinary woman who may or may not have been alive and thriving at some point couldn't be this difficult. She hadn't always had the best understanding of people's emotions, but this was too urgent to care about any of that. Again, Maggie nervously sighed and ran her fingers through her hair. Her exasperated facial expressions clearly showed her disinterest in further conversation.

"I don't know why these women were talking about you, Sara May; I honestly don't."

"This is Northtown, Mum. If those sadistic witches couldn't sniff out gossip, they'd die. You remember how they yapped about you and Dad back in the day. I moved away because of it."

"Still, they had no right saying anything!"

"What's the big deal? Who is Helena, and why is her name so tainted?" Maggie inhaled deeply before proceeding. This was it—the moment she'd dreaded for years.

"Helena is my little sister. The youngest of the three."

Sara May was stunned, sitting motionless in her chair like a block of ice. Sister? Had she got another aunt? How could that be possible? And why had no one mentioned her before? She couldn't recall ever meeting her; she hadn't even heard of her until now.

"What do you mean she was your sister? Where is she now?" Maggie let out a small breath of air before continuing.

"God only knows. She was known to be a bit of a hussy, and eventually, rumours started going around that she was having an affair with a married man in town. Nobody knew if it was true, but she never denied it, which made many loyal housewives frantic; some became downright hysterical. The story goes that at least three marriages collapsed because of this. We were so deeply embarrassed about the whole thing, especially your nan. It became so bad that one day, Helena just had enough and fled town. Never to be seen or heard from again."

"Have you guys never tried to contact her?"

"No. Your nan was humiliated by Helena's alleged behaviour, and your Aunt Marie was furious that her little sister had so wickedly tainted her reputation. So, we just let her go." No less surprised than before, Sara May struggled to find the right words.

"Have you never wondered what happened to her?"

"I've had moments here and there. But it's been so long, I don't think anything will change, I'm afraid."

She couldn't believe her ears. She never suspected that her mother was hiding such a big secret. The very predictable Margarete Rachel Jensen, the woman who'd always been so understanding and compassionate towards everyone. Even on her worst days, she always managed to put on her best smile and pretend everything was fine. Could she have perfected her mask so flawlessly that the cracks weren't visible to the naked eye? Had she become so skilled at hiding her emotional scars that no one suspected a thing? Sara May suddenly felt like her whole world had been turned upside down. Not only was there another aunt somewhere, but her mum, Grandma Gladys, and Aunt Marie had deliberately kept it from her. Why? Surely, it couldn't have been because they were ashamed of Helena's behaviour. That shouldn't have affected Sara May's life in any way. Something else was at play here.

"Do you have a photo of her?" Sara May finally asked after a long stretch of silence.

Initially, Maggie said nothing. She hadn't expected Sara May to suddenly become so interested in her family history, let alone demand photographic evidence. There was no avoiding this. She quietly stood up and wandered out of the kitchen. A little while later, she returned with a thick red photo album and placed it in front of her daughter. Reluctantly, she opened the album and skipped a few pages until she found a photo that caught Sara May's attention — a picture of three young women in their twenties standing side by side.

"There she is," said Maggie, pointing at the picture.

Sara May looked at the photograph. Those women were as different from each other as sisters could be. On the right, Aunt Marie towered over the two younger ones. She's always been taller than Maggie, causing daily distress over her unsuccessful modelling career. According to Aunt Marie, there hadn't been a shortage of suitors; a selection of eligible young men had fallen hard for those toned legs that stretched to the high heavens and offered her all her heart's desires for just a touch. Maggie stood next to her, smiling from ear to ear. This photo had clearly been taken before the storm hit. She seemed blissfully unaware of what awaited her, with her messy brown hair all over her happy little face, dressed in blue dungarees and a white T-shirt, ready to tackle whatever life threw at her. The world was hers, and she was prepared for it.

Sara May's eyes quickly fixed on the girl on the far left. There she was—Helena, her lost aunt. The smallest of the three, so innocent and pure—like a little butterfly that had yet to emerge from its cocoon. Her wavy blonde hair fell just below her shoulders, and her delicate face was perfectly framed, with navy blue eyes and thin, pale lips set neatly beneath her petite nose. Dressed in a scruffy jumper and light blue denim, she looked like she had stepped straight out of a 1990s teen magazine. Sara May looked up from the album. Standing next to Maggie was the mysterious woman from her nightmares.

"Helena?" Sara May quietly whispered. The woman was there. She had a worried look on her face.

"She doesn't know. She doesn't understand," Helena muttered, her voice slightly trembling. Maggie cleared her throat.

"That's enough for now. I need to get ready for work, and I promised your nan that I would stop by the Bread Box and remind Eric to bring her some pastries," she said as she closed the photo album and hurried out of the kitchen.

Sara May looked back at Helena. Was she really seeing her aunt? If so, it was clear that she was no longer alive. Helena stood silently by the sink, seemingly waiting for her to come to her senses, but to no avail. She'd never been so confused. What was happening? How could she dream about her aunt and see her whilst awake? One thing was certain amid the tornado of thoughts that filled her mind. Something terrible had happened, and she felt like she owed it to this terrified young woman to find out what had happened to her. She felt sorry for her. So, she devised a plan. From now on, she would set aside her emotions and find out once and for all what had gone wrong. Someone had to know something. And she knew exactly where to begin.

Chapter 15

"Nana Lou? Are you home?" Sara May called out.

She had decided to heed Eric's advice and visit the old lady she'd long believed was dead. Nana Lou had always been like a grandmother to all the children in Northtown. Her house was open at all hours and had, in the past, been the most popular spot for kids who disliked the food at school for any reason. Nana Lou to the rescue! Happy and compassionate, she always welcomed everyone with open arms; as a result, every child in Northtown claimed her as their own. Her name was Louise Charlotte Beatrice Baker, but she'd shortened it to Nana Lou when she started collecting grandchildren all over town. Her husband of fifty years, Trucker Tom, as he was known for his connection to the garage he owned and ran, had passed away a few years before Sara May moved away. His death had sent shockwaves through Northtown, as he was a hugely admired and beloved man who had somehow convinced nearly every child in town that he was Santa Claus. He had chosen this small, seemingly unknown town to reside in during the off-season. Everyone loved Nana Lou and Trucker Tom, and Chris and Sara May often envied Eric for having them as grandparents.

"Come in, let me see you!" Nana Lou replied loudly.

With her arms wide open, she bounced towards Sara May, who couldn't believe her eyes. Not only was Nana Lou very much alive, but she also looked far better than Sara May had dared to imagine. Sure, the wrinkles on her face had increased, and her hair was whiter and thinner, but aside from that, she hadn't changed one bit! She still had that same warm smile spread across her whole face and the same endlessly pleasant embrace. Nowhere else could one get a hug like that, and for the first time since returning to this God-awful place, Sara May felt like she was home again. She followed Nana Lou into the living room, admiring the home that held her greatest childhood memories. It was exactly as she remembered it—a magical cottage straight out of a fairytale. Nana Lou and Trucker Tom had always made sure their house matched the myth surrounding them, so the children who thought they were visiting Santa during his off-season got just that. Since Tom's passing, Nana Lou has developed her own unique style. Every wall was festooned with strange statues and crooked paintings; every square foot covered with plants of all shapes and sizes; stacks of colourful books, and hidden among all this were bird cages, home to her feathered friends, whom she often let fly freely through the house. The air smelled of a mixture of scented candles and herbs; the old lady used various mystical items that earned her a legendary reputation. Sara May sat on the red velvet sofa and watched Nana Lou walk into the kitchen. Seconds later, the walnut-coloured coffee table was filled with freshly baked pastries and other delights, emitting the delightful aroma of a bakery. Dear old Nana Lou. She hadn't forgotten a thing.

"So, tell me, dear. What unholy forces dragged you back to Northtown? I was so sure you'd be halfway around the world by now," Nana Lou playfully asked, adding a smile that could melt even the sturdiest icebergs.

"I wish," Sara May shrugged. "I had a little accident, and Mum thought it'd be best I stayed with her until I'm better."

"I suppose this is as good a place as any. But what

brings you here? Aside from my delicious bread buns, of course." Sara May chuckled and took a bite. Nana Lou was renowned for her buttery bread buns and often gave her son, Bill, and his wife, Laura, a run for their money.

"I wanted to ask you something. I recently found out about Helena. She was my aunt. Do you know anything about her?" The old lady leaned back in her armchair.

"I remember her very well. She was a lovely girl, an absolute gem. Always so full of happiness and life," she replied, her face beaming with joy.

"That doesn't match what I've heard. Grandma Gladys threw a fit when I mentioned her, and Aunt Marie refuses to speak to me."

"People form their opinions based on what they choose to focus on. Those rumours weren't the best, but I've always said you shouldn't judge people based on their mistakes. "There's good in everyone, no matter how hard it is to spot," Nana Lou pointed out, sipping her coffee.

Dear old Nana Lou. She always wanted the best for everyone, never uttering a single harsh word if she could help it. One would have to be mad not to care for this strange little elf queen, to whom everyone felt entitled, despite never being able to confirm the rumour swirling around her since the beginning of time. It was part of the mystery that was Nana Lou. Some believed her to be psychic; others went so far as to call her a witch. Many mysterious things had happened throughout her lifetime that people had linked directly to her. Over time, the stories took on a somewhat mythical charm, further enhancing her image as someone slightly different from most people. Rumours had it that even the most hardened sceptics had been seen walking out of her house in the middle of the night after seeking supernatural solutions to their earthly problems. Nana Lou, however, remained as silent as the grave about it all.

"Is that the real reason you're here? Or is there something you're not telling me?" She didn't have to ask. She knew precisely why Sara May was sitting across from her.

"She appears in my dreams. A lot. It's more like a nightmare. And I don't know what to do," Sara May replied, slightly embarrassed.

"Describe this nightmare."

"There's a man, or more like a figure of a man, dressed all in black. He runs past me towards Helena and brutally assaults her until she vanishes. Then he turns towards me and starts running in my direction. I always wake up right before he gets to me. And..." Sara May stopped, gathering herself for a brief moment.

"And....?"

"Not long ago, I started seeing her."

"Seeing her? You mean Helena?"

"Yeah. She always appears out of nowhere, and I don't know what she wants or how to make this go away. She talks about the evil man, which I think is the man from the nightmare, but I have no idea who or what he is."

Nana Lou sat quietly for a while before getting up from her chair. She wandered around the living room, tending to her birds that flew freely, enjoying their liberty. These birds always helped her think clearly and connected her to her spirit guides on the other side. She should have known the girl would return one day. Her spiritual assistant, Jandaya, had informed her of this. *She has a job to do,* she said. Nana Lou smiled. Sara May had always been special. Since she first came to the house as a child, tagging along with Eric, Nana Lou had kept an eye on her. She hadn't shown signs of being aware of her gift, but the old enchantress was patient. Her spirit guides had assured her that Sara May was being watched and her powers would fully emerge when the time was right. For years, Nana Lou wondered if she'd misread this message because there had been no word from Sara May. She even began to doubt whether she would live to see her become the powerful necromancer she was destined to be. Now, she understood it was her role to guide Sara May on her journey, as she was meant to solve the mystery that had haunted the town for thirty-one years. That was her destiny, her fiery initiation into the magical world of the unknown.

"Have you told anybody about this dream?" Nana Lou almost whispered.

"Just Eric," Sara May confessed.

"Good. Don't mention this to anyone else. And trust no one. Northtown is not all that it seems; you must know," Nana Lou warned, stroking Theo, her blue parrot, down his back with one finger. Sara May edged forward, unsure what to make of this cryptic warning.

"What do you mean?"

"There is darkness lurking between the trees in town, Sara May. Keep that in mind. You should go now before your mum becomes worried. And remember, not a word to anyone."

Sara May knew better than to go against Nana Lou's words. She'd always trusted her in a way that was hard to explain. Nana Lou gave her the safety she'd never felt at home while growing up, which led her to trust the old woman with her life because Nana Lou understood her soul better than anyone. Standing by the front door, about to leave, she turned around and saw Helena standing beside the old witch. Sara May smiled.

"Helena is standing next to you," she informed Nana Lou, who smiled back.

"I know," she replied.

Chapter 16

What the hell is she doing there? Pastor Evans thought to himself as he watched Sara May wave goodbye to Nana Lou. Pastor Evans had long known about the old lady's psychic abilities, and as a man of the cloth, he'd concluded that buying the house opposite hers was the safest move. That way, he could keep an eye on everyone who, for whatever reason, was compelled to seek the witch's advice or perhaps provide her with information she could use to her advantage, utilising her ghostly talents. And now, Sara May had been sucked in as well.

Pastor Evans watched her walk down the street and disappear from view. He could feel the knot in his stomach tightening. This same knot had caused him pain for years, yet he'd never been convinced to admit why. He blamed the heavy workload, which satisfied those brave enough to ask. There was something profoundly Icelandic about accepting that one's health can be sacrificed for the sake of work. It's almost a badge of honour. Pastor Evans shrugged. The girl was back, God damn it! The out-of-control little bastard who now threatened everything he'd built over the past thirty-one years. She was a stain on his otherwise spotless reputation. She was never meant to return. Her presence here threatened the comfortable life he'd carved out for himself, and he wasn't about to stand by without a fight! As he moved away from the window to plot his next move, there was a knock on his office door.

"Come in!" he called out. Simon stuck his head through the half-opened door.

"Am I interrupting?"

"No, come in." Pastor Evans gestured with two fingers

while keeping his other hand firmly in his pocket.

Simon closed the door behind him and sat down opposite the pastor. Between them was a large, old-fashioned desk made of the finest mahogany available. Those things cost a fortune nowadays. All around them were wooden bookcases, reaching from floor to ceiling and filled to the brim with books meant to enhance one's knowledge and broaden one's mind. Various pictures of Jesus hung between the bookcases, and next to most of them were crosses of all sizes, clearly indicating that this office belonged to a man of strong Christian faith. In this doctrinal office, many societal issues had been discussed and sometimes resolved over the years, often over a good cup of tea. But despite no beverage being offered this time, Simon held no grudge. His reason for visiting the pastor was more important than whether to have tea or not.

"What brings you here this time of day?" Pastor Evans asked, annoyed. When ill-tempered, he wasn't fond of visitors.

"I would like to request an extension. The pub isn't doing so well and…"

"I have already granted you two extensions, Mr. Lewis. I expect you to repay the loan," Pastor Evans interrupted.

"I'm aware of that, but surely, I would have thought that a man in your position would be more understanding. I'm in a tight spot at the moment."

"If you can't keep one measly pub afloat in a shithole like this, how do you expect to survive in the shark tank back south?"

Simon said nothing. He knew Pastor Evans was telling the truth, but admitting it would be like admitting defeat.

He should have known better than to rely on the church for help, but he genuinely believed he had the upper hand at the time. He knew something about the pastor that no one else did, and in the early years, he used it to get his way. The pastor had paid him to keep quiet. He used the money to open the Brewer, trusting the pastor's words that with hard work and dedication, the pub would succeed, and that would be Simon and Suzy's ticket into the glamorous world of the rich and famous. A world in which Pastor Evans and his wife, Paula, were already a part of. Being young and naive at the time, the couple had been captivated by the alluring appeal of the wealthy top one per cent, eager to belong above all else. But as the years went on, Simon realised the pastor's promises were nothing but the poisonous words of a devious snake. The game had been rigged from the start, and slowly but surely, it turned against him. Keeping the Brewer afloat had been tough work that constantly demanded more financial support.

"Pastor, we go way back. You can trust me," Simon pointed out in a weak attempt to garner some sympathy.

"Can I? Can I honestly trust that you'll keep your mouth shut?"

"Haven't stayed silent for the last thirty-one years?" The sheer notion that the pastor would doubt his integrity offended Simon.

"It's often been a close call, mind you."

"Please, Evans. I'm desperate," he pleaded.

"Whilst you know what you know, I can't take any chances. There's a contract between us for a reason!"

"And that contract states you finance the Brewer! If you won't hold up your end of the bargain…."

"I have, and then some!" Pastor Evans suddenly

erupted, slamming his clenched fist on the table as he quickly rose and pointed a steady index finger at Simon. "You, however, are an atrocious businessman, so why should I continue to throw away money when I get nothing in return? I must be mad!" This prompted Simon to stand up as well, not to be intimidated by the pastor towering over him.

"Because I know what I know, and all I have to do is start talking! I see no reason to shut my mouth if you're not granting me the extension I humbly request! Grant me the extension, and you'll get my silence in return."

Simon had managed to corner Pastor Evans, who angrily lowered his weapon. But this fight was far from over. Simon didn't realise this was just the start of a war. On this battlefield, Pastor Evans was far better equipped, thanks to the support of his militant allies in the capital city. Having friends in high places has always been a valuable strategy in every society.

"Very well. You've got three months. Find a way to repay me; otherwise, I'll sell this godforsaken cesspool. Men should know better than conjuring up their demons through sinful day-drinking anyway."

Simon thanked the pastor and hurried out of the office. Pastor Evans sighed heavily. By now, he had hoped this issue would be a thing of the past. If it hadn't been for this pitiful loser, he would have settled the matter years ago. Simon was a lousy businessman, but he could have climbed the ranks within any mafia in the world if he wanted to, being such a clever negotiator. There was another knock on the door. Annoyed and tired, he invited the guest in. His wife, Paula, entered the office, carrying a tray of treats fit for a king.

"I thought you might need this after this visit," she

said, placing the tray neatly on the desk before her husband.

Bless this woman, he thought to himself, giving her a coy smile as a sign of approval.

Pastor Evans considered himself a fairly fortunate man. Paula was a good woman who always knew what he needed and when he needed it. She had perfected the art of catering to his every need long ago and did so flawlessly. One might say she was the perfect housewife, even if that wasn't seen as very admirable nowadays. Paula had stood by her husband's side like a rock for nearly forty years. Therefore, Pastor Evans sometimes couldn't help but feel a bit guilty. Oh, if only she knew. Maybe she did, but he wasn't sure. If she did, she never mentioned it. Her main concern was maintaining an outward appearance of perfection. The slightest cracks, and the other housewives outside her close-knit group of faithful followers, would jump at the chance to criticise every minor detail they could find. And that was too much for the honourable pastor's wife to bear. A distinguished noblewoman couldn't stand tall behind her curtains and judge others if her home was filled with hypocrisy.

"What did he want?" she asked as she skilfully poured her husband his tea with a hint of honey, just as he liked it.

"Another extension," Pastor Evans shrugged, taking a big bite from his cream cheese bagel. Paula scoffed.

"Of course. Does he have any plans to pay back the last two loans? Given the debt he's already in, I think that would be sensible."

"Now, now," Evans calmly replied. "The man came to me on his knees. I vowed to honour such a commitment.

The good Lord won't allow me to turn away from that," he lied as religiously as he could master.

"I don't understand why you keep pouring money into that devilish den. It isn't profitable in any way, and all people do there is commit ghastly misdeeds at all hours," Paula replied with a deep inhale, placing one hand on her chest to underline how horrid that sounded.

"Watch your words, my dear. He can hear you. Our Lord is merciful; no matter how disgraceful this pub might be, it might be the only shelter these poor people have. And who are we to cast judgment on that?" Paula smiled self-righteously.

"You're right. As always," she said and kissed her husband on the cheek.

She took the tray away and left the office. In all the years of being married to a clergyman, she had learned to trust his words. After all, he was a servant of God, doing His good work on Earth. Her upbringing had taught her not to go against it. Pastors deserved her automatic respect because they represented the Christian faith, God's holy messengers, and the backbone of a stable, functioning society. She didn't always agree with what was said, let alone how things were done, but upon marrying Evans, she agreed to walk a step behind him at all times and support him in his duties. And if that meant keeping quiet and being cute, so be it. No one could say that the pastor's wife wasn't capable of her role. The very thought of such a scandal was outrageous! She couldn't bear to think of it. Her primary duty was to support her husband when needed, and she was willing to do almost anything to ensure their success.

Chapter 17

Sara May dragged her feet to the living room. They felt heavy. It had been a long day, and she longed for her soft pillows and warm duvet to give her a good night's sleep. She would have preferred her bed back in Reykjavik, but, like so many other things involving her mother, she had little to no say in the matter. Maggie sat in front of the television, watching the evening news. Senate elections were fast approaching, dominating headlines for weeks. Sara May saw them as nothing but hollow words and empty promises. Vote for us, and we will improve your life! No, vote for us because the other guys will ruin your life! That's what it was really about. It was about who could lie the most and shout the loudest. She had always voted, mainly to escape the constant bombardment about how she was messing with democracy if she didn't vote. And it wasn't as if the conversations improved after the elections. Who did you vote for? I hope your vote went to the right party! I sure hope so because all the other parties will torture us and send us straight to eternal damnation! What? You didn't vote for the same party as me? Do you want to see this country burn?

It didn't matter who got the X on the ballot behind closed doors. It was all the same swamp. All of them pretended to have nurtured the garden of prosperity, hoping to fool people into voting for them while hiding the fact that the garden was nothing but weeds and wildflowers that no one had bothered to tend. As soon as the results were in, the splurge recommenced. Senior politicians had become so corrupt after years of extortion that they no longer seemed to care. The new individuals elected had their first taste of money and power, soon becoming just as depraved as their senior colleagues. This continued until the next election, resulting in another surge of lies to hide the fact that no one had attended to the garden. No one had bothered with the weeds and wildflowers. This was a vicious cycle as old as humanity itself. Sara May had long since decided to stay clear, though she couldn't help but admire those young people just entering politics. Still naive, not yet consumed by corruption, and adorably optimistic, they could do some good and bring about change. It was almost comical to watch.

"Mister Speaker, as a counterargument against the notion that our party has done nothing but faff about for the second term, I would like to point out that my government has done an outstanding job in securing support for low-income families and polls have time and again shown that the public is very much in favour of our actions! Therefore, I see no reason not to continue with our current plans," Prime Minister Stephen Crow proudly announced, while his colleagues, clearly disagreeing with this assessment, loudly protested all around him, accompanied by a few who gave him their most enthusiastic applause.

"Oh, isn't he just the greatest? He's always been so fine. He's from Northtown, you know," Maggie gushed, fawning over him like a teenage girl crushing hard on the most popular boy at school. Sara May lowered her brow in astonishment.

"Is he? I didn't know that."

"They're the same age, him, Pastor Evans, and your Aunt Marie. They've been friends since childhood," Maggie added, practically beaming with pride.

"I thought Aunt Marie hated the pastor."

"Hate is a strong word. They're not as close as they used to be, but she and Crow have always maintained close contact. Sara May rolled her eyes.

She had always disliked Prime Minister Crow and everything he stood for. She hadn't stooped so low as to dip her toes into the muddy political swamp that was his life, but she resented the fact that his decisions affected her life. Because, more often than not, he made terrible choices! He showed no concern for the will of the people while in office. Only when elections approached did he bother to show a flicker of interest. When he wasn't campaigning, he turned his back to the wind and flipped the bird to all those he regarded as beneath him, even going so far as to mock those brave enough to point out that the emperor had no clothes. Desperate pleas for help went unheard, and protests only seemed to fuel the political fire he relied on to thrive as a corrupt politician. They revitalised his strength and enabled him to keep filling his treasure chest with the public's hard-earned money while pretending to be oblivious to the whole thing. He always came out on top, basking in the glory bestowed upon him by those who kept voting for him. Prime Minister Crow was a white-collar criminal, and the worst kind at that.

"So, that's why Aunt Marie has always been invited to all these political galas," Sara May muttered. The thought of her aunt kissing the ring was horrifying.

"Well, they've been friends since primary school," Maggie replied while flicking through the channels.

"Whatever happened between Aunt Marie and Pastor Evans?"

"I don't know. Some say he just got tired of chasing her. But I don't believe that. He desired Helena much more than Marie." Sara May's eyes went round.

"Pastor Evans was crushing on Helena?"

"Oh, yes," Maggie replied without taking her eyes off the telly. "He was like a mad dog around her, but she didn't fancy him," she continued, looking back at her daughter. "This was all before Paula, of course. Oh, your Aunt Marie loathed her. She thought she was so stiff and boring."

"You think maybe that's why Aunt Marie and Pastor Evans had a falling out?"

"Could be. Crow and Evans still talk, at least they did last time I knew," Maggie replied before looking at the clock. "Oh, dear Heavens! I need to start getting ready. I'm working a night shift, so you'll have to fix your own dinner."

"Mum, I'm thirty-one years old. I can take care of myself."

Maggie smiled and kissed her daughter's forehead before heading upstairs to get ready for work. Sara May turned off the telly. She'd had enough of the news. Usually, she avoided it altogether, but there was no way around it at Maggie's place. Her house, her rules. Sinking deeper into the sofa, she pulled her phone from her back pocket and began absorbing her daily dose of social media. Happy family posts here, a trip to the Bahamas there. Holidays, mountain climbing, and photoshopped beauties. Everything was always so excellent, so picture-perfect. Usually, this was enough to distract her and even lead her down a dangerous path of depression and self-destruction. But not this time. What did her mum mean when she said Pastor Evans desired Helena? When had that been a thing? She was sure her mum had told her this by mistake, given that it was part of the big secret no one talked about. But she hadn't realised what she'd said in the euphoria that had consumed her upon seeing Mr. Crow's face on the telly. She'd unwittingly given her daughter a vital piece of information. And just like that, with the snap of a finger, Helena appeared right in front of Sara May, frightening her half to death. She jumped, not yet used to this whole ghost thing.

"Shit!" she shouted as she steadied herself, trying to calm her rapidly beating heart.

"The tattoo!" Helena replied loudly, speaking in riddles.

"What tattoo? What are you talking about?" Sara May hissed, still not fully recovered from the unnecessary jump scare.

"The evil man! He has a tattoo on his right shoulder!"

"And you are just remembering this now?" Sara May wretchedly asked. Helena's brows lowered, her hands firmly placed on both hips.

"It's hard to remember stuff when you're in this state, you know," she replied, slightly offended. Sara May shook her head, realising she needed to keep the ghost calm to avoid another episode of *Paranormal Caught on Tape*.

"I'm sorry. I didn't mean to upset you. What kind of tattoo did he have?"

"Two hands together. As if they're praying and they're holding prayer beads.

"Okay, so I just need to find a man with a tattoo on his right shoulder. Great."

"Who are you talking to?" Sara May hastily turned around when she heard her mother's voice behind her.

"Ahh…. myself. I haven't seen my friends in a very long time. Maggie looked unconvinced.

"Are you sure you're all right? Maybe it wouldn't be the worst thing if you went out and talked to people."

"I'm okay, Mum, don't worry.

Maggie wasn't convinced but didn't have time for further discussion. All she could do was be thankful that she had the good sense to bring her daughter home so she could keep an eye on her. It was obvious that the head injury she'd sustained had caused more damage than they initially believed. Maggie closed the front door behind her, and Sara May was once again alone in the house. Helena was gone, and she knew from experience it was pointless to call for her. But that didn't matter this time, as she was now armed with new information that might help her solve this puzzle. She now knew that Pastor Evans had fancied Helena, but she was unsure how much and for how long. She also knew the vile man had a religious tattoo on his right shoulder. How was she going to find the right one? Was he still here in Northtown?

Chapter 18

Sara May parked her car on Old Gilbert's farm. The surroundings were much better maintained than she had imagined after all these years. Aside from that, not much had changed. It was probably thanks to Eric that nature hadn't overtaken this place long ago. Old Gilbert's house looked quite decent—a white-painted concrete house with a red corrugated metal roof. Even though the paint had started peeling in some places and the roof desperately needed repair, the house still had some charm. And there was the old barn, still connected to the stables that had once housed about twenty horses, until the day the old man could no longer care for them due to his failing health. Both the barn and the stables looked battered, but the overall atmosphere on the farm was appealing. Eric must really care for this place, she thought before heading on. She knocked on the door, and to her amazement, Eric opened.

"Sara May? "What are you doing here?" he asked with a stunned expression.

"Is old Gilbert home?"

"Yeah, he's in the kitchen. Why?"

"I need to speak to him."

Even more confused than before, Eric let her in. The air smelled of dusty old books, pipe tobacco, and a sheep pen, characteristic of a senior farmer like Gilbert. His whole life was within this small yet cosy little house. From dilapidated photographs on the walls depicting his many travels and achievements over the years to dirty notebooks and newspaper clippings that he, for some reason, had thought were interesting enough to keep. One wouldn't find this kind of home among the perfect

Instagram homes of the modern era. This old country style was much more suited for a museum. It was a testament to a dying generation and a way of life that was fading despite being the foundation of the present-day nation. Sara May followed Eric into the kitchen to see the old man pressing his ear against the radio, listening to the twelve o'clock news.

Bless his heart. Old Gilbert had been alone for most of his life, having never married or had children. He'd lived in Northtown longer than most, but no one seemed to recall ever seeing him with a woman. So, his immediate family was sadly very small. Eric had felt sorry for the old chap once old age began to catch up with him and offered to help care for his farm, which Gilbert gratefully accepted despite his pride. He was a kind soul who cared deeply about the children of Northtown. Everyone loved him, even though he mostly kept to himself. He'd always been seen as old by Sara May and her local friends. That's why the nickname "Old Gilbert" stuck to him like a nail to wood. Eric announced her arrival and then went off to tend the sheep. Old Gilbert beckoned her to sit down, but there was no way to get his attention until the news anchor said farewell. What was with old people and the news?

After what felt like an eternity, the old farmer finally turned off his radio and turned his attention to his guest. For a brief moment, the two sat in silence. It was truly majestic, sitting across from what looked like an ancient man dressed in a dirty, red-checkered shirt with a poorly groomed beard, merely waiting to tell her off for whatever nonsense she was about to blurt out. She felt slightly nervous. His thin, patchy hair was white and unkempt; his frail hands were so bony that the blue veins looked like flowing rivers. The wrinkled face testified to a long and challenging life. That face had seen more hardship than most people would ever know. Old Gilbert was from a generation that had laid the groundwork for what Sara May and her generation now took advantage of without giving it a second thought. Old Gilbert's generation was, above all else, selfless and could still rattle some chains if given the chance.

"What storm has washed you ashore this time?" he asked slyly.

"I wanted to ask you about Pastor Evans." The old man huffed.

"Hah! Nothing but a wretched old scoundrel he is! Best keep away from him."

"Why do you say that?"

"Sweetheart, I don't go to church to please that scallywag, I tell ya! I go to show loyalty to my Lord and Saviour!"

"But how could a man like Evans become such a beloved pastor?"

"Guess you could blame that on his conscience if he has any," Old Gilbert mumbled.

"What do you mean?"

He was a thick-headed twit. He drank like a fish and chased tails like a mad dog. And then one day, it was like someone had tightened the loose screws in his head because he started behaving like a newly christened choirboy! A year later, old Pastor Gibbons fell ill and retired. Evans studied theology in the capital city, then, God knows why, but he returned to Northtown to take over the parish. He was only twenty-two, and nobody took to him at first. The story goes that Pastor Gibbons's daughter, Paula, was involved in this unusual arrangement. But that's just hearsay.

"So, Evans was given the job just like that?"

"And the woman. In my opinion, he deserved neither. He´s a damn fool!"

Sara May listened intently. She believed the best way to solve this mystery was to talk to those who were around when the supposed crime took place. That included everyone who had lived in Northtown before Helena ran away.

"Do you remember who Pastor Evans fancied back then?" Old Gilbert let out a little air to underline his distaste for this trip down memory lane as he leaned back and crossed his arms over his chest.

"There were a few. Your Aunt Helena was one of them. She turned him down, rightfully so. A smart girl she was."

"I'm just having a hard time believing he just suddenly stopped being this nasty creep that he was before he got hitched to the church."

"Well, that's what he led us to believe. But who can tell what goes on behind closed doors? You hear rumours, but where the truth lies, well, I can't tell ya."

"What rumours?"

"Some have said that Pastor's wife Paula, bless her heart, has overlooked things that aren't exactly considered morally correct in the eyes of our Lord. But again, that is just hearsay, not to be repeated," Old Gilbert replied with a smug grin, causing Sara May to smile widely. Oh, that charming old chap.

But could it be? Had the holiest man in Northtown, the servant of God who preached about trust, honesty, and love for all, possibly struggled to stay faithful to his vows? If so, who were the women who had to carry the shame of willingly lying under such a devilish dimwit? Perhaps the same flock of women that had chased Helena out of town for the same reason?

"I heard that my Aunt Helena had been somewhat of a floozy. That she'd been having an affair with a married man in town." A half smile slid across the old man's wrinkled face.

"I guess that was one thing said. Nobody ever confessed to being the poor schmuck spoken of," he said, sipping his cold, inky black coffee.

Suddenly, the air felt freezing, and Sara May could feel sweat drip from her forehead. Her father had left the family when she was only ten, and during the argument she witnessed just before he slammed the door behind him, she'd heard him yell at Maggie that he "couldn't continue living a lie." That he'd had enough was what prompted him to leave them both. Could her father have been the man with whom her Aunt Helena was having an affair? That would certainly qualify as a dirty family secret best kept hidden. She quickly thanked Old Gilbert for the chat, got up, and hurried out of the kitchen. On her way to her car, she bumped into Eric.

"Leaving so soon?"

"Yeah, I have to go home and interrogate my mother!" she hastily replied.

"Alright. If there's anything I can help you with, just let me know.

"Thanks, Eric."

Swiftly, their eyes met like never before. She'd never noticed how navy blue his shimmering eyes truly were. They resembled the ocean — vast and enchanting. She found it hard to look away, and for a fleeting moment, she flirted with the idea of abandoning all reason for a brief spell of reckless passion. But this wasn't the time nor the place. Questioning her mother about a possible family scandal was more urgent than a fiery lovemaking with a man so hot it was almost unfair! She stepped back, thanked Eric once more for his offer, got into her car, and drove away. Eric watched longingly as she disappeared from sight. He'd be fooling himself if he didn't admit his heart's deepest longing. Just a few seconds of intense passion that defied all logic. That was all he asked for.

Chapter 19

"Mum? Are you home?" Sara May shouted as she angrily burst through the door.

"I'm in the kitchen!" Maggie loudly replied.

Sara May followed the sound of her mother's voice. Maggie had just woken up after a long night shift and still had enough energy to bake her famous chocolate cake. She was about to spread the buttery frosting on top of the two-layer cake when her daughter rushed into the kitchen.

"Where've you been? I was going to ask you to help me bake a cake, but you weren't here," Maggie said condescendingly, reminding her daughter who called the shots in this house.

"I went to see Old Gilbert," Sara May replied.

"Oh, that's nice. How is he?" Maggie asked, turning her focus back on the nearly finished masterpiece.

"Good. He told me that it had never been fully established who Helena was supposed to have had an affair with." The gleeful smile vanished from Maggie's face as she still refused to acknowledge her daughter, focusing all her attention on the cake.

"What difference does that make?" she asked, smearing the frosting, hoping it might distract her from this uncomfortable conversation.

"Was it Dad?" That sentence nearly had her dropping her spatula.

"What? Don't be ridiculous! Of course, it wasn't your dad!"

"I heard you guys fight the day he left. He said he couldn't continue living a lie! So, one can only assume that…."

"Sara May, sit down!" Maggie sternly ordered.

"What? No! I...."

"I said sit down!" The command sounded like it came from a senior military major with years of war experience, causing Sara May to become so frightened that she dared not disobey her mother's orders. She quickly sat down like a petulant child being scolded for misbehaviour.

Maggie wiped her hands on her apron, took it off, and carefully placed it on the kitchen table before sitting down. She hadn't realised how much discovering about Helena had affected her daughter. Perhaps she'd approached it the wrong way. She should have given Sara May more of a chance to ask questions. But it never occurred to her that she would connect Helena's disappearance to her father's departure. From Maggie's perspective, that was utterly absurd! What Sara May didn't know was that they had tried for a long time to save their marriage. But the boat couldn't withstand ten years of rough seas and eventually sank. There was simply nothing left to salvage. They had started a journey without making sure they were rowing in the same direction. The result of that had, over time, weakened the marriage and ultimately sunk the broken-down boat that once carried their love. Yes, Helena had undoubtedly played a part in that, but not in the way Sara May believed. Maggie took a deep breath before continuing.

"Now, you listen to me. Your father and Helena were *NOT* having an affair. That wasn't the reason he left. Helena skipped town long before your dad decided to leave us," Maggie explained calmly.

"Then why did he leave? What lies was he talking about?"

"Sometimes marriages just fail. I guess he just didn't want to pretend everything was fine anymore."

Sara May sat opposite her mother, listening attentively to every word. She had no reason to doubt her, but she still felt that much more was missing from the story. Her mother was holding something back. What hardship had they faced so severe that he had been forced to leave? What burdened him so heavily that his only way to survive was to abandon his wife and ten-year-old daughter? She decided to call her bluff.

"Bullshit. Dad would never have left me if it were just issues between you two," she wheezed, then abruptly got up from the table and stormed into her room.

She was done talking about this. The conversation had ripped open an old wound she thought had healed years ago, but in reality, it had become infected, and now the pus was gushing out like an uncontrolled waterfall. Reflecting on that fateful day brought nothing but dreadful memories and horrible feelings. She remembered how terrifying it was to see the man she once regarded as a superhero walk away from her without looking back. She remembered feeling as though it was somehow her fault that he left her. She recalled feeling incredibly alone, rejected by the one man who was supposed to love her unconditionally. She squeezed her eyes shut to stop the tears from falling. Stupid Northtown! That lousy, pathetic excuse for a town! Nothing good ever happened here; she should have caught the first bus out!

In the kitchen, Maggie was still sitting alone, fighting back tears. She should have known that the secret she'd kept so closely would eventually escape and bite her in the backside. She had always planned to discuss this with her daughter when the time was right, telling her the full story. But when Sara May decided to leave town at just eighteen, Maggie naively believed she would never return, so the issue resolved itself. Sara May had never asked questions until now, so it caught her off guard when she suddenly began probing what, in Maggie's opinion, was a matter long settled, based on senseless rumours that caused nothing but heartache and pain. John left her. He had abandoned her to handle this problem on her own, and for that, she would never forgive him. Damn coward! It would have been so much easier having him by her side, weathering this storm together; at least then, they could explain all sides of the story. Together. Sara May was right. Maggie was holding back. There was far more to this God-awful story than she could ever have imagined. But Maggie neither longed for nor had the strength to discuss it. Not right now.

Sara May did not leave her room until much later that evening. Maggie had gone for another night shift but left a note about some leftovers in the fridge. This endless cycle of arguing reminded her of the many fights the mother-daughter pair had during the difficult, emotional years of a troubled teenager nobody knew how to handle. This was far from ideal. She sat at the kitchen table and cut herself a slice of chocolate cake. She was furious with her mother, but refusing a perfectly delicious cake would be like committing a crime. The heavenly smell enveloped her, but just as she was about to take the first bite, Helena suddenly appeared, causing her to jump and drop the fork on the floor.

"Jesus Christ! Stop doing that! Can't you just float from the living room or something?" Sara May snapped as she scrambled to find the vanished fork.

"I'm a soul, an energy. "I can appear however I want," Helena replied cheekily. Finding the fork and slamming it back on the table with a frustrated sigh, Sara May looked at her aunt.

"I've been trying to figure out what you were trying to tell me. But I don't know how the evil man fits into all this. Was he the married man you were having an affair with?" Helena scoffed.

"There was no man!" she snarled.

"What do you mean? You left town because people found out you were sleeping with a married man."

"There was no man!" Helena repeated more harshly.

"What, was he some kind of a loser?"

"Talk to Nana Lou," the ghostly woman begged.

Just as Sara May was about to ask more questions, Helena vanished right before her eyes. It would take some time to get used to that. She still didn't understand why this was happening or why she was suddenly seeing ghosts. But the bandage had been violently ripped off, and she was too deep into this wound to turn back now. She quickly rose from the table and rushed into her mother's study. For the next hour, she sat glued to the screen. Website after website, all she could hear was the rapid clicking of the mouse and the occasional grunt. Nothing here, nothing there. No information, no leads, nothing. Sara May leaned back in her chair and let out a heavy sigh. This was becoming an unsolvable mystery. But she owed it to Helena to find out what had happened to her. Although she couldn't remember herself, she had given Sara May vital information by mentioning the evil man. And someone, somewhere, was whispering in her ear that Pastor Evans was more entangled in this twisted web than he would ever admit.

Chapter 20

"I came as soon as I could," said Eric as he pulled out a chair and sat beside Sara May, who initially didn't notice him. Her eyes were laser-focused on the screen.

He hadn't been to the public library for years. He had never excelled as a student and preferred manual work over dusty old books. But Sara May insisted he meet her at the library, specifically by the computer corner. Although the council hadn't bought new computers since the early 2000s, they still worked remarkably well. "Those darn robot devices can't provide people with anything they can't get from books," the old-fashioned mayor, Timothy Brown, once said when pressed on the issue.

"What's so important I had to run away from Old Gilbert's livestock?" a slightly annoyed Eric asked, realising he hadn't even gotten so much as a "hello."

"Nothing comes up," Sara May replied without taking her eyes off the screen.

"What do you mean?"

"I've checked the local listings and the national cemetery website, but nothing comes up. Helena isn't listed anywhere."

"You still think she's dead?" Sara May frowned.

"Nana Lou also sees her. Have you ever doubted her?"

"Fine, I believe you. But if she's dead, then she has to be buried somewhere. Maybe you spelt her name wrong."

"How many ways are there to spell 'Helena Jensen '?" Erich huffed, growing tired of her bullheadedness.

"Check anyway," he ordered. Sara May pouted but did as she was told.

"See! Nothing. I don't understand."

"Maybe it's an error in the system. I've got to go and finish helping Old Gilbert, but I'll phone a few cemeteries and see if anything comes up."

Eric stood up and walked away. Sara May glared at him longingly, a tingling sensation swirling in her stomach like countless butterflies soaring to the highest heavens. How had he become so irresistible? This was Eric — her childhood friend. Never in a million years did she think he'd become so sensual that it would provoke some lewd thoughts in her dirty mind. She shook her head and refocused on the computer. She had work to do, but each mouse click stretched her patience thinner. How was it possible that the woman wasn't listed anywhere? Was the system so broken that people were buried left and right without anyone tracking it? The cemeteries in Reykjavik had always seemed so organised. Perhaps there were different rules for the unfortunate souls buried outside the capital.

According to everyone she'd spoken to, Helena had moved to Reykjavik, so it was only natural to assume that's where she'd been buried. She leaned back and reviewed all the facts in her mind. She'd decided not to tell the other Jensen women she believed their baby sister was deceased because she wasn't sure how they would react. Aunt Marie didn't want to hear her name mentioned, so she probably wouldn't care. Maybe she already knew. Sara May could feel her blood boil inside her. Ever since she returned, the Jensen sisters had been so secretive and treated her like a child who needed to be shielded from the ugly truth. So, if they were determined to keep vital information from her, they sure as hell didn't deserve to know whatever she managed to uncover. She knew Helena was dead; that had to be a fact since she was floating around and appearing out of nowhere. She knew Aunt Marie was good friends with Prime Minister Crow and Pastor Evans, and the holy reverend circled Helena like a dog chasing its tail. But she'd turned him down and eventually moved out of town. That's where the trail ended.

"Sara May? What on Earth are you doing here?" she suddenly heard a familiar voice echo beside her.

"Chris? Hi! Oh, I'm just checking out some books they have here."

"Then wouldn't it make more sense just to walk around and have a look?" Chris teased. Sara May smiled.

"I guess. What are you doing here?"

"I'm studying business management at the University of Iceland. I figured it might be useful if I ever decide to grow my empire."

Sara May was lost in his deep, mocha-coloured eyes, hanging on every word that escaped his luscious lips. Suddenly, she felt caught between a rock and a hard place. On one hand, she'd been pondering some risqué, late-night thoughts about Eric, naughtier than a Sunday sin. On the other hand, she pictured a life with Chris, the perfectly sculpted man made of pure gold, who, on top of everything, was working hard to build a secure future for himself by growing his business. Why couldn't she combine Chris's good sense with Eric's lumberjack physique to create one perfect husband for herself?

"The national cemetery website? I don't know what you're into now, but I highly doubt graveyards have started publishing quality reading materials. The words quickly snapped her back into reality.

"What? Oh, no, I was just browsing." Chris smiled his impeccable Colgate smile.

"Anything I can help you with?" he asked.

"No, not really. I was looking for the grave of a woman who doesn't seem to be listed anywhere."

"Every grave is listed. It doesn't matter if people are buried in a coffin or cremated; it's all documented. So, either the information you typed in is wrong or..." He stopped himself, provoking Sara May's curiosity.

".... or what?" she impatiently asked.

"Or the person you're looking for has never been buried. At least, not in a cemetery, which would be against the law."

This left her speechless. The idea that Helena had never been buried hadn't even crossed her mind. Dead people were buried; that was just the way it was. If Helena wasn't buried in a cemetery, it could mean she had wandered away from her home, got lost, and was never found, or... no. It was impossible. She quickly stood up and gathered her belongings.

"Where are you going?"

"I need to speak to Nana Lou!"

Sara May hurried out of the library, leaving Chris behind. His confusion soon turned to amusement as he let out a small chuckle. This woman had always been different from the others, and he'd be foolish to think his feelings for her hadn't always been there. But he had to respect the boundaries. He'd once crossed that invisible line, ending his friendship with Eric. It was, in his opinion, a stupid mistake, but according to Eric, it was cruel intentions. It all seemed so logical at the time, until she ended things with him, leaving him with nothing but burning guilt towards his best mate. And now Sara May was back in both their lives. Eric had to make the first move.

Sara May hurried down the street towards Nana Lou's house. To do so, she had to run down Northtown's High Street through the town centre, if one could call it that. It wasn't anything like the high street in the multicultural city of Reykjavik, and yet it served its purpose by housing the Bread Box, the Brewer, and a few shops and cafes. There weren't many people around this Wednesday afternoon, but enough to notice the strange woman running for her life down the street. Had she not been in such a rush, she might have paid more attention to the women, often referred to as Paula's chatty minions. They belonged to her army of gossipers and had certainly taken notice of Sara May.

"Whatever's the matter with her?" one of them asked.

"Wasn't that the Jensen girl?" another woman asked.

"She's always been so strange," the third one huffed.

"I heard she had started digging up some old dirt. Apparently, it's driving Maggie absolutely mad!"

"I wonder if Paula knows anything about this?"

Nobody knew how these women managed to sniff out everything that was none of their business, but thanks to them, the only secrets that thrived in town were their own. In many people's opinion, their talents were wasted on Northtown; they could be of excellent use to any respectable police force in the Western world. No mafia stood a chance against those self-proclaimed guardians of morality. But Sara May had no time to stop and call them out. She had to get to Nana Lou quickly!

Chapter 21

"Nana Lou? I need to speak to you! Sara May shouted as she loudly banged on the purple wooden door to the old lady's home.

Something didn't sit right, but she couldn't quite put her finger on it. Of course, there was always a chance that Helena had actually gone missing and died somewhere in the wilderness. Who would have noticed? Her family had disowned her; her mother and sister didn't even want to say her name. So, if Helena had disappeared, it wouldn't have made a difference to anyone in Northtown. She'd left voluntarily, so to the locals, she was out of their lives forever. *Good riddance* said the women who suspected her of cheating with their husbands. Sara May knocked on the door again. While she waited, she looked cautiously around, half-expecting someone to surprise her from behind. She noticed Helena standing not far off, pointing her finger towards a massive tree rooted across the road. It stood slightly to the left of the pastor's house. She shifted her gaze to the tree, and that's when she noticed someone watching her. Their eyes briefly met, causing the man to run away. Just as she was about to call out to the mysterious man, Nana Lou opened her door.

"What in Heaven's name has gotten into you, child? One might think you're running from the police!"

"Can I come in?" Sara May nervously asked. Nana Lou nodded and let her in.

What on Earth is going on with you, girl?" she asked. She hadn't even had the time to offer her guest something to drink.

"When did Helena leave town?" Sara May asked, wasting no time.

"I think it was around '93 or '94. It was soon after you were born," Nana Lou replied, not sure where she was going with this.

"And she never came back?"

"Not to my knowledge, no. Nobody ever saw her after that."

"I know people say she moved to the capital, but does anybody know for sure?"

"Well, I suppose somebody does. What's this all about?"

"I was at the library earlier and tried looking up her grave because I wanted to know where she's buried. But there's no grave listed in her name. And Chris told me that all graves are listed, which must mean that...."

".... she isn't buried." Nana Lou finally caught on.

Hearing her say this so bluntly out loud was like receiving confirmation of the one thing Sara May didn't want to face, as it forced her to face the brutal truth. If Helena wasn't buried, that could only mean two things, and both were so disturbingly gruesome that she hesitated to continue the conversation, even though she knew she had to. Helena kept appearing around her for a reason. She was meant to help her, which meant uncovering what had happened to her, no matter how hard it proved to be. She swallowed hard, feeling a lump in her throat, and forced herself to ask the question she didn't want to hear the answer to.

"Could she have been murdered?" she asked, her voice slightly trembling. Nana Lou's eyes widened.

"I don't remember hearing anything about a murder, but I guess it's not inconceivable."

"Well, she's not alive anymore; we know that. Otherwise, I wouldn't be seeing her as a ghost."

"So, it's a question of how she died. I'll see if I can find any newspaper articles from around this time," the old witch declared as she turned around and bounced out of the living room.

Sara May couldn't help but smile. It was innate for her generation not to bother keeping up with the times. She couldn't bring herself to point out that in the 21st century, one could go online and find any newspaper published with just a few clicks. So, discovering what happened to Helena shouldn't be that difficult. Whether she'd wandered off and died outside in the cold or been murdered, it should have attracted media attention. Her throat tightened again. The sad truth was that if Helena had perished in a blizzard, it was very likely that nobody would've cared. A young girl nobody missed. A nameless woman of the night, struck down by the darkness of the merciless Nordic wilderness, cast out of her hometown for the only sin of being with a married man. Had she even known he was married? It all seemed so unfair. Suddenly, a knock at the door startled her. She hurried to the foyer.

"Oh, hi. Didn't expect to see you here."

"Jack? What are you doing here?"

"I could ask you the same thing," Jack smugly replied. "I came to see if Nana Lou needed anything. I sometimes check in on the elders in town. I find that it's our civil duty to look after the weak and vulnerable—a duty that, sadly, so many neglect," he continued, putting on his finest theatrical performance.

Jack Lewis, an old schoolmate of hers, was a perpetually arrogant prick. He was always so full of himself and his mediocre achievements, spouting fictitious nonsense disguised as truth, that most people avoided him altogether. His parents had ensured he never went without, constantly reminding him of his brilliance and superiority over the second-rate citizens of Northtown. Over time, this constant stream of praise turned him into an egotistical, self-absorbed arse who thrived on putting others down.

"Glad to see you haven't changed," Sara May said, shooting him dirty looks that made her thoughts about him clear as day. Jack was unfazed.

"I appreciate your concern, Mr. Lewis, but this old battle-axe doesn't need a babysitter, nor do I particularly care for one!" Nana Lou could be heard in the background as she slowly approached the door.

"Well, I guess that's that, then. I bid you good day, ladies," Jack replied, tilting an invisible hat slightly before confidently walking away.

The two women watched him leave, head held high as usual. Neither of them spoke. This unexpected visit was no coincidence. Jack never visited anyone without expecting something in return. His fake act of caring was highly strategic because, over the years, Jack had learned that the best way to climb the bloody corporate ladder was to forge powerful connections. Had Sara May and Nana Lou watched him a little longer, they would have seen him confidently make his way to the home of Paula and Pastor Evans, where he knocked on the door and was quickly let in.

"Well?" asked the pastor impatiently.

"She was there," Jack said, impressed with himself.

"And what? What did the old hag tell her?"

"I don't know; she didn't let me in."

Pastor Evans could feel his face heat up with anger. But instead of shouting at the daft-looking nitwit, he took a breath and steadied himself. *I mustn't let the feelings get the better of me,* he thought as he prepared himself. He'd spent too many years building an impeccable image to ruin it over a minor slip-up. The people of Northtown recognised him as ever so calm and collected, always ready to assist those in need. With open arms and a caring heart, he'd welcome many penniless lowlifes into his home, portraying himself as the Good Samaritan everyone loved and trusted. He was not about to let anything ruin all that hard work. A bonehead like Jack wasn't worth the hassle. Instead, the pastor cleared his throat and wore his most menacing smile as he slowly approached the young messenger.

"Jack. You know I can make you a mighty man," he said, ensuring he was heard and understood.

"Duh. Why do you think I attend those stupid Sunday masses of yours?" Jack replied, rolling his eyes, which irked the pastor, who struggled to suppress the violent anger bubbling within him.

"Then perhaps you are aware that I can also make sure you become nothing but a dirt-poor pleb that nobody will touch with a ten-foot pole, much less their filthy rich fingers! You do realise that, don't you?"

Jack swallowed the lump in his throat, as large as a snowball. The confidence that had brought him into Pastor Evans' office just moments earlier disappeared in an instant. The dream had been a promising political career with all the luxuries that came with it, but the reality was that Pastor Evans kept that dream tightly under lock and key. He was an extremely wealthy man who had built his fortune by loyally serving the church for decades. He was also a shrewd businessman who, throughout his long career, discovered hidden loopholes in the system and learned how to exploit them, transforming himself into the well-dressed white-collar criminal everyone admired. People saw him as a man of God, someone trustworthy and respectable. But they didn't realise their beloved spiritual leader spent his free time building a network of connections as strong as a trawl net. Pastor Evans and his wife, Paula, had funded many political candidates and MPs whom they believed could bolster their position within the elite circle and thus increase their influence. Only a few people seemed aware of this double life. One of them was Simon Lewis. However, he never talked about his unusual relationship with Pastor Evans. Since the pastor had agreed to fund both the Brewer and his favourite son's political ambitions only if Simon promised to stay silent about what he knew, he saw no point in airing his dirty laundry. And Jack was too self-absorbed to care whether the money was stained with blood. As long as he got what he was owed, he was fine with it. But now, he couldn't help but feel frustrated as he stared into the dark eyes of his financier. It wasn't exactly ideal to be financially dependent on someone else.

"What do you want?" he asked irritably.

"I want you to follow her. Ensure she stays in her lane and refrains from asking questions. If she tries anything, you report back to me immediately. Understood?"

Jack reluctantly nodded. Pastor Evans gave him a gentle slap on the cheek and sent him on his way. He didn't dislike the boy, far from it. He felt sorry for him. Jack was just an impoverished young dreamer with an inflated ego, a nobody who longed to belong to the world of somebodies but was too stupid to do so on his own. A perfect pawn. This wasn't about screwing him over. He participated in this ugly business just as much as Pastor Evans himself. And in this lawless game of life, it was every man for himself. Sara May had started uncovering things that were none of her business, and if she managed to find out too much, it could have dire consequences for far too many. And the ever-merciful pastor and protector of his flock couldn't allow that to happen.

Chapter 22

"Can't you just take the bus back to town?" Paige pleaded.

"I wish, but Mum's watching me like a hawk!"

"I don't know how long Dad will be able to hold your position in the kitchen, Sara May. Tommy quit because he couldn't handle the pressure on his own, so Dad had to put one of the waiters in there to cover, which means more strain on the rest of us."

"Wow, the kingdom crumbles as soon as I leave. I didn't know I was that important," Sara May joked without receiving a laugh from the other end.

"I'm serious! I thought you hated Northtown."

"I do. But like I said, Mum got me all chained up…."

"…Christ, you're thirty-one years old!" You can leave!" Paige interrupted.

"It's not that simple. Look, I'll only be here a few more days, hopefully. I'll phone you when I return, okay?"

She hung up the phone. A familiar feeling of guilt washed over her as she sighed deeply on the sofa. She'd left Eric and Chris without explanation, and now she'd done the same to Paige. It was becoming a nasty habit she didn't care for but didn't know how to break. This wasn't how she'd wanted things to happen. Her mum and aunt had kidnapped her and forcefully dragged her back to Northtown, so she was entirely at their mercy. But despite her deep-seated disgust with this hellhole, she'd deliberately not told Paige the real reason why she couldn't leave just yet. Helena sat on the windowsill and waited for her confused niece to say something. Finally, Sara May sat up.

"I know there's no point in asking you. You don't remember anything," she muttered.

"I wish I did," Helena replied.

"How can you not remember what happened to you?"

"Being dead is strange. It's as if they erase the memory of the event itself so you don't have to carry that burden around.

"Who are they?"

"I don't know," Helena shrugged. "Those who control all this, I guess. You met one of them at the hospital. She came to you."

"You mean the woman who fixed my pillow? Is she…?" Helena nodded.

"I've seen her a few times. She helped me realise I was dead."

"Couldn't she help you get where you needed to go?"

"No. She said I couldn't go there until my case was solved." Helena looked away, saddened by the thought of what she was missing out on because of the mystery still surrounding her death. Sara May's heart broke for her.

"And that's why I'm here? To help you?" she asked, offering her most sympathetic look.

"I think so. You see me. And you hear me."

Sara May was left speechless. Ever since the mysterious woman appeared in her dream and then showed up at the hospital to adjust her pillow, she felt as though her life had been turned completely upside down. Nothing made sense anymore. She still wasn't sure if seeing ghosts was just a hallucination caused by her head injury or if she was genuinely seeing them. Regardless, proving what she'd uncovered became increasingly difficult as the days went on. The dead woman she saw was her aunt, Helena—a young woman who'd mysteriously lost her fight for life far too young, and for some unexplainable reason, her name was so tainted that her own family refused to say it aloud. She couldn't make sense of it. Who cared if Helena had been a bit promiscuous? Why did it matter? That wasn't enough reason not to tell Sara May about her. If only Helena could remember more than just the measly tattoo. How could she remember that but not her death? It was nearly impossible to find a man with that specific tattoo on his shoulder; he could be anywhere in the country, or even the world. She looked over at the windowsill. Helena had gone. She seemed unable to stay longer than a few minutes each time and could never recall where she'd been when she reappeared.

"Who were you talking to?" Maggie quietly asked. Sara May nearly jumped from the sofa. She hadn't noticed her come in.

"Mum! I thought you were at work!"

"I had to come get my slippers. I need them for work. Are you sure you're all right?"

"Yeah. I was talking to my friend Paige. I work for her dad. Or I used to. I don't know how long they can cope without a kitchen porter." Maggie chortled a wee bit.

"Would that be so bad? You're way too old for a job like that. Being a kitchen porter is for teenagers, sweetie. Why don't you use this time off to start thinking about a real career?" Sara May looked away, irritated by that last comment.

"It's not like a thirty-one-year-old, uneducated woman is swimming in offers, mum."

"And whose fault is that? You gave up on college, you refused to allow your Aunt Marie to fund you...."

"... Because I don't need some fancy degree to

become a writer!" Sara May snapped back.

"Spare me the theatrics! When will you stop this ridiculous fantasy and start living in the real world? You're fast approaching forty, and you've never published anything! You haven't even written anything, God damn it!" Sara May quickly got up, seething with anger.

"At least I'm not a sixty-two-year-old lonely care home worker who couldn't hold on to a husband!"

She had barely let go of that last word when the regret hit her full force. But the words had been spoken, and it was too late to take them back. It was obvious to everyone that those two women would never see eye to eye, and all hopes of a loving mother-daughter relationship between them had long since been lost. They were too different. Sara May stormed out of the living room and went to bed. As soon as Maggie heard the door slam, the once sturdy, now shattered dam of uncomfortable memories of endless fights burst. John, that doggone coward, had abandoned ship at the first chance and left her to fight this war alone. That gutless wimp! Maggie had long suspected what was causing the rift between them, but she had to keep that secret, no matter the cost. She still believed that bringing Sara May home to Northtown was the best thing for her, even though it had brought back a wave of buried memories. She could only hope Sara May would eventually see it the same way.

Maggie entered the kitchen and poured herself a cup of tea. She wasn't in a hurry to return to work; surprisingly, they'd managed to find enough staff to cover the shift for once. Exhausted, she wiped away her tears and embraced the silence. It gave her the time and space to reflect on her thoughts. Margarete Rachel Jensen had made some mistakes in her life, but who hadn't? It was part of being human, or so they said. But she couldn't help but wonder if things had gone differently, would she have had the good sense to choose different company for herself back then? Things might have turned out differently if her teenage friends had been different. Maybe Helena wouldn't have done what she did. Had that been the case, the frigid Tuesday evening of 6th December 1994 might not have happened as it did. The visit they received that night had changed everything. Maggie sighed and finished her tea. She knew she mustn't dwell on such thoughts. The therapist who'd scammed her out of a lot of money back in the day hadn't done much for her, but he'd taught her that wishing and what-if thoughts did more harm than good. She couldn't change the past. She could only deal with the aftermath as best she could. That meant ensuring Sara May never discovered the truth about what happened on that winter evening all those years ago.

Chapter 23

"My spiritual guides and protectors from beyond, I beg of you. Show me the way. Give me some guidance. Lead me down the path that I am meant to take."

Nana Lou sat by the round oak table covered with a thin maroon veil adorned with bells and multicoloured crystals hanging from it. She had bought this veil at a rickety old flea market in a small village in Nepal many years ago. Like many things scattered around her unusual home, she acquired this particular veil from another witch who praised its powers and promised it would serve her well. Over the years, the veil indeed fulfilled those promises, giving Nana Lou's crown jewel, a mighty, forceful crystal ball, the strength to reveal its true power. The ball was given to Nana Lou by an ancient, hermit-like sorcerer in Egypt. She had met him by chance during a visit to see the pyramids many years earlier. Her trip took an unexpected turn when she walked down a narrow alleyway where he was hiding. He tried to lure her into his hidden hut, which, under normal circumstances, would have made her turn and run. But nothing about the situation was normal. They were alike in many ways. So, she accepted his offer, and he led her to his hut, nestled between two crumbling buildings.

The hut looked misty and smelled of old books, potions, and scented candles. The aged wizard, wearing a thin, slightly greyish robe that complemented his long, nearly white beard, turned to Nana Lou and told her that his time was nearing, and the crystal ball had revealed its next owner. It showed him a young woman from a distant land who would soon find him, and he was to give her the priceless artefact that had guided his light for decades. At that moment, Nana Lou didn't believe she was worthy of such a meaningful gift, but she knew that in the world they inhabited, the rules differed from those in most ordinary societies. In this world, people accepted when they were handed the torch. She thanked the elderly warlock and took the crystal ball home, dismissing people's curiosity by telling them it was a souvenir. Since that fateful journey, the crystal ball had served her well. It showed her things hidden from others and even revealed the locals' deepest secrets. But one thing she had never been able to see or solve. Gradually, she realised it wasn't hers to figure out. That was the task of the ball's next owner. That was Sara May's mission.

Nana Lou had known for some time that Sara May would eventually return to Northtown. The gods had foreseen it long ago, and it was only a matter of time before the spirits would guide her back. Nana Lou's spirit guides told her that it would take the girl a while to truly understand everything, and she would initially resist it fiercely. That was to be expected. They had decided not to activate her powers until the right moment, when she could manage it herself. The moment would come when she accepted that she'd been given an extraordinary gift. Nana Lou's role was to observe and mentor her when that time came. But now, everything was in chaos. External forces threatened to derail the plan, and she couldn't let that happen. Sara May received this gift under terrible circumstances, to help her cope with what had happened and to find her way out of it. If she didn't begin to accept it, the risk was that the demons already influencing many in Northtown would get to her as well.

"She has to understand her nightmare. Otherwise, it won't stop," a ghostly male voice whispered in Nana

Lou's ear.

"Can I help her with that?" she asked.

"You can only tell her what you already know," the crystal ball answered in a soothing female voice.

Nana Lou thanked her guides and bade them farewell. She knew what she had to do. She glanced at the large clock above the front door. It was nearly time for Sunday mass. She packed her belongings and headed out. She'd never been fond of those masses because she couldn't stand Pastor Evan's self-absorbed mannerisms. He always stood by the altar, towering over the congregation, spouting nonsense he knew were lies. They were all lies, and he knew it. Because of this, Nana Lou hadn't been the most active churchgoer. Only attending when she was compelled, and this time, she could only hope that Sara May had also been subjected to the same dreadful fate.

A group of people had gathered in front of the church. God's cheerleaders, as she liked to call them. They were the ones who worshipped the church as they did their own inflated egos, never missing a service. There were also a few who showed up occasionally to appease their conscience. Everybody mingled well during Sunday services because, despite having more things tearing them apart than uniting them, everyone could find common ground in the peace of mind those masses seemed to give them. Nana Lou looked around but couldn't see Sara May anywhere. Please, let her be here, she prayed, keeping her voice down. She slowly moved closer to the church entrance and sat on the bench furthest from the altar. Usually, she was very chatty and took her time talking to all those who longed for her attention. Now, all she could manage was a quick hello and a casual nod.

The service started at two o'clock as usual and

finished about an hour later. After Pastor Evans had given his final *Amen,* the usual chaos broke out as everyone rushed to be the first to leave. The devoted ones thanked the pastor for another excellent sermon, while others just wanted to avoid the traffic. Nana Lou tried her best to avoid Pastor Evans's eagle eye, but he spotted her about ten minutes into the sermon and hadn't let her out of his sight since. However, this time the number of God's most loyal supporters, eager to praise him to the high heavens, worked in her favour. Evans had to concentrate on them rather than the old witch, who managed to hide in the crowd like a timid mouse fleeing for its life. Finally, she saw Sara May standing next to Maggie.

"Sara May! Psst, Sara May!" Nana Lou tried calling out quietly, but to no avail.

"Well, if it isn't the great Louise Charlotte Beatrice Baker herself! Whatever do we owe this pleasure?" Paula's screechy voice suddenly pierced her ears. She muttered a few curse words before turning around.

"Hello, Paula. I figured I'd find you here."

"Oh, I'm sure you're not here to see me now, are you? If it's my husband you're after, I'm afraid he's fully booked through next week. He's been promising things left and right; you know how it is. His heart is in the right place, but Lord, help me with his head sometimes!" Paula laughed.

"Good thing God has you to do His dirty work. But, no, I wasn't here to see him. I need to see…" Paula interrupted.

"Well, whoever it is that demands your attention this time, I'm sure there will be plenty of time for it later, but right now, I must ask you to move along. We've got a christening here starting at five, and I need time to prepare."

Nana Lou forced a smile before turning and walking away. She had always hated Paula's superficial small talk, but feared it wasn't a coincidence this time. This was deliberate. Whether or not Pastor Evans had been pulling the strings, she wasn't sure, but it seemed pretty likely. He'd always had a strange, almost creepy hold over his wife, who bent over backwards to meet his every need and obey his commands whenever he snapped his fingers. Together, they operated like a well-oiled machine, maintaining control over the locals by stoking fear of hell or spreading nasty rumours that lacked any real foundation. Everyone seemed to respect the pair who ruled Northtown like royalty. However, a few rebellious individuals had managed to resist the church's powerful influence. Bill and Laura Baker, the town sheriff, Robert Decker and his wife Martha, and Nana Lou and Trucker Tom were among those. These were the people Paula and Pastor Evans publicly tolerated but secretly despised, as they saw through the fake smiles and heard the snake-like whispers after dark.

Nana Lou waited outside the church, expecting Sara May to come out. But as time went on, she realised the girl must have slipped away during her painful attempt to escape from Paula. She cursed the damn cow. Ever so spiteful she was. How dare she? It was increasingly clear that the wheels had begun to turn. Someone had figured out Sara May was on the trail like a bloodhound, rubbing many people the wrong way. Nana Lou got into her car and drove off. She needed to find a way to reach the girl as fast as possible.

Chapter 24

"Sheriff Decker? There's a woman here to see you."

"Send her in."

Northtown's sheriff, Robert Decker, sat at his desk, buried in stacks of paperwork as tall as Mount Everest. He was just over sixty, with greyish hair at the sides and in excellent shape for his age. An outdoorsy man, he enjoyed spending his free time hiking, playing golf, and hosting barbecues for his friends and family on weekends, often inviting the entire police force to join. He had been the town's sheriff for decades. Shortly after his son, Chris, was born, he promised the baby boy that he would always protect him, no matter what. That promise inspired his decision to become a police officer. His wife Martha supported her childhood sweetheart. With her help, he worked hard to become the town's sheriff. He was a very successful sheriff, known as a likeable man who didn't discriminate and often went above and beyond his duties to help those in need. People who didn't seek comfort at the pastor's house often found themselves in the sheriff's office, seeking answers from the trusted man they relied on. Despite his busy schedule, Sheriff Decker always made time to listen and offer advice. He loved the town and its people. Because of this, Sara May wasn't afraid to contact him, hoping to find answers to the complicated mystery she was now facing.

"Come in. Have a seat," Decker gestured. Sara May did as she was told. "How nice to see you again. " You couldn't have been much older than sixteen the last time I saw you," he continued, carefully eyeing every inch of her—an old habit as a painstakingly thorough police officer.

"I was eighteen," she corrected him.

"You know, Chris was heartbroken when you left."

"Yeah, guess the next round of beer is on me," she replied apologetically. Decker chuckled.

"So, what can I do for you?"

"I need information." He smiled, still not taking her seriously.

"And what kind of information do you need?" he asked, more condescendingly than he intended. Sara May pretended she didn't notice.

"Has anyone ever committed a murder here in Northtown?" Decker leaned back in his chair, needing time to dissect each word in that sentence.

"Not that I recall, no. When was that supposed to have happened?"

"Sometime between '93 and '94."

"Back then, I lived in Reykjavik, studying to become a policeman. If you'd like, I can look up some old reports, but I can't promise anything."

"That's all I ask."

"Just out of curiosity, do we suspect anyone in particular?" Sara May remembered Nana Lou's words: "Trust no one."

"No, not really," she lied. Being a seasoned officer with years of experience dealing with con artists of every calibre, Sheriff Decker saw right through her bullshit.

"Well," he finally said, leaning forward again. "I can't do much more than just look at old reports, but if I come across anything, I'll let you know."

"Thank you."

Sara May hurried out of the office. Decker was far from convinced. The Jensen girl had always been odd; there was no denying it. But she was no liar. She had always been as honest as the day was long. He had known that for years. She had been a regular visitor at his home, being Chris's best friend. He remembered many days when she tagged along with Chris and Eric, and the Deckers could always count on her to tell them in great detail what the three of them had been up to on any given day, even if it got them into trouble. He always admired that about her. Because of this, he knew she hadn't been entirely truthful with him just now. She already suspected someone; his gut told him that someone was God's self-appointed servant.

Sheriff Decker and Pastor Evans had never seen eye to eye. Certain morals in life guided Decker, causing him to dislike the pastor's volatility. That holy bastard contorted his conscience depending on how the wind blew. Pastor Evans had been a womanising drunk in his days, and for a while, it seemed he would become nothing more than a beggared old boozer whom everyone felt sorry for. It was, therefore, a great shock to everyone when he suddenly decided to apply to a university to study theology. It was such a massive behavioural change that it made no sense to anybody. Evans had always stuck to the same story: God had appeared before him one night, like the three Dickens ghosts, and shown him the way. He seemed convinced that the Holy Spirit had touched his soul that night and revealed to him that his destiny was to help those in need. Sheriff Decker, however, wasn't buying it. To him, it was as much hogwash as the pastor's superficial kindness. Such a colossal one-eighty in someone's character overnight had to have another, more logical explanation. Something had to have happened to make such a grand lover of liquor put the cork in the bottle and turn to God overnight. Something the pastor had lied about for over three decades. Outside the police station, Sara May had stopped to check her phone when she suddenly heard a familiar voice call out to her, causing her to jump ever so slightly.

"In trouble again, are we?" Eric teasingly grinned as he casually strolled over, hands in his pockets, with no care in the world.

"Jesus, you scared me!" Sara May aggressively replied, clutching her chest and dramatically faking a near heart attack.

"Sorry. I didn't mean to. What were you doing at the police station?"

"I needed to speak to Sheriff Decker."

"About Helena?"

"If you must know, yes. I thought if anyone might know something, he would."

Initially, Eric said nothing. She was far deeper down the rabbit hole than he had realised. He would need to set aside his pride and show her he supported her completely if he wanted any chance of reaching her. Or at least pretend he did. He shrugged and took a step closer to her. To his relief, she didn't retreat despite eyeing him cautiously.

"Look, I know I haven't been much help, but if this is important to you, I want to be." Sara May kept her poker face, staring him down with intense suspicion. He made another move. "Can I come over anytime soon?" he confidently asked. She dropped her crossed arms to her sides, surrendering.

"Yeah. Mum works nights; she's usually out of the house by nine. You can come around then whenever you're free."

She was taken aback by how brazen she had suddenly

become. Had she just invited Eric to come by her house like that? A half-smile flickered across Eric's face. She might be more stubborn than a mule, but she wasn't daft. If the two hadn't been so lost in each other's eyes, with her trying to stand her ground and him smashing through all her defences as if they were made of matchsticks, they would have noticed Jack standing across the street, watching Sara May's every move. Inside the police station, Sheriff Decker was still contemplating the latest encounter with the Jensen girl. This seemingly simple question had taken root deep inside him, making his skin crawl. After some thought, he grabbed his phone and dialled his colleague in Reykjavik, Chief of Police Garret Chase.

"Garret? Hi, it's Robert. Yeah, I'm good, thanks. Listen, I was wondering if you could provide me with some information."

"That depends on what you need," Chief Chase replied in a clipped tone, like only a busy man would.

"I'm investigating the disappearance of a young woman from Northtown in the mid-'90s. Helena Jensen. She's said to have skipped town and moved to Reykjavik, but nobody has heard from her since."

"Hah, you certainly have a cushy job if you have time to ponder over a cold case like this," Garrett laughed, sounding deep and somehow disturbingly sinister.

"Well, you know how it is with these small rural places. Hardly anything exciting ever happens around here," Decker joked.

"Yes, yes, we all envy you. But I've got bigger fish to fry, buddy. I need to uphold law and order in the nation's capital, so I'm sorry I can't help you. The best I can do is see if I can spare a man to look in the archive. I'll phone you if anything comes up."

"Much appreciated. Thanks for your time," Decker replied just before hearing a click followed by an empty dial tone.

Chief Chase hung up the phone and smirked. He had met Sheriff Decker at the National Police Conference in Reykjavik years ago, where the main goal was to coordinate police efforts across the country. Decker had approached him, praising him for what seemed to be an impeccable career. He enjoyed being showered with compliments while remaining reasonably cautious. Chief Garret Chase had long been a member of the country's elite society, where the rule of law didn't apply the same way as it did for the middle class. Keep your friends close and your enemies closer was a motto he lived by; that was how he had firmly overseen the police for the past twenty years. His questionable methods had gradually attracted the attention of those who preferred to do business in back alleys, hidden from the long arm of the law. In any such case, it was always better to have the Chief of Police in their pocket. He picked up his phone and dialled, waiting patiently for a few seconds. Finally, there was a reply on the other end of the line.

"Prime Minister Crow? How are you, my friend? Good. Listen, how's your campaign schedule looking right now? Aha. I see. Well, I just thought it might be worth making Northtown your first stop."

Chapter 25

"Aunt Marie? Are you home?"

Sara May sauntered through the massive steel door that sealed Aunt Marie's opulent palace on the hill. She knew calling her was pointless; given the size of this mansion, they'd have to use radios. She slowly strolled down the grand corridor. The white marble floor blended seamlessly with the white-painted walls, which were finely decorated with lavish paintings by some of the world's most renowned artists. On both sides were priceless artefacts carefully arranged on slender wooden tables of various sizes, giving the palace the feel of an exclusive gallery. The air was filtered to hospital standards, and the overwhelming absence of colours made the whole place cold and impersonal. Aside from a subtle golden hue here and there, nothing indicated that this was someone's actual home. But then, Aunt Marie had never been ordinary, so an ordinary home had never suited her lavish taste. She preferred to live like an old Hollywood starlet—a woman with exquisite taste in fine art and elaborate home décor.

"I'm here! Just go into the living room and take a seat. I'll be with you in a sec!" Aunt Marie loudly replied. The mansion's acoustics carried her voice like a wave until it reached Sara May's ears.

She sat on the most ridiculously oversized, white, velvety sofa she'd ever seen. The button-upholstered, suede couch could easily fit a family of fifty, stretching across the entire vast living room. Above it hung a huge painting that resembled two naked people cuddling. Or was it the sun and the moon? She'd never been much of an art critic, let alone a fan. On either side of the large sofa were two matching armchairs, positioned opposite each other with a generous glass coffee table between them, resting on a fluffy cream-coloured rug. Straight across the sofa, on the other side of the room, stood a gargantuan fireplace, accompanied by a single white bookcase nearby and a sizable floor-length mirror on the opposite wall. She looked around. Aunt Marie had done well for herself, having the good sense to marry rich men, not just once but four different times. She was a woman with a knack for business and wasn't afraid to put it to use.

But Sara May couldn't help but wonder if Aunt Marie's pretentiousness was not just to showcase her superiority over the poor peasants in town who still had to work their asses off for every penny, but rather to rub it in the face of the second-wealthiest woman in town, Pastor's wife, Paula. A woman Aunt Marie had hated for decades. Paula had never been one to pretend. She flaunted her feelings towards Aunt Marie proudly, making it crystal clear to everyone she despised that the seductress's promiscuous lifestyle was common knowledge. The two had been at war longer than Sara May could remember, and she'd never really been interested enough to ask why. But she was sure Aunt Marie had built her palace in Northtown, of all places, so she could annoy Paula. That had Aunt Marie's signature written all over it. Finally, the self-appointed queen of the North stormed into the living room, making a grand entrance as usual. No matter where she was, Aunt Marie ensured she was the centre of attention. Dressed in her pink silky bathrobe, wearing her fluffy slippers to match, and with about fifteen hair rollers on her head, it didn't matter whether she was dressing up for a party or the president. She had to be the talk of the town at all times.

"To whom do I owe the pleasure?" she asked, sipping her Dry Martini with two olives on a stick at two o'clock on a Wednesday. Why not?

"I wanted to return the dress I borrowed the other day," Sara May replied, handing over the plain-looking garment. Aunt Marie jeered.

"Darling, you didn't have to come all this way for that old thing." It's a rag; I was going to throw it out anyway," she replied, tossing the dress aside. Sara May bit her bottom lip and forced out a smile: nothing but the second best for her only niece.

"Going somewhere?" she sheepishly asked as she sat on the velvety sofa, remarkably uncomfortable despite its luxurious looks. Aunt Marie turned around and started admiring herself in the mirror next to the fireplace.

"Crow is coming to town with an entourage from his party. We're nearing the election, and they're campaigning. I don't know when they'll be here, but I'll be ready!"

"You want to be the hostess?" Aunt Marie hastily turned around, her mouth and nose drawn together as she gasped.

"Well, of course!" she replied, putting one hand dramatically on her chest to underline how offended she was while the other waved the cocktail, spilling drops on the floor. "You honestly think any of those run-down dumps in town are feasible for folks of their stature? No self-respecting woman with even half a brain would ask dignitaries to bunk in one of those rickety old ratholes that are popping up all over town like the plague! Whatever would people say?" She scoffed before taking another sip.

Sara May couldn't help but smile. Those words were

aimed at one particular pastor's wife in town. Aunt Marie began removing the rollers from her hair, admiring the masterpiece before her. There was no denying it; she was a stunning woman who had kept herself well despite her age. Aunt Marie had always been preoccupied with her looks. Her young, toned body had been the bait on her hunting trips over the years, landing her at least four big catches. It was, therefore, crucial that she stayed in shape if she was to have any hope of finding husband number five.

"Mum told me you and Prime Minister Crow were childhood friends."

"Did she now? I would've thought she'd never want to mention that to anyone," Aunt Marie replied without averting her eyes from her reflection, twisting and turning to get a good look from every angle.

"Why not?" asked Sara May, her curiosity piquing.

"Stephen and I didn't become friends until after they had broken up. My God, back in those days, it was considered such a scandal; you wouldn't believe it!"

"Wait. Mum and Prime Minister Crow dated?"

"Only one summer, if that. It was such puppy love. It was cute. She and I were so close in age that she hung out with any friends I made. They started dating in the summer of '84. Around the same time, I became interested in his best friend, Robbie Decker."

"Sheriff Decker?" Aunt Marie smiled as she puffed up her hair with her left hand, gripping the martini with the right.

"The one and only. Nothing came of it, though; he was so hung up on Martha, his now wife. He's been in love with her since they were teenagers, ain't that cute?" '

Sara May rolled her eyes and adjusted her posture on the

torture sofa.

"Very. Was Pastor Evans a part of this group of friends? Aunt Marie huffed.

"Unfortunately, yes. He was glued to Crow's ass like a fly on a pile of poo. Helena was drawn to him for some reason, but Paula beat her to it, so Helena became the filthy whore she was! To make Evans jealous!" Aunt Marie quickly turned around. "Just think! Sacrificing your dignity for a man!"

She turned again to face the mirror, taking a deep breath to steady herself. Much could be said about her, but nobody could ever accuse Miss Marie Magdalene Jensen of sacrificing her feminine grace and self-respect for a man. That was well beneath her. She had landed all four husbands on her own terms, never allowing a man to make her look foolish or take advantage of her. Sara May sat quietly for a while, taking it all in. Her mother never mentioned she had once dated the prime minister. That could explain why she always gushed about him and glowed whenever his face appeared on TV. But if Crow had been her childhood love, when would her dad have entered the picture? She looked to her left and saw Helena standing by the end of the sofa near the massive floor-length windows. She tried signalling that she couldn't talk without looking like a popped-out pill addict. But Helena stood firm.

"Why did you and Pastor Evans have a falling out?" Sara May asked, shifting her focus to Aunt Marie, who exhaled sharply.

"Hah! You can thank the pompous piece of a prune he married for that. The woman is so self-absorbed! She sees everyone as these puny little pests; if she tilted her head further back in disgust during rainfall, she'd drown! She almost left Evans when he decided to get a tattoo." Sara May's eyes widened.

"Pastor Evans has a tattoo?"

"He does. Not many people know about it; the she-devil he's hitched makes sure he keeps it carefully hidden."

"Do you know what kind of tattoo?"

"No. I think it's on his right shoulder, but it's been a long time since he got it. Why do you ask?"

"Just curious."

Chapter 26

Nighttime had taken over, pushing the comfort of daylight away. Sara May twisted and turned in bed like a wounded animal once again. The same nightmare kept tormenting her, causing her both anxiety and depression. She wasn't any closer to solving the mystery of her aunt's fate, which only seemed to intensify the nightmare's brutality. It had morphed into something much more sinister. This time, she was standing barefoot on a black sanded beach, with the ocean pounding her feet mercilessly, making any motion impossible. It felt ice cold but looked like red bodily fluid. She soon realised it wasn't water. It was blood. Before she could comprehend what was happening, a giant wave crashed ashore, almost sweeping her out to sea and drowning her in a gory, maroon-coloured liquid. She tried to run to safety, but her feet sank deeper into the charcoal sand with every step. Another wave hit her, so cold and brutal, leaving her soaked in blood. Right before the third wave hit, she woke up, heart pounding and sweat streaming down her face. It took her a while to gather her thoughts and calm down. As she sat in bed, shaking like a leaf, feeling utterly defenceless against the malicious entity that had taken hold of her mind, a subtle voice whispered in her ear.

"Go find Laura."'

Sara May was so startled that she leapt out of bed and quickly scanned the room. She was surely losing it! Desperately, she spun around half a circle, finally noticing Helena standing still in one corner of her room, nearly giving her niece a heart attack.

"Don't do this to me!" she begged after stopping

herself from screaming.

"I'm sorry," Helena shamefully replied.

"Were you watching me sleep?" Sara May felt cold shivers run down her spine and spread through her whole body.

"I was waiting for you to wake up."

"Were you the one planting this devilish nightmare in my head?"

"They asked me to."

"They who?" Helena shrugged.

"I don't know. The ones in control of this whole thing, I think." Sara May sighed.

"I was told to go find Laura. Do you know anything about that?"

"Laura was my friend."

"Laura Baker? At the Bread Box?"

"I think so, yes."

Sara May exhaled in frustration. Helena's memory loss was beginning to rattle her nerves. Perhaps it was unreasonable to expect a woman in her condition to remember anything from her past, so maybe it was better just to be happy with any small steps forward. She remembered the tattoo, and now she'd remember Laura. And although Sara May hadn't considered linking Laura to this mess, she knew she couldn't rule out anyone. It seemed to spread all over town. It was like every house in Northtown had cupboards full of skeletons now threatening to surface. She thought about Laura. Please don't let her be involved in this, she prayed.

Laura was one of the few people in town she'd taken a liking to. After every quarrel with her mother, she would run over to the Bread Box, where Bill and Laura would always look after her and let her stay until she calmed down. They were such a close-knit and lovely couple, drawing customers who gradually transformed the Bread Box into a community centre over the years. A place where everyone was welcome, where locals gathered to enjoy each other's company. Sara May closed her eyes and hoped to God that Laura was innocent. When she opened her eyes, Helena was gone. Booking an appointment with the dead clearly wasn't an option. She lay back down and made another attempt to fall asleep.

"Sara May, I'm home!" Maggie called out from the foyer.

She slowly opened her eyes, unaware of how long she had been asleep. Why her mother felt the need to announce her arrival like a five-star general was beyond her understanding. There was no need for alarm clocks in this house. All that was missing was a marching band announcing Maggie's return from work; at least that way, the neighbours would suffer along with her tormented daughter, who desperately craved some rest. Pissed off, Sara May threw off her duvet and stormed out of her room to greet the household queen.

"Hi, honey. I am completely drained; you'll have to fix your own breakfast," said Maggie as she took off her coat and hung it up.

"Haven't I always?" Sara May mumbled in annoyance.

"Can we not do this now? I just got home from a long night shift."

"You're always coming home from a long night shift. And if you're not coming home from work, you're on your way to work. When will it end, Mum?"

"It will end when I retire! Which should be in about seven years or so. You would know this if you had a decent job!"

Sara May took a step back. She hated hearing about her career or the lack of it. She was well aware that she'd missed the train to Triumph Town and wasted every opportunity she'd been given to achieve something. She didn't need constant reminders. Hearing it was like being punched in the face with a clenched fist.

"I just don't understand why you slave away for a company that gives you nothing in return! They're taking advantage of you! Can't you take up a part-time job?"

"No, Sara May, I can't take on a part-time job because your father left me with an enormous mortgage that I must repay if I don't want to end up on the street." On top of that, I also have to pay for food and bills. Modern society is pretty hostile to single people if you haven't noticed!"

"I know, Mum, I live alone!"

"And whose fault is that?" That was a below-belt kind of punch that Sara May felt in her gut. Clutching her shaking fists to stop the tears from bursting out, she took another step back. The fiery volcano within her was about to blow, and she was done holding back.

"Has it never occurred to you that I prefer being alone? At least then I won't have a husband walk out on me, leaving me with the sad fact that the Prime Minister rejected me!" Sara May yelled.

The marching band had left the room, leaving two gladiators standing. Neither lowered their swords. Once again, heavy words that couldn't be taken back had been spoken. It was a never-ending story. This was a home of endless battles with no end in sight. This mother-daughter duo seemed destined to always be at odds, neither willing to find middle ground nor compromise. They were too different. There they stood, facing each other. Both so proud, both so broken. This last mental sword fight had wounded them both. This time, Maggie walked away. She didn't have the energy to keep fighting, so she gave up the battle. They must have woken the neighbours. It wouldn't be the first time. And she didn't care enough to pretend everything was alright. Not this time. She no longer believed in it herself, so why bother trying?

Sara May watched as her mother turned her back on her and quietly went upstairs to her bedroom. She felt guilty but, at the same time, was furious. Why was it okay for everyone else to point out her flaws, but when she opened her mouth, all hell broke loose? She should know better than to argue with her mother like that, but she had every right to defend herself. Nobody was innocent in this. The desire for a good breakfast had turned into a wish to leave the house as quickly as possible. And she knew exactly where to go.

Chapter 27

"Eric! Can you take the cinnamon buns out of the oven?" Laura called out to her son. As usual, the Baker family had arrived early to prepare the Bread Box for hungry locals, who yearned for freshly baked pastries with their morning coffee.

Bill and Laura Baker were a close-knit team, both in business and in life. They'd always been on the same page when it came to raising their only son, Eric. That shaped him into a wholesome, down-to-earth man who enjoyed helping his parents run the family business. Just as he was about to put down the last pan of cinnamon buns, the door swung open, and the bell above it announced the arrival of the first customer of the day. As always, Bill stood behind the counter with a big, welcoming smile, ready to greet whoever was tempted by the delicious-smelling pastry.

"Oh, hello, Sara May. Fancy seeing you here so early in the morning!" Eric quickly looked up when he heard her name and hurried to meet her.

"Hey. "Is everything okay?" he asked, a slight worry in his voice.

"Yeah, why?" she replied, brows raised in confusion.

"Because you are never here this early."

"Well, I wouldn't be if Mum hadn't announced to the whole neighbourhood that she was home from her shift!" Sara May groused.

"Why didn't you just go back to bed?" he asked, a bit miffed that her storming in so early wasn't more urgent.

"Because we fought," she reluctantly admitted. Bill let out a little chuckle.

"Of course you did. Laura, honey? Do you have

anything for Sara May? She and Maggie had another fight,' he called out with a grin, almost as if he were enjoying this. Soon, Laura emerged from the back room, wiping her hands on her blue apron tied neatly around her waist.

"I'm sorry, I don't. But if you wait just a few minutes, darling, I'll have freshly baked croissants and bread rolls for you if you'd like."

"That's okay; I'm not that hungry. I need to chat with you, Laura. Is that okay?" Laura looked at Bill, quite taken aback by this response.

"Well, yes, of course. Just give me a second."

Laura returned to the back room while Sara May promised Eric she would tell him everything later. He didn't seem convinced, but he knew better than to second-guess the stubborn mule. He didn't know what he saw in her beyond her insane beauty. But he couldn't deny that everything about her, all her pros and cons, intrigued him more than he cared to admit. She annoyed him as much as she captivated him, a dangerous mixture he didn't know how to handle. Sara May sat by one of the large floor-to-ceiling windows that faced east so that customers could watch the sunrise. She was shaking nervously, something she'd never experienced when near Bill and Laura. She'd always felt so at home at the Bread Box. But not this time. She had no idea how to proceed. She feared that Laura was somehow involved in this mess, and by opening up this can of worms, she'd ruin the day for the poor woman. Maybe this wasn't such a good idea. She quickly got up from the table, but as soon as she took the first step forward, she noticed Laura heading her way. It was too late to back out now. Ashamed, she slowly sat back down as Laura took the seat across from her.

"What's going on, dear? I heard you and your mum had another fight." Sara May leaned backwards and shrugged.

"Yeah. It is what it is. We just don't get along."

"Well, you're both grown women now. Don't you think it's time the two of you had a proper chat and at least tried to find some common ground?" Laura asked in a motherly tone. Sara May tilted her head slightly to the right.

"I guess. But that's not what I came here to talk to you about." Just as she let go of that last word, Helena appeared behind her old friend.

Laura leaned back in her chair and waited to see what would happen. She sensed something was off, but couldn't quite explain it. She looked around, half-expecting someone to be standing nearby. She tried to stay calm. This wasn't the first time she'd felt the presence of people around her who couldn't be seen with the naked eye, but she'd always ignored it because she liked to think of herself as a sensible woman who didn't believe in this kind of nonsense. She stayed clear of churches and dismissed all ghost stories. Partly, it was because of the Bread Box; she was convinced that it would tank the business if rumours started spreading that one of the owners had her head in the clouds. But despite her efforts, she could never fully shake the feeling that there was more to this existence—something she wasn't meant to understand. That same feeling had never been as strong as it was at that moment.

"What do you need to tell me, Sara May?" she asked, more nervous than curious.

"I wanted to ask you about Helena."

Laura's whole body trembled at the mention of that name, and within seconds, a flood of thirty-one years of memories clouded her ability to breathe. How did she find out about Helena? Who had blabbed? How much did she know? She could feel her palms becoming clammy, and her heart beat faster than a hummingbird's wings. She'd woken early on this cold winter morning, not expecting the day to be any different from the others. Quiet and full of people gathering at the Bread Box to natter over hot tea and pastries. Laura had always loved how this little bakery drew folks from all walks of life, who would take a few moments out of their busy schedules to stop for a quick bite and a chat. But never in a million years did she imagine the secret she'd guarded so closely for thirty-one years would catch up with her so fiercely! She took a moment to compose herself. She had to choose her words carefully.

"Sara May. Who told you about Helena?" she calmly asked.

"Some ladies here at the Bread Box said I looked like her. So, I started asking around."

"And why did you think to come to me?"

"Because you've lived here so long, I thought you might remember her and be able to tell me about her." She was surprised by how quickly she'd thought of this lie.

"Very well. Let's go somewhere private and talk. I'll get Bill and Eric to cover for me."

The father-son duo needed no convincing. Laura's vision of raising a strong, united family had paid off many times before, and she knew she didn't need to worry about the bakery while she was away. A short while later, she placed a tray of pastries on the table in front of Sara May, who sat quietly in the Baker's family dining room. Laura wasn't used to being the host. Despite her and Bill being a well-liked couple, whom people enjoyed visiting, Laura had always avoided women's clubs and gossipy gatherings. It wasn't her preferred company, and there was a reason for that.

Now, she was sitting opposite Sara May by the elegant dining room table Bill had bought and given her one Christmas. The young guest looked around. It had been over thirteen years since she last set foot in this lovely home she'd always considered hers; that's how much time she'd spent here as a child. The house was stunning on the outside and both warm and cosy on the inside. The Bakers had never been ones to flaunt their success. All over the walls were photographs of treasured family moments. The décor mainly consisted of flowers and other personal items, giving the home a stylish yet inviting atmosphere. Sara May had always felt at ease in the Bakers' house.

"Well, darling. Tell me what you know, and I will tell you what I know," Laura said after a long silence.

"I don't know much, to be honest. Just that she was a dirty whore who had affairs with married men. That's it." Nana Lou's words were still fresh in her mind. "Trust no one." So, she deliberately held back. Laura scoffed.

"You've spoken to your nan and Aunt Marie, I hear."

"Among others, yes."

"Well, let me tell you something, Sara May. Helena was no whore! And there was no married man; that was nothing but idle chatter!" Sara May's ears perked up.

"How do you know that?" she asked.

"Because I was with her almost every day. She was my best friend. I was the one she trusted the most."

"Then you must know more than Grandma Gladys and Aunt Marie."

Laura hesitated. She knew more than most in this loose-lipped town, but over time, she'd learned not to reveal too much, no matter who asked. Helena had been a much-valued friend, so she wouldn't disrespect her by blabbing about their deepest, darkest secret.

"Helena was a wonderful person. She was a kind, gentle-hearted soul who treated everyone with equal kindness. So genuine and beautiful, both inside and out. But she was also very innocent; some might say naïve. And maybe that caused her downfall. She was an easy target for some pestering nuisances in town," Laura explained, sipping her tea.

"Aunt Marie told me she'd been hanging with her, Maggie, and their friends."

"From time to time, yes. Mostly when it was convenient for them. Your mum and Aunt Marie were so close in age, but Helena was a few years younger, so, to nobody's surprise, they couldn't always be bothered with her."

"What about Pastor Evans? Did she like him?" Laura nearly choked on her tea.

"Heavens, no! That's why he chased her non-stop, with the rock-hard cock in his trousers, being all perverted and obnoxious. She didn't fancy him one bit; she thought he was disgusting! Mind you, we were only fourteen when this all began. The boys were all around nineteen at the time. Prime Minister Crow and Sheriff Decker had the good sense not to meddle with such young girls, but Pastor Evans, he was a dirty devil, he was."

Sara May listened carefully. Laura was describing a

very different image of Helena, and now she understood why she had been told to speak with her. With this new knowledge, she found it easier to grasp the dark nature of Pastor Evans. According to Old Gilbert, the pastor had previously been an alcoholic womaniser, a point that Laura had largely confirmed. Furthermore, Old Gilbert mentioned it was a near-instant celestial turnaround in the pastor's behaviour, almost overnight, so to speak. Suddenly, he had transformed from a predatory drunkard to a seemingly innocent choirboy. Things were not looking good for Pastor Evans.

Chapter 28

Sara May spent most of the day chatting with Laura, and afterwards, she took a long walk to try to put things into perspective, using all the information she'd been given. Most of it seemed to point to Pastor Evans's severely dark conscience. But what didn't make sense was Helena's talk of the evil man with the tattoo. Aunt Marie confirmed that the pastor certainly had a tattoo. However, according to Laura, Pastor Evans never had any luck with Helena despite many bold attempts. So, it couldn't have been him that she ended up having a relationship with after moving to the capital, the man who'd abused her so abominably. The timeline didn't make sense, either. What were the consequences? Had the unknown man beaten her up so badly that one day he just took it too far, and that's why she always vanished into thin air in the nightmares? Or had she escaped the ordeal but been stricken by the merciless Mother Nature? If so, why had she never been found? These were all questions that Sara May desperately needed answers to.

The cold, gusty wind blew gently through town, wrapping around her like a ribbon. She quickened her pace in hopes of generating more heat. It was early November, but nothing pointed to it. Frigid snow flurries covered the ground like a thin blanket, giving it a frosty glow. She silently cursed the cold. One day, she would save enough money for a tropical holiday. Maybe she wouldn't even return. She hated the cold. As she walked past Simon and Suzy's home, she heard a loud argument that swiftly snapped her out of her thoughts. She paused to listen. Was this how people experienced the fights between her and her mother? She felt forced to face the idiocy, which made her cringe. The house's front door slammed open a moment later, and a distraught Simon stormed out. Suzy desperately called after him, her voice breaking, her hands trembling. Livid, Simon stomped off, away from the house, without giving his frantic wife a second glance.

Sara May shook her head and kept walking, puzzled as to why this fight had caught her attention. This sort of thing happened all the time in this dump. Every day, loud arguments could be heard across town, objects were thrown, and rumours spread; judging, cheating, lying, and betraying were the four sacred words that had defined Northtown for decades, though the council had yet to inscribe them on the town crest. Behind every closed curtain was a story being spun because no self-respecting person dared air their dirty laundry for all to see. The thin mask was so finely polished that it was difficult to see the cracks. The skeletons filled most closets, constantly threatening to surface, but were always carefully locked away. Sara May looked around. She'd never managed to get hold of those rose-coloured glasses that made Northtown appear as most people imagined a perfect little countryside village should be. She'd always known about the fissures the locals tried so hard to hide. It was pathetic. That's why she never felt like she belonged. That's why she left.

It was nearly nine o'clock when she finally arrived at her destination. She hoped and prayed that Nana Lou was home and still awake at this hour, sighing with relief when she saw lights shining from the old lady's kitchen window. She knocked on the door and waited patiently until Nana Lou answered. Surprised, she immediately let her in. As always, Sara May walked straight into the strange but cosy living room and sat down. While Nana Lou was preparing something to eat, she looked around, her gaze fixed on the large, peculiar crystal ball on a well-decorated round table across from her. The more she looked, the stranger everything seemed. A weird, slightly blue glow formed around it, and soon she could see the outlines of oddly shaped humans circling the table. She didn't recognise these people. They appeared to be of all ages but seemed to have no awareness of one another. They just stood there silently. Suddenly, they all looked at her in unison, so quickly that she nearly screamed. The moment she jumped, they vanished, and Nana Lou entered with a tray of fresh pastries, none the wiser.

"I hope this is enough. I didn't expect company tonight, to be perfectly honest," she said as she laid down the tray. When she failed to get a response, she looked at the girl who sat frightened opposite her.

"Is everything alright, dear?"

"Huh? Oh, yeah. I'm good. I just saw this crystal ball over there, and I…" When Sara May was unable to continue, Nana Lou looked at the ball but saw nothing. But she knew exactly what had happened.

The crystal ball had been passed to its new owner. It had done the same to Nana Lou when she visited the strange old wizard in Egypt just before he handed it to her. The ball began giving off a radiant blue light, and from it emerged people, none of whom Nana Lou had ever seen before. She quickly realised that those people were not of this world and had never been. Yet despite their unusual appearance, she knew she could trust them, and from that moment, she worked closely with these bizarre beings in the light until last year, when it became increasingly difficult to reach them. She knew why. Her time as the owner of this powerful crystal ball was coming to an end. She grinned. She'd always known she wasn't meant to find her successor. That was up to the ball itself. Whether she knew it or not, Sara May was destined for great things. Nana Lou smiled and turned her attention back to the frightened girl.

"Yes, this is a mighty ball, you see. But you didn't come over here to talk about that now, did you?" The old lady's calm demeanour seemed to calm her down, and she composed herself.

"No. I spoke to Laura." Nana Lou's smile widened.

"I was hoping you did."

"Did you know she was friends with Helena?"

"I wasn't born yesterday, my dear. I've lived here longer than most people."

"Then why didn't you tell me?"

"It wasn't mine to tell. There are some things you have to discover for yourself."

Sara May rolled her eyes. She knew Nana Lou was right, but it would have been nice to get this vital information sooner. It had been over a month since she returned to Northtown, and she felt stuck. She was sleep-deprived from suffering horrible, recurring nightmares that caused her major anxiety, so she accepted all the help she could get at this point. Knowing that Nana Lou was hiding things from her was infuriating!

"Did Laura tell you anything of value?" Nana Lou asked, sipping her tea.

"She said that Helena hadn't been the slut everybody made her out to be. That she had never had an affair with a married man, those were just rumours. Maybe she did, but was afraid to tell her best friend."

"That's possible."

"She also told me that Pastor Evans had circled her like a horny dog but never had any luck. That doesn't match what Aunt Marie told me, and it doesn't add up because if they were never together.... then...who abused her?"

Nana Lou sat in silence. Her memory wasn't as sharp as it had been, but her feelings remained unchanged. She'd always disliked Pastor Evans for many reasons, primarily because of his unnerving presence. She couldn't quite explain it, but it was like a dark, misty cloud of hatred and evil trailed him wherever he went. In his youth, he had been a notorious skirt chaser, known for being very aggressive, especially after heavy drinking. But then, one day, it was as if someone had just flicked a switch in his head. He enrolled at university to become a priest and returned to Northtown, clean as a whistle. A married man of God who easily resisted all temptations, leaving behind all his former sins. He even got a tattoo to mark his victory. Despite not completing his studies following the sudden death of his father-in-law, the then-pastor of Northtown, nobody seemed to hold it against Evans. He had served the town well and obtained the degree he needed somewhere along the way. While most people in town had nothing bad to say about him, a few secretive souls saw through the facade. Nana Lou and her beloved Trucker Tom were among them. The pastor's false behaviour didn't fool either of them.

"I wouldn't put the pastor behind me just yet if I were you," Nana Lou warned. "There is something more to him; I am sure of it."

"But if Helena moved to the city and met a man there, it couldn't have been the pastor because he never returned after being called home to serve the church."

Before Nana Lou could answer, there was a knock on the door.

"Who the hell could this be?" she asked, more miffed than surprised, as she got up to answer the door. "Speak of the devil!"

"My dear, is this the right way to greet a servant of God?" Pastor Evans asked with a hellish smile, pretending to be offended.

"We've never been so close that I should require his service," she hissed. "What do you want?"

I was just on my evening walk and decided to come and see how you're doing. Is that such a crime?"

"Bothering people at this hour borders on unlawfulness." That wiped the smirk off the pastor's face, replacing it with frustration.

"Is Sara May inside?" he sternly asked. Upon hearing her name, Sara May got up from her chair and walked confidently to the front door. Pastor Evans's face lit up when he saw her approaching.

"Hello there, young lady. I saw your mother earlier, and she's starting to worry about you," he said, lying through his teeth. "I think it would be wise if you hurried home. You don't want to cause her more suffering than you've already done," the pastor continued with the devilish smirk on his face that made him so unappealing.

Sara May stood between Nana Lou and the pastor. As he uttered that last word, the same black smoke as before began to swirl around him, and the horrid grin on his face grew so terrifying it almost appeared demonic. It sent shivers down her spine, gripping every nerve and igniting them. It caused her physical pain, but before it became too obvious, the smoke slowly started to fade, driven off by a warm, glowing light coming from behind her. At that very moment, she felt a hand resting on her shoulder as a sign of support. She didn't need to turn around to know she was being protected. Those beings held back the evil, ensuring the darkness couldn't reach her. Neither Pastor Evans nor Nana Lou noticed what was happening, and Sara May decided not to risk bringing this malicious energy into the old lady's home. She thanked her for her time, and before she strode past God's servant defensively, she cast a spiteful look, making sure he knew she wasn't afraid of him in the slightest.

Chapter 29

Sara May hurried down Northtown's High Street, her hands jammed firmly in her pockets and her head bowed. Only a few people were about, but she couldn't shake the feeling that someone was following her. She was certain that Pastor Evans's visit wasn't a coincidence. Someone had tipped him off. He knew about Nana Lou's psychic talents, as did everyone else, but he seemed more afraid of it than most. This made Sara May believe he was hiding something—something Nana Lou's powers could reveal. She sped up, eager to get inside. It was nearly eleven o'clock at night, and most places were probably closed. This certainly wasn't the capital city. Just as she was about to curse herself for not being at home, she noticed a tiny speck of light coming from the Brewer. *Weird,* she thought to herself. This dilapidated place always shut early on weekdays, much to the annoyance of the town drunks. Shivering, she hurried towards the light and slowly pushed the front door open.

To her surprise, all the lights were out. The only illumination came from a small candle on one of the modest tables by the street-facing windows. Sitting on one of the chairs around the table was Simon, drunkenly clutching a half-empty cognac bottle in one hand and holding a full glass in the other. He looked plastered, which didn't surprise Sara May. Over the past few years, Simon had developed a taste for the alcohol he so openly sold to others. His highly publicised problem had become a spectacle for the town's busybodies, who gleefully fed off his misery. Sara May gently closed the door and slowly approached Simon, who initially didn't notice her. As she lowered herself into one of the chairs, he looked up, his glazed eyes squinting, trying to see who was sitting across from him.

"We're closed!" he slurred out the best he could.

"Simon, it's me. Sara May." He tsked.

"The Jensen kid. I should have known," he garbled, tightening his grip on the bottle.

"Are you okay? Did something happen?" she asked, remembering the argument she'd witnessed earlier.

"That son of a bitch! He thinks he won this war!" Simon yelled and angrily slammed his clenched fist on the table, scaring Sara May, who tried to keep calm.

"Who are you talking about?"

"Evans. That vile sack of shit! That…that…. devil!"

"Pastor Evans? What has he done to you?" she asked, acting clueless. Simon let out a sinister laugh.

"He thinks he's so slick. He thinks he can hold this over my head and then take my boys!" he replied, giving the table another hard slam before trying to pour some more alcohol into the already full glass and failing miserably.

"What do you mean by taking your boys?" Simon focused on steadying the bottle, seemingly not noticing the mess he'd previously made.

"You think they're mine? No. That bloody whore couldn't resist the devil's dick! She's nothing but a filthy, bed-hopping tramp, she is!" Sara May's eyes widened.

"I don't understand. Are you saying Pastor Evans fathered Jack and Jake?"

"He can have them. He can have it all! He knows that I know!"

Sara May felt more confused than ever before. Had Simon become so intoxicated that he didn't know what he was saying? Or was it his words that had driven him to

174

this state? What on Earth had happened between him and Suzy? If Pastor Evans was the twins' father, then Simon and Suzy were also caught up in this web of lies and secrets that had poisoned the town for the last thirty years. Given the state of the poor man, it was apparent that he hadn't had any idea of his wife's infidelity until recently, and he was clearly not taking the news well. Sara May wondered if Jack and Jake knew, or if the pastor's wife, Paula, was aware. She and Evans had never been able to have children. If she found out, it could send her to an early grave! Sara May didn't know what to think. Suddenly, Simon quickly stood up from the table, almost knocking over the candle and the cognac bottle. The anger sizzled inside him, burning like wildfire. The dim glow of the shrinking candle distorted his drunken face, and Sara May realised she'd never feared another person as much as she feared Simon at that very moment.

"He will pay for this! That evil, hellish, homewrecking, vile piece of scum!" he shouted before hastily storming to the door. There, he suddenly halted and turned around. With a chillingly ice-cold gaze in his eyes, he stared into her soul so intensely she was unable to move.

"He'll be coming for you, too," he warned.

With that said, he rushed out and slammed the door so forcefully behind him that two vodka bottles fell from a shelf behind the bar and shattered into pieces. Sara May felt like crying. Shaking uncontrollably with fear, she could feel her nervous breathing growing heavier and heavier, almost as if someone was pressing down on her chest with full force. What did he mean by this ominous threat?

Chapter 30

Sara May hardly slept the following night. The nightmare haunted her like never before, becoming increasingly violent. The strength of the shadowy man had grown so much that, in the end, another person had fallen victim to his brutal rage. A man in his mid-sixties. She didn't see who it was, most likely just a faceless no-name who had struggled in life. Watching him collapse was extremely distressing, and when she looked down, she noticed she was standing in a murky puddle of blood, ankle-deep. Paralysed with fear, she looked up again and saw the shadowy figure sprinting towards her like a madman in a frantic fury. Then, she abruptly woke up, soaked in sweat and terrified beyond reason. This was beginning to take a heavy toll on her mental health, causing her crippling anxiety.

The following day, she woke up feeling confused after another night disturbed by night terrors. Finally, she dragged her feet to the kitchen, wishing she could stay under the covers all day, but sadly, that wasn't an option. She dreaded facing the outside world. What awaited her out there besides a slim chance of bumping into Eric? He had been the carrot that pulled her out of bed these past few mornings, but the fear of him discovering her true feelings and rejecting them kept her at a distance. Now, she stood in front of the toaster, making herself a half-decent breakfast and waiting for the usual lecture from her mother. But not this time. Maggie entered the kitchen soon after her daughter and sat down silently, without making her usual bitter remarks about Sara May wasting her life with no ambition. Instead, there was only silence, which sparked concern.

"Mum? Are you okay?"

"I don't know. Suzy called me this morning right before I got home from my shift. She wanted to know if Simon stayed at my place last night."

"What? Why would she ask that?" Sara May asked, feeling her skin crawl with the thought of her mum and Simon sharing a bed, doing the nasty, as she focused on her toast and orange juice.

"Beats me. Apparently, they got into an intense argument last night, and he left the house. She hasn't seen him since then." Sara May quickly turned around.

"You mean he never came home?"

"Evidently not." Maggie shrugged her shoulders. "I'm sure it's nothing to be concerned about. He's probably just staying with a friend until he calms down. I told her he wasn't here, but I would keep an eye out for him."

"Why doesn't she just call him?" Sara May asked and took a bite out of her toast.

"He's not answering. She's absolutely distraught, thinking something might have happened to him."

Sara May listened carefully, fearing the worst. Simon had been visibly upset that night at the Brewer and rushed out the door without saying where he was going. He'd been furious with Pastor Evans for a good reason. As she often did before, she remembered Nana Lou's wise words about trusting no one, so she decided not to tell her mother about her meeting with Simon the previous night. She didn't have any proof to link the pastor to anything suspicious yet, so going to his place and accusing him of a violent act was unwarranted. But she couldn't shake the troubling feeling that something wasn't right.

"What are you going to do?" she asked her mother.

"I told her I needed to rest after my shift, but if Simon

hadn't returned when I woke up, she should come here."
Sara May's brows lowered in confusion.

"Here? Why?" she asked with a mouth full of marmalade toast.

"For moral support." Sara May nearly choked as she swallowed the last piece.

"Mum, you know that if she comes, they all come! Every busybody in town! And they'll gossip!" she warned after a vicious coughing fit. Maggie was having none of it.

"Oh, don't be silly. They won't start jabbering with Suzy in the house."

"That has never stopped them before!"

"Sara May, I will not tolerate this kind of talk in my house! I've already invited Suzy over to show support because that's what good neighbours do! If that upsets you, you are welcome to go and stay somewhere else!"

Maggie quickly left the kitchen, leaving Sara May sulking by herself. It gave her a moment to reflect. Could something have happened to Simon? No, surely not. He probably just passed out in someone's garden, with his bum in a bush. Worst case, he'd catch the first bus out of town. Stranger things had happened. She wouldn't blame him; she'd done the same at just eighteen. And, considering everything, she was amazed that Simon had lasted in Northtown as long as he had. Suddenly, feeling like she wasn't alone in the kitchen, she looked up and saw Helena standing nearby, looking very worried.

"What do you want?" Sara May asked, annoyed.

"He's an evil man," Helena replied in a shaky voice.

"Who? Simon? Nah, he's alright. Maybe a little disgruntled and could have treated Jake better, but other than that, he's okay."

"Things are not as they seem."

"What do you mean?"

"Find Simon."

And just like that, she was gone again. Sleep-deprived and agitated, Sara May wasn't in the mood for guessing games. Helena spoke in riddles, and because she hadn't had a good night's sleep, she barely had enough brain cells left to function, let alone act like Sherlock Holmes. She threw the rest of her breakfast away and left the house. The grey-clouded sky above looked as if it was preparing to dump a month's worth of rain on everything in sight, almost as if it was holding its breath, waiting for the perfect moment to unleash. Walking quickly down the high street in town, she slowed as she approached the Brewer. Perhaps Simon had gone back there after she left. Maybe he was just sleeping in the wine cellar without anyone thinking to look for him there.

Aside from three or four staff members, only a handful of lonely souls lingered at the pub on that cold November morning, clutching their first alcoholic drink of the day. Standing in the centre of the wooden tavern with a broom in hand was Jake, wearing his headphones, sweeping up last night's crumbs and minding his own business. Behind the bar, Bob the bartender was chatting with Chris. Sara May felt her heart race skyrocket. She was almost certain her heart and mind belonged to Eric at this point, but she couldn't help but admire the sight of Chris, a stunning picture of human perfection, leaning against the shelves with his legs and arms crossed while talking to Bob. His perfectly sculpted face lit up when he noticed her.

"Hey there, kitten. What brings you here on this fine

Thursday morning?" he gleefully asked.

"I was just wondering if Simon might have dropped by?"

"No, we were just talking about that, actually. He wasn't here when I showed up earlier. It's not like him to be late," Bob replied, putting down a stained glass he had just finished polishing.

"That's odd," she said, becoming increasingly concerned over the whole thing.

"Well, something happened here last night. When I showed up, everything was a mess. Two broken bottles and alcohol everywhere."

"You think someone broke in?" she asked, putting on her best poker face and pretending to know nothing about how that mystery occurred. Bob shook his head and looked around.

"No sign of a break-in. Guess the old geezer just had one too many last night," he said, sparking a laugh from Chris.

Sara May smiled, even though she saw nothing remotely funny about the situation. She was convinced that the things she knew were vital to the bigger picture, but she also knew that saying too much too soon could cause more problems. The timing wasn't right. Bob picked up another glass and started polishing it.

"I'm sure he's fine. I reckon the men will go out and look for him if he's not home before dinner," he added.

Sara May forced out a fake smile and bade the men farewell, then hurried towards the front door. Just as she reached the threshold, she heard her name whispered subtly but loud enough for her to stop and turn around, seeing Jake standing just a few feet away. She wasn't sure if she was hearing things because Jake wasn't known for his social skills. He hardly ever approached people if he could help it. Known for his eccentricity, he was a man who prioritised his solitude above all else and disliked mingling with others. Locals had branded him either daft or an ingenious oddball, depending on who was asked. "He's a right crackerjack he is" was commonly used to describe the poor boy. The reason was either said to be his parents' awful treatment or his high intellect, that he didn't function well among the average IQ public.

Whatever the reason, one thing was clear. Jake was not a man to get close to, so Sara May wasn't sure if he'd called out for her or if she was losing her mind. Jake was looking directly at her, something he usually avoided at all costs. She felt trapped in an uncomfortable staring contest. It was almost like Jake was trying to break her mentally with just his mind alone. She could feel her body stiffening, and fear gripped her like invisible chains, trapping her. She looked around, expecting Chris and Bob to say something, but saw no one. Not even the town drunks, who had, just a few moments earlier, been dispersed all over the pub, looking defeated with their bottles of beer in hand, broken down with shame and disgust at their weakness. Jake stepped closer without breaking eye contact, still clutching the broom.

"I saw Pastor Evans. And I know you know more than you're telling," he muttered ominously. Sara May took a deep breath and tried to break free from the awful spell he was casting on her.

"When… when did you see him?" she stuttered, her voice shaking with fear.

"The night Dad went missing. I was walking home around three am when I saw Pastor Evans. He got in his car and drove away. A bit odd, innit? Go out driving so late at night. But who'd believe a thick-witted mute like me?" he shrugged.

And just like that, he went back to sweeping, acting as if nothing had happened. Sara May stood like a statue, utterly baffled. Never before had she felt such terror, yet she was also deeply curious. Jake had given her crucial information, but the puzzle was still scattered across the table. The frame was gradually taking shape, but the most vital pieces were still missing to complete it. She thanked Jake and stepped back onto the high street. She needed to find a way to connect the dots; only then would she be able to link Pastor Evans to the whole thing.

Chapter 31

When Sara May got home that evening, it was as if she'd fallen into a bird's nest by mistake. The squawking noise was so loud it could shatter glass, yet no one thought to tell them to quiet down. A group of women had gathered in the living room under the pretence of supporting Suzy during this tough time. After all, that's what good neighbours do. But Sara May knew better than to buy that bullshit. The women of Northtown were the undisputed champions of hypocrisy. Cleverly disguised as love and care, it was a golden opportunity for those meddlesome busybodies to cluster like rats around rubbish and feast on one of the biggest, most newsworthy carcasses they'd seen in ages. The fact that Simon was nowhere to be found was the perfect ingredient for whatever they planned to cook up in their kitchen of gossip and lies.

"I bet he's run off with some hussy," one said.

"I heard they had a huge fight last night," another added.

"Well, I'm not surprised. If she found out about his mistress, she was bound to kick him out. "I would have!" the third yenta added.

"If I were her, I would've buried him alive!"

"You think she did? Killed him, I mean?"

Sara May rolled her eyes and threw her hands up in exasperation, only to let them fall just as quickly before stepping into the kitchen. She wouldn't be at all surprised if Simon ended up being labelled a sleazy pimp, secretly gay, or a sex-crazed drunkard caught up in a midlife crisis, running away with a younger woman. Sadly, that wouldn't be unusual here. In the kitchen, the scene was just as lively. A group of women, equally loud, had gathered around the table, chatting simultaneously while trying to put together some sort of feast, as was the custom in times of crisis. It was like watching a blender on the verge of exploding. Suzy sat like a broken doll by the table, with at least four women fussing over her, trying to patch the poor woman together, and an additional five were all over each other, holding plates of food and occasional cake for dessert, talking over each other in an attempt to organise things the best they could. It was utter chaos. Amidst all the commotion, Sara May spotted her mother holding a beautiful three-layer cake and called out to her.

"Mum, what the hell is going on?"

"Simon still hasn't turned up, and we fear the worst! The men are out looking for him!" Maggie replied with a distressed look on her face, narrowly dodging an elderly lady with a casserole.

"What's with all the food?"

"You can't worry about someone on an empty stomach, Sara May!" Just as she was about to think of a clever comeback, she was interrupted by a distant yet familiar voice.

"I tell ya, he's a right old twit he is! He got his nose all up in them young arses, that grey-haired geezer!" Grandma Gladys huffed as she stomped past the kitchen. Too stunned to reply, Sara May turned to her mother again, pointing after her grandmother, palm up in demand of an explanation.

"What's she doing here? I thought she hated everyone in town."

"Hate is a strong word. I asked her to come," Maggie replied, still trying to keep the cake intact.

"And she just showed up, just like that?"

"No, I told her if she wouldn't come, I wouldn't drive her to church anymore. It's cold negotiating."

"It's called blackmailing!"

"Not the point. Can you please not argue with me on this one?"

"Me? You should be worrying about Grandma Gladys!"

"I'm not fighting with you right now! That's the last thing Suzy needs."

Sara May took a deep breath. With the gossip club in the living room and the noisy chicken coop in the kitchen, there wasn't much space for her anyway. Just as she was about to reply with a carefully considered answer, Didi Donnelly, from two blocks away, barged uninvited into the conversation. Her face was a mask of shock and disgust. Sara May stepped to one side. The woman looked like she was about to blow.

"Maggie, I cannot believe my ears! Is your sister throwing a lavish gala for Prime Minister Crow and his entourage tonight?" she asked, her nose twitching upright with repulsion. Ashamed, Maggie looked away.

"Yes, yes, she is." Didi placed a palm on her chest before loudly gasping.

"I cannot believe this! How dare she cater to those filthy rich fat cats in times like these? This is hardly the time to celebrate! Has she no shame?"

"No, Didi, she doesn't, I'm afraid."

"I heard the whole town council is attending. Pastor Evans and Paula, as well. I hope they'll all be crippled with guilt!" a woman named Sharon Mooney chimed in as she poured wine into a liquor glass which she then tried to interest Suzy with.

Didi huffed as she pushed past Sara May and stormed

into the living room, furious over what she had just heard and desperate to share it with the rest of the judgmental gasbags. She had, however, inadvertently planted an idea in Sara May's mind. Suppose it were true that Pastor Evans and his wife were away. That would give her the perfect chance to sneak in and hopefully gather more information about what had happened to Helena. It couldn't be a coincidence that Simon was also missing after his encounter with the pastor. At this point, she was convinced that his conscience was darker than the devil's heart. She looked into the kitchen and saw Suzy sitting silently by the table amid the chaos.

That poor woman. She looked like she was on a completely different planet, unaware of the utter chaos around her. They meant well, this lively flock of hens they were, but they didn't know what Sara May knew. She couldn't tell from Suzy's emotionless expressions whether she was in shock over her husband's disappearance or if she was just so overwhelmed with guilt for causing it. She must have told him that Jack and Jake weren't biologically his; they belonged to Pastor Evans. Something had gone terribly wrong with this group of friends all those years ago, and Sara May was confident the key to solving this mystery was in Pastor Evans's pocket. The more she dug into their past, the closer she'd be to uncovering the truth. She quietly slipped out of the house. The women were too busy gossiping and chattering to notice she was gone. Maggie was busy caring for Suzy, and Grandma Gladys couldn't care less about where her only grandchild was half the time anyway. She shut the front door behind her just as Laura Baker headed towards the kitchen. She was also about to leave, fed up with not being able to hear her own thoughts over the loud noise. She had only one thing left to do.

"Maggie! Hi!" she called out. Maggie turned around and vaguely smiled.

"Oh, hi, Laura. Good to see you."

"Thank you. Although this isn't exactly a happy occasion."

"You're right about that," Maggie sighed, finally managing to put down the cake she'd protected from the swirling group of women coming and going, fumbling over each other in the kitchen like a group of nervous actors about to take the stage.

"I spoke to your daughter the other day," said Laura.

"Did you, now? That's nice," Maggie replied, instantly feeling uncomfortable. She attended to the dessert, quietly hoping this conversation wouldn't continue.

"She knows about Helena," Laura pointed out, determined to get answers. Maggie sighed in annoyance.

"Yes, I was told someone at the Bread Box let it slip."

"Has she said anything to you?"

"Please, Laura, this is not the place nor the time for this discussion."

"Don't you think she ought to know the truth? It has to come out eventually. You don't think now's the right time?"

"No, I don't think so. And if everyone honours their end of the bargain and keeps their mouths shut, we don't need to worry!"

Maggie pushed past Laura, who let out a heavy sigh. Given the circumstances, she'd hoped Maggie would show some understanding, but that was just wishful thinking. Laura had known for some time that Helena was dead. She based it on the fact that Helena had left without telling anyone. She hadn't even bothered to tell her best friend. Since then, she hadn't heard anything— not even a phone call. Laura knew their friendship meant more to Helena than that. Something had to have happened to her. However, since Maggie saw no reason to be honest, Laura saw no reason to share what she knew was the sad truth about this awful mess. And with that, she left the house. Troubled by her encounter with Maggie, she didn't notice Sara May standing just a few feet away, staring at her phone. It was cold outside, and the night somehow seemed darker than usual. Shivering, Sara May dialled Eric's number.

"Hi, Eric? It's Sara May. Are you up for a little adventure?"

Chapter 32

Aunt Marie's mansion was bustling with high-society socialites. Someone had informed the media earlier that Prime Minister Crow and his entourage of political sycophants planned to launch their re-election campaign in Crow's hometown up north. Once there, they would meet with voters and hopefully persuade one or two undecided individuals that voting for their party was a safe choice, despite a long history of broken promises. All was forgotten; elections symbolised a fresh start and a new, bright beginning. Aunt Marie had always maintained good relations with her childhood friend, now Prime Minister, and had agreed to host the welcoming gala when asked. The guest list was limited to those who had proven themselves essential in business. Besides their precious votes, Prime Minister Crow and his like-minded associates believed the inferior peasants had nothing valuable to offer and should, therefore, be excluded from this lavish celebration. The luxury that flowed through the wide hallways and enormous rooms that evening was reserved only for those deemed worthy by society's upper class.

Among them were Mayor Timothy Brown and his wife, Pastor Evans, Paula, Jack, and many other shrewd businesspeople, as well as easily bribed politicians and their trophy wives. Aunt Marie had invited Simon and Suzy, fully aware of their desperate attempts to join the glamorous world of the rich and famous. But fate thwarted her efforts. She knew many would curse her for proceeding with the gala despite the circumstances. They would call her cold-hearted and insensitive. But the public's opinion of her had never been something to boast about anyway, so she had learned to dismiss it, no matter how nasty the rumours became. She was her own boss and critic, which gave her the freedom not to care what others thought. Of course, she felt sorry for poor Suzy. But cancelling the party wouldn't have made any difference. That was out of the question. It was too short notice, and the guests were too important! So, instead of withdrawing, Aunt Marie glided among the pretentious aristocrats, dressed to impress, capturing everyone's attention as she moved. She was on her A-game.

"Hello. Nice to see you. Glad you could make it. Love that dress," the ever-so-boastful socialite flattered her way through the group.

Only one woman despised her false adulation. Paula had loathed her wealthy neighbour for decades solely because of what she represented. Aunt Marie's lifestyle starkly contrasted with the Christian values that Paula upheld, and the fact that she could live so scandalously and still wield such influence within the circle of business elites was more than the virtuous Pastor's wife could bear. That shameless scarlet jumped from one husband to another and appeared utterly indifferent to the notoriety her disgraceful actions had gained her. But worst of all, she seemed to have avoided any punishment for her sins. If anything, she grew wealthier and more powerful with each divorce! She mingled with the high society, socialised with the prosperous, and walked around with her head held high despite Paula's numerous attempts to tarnish her reputation. No one realised just how much it bothered the honourable pastor's wife. Aunt Marie had always known she was like a malignant tumour on Paula's soul, and she enjoyed every bit of it. Over the years, it became a hobby to flaunt her lavish wealth before the grandiose Mrs. Perfect. Because, despite her ambiguous image, Aunt Marie despised privileged, gossiping snakes who fabricated stories about kind-hearted people of lesser means for amusement. Wealth be damned, Aunt Marie was a woman of high morality. She didn't associate with the working class, being the high-class fashionista she was, but she didn't tolerate injustice in any form. She hadn't been raised in wealth and never forgot her roots.

She enjoyed being a hostess, but most of all, she relished seeing Paula's seething expression. It looked as though she was about to erupt like a volcano over the party's success. The elegant guests indulged in all that being upper-class had to offer, and Aunt Marie loved every moment. But where were Prime Minister Crow and Pastor Evans? She quickly scanned the room but couldn't see them. It wasn't unusual for the Prime Minister to slip away from a party for a private, important conversation. However, the absence of Pastor Evans was concerning. Her palms grew clammy, and her heart raced. She forced a smile so no one would notice her inner panic as she slowly slipped out of sight. Acting as if everything was under control came naturally to her. Years of pretending had turned her into a master of deception. Moving through the crowd, nodding politely and exchanging casual greetings, she finally disappeared without being noticed. Her anxiety increased as she searched each empty room. Where could they be? It shouldn't have been a worry that they had vanished. But if they planned to use her party for an unethical political scheme, that was a different matter entirely.

After thoroughly checking every room, she was about to give up. They must have left. Damn it! Aunt Marie knew that Crow was under Pastor Evans's spell. They'd been like two peas in a pod since childhood, and Evans had been a loyal supporter of Crow's political career from the very beginning. So much so that many believed the Pastor's political connections eventually secured Crow the cushy job as Prime Minister. However, the voters didn't realise just how much Pastor Evans influenced Crow's political choices. In exchange for a hefty donation to his campaign, Crow favoured his old friend's opinions over most others and followed his advice meticulously. He'd also been very generous, fulfilling Evans's wishes and commands, although he tried to hide it most of the time. When the two met, it never ended well for the ordinary voter, but it greatly benefited the wealthy business elite. Aunt Marie knew the rules of the game. If the media found out that Evans and Crow had used her party to hatch another political plot, she, too, would suffer the consequences. Suddenly, she heard faint muttering from one of the rooms, the last one she hadn't checked. She moved closer and pressed her ear against the slightly open door. Bingo. Her first thought was to burst in and chase them out. The nerve! But she held back and chose instead to listen in.

"I'm not saying they'll link you to this, but if you've had anything to do with it, I need to know now," Crow commanded, towering over the sitting Evans with both hands firmly on his hips. Evans sat with his legs crossed, visibly calmer than Crow.

"I'm not confessing to a damn thing. Besides, the less you know, the better it is for you, you know that," he reminded him. That didn't appease the Prime Minister, who became instantly enraged.

"Jesus Christ, Evans, we're only minutes away from

re-election!" If so much as a snippet of hair is found...."

"It won't. Don't worry, I've taken care of it."

Aunt Marie felt her body suddenly cool down sharply, rendering her unable to move. She struggled to understand these cryptic conversations, but to no avail. Without warning, a hand was firmly placed on her right shoulder, causing her to turn around swiftly.

"It's hardly good manners to leave one's own party to listen in on private conversations," Paula reprimanded the hostess, her brows furrowed to show her disgust. Aunt Marie snatched her shoulder free from Paula's grip.

"In this house, we believe in one's freedom to do what one chooses," she clapped back.

"Well, then, a confidential discourse shouldn't be of any interest now, should it?" Paula replied with a snide grin.

Aunt Marie chose not to retaliate further, instead taking the high road as she walked gracefully past Paula. Nobody would accuse her of being the lesser of the two. She still had her dignity. Paula, however, was not about to let this go and chased her nemesis back into the main hall. Too often, she had allowed this pitiful excuse of a woman to walk all over her because of her connections to the Prime Minister and his influential friends. But not this time. Both Evans and Crow had heard the commotion on the other side of the door and hurried to see what was happening, as they saw the two women rushing back into the main hall.

"Is this how you choose your husbands, Marie? Spying on conversations that are none of your business, in the hopes that someone will throw you a bone?" Paula mocked. Aunt Marie hurriedly turned around, seething with anger.

"You're one to talk! You miserable, loose-lipped cow who does nothing but hate on those you deem below you!" Aunt Marie yelled through gritted teeth. Paula gasped.

"At least I'm not so desperate that I need to screw my way around to maintain my status among those who matter!"

"That's because no one can stand you long enough to give you a second look, you flabby old gasbag!"

The crowd stood stunned and silent. It wasn't unusual to see two giants going head-to-head in political parties, but it was less common to see it aired so publicly. Nobody dared say a word. After what felt like forever, Paula turned around, grabbed her husband's arm, and stormed off in fury. She had made her point. Nobody should think the Pastor's wife wouldn't fight back when threatened. She still carried her grandeur, if nothing else. When the pastor and his wife left the party, Aunt Marie instructed the band to keep playing to distract the crowd. Soon, the party returned to normal, and the mansion was once again alive with cheerful chatter and the clinking of champagne glasses, blending seamlessly with the smooth jazz soothing everyone's senses. Aunt Marie decided to put everything behind her as best she could and avoid eye contact with Crow. She wasn't in the mood for an awkward interrogation. Luckily, he felt the same, so the two childhood friends stayed clear of each other for the rest of the night.

Chapter 33

"Have you lost your damn mind? How is this a good idea? "a furious Eric asked as he slammed the car door behind him.

"I never said it was a good idea! "Sara May clapped back.

Eric shook his head in frustration, firmly placing his hands at his sides. He'd often wondered why he always went along with her craziness, never more so than at this very moment. It'd been adorable and funny when they were children, but this situation was downright awful for a grown man who hoped to benefit society as a law-abiding citizen. To break into someone's house was bad enough, but invading the Pastor's private residence, the most sacred of all homes in Northtown, carried so many negative points that not even the Pope himself could grant absolution. Yet he followed her blindly. He couldn't explain it; she had him under a spell. Perhaps it was her dazzling beauty. Maybe it was her courageous stupidity. Whatever it was, despite every fibre of his being objecting to it, he couldn't fight the feelings growing within him towards this enchanting yet utterly crazy vixen standing before him, her hands just as firmly on her hips, signalling she wasn't backing down and she certainly wouldn't let him tell her otherwise. He threw his hands up, surrendering to her will.

They managed to sneak into the back garden unnoticed. The rest was pretty straightforward. The lock on the back door was still broken, just as it had been since they were young. Paula persistently complained about her husband's reluctance to fix it. *My dear, it's Northtown. Who'd want to break in? Besides, I am the*

town's pastor; my doors are always open to those in need,
he had said with the best Christian smile he could muster.
Now, his laziness was working in their favour. Slowly but
surely, they slipped inside through the back door. They
had to find their way around in the dark because turning
on the lights risked them getting caught in the act by any
of the watchful locals who never missed a chance to spy
on their neighbours.

"What are you looking for exactly?" Eric whispered,
nearly tumbling over an end table near the brown leather
sofa in the living room.

"Evidence," she replied.

"What kind of evidence?" he asked, hitting his foot on
a matching ottoman in front of a recliner armchair close
to the fireplace.

"Something to prove those two cases are connected.
That Pastor Evans has something to do with Simon
vanishing and my aunt's disappearance."

"Your aunt moved to the capital, and Simon's
probably just sleeping in a drunken stupor on someone's
sofa," Eric reminded her harshly, annoyed by all the
obstacles as he fumbled through the darkened house.

"And yet they are both missing! If you're not going to
help me, I suggest you leave now, and I'll do this alone,"
she warned him.

He wanted to stand his ground but knew it wouldn't
matter. When she made a decision, she followed through
on it. Her stubbornness had often landed them in trouble
while growing up, and it seemed nothing had changed.
Eventually, he agreed to split up so they could cover
more ground. Sara May slowly moved towards the stairs
leading to the upper floor. This house wasn't quite as
grand as Aunt Marie's mansion, but it wasn't bad either.

Serving God and preaching His words was clearly a profitable job. After a brief search, she found what appeared to be an office. Every wall was carefully concealed behind thick, wooden bookcases filled with dusty, old books, mostly in shades of brown, and holy statues. Much of the floor was covered with books, papers, and occasional folders, giving the room a musty smell. In the centre of the room stood a large mahogany desk, accompanied by a light-brown leather chair with a button-back that resembled a throne. Who did he think he was? It was obvious she had discovered Pastor Evans's office. If she hoped to find anything, it would most likely be there.

Carefully stepping over stacks of books to avoid messing anything up, she examined the bookcases one by one. After a while, she found what seemed to be diaries marked 1993 and 1994. She pulled one out and carefully read through it, page by page. It had to hold some clues. She took out her phone and started taking photos, hoping something was hidden between the scribbled words on each page. Halfway through, the room suddenly lit up from outside as car headlights swept across the window. She gasped and hurried to the window facing the driveway. Damn it! Why were they home so early? Panicking, she tried to put the book back as neatly as possible but failed. It fell to the floor just as she rushed out of the room, terrified they'd been spotted. She had to alert Eric before it was too late! She reached the stairs, the second step from the top, when she saw him in the living room rummaging through folders stacked on a dresser by the back door.

"Eric!" she quietly called out, waving her arms to grab his attention. "They're home!" she whispered before hearing the keys turn to unlock the front door.

"Shit!" Eric quickly slid out through the back door just in the nick of time. Terrified, Sara May swiftly looked around, noticing large closet doors next to the master bedroom. She promptly jumped towards them and managed to hide a moment before all the lights were turned on in the house.

"She had no right talking to me like that! She knows who I am! Is it too much to ask that she show me some respect, if nothing else!" Paula shouted, clearly upset.

"There, there, my dear. I'm sure she didn't mean it that way," Pastor Evans replied in a calming tone.

"She called me a flabby old gasbag! And you just stood there and said nothing! Effing gutless coward you are!"

Sara May stood trembling with fear and on the verge of tears inside the darkened closet, too frightened to move a muscle. She didn't catch every word, but she knew exactly who Paula was referring to. Aunt Marie had hated the Pastor's wife for as long as she could remember, yet she never knew why. But this was no time to find out. She had to figure out how to escape the closet unnoticed; otherwise, she'd be in prison for the rest of her life. Then, as if by some divine miracle, the doorbell rang, prompting Pastor Evans to answer. Sara May could faintly hear Eric's voice.

"Hello, Pastor. Sorry to bother you, but my car broke down in front of your house, and I was wondering if you could help me get it fixed?"

"Of course, my boy! Never shall it be said that Pastor Evans turns away a fellow citizen in need!" the Pastor replied loudly, glad to be pulled away from his seething wife.

Sara May mentally thanked Eric for his rescue attempt, but that was all it was. Paula had no interest in cars, so she remained inside the house. The gripping fear had begun numbing her body just as she cautiously emerged from the closet. From there, she tiptoed towards the stairs, where she could get a good view of Paula in the kitchen. That meant the escape route through the back door was blocked. Suddenly, Helena appeared in front of her out of thin air, smiling like she was enjoying the whole thing.

"You sure do know how to get yourself into trouble, don't you?" she gleefully asked.

"Jeez, thanks! I could use some help here!" Sara May whispered harshly. Helena smiled as she assessed the situation.

"All right. But only because you're helping me."

This was no time to argue. Sara May watched as her aunt's ghost floated gracefully down the stairs and into the kitchen. She didn't try to follow her, fearing she would provoke the fiery wrath of the Pastor's wife. Her temperament was frightening enough; dealing with her unpredictable mood swings was not for the faint-hearted, often likened to a blazing inferno on an icy lake. Just as Sara May let go of that last thought, she heard high-pitched screaming from the kitchen, loud and piercing enough to shatter every glass in the house. Cupboard doors were slammed open and shut, drawers yanked out forcefully, chairs tipped over, and dishes and cups flew from the cupboards, smashing into countless pieces on the floor. Paula shrieked in terror and shot out of the house like a rocket. As soon as the front door banged shut, Sara May swiftly descended the stairs, only to be met by the victorious ghost.

"What did you do?" Sara May asked between heavy breaths.

"I just scared her a little bit," Helena replied with a big smile.

"How did you do all this?"

"What's the point of being dead if I can't have a little fun with it?" She shrugged.

Sara May chuckled, but the joy was cut short when Paula and the Pastor tried to open the front door again.

"I locked the doors, but only for a little while. Hurry before they catch you!" Helena warned.

She obeyed without hesitation. She darted into the living room and slid like a seasoned spy through the back door. At that very moment, Pastor Evans burst open the front door with his wife and Eric in tow. Paula was still screaming from the frightening ordeal, trembling and crying uncontrollably. Pastor Evans did his best to calm her down and assess the situation. Eric slowly backed out through the door without the couple noticing. He was not about to spend another second in this eerie ghost house. He hurried to his car, which had barely managed to stay intact after Evans's failed attempts to show off his poor mechanical skills. Just as he was about to drive off, Sara May raced over. She leapt into the front seat, shutting the door behind her, and gasped from the narrow escape.

"I don't give a shit if you show up naked next time you ask me to commit a felony with you; I'll never do this again!" Eric shouted.

With adrenaline rushing through her body, she didn't listen. Her mind was filled with excitement and relief at having heroically escaped the house. Overwhelmed by a mixture of emotions that clouded her judgment, she hurriedly pulled Eric towards her and kissed him passionately. She was grateful he had tried to save her, but mainly for agreeing to join her in this risky adventure. It brought back memories of old times; those moments with him were the only real moments that gave her troubled teenage years any meaning. He'd always been there for her,

ready to lift her up whenever life pushed her down and to help her forget her problems at home. He'd come through for her once again, despite his strong objections.

"Fine. You can show up naked next time," he said in a daze once their lips parted.

He didn't understand those emotions that overpowered all reason and pushed logic aside. He'd only been in love once, or so he thought. But that was nothing compared to this raging storm of feelings he experienced towards Sara May. All she had to do was blink those big, beautiful, heavenly blue eyes, and he melted like butter. This adventure had been far too dangerous. But he wouldn't hesitate to do it again in a heartbeat if she asked. At this point, he'd go to hell and back for this petite yet fiery Valkyrie who had captured his heart. Oh, how he longed to touch her, to feel her body pressed against his in a moment of reckless passion. But now was not the time. They had to get the hell out of there before Pastor Evans realised that he still hadn't fixed the car.

Chapter 34

Maggie had offered for Suzy to stay with her while the men searched for Simon, but she had politely declined. She couldn't bear the thought of leaving their two sons at home alone during this difficult time. Sara May had to bite her lip upon hearing those words. Perhaps it had just been Simon's drunken mumbling, but Suzy's confession that the twins were not his had to have been the cause of all this. Such a bombshell could make even the hardest men drink themselves senseless and, as a result, do something crazy. Poor Simon. His whole life had been one big lie. He'd been raising another man's sons. A man he'd loathed for most of his life but had been forced to interact with due to his wife's desire to belong to the elite society of the rich and famous, a society only Pastor Evans could grant them access to. For most of his adult life, Simon had been a servant to the pastor. Evans had financed the Brewer for reasons unknown to most locals. Those reasons were carefully kept hidden as part of the town's many secrets.

Maggie respected Suzy's wish to go home to her boys and walked her to her house, making sure she arrived safely. Most of the women who had previously visited had already left, much to Sara May's relief, as her sanity was hanging by a thread. She lay flat on the sofa and flicked through the blurry photos she had managed to take at Pastor Evan's office before being hurried out. Some were too blurry to identify anything; others didn't contain anything interesting. She was losing hope. Of course, she'd messed things up again, like everything else in her life; typical! She was thirty-one and couldn't even take decent photos! She sighed and put the phone down.

The weeks since her accident had been chaotic, full of secrets, lies, and frustration. Not the peaceful recovery she'd hoped for. Slowly, her eyes filled with tears that poured down her cheeks like a torrential waterfall, blurring her vision. She felt so alone and overwhelmed by self-pity, a feeling that had been building for years. She wasn't making progress in life! And she kept being reminded of it.

She was certain that Pastor Evans was responsible for Helena's disappearance, but that feeling alone wasn't enough. Prancing around like a peacock, confident in her knowledge, and spreading the word like a prophet was foolish at best. Pointing out that the emperor had no clothes was pointless if she wasn't absolutely sure. She wiped the tears from her face and picked up her phone again. She wanted to smash it into a thousand pieces, but she knew that if she gave up now, Helena would haunt her forever. She began skimming through the photos again, just in case she had missed something. And then, out of nowhere, a picture she'd somehow overlooked appeared. She examined it more closely: 29th October 1994.

She had a kid! That filthy whore!

Sara May stared at the screen in disbelief. How dare a clergyman write something so foul? What kind of code was this? Did Pastor Evans have another child in Northtown? He had, notoriously, been an inebriated womaniser before he was ordained, a mixture that half the nation could credit their existence to. But nobody had ever mentioned Jack and Jake in that sense, or this mystery child the pastor seemed to be referring to. No matter how hard she thought about it, she couldn't make sense of it. There were far more questions than answers, and nobody seemed willing to talk. What had happened with this group of friends all those years ago? She could feel her eyelids growing heavier and heavier. Her thoughts became cloudy; before she knew it, she had drifted into a blissful sleep.

She stood frozen in her tracks. In front of her was an empty bassinet that swayed gently from side to side. She saw Helena walking calmly into the room, holding what looked like a newborn baby, who was crying softly. Helena cooed at the tiny bundle, trying to soothe it, and gently ran her fingers across the child's small face. It seemed to work. The baby settled down, appearing to find peace and safety in her loving arms. Suddenly, the room went dark, and Sara May felt a cold, familiar terror wash over her. In an instant, the violently monstrous man, dressed in all black, stormed into the room, completely deranged. Consumed with anger and hatred, he began mercilessly attacking Helena, again and again, despite her desperate pleas to stop. She tried to shield the infant the best she could, but it was of no use. The monster ripped the baby from her arms, threw it into the bassinet, and then continued assaulting her with gruesome force until she suddenly vanished into thin air, and her crying stopped. Sara May tried to scream in a desperate attempt to intervene, but she couldn't move an inch. It was like she was chained with shackles made of pure terror. She couldn't run, and her screams came out silently. All she could do was stand still and wait for the evil monster to notice her. Eventually, he did. His sinister eyes pierced into her soul. He grabbed the crying baby and started running towards her, determined to end her life in the same brutal way he had erased Helena from existence. Then she woke up, heart pounding like a freight train, scared out of her wits.

Early the next morning, she sat half-asleep at the kitchen table, trying her best to figure out what kind of riddle this nightmare had been. Where did the baby come from? Based on the nightmare, it was Helena's, no doubt. But why had nobody mentioned a baby? What had happened to it? She closed her eyes and took a deep breath. She couldn't bear the thought of that fragile little infant perishing in the same way as its mother. Such an innocent soul just beginning its life couldn't have done anything so terrible to deserve such a cruel ending. She was pulled out of her train of thought by the sound of Maggie's bedroom door opening and her bare feet tapping on the wooden floor towards the kitchen. Typical. Did the woman not know how to sleep in on her days off?

"Why are you up so early?" Maggie asked, stunned at the rare sight of her daughter being up before dawn.

"I didn't mean to," exhausted Sara May replied, leaning forward on the table, head buried in her hands.

"Did you have another nightmare?" asked Maggie as she poured herself a cup of tea. Sara May nodded.

"Maybe someone out there hates me, she mumbled into her hands.

It was a feeble attempt to lighten the mood. She hadn't told her mum what the nightmares were about, despite her many pleas. Perhaps it was her resentment towards Maggie for not telling her about Helena. But mostly, it was because, despite everything, she didn't want to cause her any more pain than she already had. While Maggie didn't know that her sister was dead, it wouldn't do her any good to find out this way. It would undoubtedly have a profound impact on her life. Therefore, Sara May decided it was best not to say anything for now. Maggie sat down and took the first sip of the steaming hot tea.

The aroma filled her senses and brought a relaxing smile to her face, one that only a good brew could.

"There's nothing like the first cup of the day," she said in peaceful bliss.

"I'm too tired for tea, Mum."

"Worth a shot." For a brief moment, the two sat in silence. Finally, Sara May decided to ask. Perhaps the euphoria the morning cup had brought would ease the blow.

"Mum? Did Helena have a child?"

Maggie nearly choked on her tea, triggering a violent coughing fit. How the hell did she know about the baby? Who had she been talking to? Everyone who knew had been sworn to secrecy, and the younger generation of locals knew nothing about it. Maggie's hands trembled as she lowered her cup. Her heart pounded so loudly it felt like it was about to explode. Maybe she was having a heart attack? It had been hard enough telling Sara May that she, in fact, had another aunt. It was even tougher explaining that Helena wasn't her father's mistress. She wasn't ready to discuss what happened that fateful Thursday evening thirty-one years ago. For that, she needed a lot more tea. There she sat, her daughter. Her lovely blue eyes were full of questions, her lips eager to ask them. These were questions Maggie knew the answers to but was not prepared to share. Yet knowing Sara May, she wasn't going to back down. Maggie knew she'd have to play her cards carefully; otherwise, everything could blow up and irreparably damage their relationship.

"Yes. She had a child," Maggie said, nervously tapping her thumbs against the teacup, avoiding eye contact.

"Whatever happened to it?"

"It was given up for adoption."

"Why didn't she take it when she left town?" Maggie sighed and stood up from the table to pour the rest of the tea into the sink.

"God only knows. You'll have to ask her about that. She sure as hell wasn't stressing over keeping us informed."

"Who adopted it?" Maggie exhaled as she swiftly turned around to face her daughter.

"I don't know. Why are you asking me all this?" she asked, feeling the grievance build up within her.

"Because I want to know the truth!"

"Who told you about the baby?" Maggie asked, raising her voice.

"Nobody! I'm just curious!"

"I can't do this anymore," she said, throwing her hands up. "I don't want to discuss those things, and I want you to respect that!"

The elephant in the room had burst in, growing so enormous it filled the entire kitchen, making it difficult for both women to breathe. Neither said a word; the air was so thick it was almost unbearable. The kitchen table seemed to stretch on endlessly; the canyon between mother and daughter had never been wider. Sara May despised her mother for withholding such vital information. She couldn't understand why. Maggie, however, was fed up with her daughter's endless curiosity that only served to reopen old wounds she couldn't possibly understand. She needed time, and this constant questioning put her in a tight spot she disliked. After what felt like a century of insufferable silence filled with anger and resentful glances, Sara May realised her mother wasn't going to back down. This time, she stood her ground, and it was clear she wouldn't be getting any answers. To show her disappointment, Sara May stormed out of the kitchen, leaving her mother hurt and mentally exhausted. She didn't have the energy to chase that stubborn mule of hers. She needed much more tea to cope with that.

Chapter 35

Sara May finished the last drop of the steaming hot chocolate she'd allowed herself at the Cocoa Bean, the charming little café in town. She sat there so long that at least two people approached her to ask if she was okay. She smiled and gave the usual *Yeah, I'm alright* answer. The truth was, she didn't have the faintest idea how she was really doing. Never in her life had she felt so confused. Not only had she discovered she had another aunt, but no one had thought to mention that the aunt had a child. According to Maggie, the baby had been given up for adoption shortly after birth, meaning it didn't suffer the same cruel fate as its mother. Which was, of course, excellent news, but it raised the question of what had happened to it. Had their paths ever crossed without either realising? Had Sara May worked with this now-grown individual, perhaps? Maybe it was Tommy! No, he was too young. She threw away her paper cup and hurried out of the café. She made her way to Nana Lou's house with her hands in her coat pockets. It was getting a bit nippy, but there was no real snow yet. Just a light flurry cover, hardly anything. Suddenly, she felt Helena beside her, unaffected by the cold in her ghostly form.

"You had a child," Sara May muttered, keeping her eyes on the endless pavement.

"Yes. Isn't that fascinating? " Helena replied.

"That would have been nice to know earlier!"

"I would have told you, but I didn't remember." Sara May's brows drew closer to one another as she looked at her aunt,

"How can you not remember giving birth?"

"It's a weird thing, being dead," Helena replied,

gazing off into the distance.

"But you remembered the tattoo. On the evil man's shoulder."

"Yes. Isn't that fascinating?" she replied, sounding like a broken record.

Sara May sighed and quickened her pace. She'd had enough of guessing and speculating. What good was it, dragging a ghost along if the ghost didn't remember a damn thing? As she passed Simon and Suzy's house, she stopped. At least five cars were parked outside. A lot could be said about the people of Northtown, but they knew how to stick together in a crisis. Even though these belonged to some of the town's biggest tattletales, Suzy had to be grateful for the company. Sara May smiled and carried on walking. Suddenly, she heard her name called from afar, making her turn around and grunt as she watched Jack rush towards her.

"Sara May!" he called again, waving his arms to get her attention.

Great, she thought to herself. She was in no mood to deal with the town's biggest twat,

"Would you like to come in for some tea?" He casually offered as he stopped a few feet from her. She kept up her guard.

"No, thank you. I'm in a hurry."

"Where are you going?"

"That's none of your business."

"Forgive my bluntness. May I interest you in a little walk, perhaps?" His pretentiousness was getting on her nerves, and she was struggling to keep her composure.

"No, you may not. I have to go," she replied and walked away, growing more irritated with each step.

"If you need me, you know where to find me!" Jack

called out from a distance.

She pretended not to hear those last words as she quickened her pace. Jack's renewed interest in her irritated her, but she knew it wasn't a coincidence. The worst part was that she wasn't sure if she was simply losing her mind. She felt as if everyone was watching her and whispering as she passed. 'Trust no one,' echoed in her mind like a broken record, and it was almost as if the judging eyes in town had multiplied overnight. She pulled her light brown jacket tighter around her waist and ran. She didn't know why she was running. It just felt safer. After a short while, she found herself at Nana Lou's doorstep. She knocked loudly and waited patiently for the old lady to answer.

"Come in. I was expecting you," she said quietly, ushering her in.

Nowhere else in Northtown did Sara May feel as safe. Jack and Pastor Evans would probably come knocking when they heard of her whereabouts, demanding to be let in, but Nana Lou wouldn't allow them. That's what made this place so safe. It was filled with an indescribable energy that gave the whole house the feel of a medieval castle—protected by some unseen forces. Nana Lou spent years cultivating this inviting yet powerful energy, mainly by showing love and affection to all those who sought her help and incorporating a touch of white magic into the mix.

"So, where do we stand?" the old witch asked, sitting across from Sara May.

"Helena had a child."

Nana Lou silently slid back in her green wingback chair. Her suspicions had been confirmed. She had spent the past few days trying to recall every little detail from that time, but had only managed a few snippets here and there. She remembered the youngest Jensen sister going strangely quiet and avoiding most people to hide her condition, but as her stomach enlarged, so did the suspicions. Her pregnancy had only fueled the fire she was allegedly accused of creating with her notorious promiscuity. *Slut!* people had shouted, seething with anger. *Who was the father?* Everyone thought they knew the answer, but the other Jensen women turned away and refused to comment. Nana Lou had kept out of all this drama, but she couldn't help but occasionally overhear. That was the cursed price to pay for living in a small town. Despite her best efforts, she couldn't remember what had happened to the poor baby who'd been born into the saddest of circumstances, completely beyond its control.

"Do you know what happened to the child?" she asked. Sara May shook her head.

"Mum said it was put up for adoption. That's all she said. She became furious when I pressed for more information." Nana Lou rolled her eyes.

"No surprise there," she muttered.

"I know Pastor Evans is behind all this; I just know it."

"All rivers seem to flow in his direction, but we mustn't be too hasty," Nana Lou cautioned.

"Helena told me the evil man had a tattoo, and Aunt Marie confirmed that Pastor Evans got one shortly after he started his theology studies."

"That's not enough to link him to such a serious matter, Sara May. We need to be careful until we get something concrete to back this up."

Sara May sat in silence. Nana Lou was right; she knew

better than to doubt her words. But she felt like they hadn't made a breakthrough for days, which tested her patience. If Pastor Evans suspected they were accusing him, he would immediately destroy every piece of vital evidence and rally his defence. The longer they waited, the more advantage he had. Something had to happen quickly.

Chapter 36.

A body discovered in Northtown!

The headline was as terrifying as it was cold. Since the body was discovered in the abandoned cabin near Old Gilbert's farm, it had taken over every conversation in town. Two siblings, Sheriff Decker's grandchildren, found the body while sneaking around the cabin, just as many children in town had done before them. Frightened by what they had seen, they ran home and told their mother, Chris's older sister, Sophie. She was visiting her parents with her children and had not expected this visit to be any different from the rest. She'd been sitting on the porch with her mother and brother when her children, ten-year-old Aiden and eight-year-old Lucy, came running frantically.

"Mummy, mummy! We found a hanging man!" Lucy yelled.

"He's dead, for sure!" Aiden added, startling the group of grown-ups to their feet.

"What are you on about?" asked Martha. She'd never seen her grandchildren so frightened, which greatly upset her.

"At the cabin!" Aiden loudly explained, pointing his finger in the cabin's direction. "He's hanging in a closet!"

"Chris, phone Dad," distressed Sophie pleaded as she tried to calm her children.

Chris didn't need to be asked twice. He quickly pulled out his phone and called his father. As soon as the call ended, Sheriff Decker dispatched every available police force in town to the abandoned cabin. Shortly afterwards, it was confirmed that the body, hanging in a broken-down closet, was that of Simon Lewis. Initially, the police ruled out foul play, but Sara May refused to accept that. She was certain her aunt Helena had met the same fate, and the same man was responsible for both cases. Nobody had mentioned Simon's confession that Jack and Jake were the pastor's sons, and she didn't want to reopen such an old, still-infected wound at a time like this. But the fact that Simon had lashed out at the pastor and was found dead a few days later was too much of a coincidence.

Suzy was informed later that same day. Sara May had gone with her mother to the Lewis home to show her support. As she had suspected, the house was full of people wanting to comfort poor Suzy and extend their condolences to the newly widowed woman. She was utterly distraught with grief. She blamed herself, repeatedly saying she never should have said anything. Amid her frantic crying, her incoherent screams made everyone's hearts ache with sympathy for the poor woman who was slowly losing her grip on reality, overwhelmed by heavy sorrow. Jack stood in one corner of the living room, so shocked that he gazed motionless at the chaos before him, unable to speak. Jake had locked himself in his room with no one trying to reach out to him. It was one of the saddest sights Sara May had ever seen.

She stood a few feet from the front door, watching the distressing scene unfold, when she suddenly began shivering from the cold, so much so that she could see her breath. The house darkened, and she felt almost paralysed by fear. She didn't know what was happening to her until a few seconds later, when Pastor Evans and his wife, Paula, walked through the door and were immediately greeted by their loyal fans. Everyone seemed in desperate need of comfort during these unprecedented times, and Pastor Evans had mastered the role of the Good Samaritan. A role he had practised throughout most of his adult life. But Sara May saw through the act straight away. She noticed the thick, black plume of smoke surrounding him, even if no one else did. He was a good actor. His loyal followers led him and his wife into the living room, where the grieving widow had hysterically fallen to her knees in anguish, pleading with her Pastor for answers. Thinking he was a kind-hearted and well-meaning servant of God, who only had her best interests at heart, she trusted him. Like so many had done over the years. The pastor, performing an Oscar-worthy act, promised her peace of mind and the holy Father's almighty love and blessing if only she had faith in God, her church, and, most of all, in her Pastor. Sara May turned around and left upon hearing those lies, all covered in thorns. She'd had enough of the theatrics. It was one thing to act like the embodiment of all that was good in the world, prancing around like a peacock in the process, but to promise salvation to a grief-stricken widow if she put all her faith and trust in him was a step too far.

Sheriff Decker sat at his desk in the police station, reviewing the facts of this peculiar case. They were painfully few. Simon's body had been sent to the capital for further examination; all Decker could do now was wait for the results. Everything pointed to this being a suicide. But the fact that his grandchildren had been the ones to find the body had caused him more pain than he was willing to admit to anyone. Aiden and Lucy seemed to be doing all right after the distressing ordeal, and Decker hoped they were too young to fully grasp the gravity of the situation. The family had wrapped them tightly in their arms; not much more could be done. Sophie eventually went back to Reykjavik with the children to get them back into their routine as quickly as possible in the hope that it would prevent future trauma. It had now been four days since the body was discovered, and Decker had spent most of that time in his office, pondering the case. Things didn't add up. Simon had never shown any signs of being suicidal. Of course, it could very well be that he had simply been able to hide the pain behind a well-polished mask, but still, it felt like such an extreme reaction to what seemed to have been just a typical fight between a married couple. He leaned back in his leather chair and sighed. There was a knock on the door.

"Heya, boss!" Biggie Mac called out in his loud, friendly voice.

"Hi, there. Any news?"

"Nah, I'm afraid not. But give it time; it's only eight o'clock."

"I guess. It's just driving me mad." Decker shrugged before pushing himself towards his desk.

"Maybe it's worth giving Chief Chase a call. See if he knows anything."

"Yeah, maybe. Thanks, mate."

Biggie Mac nodded and closed the door behind him. Decker smiled. He could always rely on this friendly giant to uphold the law and order and provide his boss with solid advice in a crisis. Matthew McAllister, also known locally as Biggie Mac, was an unusually tall and muscular man in his forties with an affectionate smile and the biggest heart in town. He had worked as a police officer in Northtown for the past nine years. Some locals slightly feared him because of his size, but everyone loved and respected him. They felt safe knowing Biggie Mac was patrolling the streets; nobody dared to commit a crime when he was on duty. He had married his high school sweetheart, Mary, who was physically the complete opposite of her husband. She was a very petite, somewhat scrawny woman, about the size of a medium-sized fence post. Together, they formed one of the oddest-looking couples in town, though they were loved by all for their kindness and hospitality.

"Chief Chase? It's Sheriff Decker."

"Yes, hello. What can I do for you?" Chase replied, trying to sound busy.

"I was wondering if there is any news about Simon?" Chase let out a quick laugh.

"Isn't it ironic? Finally, something happens in this pathetic little town of yours, and it's nothing more than a pitiful wino offing himself." Feeling the frustration mounting up, Decker contained himself. He was, above all else, a professional.

"Is that confirmed?" he asked.

"We haven't gotten the autopsy results yet, but everything seems to point to that being the case, yes."

"Right. Thank you," said Decker and hung up. Chase smirked as he put his phone away.

"Was that Decker?" asked Prime Minister Crow.

"Yes. He's getting impatient."

"Just make sure the autopsy results are indisputable. The man killed himself; there is no reason to dig any deeper. If so much as a letter about this leak to the media, you can kiss your cushy job goodbye!"

Back in Northtown, Sheriff Decker sighed deeply, hoping for peace of mind. It had taken every bit of strength he had not to shout at Chief Chase for his comment about the small country town Decker loved so dearly. It reeked of typical big-city arrogance. As he calmed down, he began reviewing the timeline of events leading up to Simon's death. Something didn't add up. Simon had never shown any signs of mental disturbance, desperation, or depression. He'd been an old classmate of Decker's in primary school and had always been the class clown, making people laugh. As he grew older, he became a very ambitious man with a plan, a plan that was, unfortunately, funded by the local clergyman and his wife. Nobody had ever understood why, because Simon had always refused to discuss it. It was all so strange. Why would a man, claiming to be doing God's holy work, fund a measly pub when he despised drinking? It had always seemed so random. Apart from that, there had never been anything unusual about Simon. He was just a regular bloke, a devoted family man, a well-liked member of a small community, and a small business owner. Sure, he could have treated his twins a bit more fairly, and he thought too highly of the sinful lifestyle of the rich and powerful, but other than that, he was an alright chap. After a short while, he called Biggie Mac back into his office.

"Can you go and look up how the Brewer is doing? Financially."

"You think he did this because of financial troubles?"

"I don't know. Could be. As police, we must turn over every stone in search of the truth, right?"

"Right. I'll get right on it."

Biggie Mac did as he was told. Sheriff Decker picked up the phone again, realising he needed to keep his cards close to his chest to gain the upper hand in this deadly game of poker. Chief Chase didn't know his colleague up north had friends in more places than Northtown.

"Mike? Hi, it's Sheriff Decker."

"Hello, mate. Nice to hear from you!"

"Likewise. So, what can you tell me?"

"What has Chase told you?"

"He was swift to rule this a suicide. Too swift if you ask me."

I thought he might. I can tell you, this man didn't kill himself. At first, the injuries on his neck looked like they were from the rope, and I was almost convinced of that myself. But then I took a closer look, and I saw two dark spots on either side, indicating that somebody had used force to strangle him. Spots like these only form when thumbs are pressed heavily on the neck, cutting off airflow. Whoever hung the body in that closet must have done so hoping the injuries from the rope would throw us off. This man was murdered.

Sheriff Decker thanked his friend for trusting him with this information and hung up the phone. He felt his blood run cold and his pulse quicken. This was serious— perhaps the most important matter he had ever dealt with. Someone in Northtown carried murder on their conscience, and Chief Chase seemed to be involved. Why else would he have tried to dismiss this so quickly? Nobody in Northtown had ever seen anything like this before. The peaceful country life they had known was about to be upended.

Chapter 37

Sara May paced impatiently back and forth, glancing at the clock every few seconds. It was nearly ten o'clock at night. Maggie had left for work about half an hour earlier, but there was still no sign of Eric. She didn't understand why she was so anxious. It was Eric! The adorably awkward little Eric had always been by her side during every childhood adventure. Sometimes, they searched for treasure near the riverbank. Sometimes, they pretended to be brave enough to spend the night at the abandoned cabin, but they always chickened out after the first twenty minutes and ran over to Old Gilbert's farm to seek refuge until their parents came to collect them. Chris and Eric had been her anchors in an unstable life after her parents' divorce, so she cared deeply for both of them.

Recently, however, she began experiencing more profound, more passionate feelings for Eric—something she'd never felt before. He had blossomed from a skinny little weirdo into the most attractive man she'd ever seen. Since seeing him in the Bread Box on her first day back, she had fought hard against those naughty, after-dark thoughts that constantly filled her mind, making it increasingly difficult to focus on more important things like solving Helena's case. These thoughts had now led her to prepare a cosy picnic in front of the fireplace, eagerly waiting for her prince charming. At last, a knock on the door made her heart race and her stomach flutter.

"For God's sake, get it together, Sara May! It's only Eric!" she firmly reminded herself before opening the door.

"Hi. Sorry, I'm late; I had to help Dad close up the bakery for the night. "

"No problem. Come in."

"Wow. I haven't stepped foot in here since I was a teenager," he said as he looked around in amazement.

"It hasn't changed much. Other than maybe piles of crap here and there Mum has collected over the years," she replied as she followed Eric into the living room.

"I see you've outdone yourself once again," Eric teased with a grin upon seeing the display on the floor.

"I hope it's okay. I just wanted to do something different."

"It's fine. I just didn't picture you as a huge romantic."

"I'm full of surprises," she replied, smiling widely

The evening passed quickly. Before they knew it, the pizza was gone, apart from a few crumbs still in the box. Their laughter echoed for miles as they reminisced about many treasured childhood memories. Sara May enjoyed sitting close to her old friend in front of the fire. She felt she could truly relax and be herself for the first time in years. She had lowered her armour, trusting him completely. She'd been walking through her adult life, gradually building a wall around herself brick by brick. It'd never been an option to lower her guard, not even for a moment. But Eric had shattered all her defences like Hulk himself, smashing them to pieces until he reached her frozen heart. How was she supposed to resist this handsome devil? The man looked as if he'd been plucked from a cheesy romantic Hallmark film, with an added touch of sinful allure.

Eric was also enjoying the evening. At that moment, nobody existed except the two of them. Oh, if only she knew how insanely beautiful she was. How much the glow from the fire made her look like the epitome of a perfect goddess. She sat on the floor beside him, with her messy hair in a bun, wearing a large white turtleneck jumper and silky blue shorts. So ordinary, yet so irresistible. He hadn't felt this way about anyone since... no. He couldn't allow himself to go there. This night was about him and Sara May. He never thought he'd see her again; therefore, he wasn't prepared for how easily she had captivated his heart and soul.

"So, what've you been up to since you skipped town, kitten?" he asked, reaching for one of the leftover breadsticks.

"I wish I could tell you I'm the proud owner of a company or a CEO with five university degrees," she hesitantly replied.

She could feel a familiar sensation wash over her. Usually, she managed to avoid this question by giving a vague answer, such as "I work in the restaurant business." That seemed to satisfy people. The truth was, she was ashamed. Icelanders had always been a highly ambitious nation. No marathon in the world could rival the race of life held daily in that country. Anyone who didn't adorn themselves with fancy degrees or grand job titles was seen as unworthy—Eve's dirty children. Being an uneducated kitchen porter in her thirties was unacceptable. People like her were never invited to fancy parties, film premieres, or opening ceremonies unless it was to clean the dirty dishes afterwards. They were rarely pictured at social events, headline: *Who was where?* No, they were kept in the back, scrubbing pots and pans. It was like Eric had read her thoughts.

"Those job titles are overrated. It's nothing but fragile, attention-thirsty egomaniacs seeking any form of validation." She shrugged.

"Maybe. I just never felt like I belonged anywhere.

223

I've no interest in being a skinny, blonde-haired influencer or an entrepreneur inventing the next app to go viral. I just want to write books. I want to sit at home or in cafés and write books that will sell. Is that too much to ask?"

"No. Not at all."

He hadn't realised just how broken she was. When they were younger, she had never hesitated to climb the tallest trees or crawl through the darkest tunnels. She had been an unstoppable little fighter. Now, it was like he understood that all her bravado was her way of coping with a hostile world that had turned its back on her. She was a delicate soul who had never truly learned how to face life's obstacles. Suddenly, he felt compelled to embrace her. She looked into his eyes, and for a moment, time seemed to stand still. Slowly, she took his hands and gently guided them to her breasts. He gave each a light squeeze, sending electrifying shivers through her whole body. She desired this man and knew he wanted her just as much. His tongue caressed her sensitive skin, beginning with the nipples, moving up to her neck, until finally entangling playfully with her eager tongue. Soon, two bodies had become one, deriving intense pleasure from the rhythmic movements and igniting the fire that would forever conceal the raw, almost beastly lovemaking on this cold November night.

Many hours later, the pizza box was kicked under the sofa, and at least one wine glass was broken. The sofa blanket now served as a towel, and the pillows neatly arranged earlier in the evening were scattered all over the living room floor. Two sweaty, exhausted bodies lay next to each other, proof of how sinfully good the sex had been. Sara May pressed herself as close to Eric as possible, unbothered by how sticky they'd both become. She was at ease, finally free from stress or anxiety. She felt safe, as if nothing could hurt her, as long as she lay beside him, held by his muscular arms. She wanted to trust him.

After a long silence, she suddenly asked, "Do you believe in life after death?" Eric shrugged, looking up at the ceiling.

"I don't know. I haven't really thought about it."

"Why not?"

"Death is so depressing. It's so... final."

"Not if you believe in the afterlife." He turned to face her.

"What do you think?"

"I thought it was bullshit, to be honest. But then, I started seeing Helena."

"What do you mean 'see her?" He sounded confused.

"I see her. Just as clearly as I see you." She felt his body shift as he turned on his side, putting his arm up and resting his head on it.

"Can you talk to her? Can she hear you?"

"Yes, and yes. She's helping me solve her case."

"Is she here now?" he asked, slightly nervous he'd just been watched doing unspeakable things to the woman beside him.

"No. She comes and goes; I can't control it."

Eric didn't respond to that last comment, lowering his arm and lying back down, shifting his gaze to the ceiling. He didn't want to spoil this magical night, nor did he want it to end. But this seemingly random conversation about death and ghosts after one of the most extraordinary nights he'd ever experienced threw him off course. He was the grandson of Nana Lou, a woman everyone knew had powers that defied all logic and reason. But he'd always just considered it part of her peculiar personality, not something to be taken seriously. He'd always had doubts about anything classified as supernatural or spiritual. Sure, he enjoyed a good horror film and could even listen to decent ghost stories, finding them entertaining at best. But he'd always avoided those who believed all this voodoo nonsense to be true. His grandmother was the only exception, as he'd been taught to respect his elders. Besides, she always seemed to have a different connection to the spiritual than most people, which scared him too much to question. Those who walked around claiming they talked to fairies and trolls would never find their way into his inner circle. They were on par with those who claimed God himself wrote the Bible. Nutters. Not in the mood for an argument, he decided to hop on board the insanity train and pretend to believe her for the sake of peace.

"Next time she shows up, tell her not to bother us," he teased as he leaned back over her, gearing up for the next round. Anything was better than continuing this crackbrained conversation.

Chapter 38

The sun peeked between the mountains, and the first early birds were already about in Northtown. Didi Donnelly and Evelyn Thomas were two virtuous women known to be Pastor's wife Paula's closest companions. For years, they had been among the first to walk the streets of Northtown early in the morning, searching for gossip and general hearsay they could share at the next gathering of the town's scandalmongers. The walks allowed them to exchange stories and sniff out anything new that might have happened the night before. Most often, they came up empty-handed, aside from gasping at slightly overgrown gardens, which, in their opinion, said a lot about the homeowners. But every so often, they managed to stumble upon a carcass so big the whole town could feast on it for days. This was one of those times.

"Can you believe it? The Miller kid has dropped out of law school!" Evelyn huffed, wheezing in shock.

"No! After he paid all that money in tuition?" Didi gasped.

"Well. The story goes that he didn't pay a dime. It was his grandfather, whom I heard became affluent doing shady business in his car dealership. Some said dealt more money than cars at that place."

"Oh my! So, now what's he gonna do?"

"Naturally, George is furious and poor Agnes is beside herself! Just imagine! How could he do this to his own mother? The woman damn near had a heart attack after finding out!" Didi's nose twitched in disbelief.

"Tell you what, I would've smacked that boy silly had he been mine, pulling a stunt like that! What does he plan on doing now, then?"

"I heard he's involved with some homosexual organisation in the capital. Can you believe it? Apparently, he likes them sausages!" Evelyn said, whispering that last part.

"You're lying!"

Before Evelyn could say another word, the pair suddenly stopped. Something over at the Jensen house had caught their attention. It was so early that not even the birds had started their morning chirping, yet someone was sneaking out of Maggie Jensen's home. The young man carefully shut the door behind him, looked around quickly, then hurried to his car and drove off. Didi and Evelyn watched the whole scene like hawks, their eyes wide with amazement.

"Wasn't that the Baker kid?" a stunned Didi asked.

"I'm sure it was," Evelyn replied, equally baffled. Didi looked at her friend.

"What was he doing at Maggie's house? You don't think...."

"No. It can't be. Can it?"

The two women looked at each other in total confusion. No words were needed. They understood the mission. Every moment was vital. Like professional sprinters, they hurried to Maggie's house. After a gentle knock, a tired-looking Sara May opened the door, only to be startled at the sight of two elderly women, eerily smiling like they had just finished eating a handful of clothes hangers.

"Hello, my dear. Is your mother home?" Didi gleefully asked.

"No, she's working the night shift at the care home. She'll be back in an hour or so."

"Interesting. Well, don't let us bother you then,"

Evelyn replied.

The pair walked off, giggling like a couple of schoolgirls. Sara May watched them turn the corner, puzzled by this unexpected visit, but she decided not to dwell on it. The insane asylum must be on a field trip, she thought before shutting the door. Didi and Evelyn hurried to Northtown's High Street. This had to be shared with anyone willing to listen. The heir to the Bread Box had been seen leaving the Jensen house early that morning, which could only mean one thing. The women entered the Brewer, located across the street from the bakery, as it was one of the only two places open this early. Scattered around were a few of the town's drunks, downing their first pint of the day. The boozers kept to themselves, completely unbothered by the two blabbermouths who suddenly rushed in, eager to share their discovery. The yentas went straight to the bar where Bob, the bartender, was chatting with Jack Lewis. Chris stood behind the till, counting yesterday's takings.

"Good morning, gentlemen!" Evelyn loudly greeted the men.

"Hello, ladies. What can I get you today?" asked Bob.

"Ask, instead, what we can offer you," Didi replied with a big grin.

"That's very tempting, Mrs. Donnelly, but as you know, I'm a happily married man," Bob replied, laughing at his witty comeback. Jack was not at all pleased with this unwelcome interruption.

"This isn't one of your gossipy group chats. If you're not gonna order anything, I suggest you get the hell out!" he hissed.

"Well, would you listen to that muddy mouth!" Evelyn gasped.

"Don't you be telling us off, Jack Lewis, or I'll be telling your mama!" Didi threatened, pointing a steady index finger at him to underline how serious she was. "You know damn well not to disrespect your elders," she clapped back. Chris and Bob couldn't contain their laughter as Jack, red-faced and deeply embarrassed, took a few steps back.

"What washes you two ashore so early?" Bob asked after a good laugh.

"Who do you think we saw sneaking from the Jensen home just now?" Evelyn asked, beaming with excitement.

Jack and Chris both looked up at the same time, with Jack instantly regretting being so nasty to the two women. He should have known better. Those women were Paula's most trusted minions, the unofficial detectives of Northtown. They were the town's bloodhounds, something he could use to his advantage. Still counting the money, Chris occasionally side-eyed the two as he waited for confirmation of what he already knew.

"We saw the Baker's son come out of Maggie's home this morning. He looked very sneaky; he obviously didn't want anybody to see him leave," Didi announced as if she were laying out facts amid a crime investigation. Bob was confused.

"Wait. Are Eric and Maggie...? " Evelyn quickly caught him off.

"No, no, no. Maggie's still at work. But Sara May...."

No other words were needed. Everyone at the pub, including the winos, knew the rest of that sentence. Although this little tidbit held different levels of significance depending on who heard it, it was obvious that a new rumour had started. Chris finished counting the money in the till and bade farewell to the group. Usually, he would have gone straight to bed after a long night shift because looking after the town's most unfortunate people was often exhausting. But now, he needed to speak to Eric. They had a falling out years ago, which he knew was mainly his fault. But he believed that Eric should have forgiven him by now, considering how close their friendship once was. They had been inseparable as children; those bonds shouldn't break so easily. Yet for Eric, Chris's unforgivable actions were the ultimate betrayal. It had hurt him so deeply that for years, he couldn't bear to look him in the eyes. I have to try, he thought to himself as he hurried towards the Bread Box, knowing Eric would be there to help his parents open up.

"You seem hellbent on not keeping it low-key," he blatantly announced to a less-than-impressed Eric as he entered the bakery.

"What do you want?" Eric aggressively grumbled.

"I just got back from the Brewer. Evelyn Thomas and Didi Connelly stopped by. They said they saw you sneak out of the Jensen house this morning."

"Yeah. So?" Eric replied, not liking where this conversation was heading.

"I'd start looking over my shoulder if I were you. You know how things are around here. The rumour mills are already turning." Chris warned.

"Are you jealous I won this round?" Eric smirked. He took great pleasure in knowing he'd gotten under Chris's skin. It felt like a small revenge for his disloyalty.

"I'm just saying. As your friend…."

"You're not my friend!" Eric loudly fired back. "You haven't been my friend since you decided it was a good idea to run away with my fiancé! She left me at the altar in front of everybody!"

"She was a frigging floozie, man! She would've banged old Gilbert had he fancied her!"

"Don't you bloody dare! She was the love of my life!" Eric threatened, seething with anger.

"Bullshit!" Chris hollered, having none of it. "We both know Sara May is the love of your life. Always has been, always will be!" This revelation shocked Eric. He never thought his feelings toward her had been so obvious. Up until now, he'd considered it his best-kept secret.

"And you don't care?" he asked, sceptical. Chris shrugged.

"I like her too. But she's made up her mind. And I love her enough to respect that."

Eric remained silent. He hadn't spoken a word to his former friend in eight years. Before that, they'd been like two peas in a pod. Chris had walked Franziska down the aisle after her father had passed away two years earlier. Dressed in a white gown that made her look like an angel, she had walked confidently towards a besotted Eric, smiling and seeming the happiest she'd ever been. That beautiful bitch. That malevolent minx. What Eric didn't know was that the man walking beside her had been having an affair with her for an entire year before the wedding—his childhood best friend.

Halfway through Pastor Evans's speech, Chris couldn't bear it any longer. He rose to his feet, strode directly to the altar, passionately kissed the fickle bride, and persuaded her to elope with him. She happily agreed, captivated by a twisted and sickening form of romance. They fled from the church, hand in hand, leaving the wedding in complete chaos. People whispered, gasped,

232

shouted, and at least two women fainted. Pastor Evans did his best to calm the crowd, but to no avail. For the most part, Eric had blocked out the memory of that traumatic day. The shock had been too much. All he remembered was the trauma it caused him and how all his energy went into standing upright with his head held high.

Two years later, it was announced that Chris and Franziska had split up. The German Jezebel had started an affair with a lorry driver from Reykjavik, who made regular stops in Northtown while exporting goods. Eventually, Franziska left town with the man, and that was the last anyone saw of her. Chris felt hollow and hurt, but Eric couldn't help but cheer, although he hadn't been bothered prancing around his former friend and rubbing it in. Being all too familiar with such heartache, he kept his distance, understanding the man's soul-crushing pain. That was punishment enough. But now, his arch-nemesis of the last eight years stood before him, armed with knowledge he didn't care for, because it belittled Chris's betrayal. If Sara May had always been his true love, he'd have to admit that the incident in the church was insignificant, and that Chris had actually saved him from a woman who didn't matter in the grand scheme of things. And he wasn't sure if he was ready to take that step to repair their friendship.

Chapter 39

Maggie hurried to her car, having just argued with her daughter and feeling close to breaking down. Sara May demanded to know everything her mother knew about Helena, Pastor Evans, and what went on in their dysfunctional friends group. Maggie felt ambushed and hadn't handled the situation well, which led to yet another big argument. This was exactly why she'd never thought she belonged to the town's gossip circles, which spread rumours and thrived on others' misfortunes. She was a private person who believed any woman with a shred of decency should keep her secrets close. With Sara May's demands, she felt like she was being held hostage. She sighed and started the car. Only one man could help her now. As she neared the church, she saw its doors wide open. Pastor Evans never liked to lock them, in case a poor, unfortunate soul needed God outside of working hours. That had earned him a few popularity points over the years. Maggie slipped in quietly, relieved to have entered unseen. At least she wasn't disturbing someone's confessions. Pastor Evans stood by the altar, preparing his Sunday sermon. He quickly turned around as he sensed someone approaching.

"Ms. Jensen. How lovely to see you."

"Same to you, Pastor. Unfortunately, this isn't a celebratory visit, I'm afraid."

"Is that so? Well, in that case, why don't you have a seat so we can chat?"

Maggie sat down as the Pastor grabbed a chair and sat opposite her. Her relationship with him felt strange. They'd been friends since childhood, yet he seemed so distant, as if he were on a much higher pedestal, towering over her, so far away, so untouchable. She didn't know if it was because of his role or just the unexplained holiness often surrounding those who served the church. Whatever it was, they led very different lives, which undoubtedly created a rift between the two long-time friends. But right now, she felt the need to trust him as both a Pastor and a friend.

"It's Sara May. She's constantly bombarding me with questions these days." Pastor Evans's ears perked up.

"What is she asking you about?"

"Helena, mostly. She thinks she's entitled to know everything about her and what happened back then. I don't understand why; I don't know who she's been talking to, but I feel pushed up against a wall, Pastor. I don't know what to do."

"It sounds like a classic case of rebellion. Perhaps she feels angry about her situation and is taking it out on you," he replied reassuringly.

"Is there anything I can do?"

"I think it's best you leave it with me, my dear. I've always found that the best solution for lost souls is to read God's word and be reminded of his unconditional love for them, regardless of their hostile behaviour."

"I don't know. Sara May has never been very religious; she'll just push back on it."

"Don't worry. I've dealt with worse demons. It's going to be okay. Trust me,"

Maggie stood up and thanked the Pastor for his time. She felt as though a heavy weight had been lifted from her shoulders, but she couldn't help but wonder if she should have dealt with it herself. It seemed wrong to involve a third party in such a personal dispute. But the damage was done. Pastor Evans now understood the gravity of the situation and promised to handle it. Hopefully, she had done the right thing.

Pastor Evans escorted Maggie to the door and bade her farewell with a smile that vanished as soon as he closed the door behind her. He instantly became consumed with blinding rage that surged through his veins like molten lava bubbling in the earth's crust. That infuriating, meddlesome she-devil! How dare she return to Northtown? Hadn't she been in a self-imposed exile? That's what he'd counted on! Now, she was back, threatening the stability he had spent years building for himself and those around him. That bloody harridan! If only he had handled things properly when he had the chance, he wouldn't be facing the consequences all these years later! He only had himself to blame. After a few deep breaths, he regained his composure. It didn't serve him to let anger and hatred control him. He was facing a problem that had to be addressed; to do so, he needed to be deliberate, almost cold-blooded. *She mustn't find out more,* he thought. He would make sure of that, whatever it took.

At the same time, Maggie went to seek the pastor's advice, her sister headed to the police station. The conversation between Pastor Evans and Prime Minister Crow at her party had stirred something within her and kept her awake ever since. It wasn't the first time she'd overheard the pair scheming politically; that wasn't unusual among the rich and powerful. Bending the rules to serve their agenda was as normal as breathing. Reshaping society to maximise personal profit regardless of the outcome was a regular occurrence. But something about that particular conversation unsettled her deeply and caused her great concern. So, she decided to speak to her old friend, Sheriff Decker. Unlike Maggie, Aunt Marie was confident she had done the right thing by trusting Decker with this information. She was so sure of herself she hadn't even looked around as she stepped into her black Cadillac SUV and drove off. Had she done so, she would have seen her niece approaching the police station. Sara May walked confidently into the station. She hadn't made an appointment; she just relied on the fact that it wouldn't be too busy, given that it was, after all, a sleepy little town. Therefore, Sheriff Decker could spare a minute or two of his time.

"Send her in," he signalled with a heavy sigh to the woman at the front desk. He was in no mood for a chat and was, therefore, less than pleased when Sara May walked in and took a seat.

"I was wondering if there is any news about Helena?" she asked, getting straight to the point.

"No, I'm sorry. I haven't found anything about any murder around the time you've mentioned, and I've been pretty busy trying to solve the mystery surrounding Simon's death. You understand that, right?"

"Yes. I do, " she replied, crossing her arms, slightly offended by this subtle dig at her intellect.

Sheriff Decker gave her a sympathetic look. She was thirty-one years old, yet still remarkably naive. Life had so much more to teach her. Legally, he wasn't allowed to tell her that Simon had been murdered; therefore, he couldn't reveal that the information from her aunt had shifted his perspective. He now understood that Pastor Evans wasn't what he appeared to be, and he was most likely connected to both cases. Decker recalled how aggressively Evans had pursued Helena in the past, no matter how hard she fought him off. At that time, Decker's wife, Martha, had been good friends with Helena and Laura Baker, often helping them ward off unwanted attention from the man who later became one of Northtown's most respected figures. He cleared his throat and continued carefully.

"It did, however, notice that The Morning Paper briefly mentioned the disappearance of a woman in the mid-nineties, but that was about it." This lit a spark of curiosity within Sara May as she rose to the edge of her seat, her questioning eyes widening.

"What do you mean? Did no one search for her?"

"Doesn't look like it. I found a small online newspaper article where people were asked to be on the lookout, but it's almost as if there wasn't enough public interest in the case for the media to continue writing about it. It just died out."

"Is there nothing in the police records?"

"Only that someone reported her missing. It seems like the police at the time had even less interest in this than the media." An uncomfortable feeling crept up Sara May's spine, causing a wave of worries to crash upon her.

"Who reported her missing?"

Chapter 40

"Yes, I'll admit, I was worried," said Maggie as she poured herself a cup of tea.

"Then, why didn't you go to the city yourself to search for her?" Sara May demanded, slamming one hand on her hip while the other had a firm grip on the kitchen chair in front of her.

"Times were different back then. I wasn't even allowed to mention her name near Mum or Marie. I was afraid they'd shut me out if they ever found out I'd gone to look for her. I couldn't risk it; the family was broken enough."

"She was your little sister," Sara May reminded her mother with a hint of sadness in her voice."

"There was nothing I could do. The circumstances didn't allow for a heroic quest that couldn't be explained. Your dad was fed up with this nonsense, and when he left, Mum and Marie were the only family I had left."

Sara May remained silent. She tried to understand both sides, but it was hard. She looked at Helena, who was standing beside Maggie. As an only child, Sara May couldn't imagine her mother's feelings, having lost contact with her baby sister in that way. Seeing them standing side by side, worlds apart, reminded her that she was still far from solving this mystery. If sisterly love had been as strong as Maggie described, she wouldn't have let anything stop her from searching for her. It also didn't explain why Sara May was kept in the dark about her existence or why her father suddenly just had enough and left. The more she searched, the less she found, and it was frustrating. Maggie sat quietly as well. She knew her daughter would eventually uncover the truth. She just hoped Pastor Evans could speak to her before that happened.

"Are you joining me for Simon's funeral?" Maggie then asked.

"I guess so," Sara May shrugged, her arms crossed.

While the mother-daughter duo fought another battle, Eric visited his grandmother. It wasn't often he had days off, and his guilt over not visiting had grown considerably. Growing up, he had the privilege of calling Nana Lou and Trucker Tom his real grandparents, much to the envy of his classmates at school. He'd never thought of it as a big deal. He was just one of dozens of children the eccentric old couple embraced as their own. Trucker Tom kept them entertained with magic tricks and silly play, while Nana Lou served them a buffet of the most delicious baked goods known to man. Nobody ever left their home sad or hungry. On his way to see Nana Lou, Eric remembered how the children at school argued over whether Trucker Tom and Nana Lou were Santa Claus and his wife, or perhaps a great wizard and his witch wife. Part of the charm had always been that neither of them denied the rumours. They enjoyed seeing the little faces light up with excitement as they tried to solve the giant mystery surrounding them. They saw no reason to spoil it with the truth.

Nana Lou opened the door for her favourite grandchild and gave him a warm squeeze. He knew she only said that to humour him, which it did. As she made her way to the kitchen to prepare some of her most famous baked treats, Eric settled himself in the living room and looked around. His grandmother wasn't about to let old age diminish her quirky sense of style. He smiled. Growing up, he'd always hated how eccentric his grandparents strived to be, and many times, he wished they could be just a little more normal, like the kind of people who knitted ugly sweaters, smoked pipe tobacco while reading the newspaper, and fussed over politics. But as he grew older, he began to appreciate and even respect how his grandmother had preserved everything that made her stand out from the crowd. There was nobody like Nana Lou if her home was any indication. He was flooded with nostalgia, rushing through his body like wildfire, mixed with a mournful longing for his grandfather. There were pictures of him all over the house. He had been the love of Nana Lou's life for decades and the only one Eric could always rely on to lift him up when he fell down. A kind-hearted giant with a deep, baritone voice, troll-like hands, and a belly laugh that won the hearts of locals in town. He was deeply missed; not a day went by that Eric didn't think of him. He wiped away a tear just as Nana Lou strolled into the living room, carrying a tray of pastries and tea, which she set on the table before her grandson. Waiting patiently for him to dig in, she sat on her throne across from him.

"So, what's troubling you, my dear?" she asked. He should have known she'd guess something was up. He'd never been able to keep anything from her; she always found out. Taking a bite out of a well-buttered bread roll, Eric eased into it.

"Sara May," he replied with a mouth full. "I always thought that if I ever saw her again, things would be different."

"Different, how?"

"I thought she'd be….I don't know….normal." Nana Lou let out a laugh.

"Honestly. Has this girl ever been normal?" she asked

with a wide grin.

"No. That's the problem."

"It's not a problem, my dear boy. It's the reason you love her."

"Nan, please." Eric rolled his eyes, much to his grandmother's amusement.

"Oh, don't be so sensitive. Don't you think I know what love is? I may be old and wrinkly, but I'm not daft, despite what some might think. I was happily married to your grandfather for years. I know what love looks like." Eric finished his bread roll.

"That's not the point. She's always been different from the rest, but I'm worried this blow to the head has made it so much worse. She says she's seeing ghosts." Nana Lou didn't raise a brow over this revelation.

"She does." Eric shifted uncomfortably in his seat.

"What do you mean?" Nana Lou shook her head. Would the boy ever learn?

"You've always been so black and white. So square in your way of thinking. Sara May sees ghosts. She can hear and talk to them. She's never been normal. We both know that."

"Are you saying she's like you?" Nana Lou smirked.

"No. She's much more powerful than I am. Stop fighting this so hard. You're not getting out of this any time soon; you're just making it worse for yourself."

Eric tried to read his grandmother's expression. He knew she was serious but didn't want to admit it. She had always lived in a different dimension from most others. Despite not being highly publicised, everyone in town knew it. Nobody ever dared to defy the unofficial witch of Northtown. The enchantress who always knew everything, the conjurer that everyone sought out but no one admitted to seeking. Being one of her beloved grandchildren, Eric had often received free advice from her without asking. Most often, the advice related to his love life, which had been on hold after the incident at his wedding. Much to Nana Lou's dismay. She kept reminding him that a woman would walk into his life one day, and he wouldn't be able to resist. And now, when that woman had burst into his life like water through a broken dam, the old necromancer was not about to keep her peace. Eric looked at a photograph of his smiling grandfather. If only he were alive. He could surely give him sound advice on how to survive a relationship with a crackpot.

Chapter 41

The day had come when Simon was laid to rest. The heavens had taken notice, gathering grey clouds that threatened to pour a month's worth of rain on the grieving crowd. Saddened and dressed in black, the locals gathered at the church, waiting for the sermon to start. A few women gathered around Suzy, supporting her as she stood like a statue, trying to hold back her tears and failing miserably. She could barely stand, so the women formed a protective circle around her to keep her upright. Jake stood beside his mother, linking arms with her and bowing his head, refusing to meet anyone's gaze. Jack was nowhere to be seen.

Sara May had hitched a lift with Aunt Marie to church because Maggie had been asked to help organise the funeral procession. The two sat in uncomfortable silence the whole way there. What could be said in times like these? If things were different, Sara May would have already told her aunt everything she knew about this case—how she suspected Pastor Evans was behind Helena's disappearance, which had ultimately led to her death, and how he also seemed connected to Simon's untimely demise. The pastor's conscience was as black as ink. But this wasn't a perfect world, far from it. So, she bit her tongue and kept quiet for now. The bleak landscape whizzed past as Aunt Marie's luxury car cruised down the country road, leaving a trail of dust.

A good twenty minutes before the funeral began, Aunt Marie parked her car. Sara May stepped out and looked around. A large group of people had gathered outside the church. It was a much bigger crowd than expected; she wondered how everyone would fit in the small chapel.

She saw Bill and Laura Baker, Sheriff Decker and his wife Martha, Old Gilbert, Biggie Mac and Mary, Bob the bartender, and Pastor's wife Paula and her band of gossipy minions. Even the local drinkers had turned up, looking smart, to pay their respects to the deceased, some with worried expressions mixed with deep sadness. Where would they get their alcohol now? Sara May greeted a few folks before heading inside. Halfway to her seat, she saw Chris standing near the coffin. She approached him slowly, tapped him on the shoulder, prompting him to turn around and smile before she hugged him tightly.

"Have you seen Eric?" he asked after letting go.

"No. I guess funerals are not a preferred choice of entertainment," she shrugged. Chris chuckled.

"Are they ever?" he asked.

"I guess not. Hey, you never told me what happened between you two."

"I could ask you the same thing," he replied with a wide grin, nudging her on the shoulder. Her face instantly turned bright red.

"How did you know about that?" Chris huffed.

"Come on. It's Northtown. Home of the most efficient rumour mill known to man."

"Well, this is one rumour I prefer to keep to myself, thank you very much." She turned to face the coffin.

"Tell me, and I'll tell you," Chris negotiated. She slowly crossed her arms as she looked back at her friend, her brows lifting with pretend shock.

"Chris Decker, are you bribing me?"

"It's called negotiations." Sara May growled.

"Damn you businessmen and your bargaining!"

"What can I say? I'm a natural," he said with a smile,

placing his hands in his pockets.

"Fine. But not here. Paula's army is already out hunting for the next slander; I don't want to give them more ammunition than they already have. It's bad enough they made my aunt out to be a sex-crazed whore; I don't want them to think the same about me."

Chris laughed, turned around, and walked back down the aisle, leaving Sara May alone with her thoughts. She stood briefly by the end of the white coffin, which was firmly placed at the altar. Multi-coloured flower wreaths sat on either side, decorated with white and gold ribbons bearing Simon's name, written in black. She couldn't help but admire the peaceful scene. It all seemed so surreal. She'd sat against the man the night he disappeared, and now he was lying here, in a coffin, cold as ice, never to wake up again. It didn't make any sense. Suddenly, she looked up and saw Helena standing at the other end of the coffin, looking sad.

"Simon needs justice. Just like I do," she said as she ran her hand over the lid.

"He took his own life. He'll have to deal with that on the other side," Sara May replied, more harshly than she intended.

"No, he needs justice!" Helena repeated in a firmer tone.

"And he'll get it, once he understands what he did."

She wasn't in the mood for a guessing game; it wasn't the right time for such nonsense. Instead of asking more questions, she watched a disappointed Helena vanish. She'd grown used to it by now. Frustrated, she shook her head and, realising she couldn't hold it any longer, went to find a toilet. She wasn't about to sit through an hour-long service when she badly needed the ladies' room. On her way, she passed a small back room where Pastor Evans used to change into his robe. Curious, she crept towards the half-open door to take a look. She gasped.

Behind the door stood Pastor Evans, bare-chested and about to put on his robe. There it was! The tattoo! On his right shoulder, just as Helena had described, two praying hands holding prayer beads with a cross. Sara May slowly stepped back from the door and hurried to find a seat. The ladies' room was no longer needed. Before she could fully process what she had seen, the church was filled with mourners, so many that there was barely enough room to move, let alone anything else. Soon after, Pastor Evans appeared before the crowd, his ever-so-holy presence cloaked in the same thick, black smoke as always, seemingly invisible to everyone but Sara May. The smoke was so suffocating that breathing became difficult, and she felt as though she was standing inside a burning building. She sensed herself drifting away, struggling to focus, until an annoyed Maggie nudged her.

"Sara May! You're not five years old anymore! Sit up; this is embarrassing!"

This was neither the place nor the time for an argument, so she reluctantly did as her mother had asked. The service felt endless. It was absurd sitting there and listening to the pastor preach about how loving and caring Simon was, knowing he was, by all accounts, the one who killed him! In a weak attempt to avoid eye contact, Sara May stared down at the floor, only occasionally lifting her head to watch the other mourners. Sitting at the front, she could see a numb Suzy staring, entirely void of all emotion, at her husband's coffin. On the other side of the aisle sat the pastor's wife, Paula, who admired her man with stars in her eyes—painfully contrasting situations. One woman was grieving for the love of her life, and the other was watching hers proudly. The few times Sara May felt like Pastor Evans had caught her eye, she felt like he was glaring at her. His grotesquely deformed face reminded her of the Devil himself. At one point, it was as if they were the only two people in the church. There he stood, condemning her to hell for meddling in his affairs.

When the service finally ended, six people—three on each side—carried the coffin out of the church and into the cemetery, followed by the crowd of mourners who had been touched by Simon's life. Sara May struggled to focus on what was happening. She watched the coffin being lowered into the ground but couldn't quite grasp how this had happened. How could a middle-aged man seem so alive one day and be gone the next? It just seemed absurd. Glancing around, she suddenly felt as though something had moved behind the large oak tree in the centre of the graveyard. Squinting, she couldn't tell who or what it was, and it felt wrong to leave in the middle of a burial. So, she dismissed it as a trick of her mind. Who would sneak around at a funeral anyway?

Chapter 42

The funeral reception took place at the Brewer at Suzy's request, who said that Simon would have wanted it that way. With all the alcohol being served, it looked more like a celebration, as people's sombre spirits gradually lifted, and tears turned into laughter. Someone called it a celebration of life. Bob was back on duty, standing behind the bar and serving thirsty mourners the pints they craved after a long and rather daunting funeral. Everyone seemed happier; multiple conversations were happening throughout the Brewer, merging into a loud, indistinguishable murmur. Sara May stayed close to Chris, who was busy talking to Bill Baker. This was the perfect opportunity to be on the lookout for suspicious behaviour and hopefully catch someone accidentally revealing themselves as a co-conspirator.

She focused on Aunt Marie, who had never been comfortable in sleazy pubs among the poor peasants. Her natural habitat was among the upper class, so seeing her out of her comfort zone and forced into this less-than-glamorous downgrade to a fancy chateau was quite interesting, to say the least. Sara May was surprised that she had even agreed to attend; there had to be a reason for it. She watched her aunt intently as the wealthy socialite approached Sheriff Decker, pulling him aside for a quick chat. She cursed that she wasn't close enough to overhear what they discussed. What was so crucial that it couldn't wait? Aunt Marie had to know more than she let on. Otherwise, she would be halfway to New York by now. Sara May knew her aunt had no interest in gossip or drama, which had always annoyed the pompous town blabbermouths and often made Aunt Marie the focus of their chatter. She never spent a penny on those old busybodies because she was busy living life on her own terms. So, it was a bit odd that she was still in Northtown; something was holding her back. Something Sheriff Decker knew all about. Sara May glanced at the group gathered at the Brewer and quickly spotted Laura Baker. She jumped off her barstool and headed her way.

"Oh, hello, dear. Nice to see you."

"Yeah, you too. Could I talk to you for a second?"

"Of course," Laura replied and put down her pint.

"I'm just gonna get straight to the point. Mum told me that Helena had a baby, and it was given up for adoption. Do you know anything about that?" Sara May bluntly asked.

Suddenly, Laura's face drained of all colour. Who had she been talking to? It was impossible that Maggie had mentioned anything about the baby. It had been Northtown's best-kept secret since 1994, simply because nobody wanted to face the consequences of revealing it. Over time, this little secret became an integral part of everyday life in Northtown, something people either forgot or didn't think much about. Laura's mind raced back to that terrible decade. Sara May's question had reopened a deeply infected wound she'd always hoped was healed, only to be harshly reminded that it was far from so. The memories overwhelmed her like a tsunami. She remembered the day her best friend told her she was pregnant. It had come as a shock to both of them. But no matter how much she begged, Helena always refused to reveal who the father was.

It had all been very strange. Helena didn't have a boyfriend at the time, and Laura wasn't even sure she'd ever had one. But she remembered how much her friend's behaviour changed after discovering the pregnancy. She became withdrawn and timid, almost like a frightened deer. She mostly kept to herself, not wanting to mingle with others. As her belly grew, so did her depression. She isolated herself in her flat and refused to discuss the child she was carrying or the man responsible for it all. She was terrified that Paula's informants would find out about her condition, which would've confirmed the nasty rumours about her having an affair with someone's husband. Everyone seemed to believe it, even though it wasn't true. It would've confirmed people's opinion of her—that she was nothing but a trashy trollop who seduced married men for her own pleasure. None of it was true, but at just twenty years old, she didn't stand a chance. She was condemned to carry the weight of harsh societal judgment, imposed by the very same people who had branded her an outcast and turned her own mother and sisters against her. Nobody came to her aid, and she rejected the help of the only person who stood by her through it all—her best friend, Laura Baker.

"What exactly did your mum tell you?" Laura whispered, mindful of her words and looking around as if the whole pub was watching.

"That Helena had a baby, and it had been given up for adoption shortly after she left town. I thought, since you were her best friend, you might know something about..." Laura raised her hand dismissively.

"Please, Sara May. It's not something I want to discuss, so please, I beg of you, leave it be. Laura's tone had shifted from enthusiastic to pure fright.

"Why can't I ask questions?"

"Because I can't answer them. I wish I could, but I can't help you with this one. I'm sorry," Laura quickly replied before grabbing her pint and rushing past Sara May, leaving her speechless.

What was going on? She'd been so eager to talk the last time they spoke. What had changed? Sara May felt her mood swiftly shift. Anger and frustration built within her like a tornado in an open field. It was irritating, as if she were being kept in the dark deliberately to protect people's fragile egos. She spotted Nana Lou, who stood close to the bar, and decided to speak to her in hopes of uncovering something. But before she could take the first step, she felt a sudden rush of cold air sweep through her, tightly wrapping around her like a rope. Jack stood a few feet away, closely watching her every move. With a glass of whisky in one hand, he was ready to strike. He was the panther, she was the prey. She ignored him, showing no interest in a conversation with the man she'd come to loathe.

"I need to talk to you," she said, pulling Nana Lou away from the bar.

"What's wrong?" the old lady asked, sensing the fear in her voice.

"Helena's baby. It's like I'm poking a tumour every time I mention it."

"Yes, I've been thinking about this. I remember people saying the father had to be one of those married men she was allegedly having an affair with, but I never believed it."

"Could the evil man have had something to do with it?" Sara May whispered in case anyone was listening in.

"You mean, could he be the father? Well, I guess it's not impossible. If I remember correctly…." Nana Lou didn't finish her sentence due to Jack's unwelcome appearance, which brought the same dread as a snowstorm in July.

"Hello, Sara May. I couldn't help but notice you. You're simply stunning in that dress! Care to join me for a drink?" he lewdly asked, raising his brows and forcing out a filthy smirk only a true scoundrel could. Sara May looked around, confused, before turning her attention to Jack.

"I'm sorry, did you mean to say that out loud?" she asked.

The gruesome grin on his face only widened as he showed no signs of taking no for an answer. He never had, so there was really no way out of this dreadful situation. Despite his obnoxious personality, she was starting to understand how he had managed to climb the bloody high-end ladder of the elite corporate world. However, she might as well listen if he had any information. Facing Jack, she put on her best poker face, making him think he had won this round.

"Ugh, fine. Since you just lost your dad, and I'm not a total monster, unlike some, I'll accept."

Jack simpered as the two walked away from Nana Lou and found a spot by the bar. While he ordered two drinks, she bowed her head, fearing that if anyone saw them sitting together, the rumour mill would start up again. Consequently, she didn't notice how closely Chris was watching the situation. He didn't trust Jack one bit. Bob pushed two pints towards them, receiving a hollow thank you from Jack.

"Okay, what's this all about?" Sara May grumbled. She had no interest in superficial small talk about his inflated ego.

"Can't a man enjoy the company of a lady without it coming with a catch?" Jack smugly replied as he took a sip of his beer.

"I'm no lady, so there's that. Besides, there's always a catch with you," she responded, prompting a chuckle from the prick beside her.

"Ouch. That hurt." Jack joked and put his pint down, wiping the foam from his mouth. "I just thought it might be good fun, sitting here with you, drinking fine ale, and reminding you to look over your shoulder occasionally."

"What do you mean?" Jack laughed.

"You didn't think you could get away with meddling in people's business without ruffling some feathers, now did you?"

"Maybe I'm just that good," she teased, still cautious and trying not to let the fear get hold of her. Now was not the time to break. Jack smirked before leaning in closer.

"Let's just say some folks in this town are not overly fond of having their private lives on display for all to see," he warned, no longer smiling.

"And I suppose you know all about that?"

"I know more than most. So, if I were you, I would ask myself if it's really worth it, having me as your enemy." Jack felt a growing grievance. Her resistance was infuriating.

"Why should I trust you?" she asked, sure he wasn't playing a fair game. Jack leaned even further toward her and whispered in her ear.

"Because you can't afford not to."

He leaned back, his sinister grin widening. He reached for his pint and, without saying another word, made his way back to the party, leaving Sara May feeling creeped out. It was well known that Jack Lewis often flaunted stolen feathers, and it wasn't unusual to hear him falsely boasting about himself if he thought it might improve his situation. Given his history as a compulsive liar, it was impossible to know if he was telling the truth. Again, she remembered Nana Lou's warning about trusting no one. But would it really be so bad if it turned out he knew something? She shook her head and gulped down a large sip of her drink. She had to be mad even to consider it!

Chapter 43

Simon's funeral reception had come to an end. The last guests left the party around 3 am, some so intoxicated they could barely put one foot in front of the other. Suzy had left the pub around midnight with a few of her closest protectors, who had been shielding her ever since Simon's untimely death. Aunt Marie left soon after. Sara May felt thwarted that she hadn't managed to speak to either her or Sheriff Decker to find out about their earlier conversation. When most of those who might know something had gone, she also left, having no reason to stay. Eric never turned up, much to her disappointment.

After the funeral reception, Chris took on the role of bouncer, ejecting the last boozed-up lowlifes out and helping Jake and Bob tidy up. Later, he asked to stay longer, and Bob was happy to agree since it meant he wouldn't have to stay behind to lock up. When morning arrived, Chris sat in a booth next to a window overlooking the high street, sipping a half-full pint and reflecting on the past few days. They had been nothing short of crazy. He had gone from greeting Simon at the start of every shift to sitting alone in the pub that had belonged to him and his wife longer than he could remember. He didn't know what Simon had done to deserve such a cruel fate, but he hated it. The man had never shown any signs of being suicidal. He had never seemed so fragile that a petty fight could push him over the edge. Suddenly, there was a knock on the door.

"It's open!" Chris called out. Eric slowly stepped into the pub.

When he saw the empty place, he jokingly asked, "Am I interrupting?" Chris looked at his watch.

"No, I reckon the town drunks won't be here for another hour."

Eric carefully closed the doors, making sure no one followed him. Those beer-loving booze hounds could scent the smell of an open door from miles away. Sitting opposite Chris, Eric realised they hadn't sat at the same table for years. It had been a long time since they had been in the same room, let alone at the same table. No matter how much he wanted to deny it, he couldn't shake the thought that maybe it was time to let go of the anger and hurt he'd held onto so tightly all this time. He missed his best friend. And with Sara May back in town, it felt like the trio was complete again. Perhaps Chris was right. Had Franziska not been the filthy whore she had been, he would be in a tormenting tug of war right now, trying to split his heart between two women. It was better this way.

"So, what's up?" Chris casually asked, taking a sip of the beer.

"Not much. What are you doing, hanging around here like a shabby wino?"

"It's a good place to think."

Eric looked around. "What will happen to this place now that Simon is no longer here to run it?"

"I was thinking of buying it," Chris replied, swirling the drink around in the half-empty glass. Eric looked at him, puzzled.

"You? Why?"

"I own the Pizza-Lot. I was thinking of combining it into a Friday Night offer. Pizza and a pint."

"Come on, Chris, this place is a dump. You'd just be taking over a massive debt."

"Believe what you will, but I do damn well in business. Besides, Jake has no interest in this place, and we both know Jack will never give it a second thought. His head is too far up the ass of any politician that gets a kick out of it." Eric let out a subtle laugh.

"Maybe it's for the best. Hopefully, then, he'll get his raggedy ass out of town." Chris smiled and took another sip.

"You didn't attend the funeral," he reminded Eric.

"No, I offered to look after the farm so Old Gilbert could go. He doesn't like leaving his animals behind. Did I miss anything?"

"Not really. Aside from Jack circling Sara May like a hungry hyena." Eric's smile faded as he gave Chris a stern look, which he was too busy downing the rest of the beer to notice.

"Did he hurt her?" Chris shook his head, putting down the empty glass.

"No," he replied, wiping his mouth with his sleeve. "She fought well."

Eric smiled with relief. He wasn't surprised to hear that Jack had been buzzing around her, but it still made his blood boil. Jack had a nasty reputation among women who knew him as a sleazy, pathetic perv who threatened those unwilling to bend to his will. As a result, he'd never had much luck with the women of Northtown. They had long since branded him as a sad little sicko, not to be taken seriously. Due to his upbringing, however, he believed women owed him all the attention he thought he deserved. His demands, combined with hidden desperation, had pretty much ruined any chance he'd ever had of finding a girlfriend. As he grew older and began to get a taste of the luxurious life of the elite, he realised that not having a desirable trophy wife was seen as a failure. So, it wasn't a surprise to Eric that he'd gone after Sara May, the most beautiful woman in town. She'd most likely twisted his arm and pinned him to the floor by the sounds of it. He smiled at the thought, feeling proud that his woman was no damsel in distress. She knew how to take care of herself. But at the same time, she also seemed to be experiencing an alarming after-effect of her accident.

"I worry about her," said Eric, pushing Chris's empty glass to the side.

"Who, Sara May?" Eric nodded.

"She's acting strange. She told me the other day she was seeing ghosts." Chris frowned, his brows lowering.

"Ghosts? Like dead people?"

"Yeah, she said something about her deceased aunt. Nana Lou wants me to believe it's all true, but you know how she is."

Do you think it could be related to the accident?

"Could be," Eric replied.

He'd barely finished that last word when they were startled by a loud bang. Something had fallen behind the bar, shattering and sending chills down their spines. Suddenly feeling very exposed and alert to their surroundings, neither wanted to admit to the other how utterly terrified they were. It was crucial to stay composed. Be a man. Surely, it was just a bottle precariously close to the edge, knocked over by the vibrations of passing cars outside. The terror heightened when there was a loud knock on the front door Eric had shut moments earlier. A few seconds later, Sara May peeked her head in.

"Hi, guys. I saw you through the window. Can I sit with you?"

The two men sighed in unison, relieved that this chaos

had logical explanations. She closed the door and hurried to the booth, making Eric slide over to give some space. Seeing them sitting together made her happy, but she had no time to dwell on the details of their fallout years earlier. She was a woman on a mission.

"What brings you here so early?" Chris asked after calming down his rapidly beating heart.

"I need to go and research the abandoned cabin where they found Simon," she confidently replied.

"What? Why?" asked Eric, bewildered over this sudden revelation.

"Because I need to do my own investigation. I'm convinced those two cases are linked and need proof."

"What two cases?" He was more lost than ever before.

"Simon's death and Helena's disappearance." Eric rolled his eyes and leaned back in frustration, crossing his arms defensively.

"Simon killed himself, and this aunt of yours vanished years ago," he reminded her rather harshly. Chris shot daggers at him, making him uncomfortable.

"Thirty-one years ago. She came under heavy fire when some blabby bitches started accusing her of having an affair with multiple married men in town. Eventually, it all became too much, and she fled. She was never seen after that, and nobody cared enough to look for her. She even left her newborn baby!" Sara May informed both men, who sat like scolded children, not daring to interrupt. Their eyes widened, however, at the mention of a baby.

"She had a child?" asked Eric, raising his brows. Sara May felt a sense of victory.

"Yes. I know these two cases are connected, and there's something in the cabin that can help me puzzle this together." Eric shot Chris a quick look as if these words confirmed what he'd just said.

"And, what exactly do you want from us?" Chris hesitated to ask, fearing he already knew the answer.

"I want you to come with me. I can't do this alone."

Chapter 44

The Nordic nights were darker than ever during winter. The galaxy's shadowy black holes twinkled in comparison. Chris and Eric struggled to keep p with their overly eager friend, who didn't seem to care at all about the freezing blackness around them as she hurried towards the cabin. Neither spoke a word. They both knew they'd made a terrible mistake by agreeing to this madness instead of trying to talk her out of it. Both silently cursed their foolishness; they should never have listened to this petite little warrior; nothing good ever came of it. The stormy winter, with its icy temperatures, had swept across the country a few days earlier, keeping it hostage with all its might. But that didn't slow Sara May. She marched confidently forward without a hint of fear, as if guided and protected by some unseen force, which gave her the courage to carry on.

After about a twenty-minute walk, the cabin appeared in the distance, standing alone like a forgotten relic. It was even creepier than they remembered. The boys both squinted but couldn't make out much more than the outlines of the crumbling hut. The cabin had been empty for as long as they could remember. It had been a popular destination for curious kids in Northtown for generations, and the three of them had been no exception. It had been the source of many of their countless adventures, acting as a pirate ship, a castle, and the cave of a fire-breathing dragon they'd heroically fought countless times. Now, it looked like a haunted hut on its last legs. The childish magic that once had the power to turn this creepy place into something else entirely was long gone. The ability to imagine something other than an eerie shack had been left behind in the innocence of childhood. The rational thinking of adulthood provided no solace as it was riddled with paralysing fear that defied all logic.

Sara May finally slowed down, and the trio cautiously approached the cabin. The light-brown paint had peeled in several places, the glass windows on all sides were shattered, and the weathered walls were covered in graffiti. Inside was no different. A sudden shaft of moonlight streamed through the front windows, casting ghostly shadows across the dusty floor, which was strewn with debris, broken glass from the windows, and muddy leaves. The few remaining doors were either hanging by a thread or had been entirely removed, and the entire structure seemed so fragile that Chris and Eric wondered how it was still standing. They hesitated to go further, but Sara May was determined. Driven by an unexplained force, the two men had no choice but to follow her, as leaving her alone was not an option. They could only hope that whatever gave her strength to carry on would somehow rub off on them. Carefully watching every step to avoid nails or glass, Sara May led the way. Guided only by the faint moonlight, she relied on her senses to find her way. She tried to remember the house's layout, but that only took her so far. Behind her, Chris and Eric did their best to keep up, trying not to show how utterly terrified they were.

The old cabin certainly had its charm, though. Located just outside the borders of Old Gilbert's land, it had been the subject of many town conversations over the years. Many believed it should have been demolished long ago, while others passionately argued for its preservation, citing its historical significance. It was among the oldest houses in town and had once been the home of

Northtown's first elected mayor and his wife. According to historical records, the couple had three children, but one night, none of them returned home after playing outside, despite their mother's desperate pleas. A search party was dispatched, and it was later discovered that all three children had drowned in the river flowing near Northtown.

The mayor's wife never recovered, and some said she completely lost her mind after the tragedy. According to those same people, the mother eventually became overwhelmed with grief. She took her own life in the house, prompting her distraught husband to resign as mayor, move out of the house and out of town, vowing never to return, and thus giving rise to the legend that the cabin was indeed haunted. Locals said the ghost of the disturbed mother, still in a state of ocean-deep grief, roamed the cabin, searching for her children and calling out for them in complete panic. That had reportedly been confirmed by everyone who tried to live in the cabin after this calamity, all of whom had eventually given up and sold the property. The cabin had stood abandoned since the last owner moved out four decades ago. Nobody had attempted to demolish the house, so it had simply been left to decay, allowing nature to take its course, with occasional help from looters and vandals hellbent on vandalising it. But even they had not been spared; some even swore to God that they heard a woman crying and children screaming, despite no one being around.

And now, the trio had returned. Chris and Eric were far less brave than their adrenaline-fuelled friend, but they knew they had to be strong and ensure she didn't hurt herself during this ridiculous quest. They promised each other not to separate, as neither wanted to become the house's next victim. The frosty wind howled outside, with chilling gusts encircling them like an ambush. Every blast sounded like the cries of the dead; every creaking floorboard resembled the movement of something so demonic it had to stay hidden from plain sight. Moving slowly and carefully, calculating their every step, it was almost as if they were expecting to be violently attacked by the mayor's deranged wife. They had heard stories over the years from people who swore they had seen her running aimlessly, flailing her arms, frantically searching for her children. Chris and Eric agreed that if they felt even the slightest breath, they'd run out of this hellhole faster than a firecracker. Sara May wandered in a trance-like state, completely unaware of how utterly petrified her friends were. She felt as if she was being led towards the staircase. Something told her to go upstairs, despite the steps looking more treacherous than a landmine. As she took the first step, she suddenly stopped dead.

"What's wrong?" Eric asked in a shaky tone, deathly afraid of the answer.

"He's up there," Sara May replied, staring in a daze at the top of the stairs.

"Who?" asked Chris whilst trying to steady his feet so he could run in the other direction as soon as possible.

"Come on, this is crazy! Let's just leave!" Eric begged.

Their desperate pleas went unheard. Sara May slowly continued up the stairs, one step at a time, as if under some spell, unaware of her nightmarish surroundings. The stairs were covered in rubbish and dust, and each step creaked under her weight, but she kept going. The two men waited at the bottom of the stairs, holding their breath and nervously watching as she floated upward, only exhaling in relief once she reached the upper floor. When she arrived there, she was met with nothing but pitch-black darkness. All the windows were broken, most covered with ripped, see-through curtains billowing in the wind. She was being pulled towards a room directly in front of her. The door had been ripped off its hinges; the peeled-away wallpaper had been replaced with colourful graffiti, and the worn wooden floor had turned grey from the accumulation of rubble and dirt. Aside from a dismantled bed and a broken closet, the room was empty—a dreadful place engulfed in years of encrusted sadness and desolation. Suddenly, a sharp gust of wind swept in and blew the battered door of the decrepit closet wide open, revealing its horrifying secret. Sara May jumped back. Inside the closet door, she saw Simon hanging lifeless with a belt around his neck. His bloodshot eyes stared wide open, his body so ashen it was almost transparent. At first, he looked like any deceased person. But in a split second, his head turned to face Sara May, jolting her to the point she almost fell over. Out of the body stepped the ghost of Simon Lewis, consumed by an inflamed anger that had overtaken him beyond the state of death.

"He's a pitiful demon, he is!" Simon screamed in a high-pitched voice, prompting Sara May to cover her ears. "He thinks he's won this war! He can have them! He can have it all! He knows that I know!"

He whirled around the room like a madman, leaving her numb with fear. She watched as he threw the bed across the room and tore down what was left of the flapping curtains, but she couldn't tell if it was real. She was traumatised, losing all sense of what was real and what wasn't. There was no time or space—just this place, this room, this moment. Simon's outburst had sent her back into that trance-like state that had pulled her up the stairs in the first place, and now, his wrathful energy was drawing her in. She had no concept of anything except this strangely alluring madness she was unknowingly approaching.

"He will find you! He will get you!" Simon yelled even louder than before, dry-heaving with rage and pointing his shaky, dusky finger towards Sara May, who stopped in her tracks.

"We have to get out of here!" Eric suddenly called out, snapping her out of her stupor.

At first, she resisted, but Eric proved to be stronger than she had thought. With Chris's assistance, he managed to bring her back and help her down the stairs. It was then that she realised Simon's fury, which had caused him to throw the bed, was indeed very real and had been witnessed by Chris and Eric, who immediately recognised their grave danger. Simon's ghastly screams pierced their ears and sent them rushing towards the front door, only for the wind to stir up piles of dust and debris, blocking their escape. The cupboard doors in the kitchen, still hanging by a thread, were slamming open and shut, adding agonising noise to the frantic wails of a confused ghost who didn't understand his situation.

"The window!" Chris yelled and pointed to a large, shattered window next to the front door.

In a bone-chilling frenzy, the hysterical trio leapt out of the window and ran for their lives. None of them knew where they were headed; none of them cared. All they could focus on was escaping with all fingers and toes intact and getting as far away from this hellish hut as possible — a hut that had once been their whole world, filled with childlike adventures and wonders. It was nothing like they remembered. All of them could recall how disappointed they'd always been after spending an entire day there without noticing anything abnormal. It was said that the ghost of the mayor's wife welcomed children into her house, allowing them to play freely without revealing herself. She enjoyed hearing their laughter and feeling their joyous energy surrounding her. Therefore, the children of Northtown had never experienced the cabin in the same way adults did. Some said the ghost blamed adults for failing to rush to her children's aid and save them in time, which bred her hatred towards grown-ups. After years of no supernatural encounters, the trio nearly stopped believing the stories, dismissing them as mere made-up tales meant to scare kids like themselves. But now, all they wanted was to forget the whole ordeal. Experiencing the supernatural was not worth the risk to their sanity. Finally, after running aimlessly in a semi-conscious state for what felt like hours, they stopped, safe beneath Northtown's streetlights, which cast their glow on patches of the pavement below.

"Never again, Sara May! I love you, but this is where I draw the line!" Chris yelled out as he gasped for air.

"What the hell were you thinking?" Eric angrily shouted at Sara May, who was trembling with fatigue.

"I saw him!" she replied, trying to catch her breath.

"Who?" Chris was in no mood for a guessing game.

"Simon. I saw him! He's still there!"

"What the heck are you on about? They found him; he's dead!" Eric, still hunched over with his hands firmly placed on each hip, harshly reminded her.

"If not, then burying him was a big mistake," said

Chris, squatting down and clutching his knees, trying not to have a full-on heart attack. Sara May's brows furrowed in frustration.

"Not him physically. His spirit's still there. He's angry! And he spoke about Pastor Evans!"

Chapter 45

"Nana Lou! Nana Lou!" Sara May frantically called out as she vigorously knocked on her front door.

After some time, Nana Lou reached the door. Alarmed to see the girl's distressed state, she quickly let her in before briefly checking the area to ensure she was alone. She had been communicating with her spirit guides over the past few days. They warned her that a storm was approaching and Sara May would be at the centre of it. She would need protection. Malevolent earthly forces planned to harm her, which didn't surprise Nana Lou. She knew Sara May's determination to uncover the town's darkest secret would attract those eager to keep it hidden. Behind closed doors, some believed it was in their best interest that this matter stay buried. With high stakes involved, people were willing to do almost anything to protect their fragile reputations from being tarnished. The old witch had noticed people sneaking around her house at all hours but decided not to warn the girl, not wanting to discourage her. When she entered the living room, she found Sara May pacing back and forth, shivering and rubbing her hands. She finally stopped when she realised she wasn't alone.

"I went to the cabin. Where they found Simon," she said, forcefully dragging out the words because her body was still on high alert. Nana Lou sighed heavily.

"I was afraid of that."

"He's still there. He's furious at Pastor Evans."

Nana Lou stayed silent. Sara May had just confirmed her fear: that Simon's death was not a reckless act born of madness. If Sara May was telling the truth, Simon remained in the same terrified state of mind as he had been in during the last moments of his life. What she hadn't anticipated was how directly Sara May had linked Pastor Evans to Simon's death. Could the cold-hearted bastard really be evil enough to kill someone and then lovingly bury them a few days later?

"What did Simon say?" Nana Lou asked, lowering her brows, preparing for the worst.

"He said that Pastor Evans knew that he knew. And that he would be coming for me."

The old enchantress had heard enough. She was ready to go to the cabin to soothe Simon's restless spirit and help him find his way into the light, but she hadn't expected that he would hold such valuable information. This was bigger than she had thought. She looked at Sara May, who had drifted into a haze as the shock began to fade. It was clear that whoever had gifted her with her talents intended to throw her quickly into the line of fire. Nana Lou had always known that her successor would be someone from Northtown. When that time came, it would be her role to teach and guide, should there be any demanding tests for that person. But nobody had warned her just how heavy the transition would be. Sara May was more powerful than she had ever dared to imagine. And yet, she was so lost. So helpless.

"I'll see what I can do. Talk to Sheriff Decker to see if he's found anything related to Helena's disappearance. Perhaps we can establish a solid foundation on that."

Sara May thanked Nana Lou and hurried out to do as she was told. The old lady had never led her astray. So far, she had been the only one who believed her. She hadn't judged or doubted her; she'd only shown her understanding, love, and compassion. It was what kept her afloat. Knowing that, amid an angry crowd of finger-pointing people with pitchforks, eager to burn her at the stake, there was one who wholeheartedly supported her. It was hard enough, having to carry the heavy burden of suddenly seeing dead people as if they were alive, but constantly having to defend herself against the never-ending ridicule was enough to break even the strongest souls. Sheriff Decker was going through a pile of papers when Sara May burst into his office unannounced. Being accustomed to this sort of thing, Decker didn't look up from the files, calmly awaiting an explanation for this unwelcome intrusion.

"Hello, Sara May. What can I do for you?" he asked nonchalantly.

"Do you have any new information about Helena's case?" Sara May blurred out.

"No. I told you I would let you know if I did."

"I know. I was just wondering, what if there is a connection?" Decker finally looked up from the paperwork.

"Between what?"

"Between Helena's disappearance and Simon's death." The Sheriff, accustomed to dealing with almost anything after years on the force, leaned back in his chair and exhaled loudly.

"Simon committed suicide." Sara May held her ground, staring so intensely into the sheriff's eyes that he questioned who was in charge, making him uneasy. He hated not being in control.

"I don't think he did," Sara May stated firmly.

Those words threw Sheriff Decker off. He maintained intense eye contact with the infuriatingly persistent woman standing before him, who had just thrown him a curveball. Who had she been talking to? Nobody knew that Simon had most likely been murdered. That was information he had intended to keep to himself until he received proof in writing that it was a murder. He knew that kind of news would turn the whole town upside down and probably send the poor grieving widow to an early grave. She was already halfway to La-La-Land, suffering from both loss and tremendous guilt. After a long silence, he gestured for Sara May to sit down.

"Alright," he said as calmly as he could. "What do you know?" Sara May pondered her next move. Trusting no one had served her well so far, but she needed people on her side if this case were to be solved.

"The night Simon vanished, I saw him storm out of his house after a fight with Suzy. He looked distraught. Later that evening, I saw him sitting alone at the Brewer. So, I went to check on him. He was heavily intoxicated and furious with Pastor Evans." Decker listened intently but without any notable emotion. He wanted to see where this was going before making a judgment call.

"Why was he angry at him?"

"I don't know. He said something about the pastor knowing that he knew. I don't know what that means. Then he stood up and left, slamming the door behind him with violent force. Jake told me he had seen Pastor Evans drive from his house at 2:00 a.m. A rather odd time to go out for a drive, don't you think?"

"Did Simon tell you anything else that night?"

"No. I think he was upset because he had found out Jack and Jake are not really his." Decker's brows lifted as his eyes widened.

"What?"

"He said that Pastor Evans could keep them. So, I guess they're actually his, not Simon's."

Sheriff Decker sat, frozen in his chair, unable to move. His hands suddenly felt clammy; his skin turned cold as ice. He recalled his younger years, when he and Prime Minister Crow ran with the same crowd. They were so young and hopeful, their lives filled with ambition and dreams. As they entered their teenage years, Evans had begun to change. He had been a sexually driven young man who didn't know how to approach the girls in the glass, who quickly cut him off as a sleazy pervert they all avoided. Decker remembered him and Crow trying to talk some sense into him and teach him how to behave around the ladies. But Evans had ignored their advice, convinced his sordid persistence and aggressive behaviour would eventually pay off. Things escalated after the trio took their first sip of the age-old cognac that Crow had stolen from his father's liquor cabinet when they were fifteen. It was as if the alcohol completely unmasked the terrifying demons that had occupied Evan's mind and body. He became increasingly threatening towards women, not accepting no for an answer, regardless of how young they were. To everyone's surprise, he quickly homed in on the youngest Jensen sister. Being only fourteen then, she wanted nothing to do with the nineteen-year-old sleazeball and tried her best to avoid him at all costs, with the help of her best friend, Laura Baker.

Decker ran his fingers through the thick hair that had grown increasingly grey over the past few weeks. Sara May's revelation had triggered an avalanche of memories he had long tried to forget, for good reason. He didn't want to remember how utterly vile the pastor had been. But with everything unfolding, he felt compelled to refresh his memory. He remembered a certain girl who, for reasons unknown, fell head over heels in love with

Evans despite his lack of redeeming qualities—Suzy Lewis. A classmate of theirs, she was always a bit eccentric. Mostly a loner, having failed to make friends with Paula and her followers, who regarded her as nothing but pathetic trash, as dictated by Paula. She was their queen bee; her words were gospel. She had never seen a reason to humour Suzy with any attention. In their early twenties, relationships began to form. Decker had snatched Martha at eighteen, having loved her since they became partners in biology at school. Crow had moved south to the capital city to study political science at the University of Iceland, where he met Charlotte, whom he later married. Suzy became engaged to Simon, a kind-hearted simpleton who had moved to Northtown with his parents a few years earlier.

But Evans hadn't given up on Helena, who fought him off like a wounded animal. Her resistance had angered him, so he agreed to marry Paula on a whim. Many believed this was one of her father's conditions for Evans becoming his successor as the pastor of Northtown. Decker thought this was the turning point in Evans's life. Almost overnight, he became deeply involved in the church as a committed Christian. He stopped drinking without ever going to rehab and studied theology, funded by his father-in-law, who acted like the puppet master of the whole affair. Decker had always wondered how Evans managed to turn his life around so quickly. And now, Sara May, the daughter of Maggie Jensen—Decker's schoolmate—was sitting in front of him, telling him that Evans's lifestyle change hadn't been the U-turn everyone thought. Evans never had romantic feelings for Suzy Lewis. But it wasn't entirely impossible that he had fallen off the wagon at some point and let his predatory tendencies take over. If he could sneak past Simon and knock up his wife without him knowing, after swearing his loyalty to God, there was no limit to what he was capable of.

Chapter 46

Pastor Evans fastened his freshly ironed white shirt. He had been distracted for the past few days and couldn't focus on his service to the church as he usually did. With the help of his loyal wife, he had convinced his most devoted parishioners that he was battling a cold and would return to his usual self soon. It was a half-truth; in a sense, his mental health had plummeted ever since that fateful night two weeks ago. Since the night a heavily intoxicated Simon had stormed into his office, blinded by fury, Evans hadn't slept. The beast within him, which he hadn't unleashed in almost forty years, was awakened, and without hesitation, he dealt with the matter without showing emotion or remorse. But it also revealed to him how powerful he truly was. By doing what he did, he had chosen to side with evil forces, and that caused him anxiety, which kept him awake. The line between heaven and hell was stretching thinner than the belt he had hung around Simon's cold, dead neck.

But what was most alarming was how empowering it had been. He did what he had to do. Anyone would have done the same in his position, having to defend oneself from a crazed lunatic. The man had been so enraged that he threatened to expose the pastor's most intimate secret. At that moment, the Devil had whispered in the pastor's ear, and he had listened. Evans had known for years who his true master was. And he didn't wear a white robe, listening to an angelic choir in the sky. Paula hadn't been home that evening, so she was unaware of what had happened just moments before she arrived home from her Gossip Girl meeting. Luckily for Evans, she wasn't a light sleeper, so sneaking out at two o'clock in the morning to drive to the abandoned cabin with a body in the boot hadn't been an issue. There, he had placed Simon's body in the ruined old cupboard, ensuring the belt was tight enough so no one would doubt what had really happened once Simon was discovered. He knew he would. There had never been a shortage of kids snooping around the cabin in search of hidden treasures. On the way back, he thought about how easy it would have been to dispose of the body in the same way he had done with Helena back in the day, but the risk of someone linking the dots due to similarities was too high. Therefore, it would be preferable if Simon's body were found. He just hadn't expected it to happen so quickly.

Since the day the body was discovered, Evans had wrestled with a knot in his stomach, weighing him down like a heavy stone. It wasn't because of regret or fear of the consequences of his actions. It was because of the town's unrest. He knew the locals well enough to see that the ocean had started to grow rough. Waves were forming, getting bigger by the second. He knew that if he didn't do something quickly to calm the crowd, the waves would turn into a massively destructive force, reducing this tiny town to rubble and leaving nothing but utter devastation. Nobody would be spared, especially those with something to hide. That damn Jensen girl! he quietly cursed himself. He should have known she would be his downfall. This was God punishing him for the lustful thoughts he'd had about Helena. She was the most beautiful girl he'd ever seen. Her light-blonde, wavy hair flowed down to her perfectly shaped shoulders, and her deep-blue eyes, like two diamonds, shimmered in the sunlight. But she had never wanted to act on her feelings for him. She was afraid of them. So, he had helped her understand and accept them. He had taken what belonged to him. If only he had known.

He shook his head, snapping out of his reminiscing daze, and finished buttoning up his shirt. He couldn't get away with cancelling yet another Sunday mass. The flu excuse could only stretch so far. He cleared his throat before walking with his head held high to greet the faithful flock that awaited him with anticipation. As he stood by the altar, ready to begin, he spotted Sara May sitting between Maggie and Grandma Gladys in the third row to the left of the aisle. She stared at him intensely as if cautioning him to go further. She knew something he didn't, sending him into a downward spiral of anxiety. She was challenging him, and he wasn't prepared for it. At that moment, he realised that he had to act. Otherwise, this feisty little vixen would beat him at his own game. He would have to stay one step ahead of her, no matter the cost. He finished the Sunday service on autopilot, preaching the same mantra he knew by heart, interspersing a few familiar Bible verses with repeated words about kindness, love, and compassion. He fought hard to stay focused. Aside from Sara May's ice-cold gaze, he could feel the shadowy figures around him filling his mind with dark thoughts. If she didn't back off, she would suffer the same fate as Helena. Of that, he was sure. He had no problem obeying his master's orders.

But there was something about her. As she sat on the wooden bench, looking like an emotionless assassin ready to strike, he suddenly felt light-headed. He knew taking her out was not going to be easy. Something was different about her; it was almost as if she were surrounded by an invisible army that gave her the strength to face this fight. She sensed his insecurity, his anxiety. It was a weakness she could exploit, making him afraid she could somehow read his mind. No! This was not the time to falter. He had to strike!

Sara May hurried out of the church as soon as Pastor Evans finished speaking. She hated those pointless sermons about things she strongly doubted were even real. She had never been religious, always finding those high praises of the man above to be nothing more than wishful thinking that he was there, listening in. All around her, all she could see were adults playing make-believe, living in a world where their imaginary friend had become such a big part of their lives that they couldn't see how absurd it was. It was cringey at best. Pastor Evans had hoped to catch her before she left and perhaps get her to confess to a sin or two in the name of Jesus Christ. He nearly lost his temper when he realised she had slipped through his fingers again. That meant he had to believe Jack was as good a detective as he claimed to be. Otherwise, that boy's political career would go straight into the bin.

Later that day, Evans dragged his tired feet home, exhausted from lack of sleep and battling the urge to go straight for the kill. It was draining to wear that fake smile and pretend to embody all the goodness that God had given him. It was a carefully crafted image he had maintained over the decades, a rehearsed performance that secured his place in society as the epitome of kindness, from whom all moral guidance was drawn. In reality, it was nothing more than an empty vessel, and it had become increasingly difficult to pretend just to appease those desperate enough to seek his comfort. He removed his jacket and shoes. The heavenly scent from the kitchen overwhelmed his senses and drew him in, where he found his wife standing by the stove.

"What are you cooking, my dear?" he asked as he sat by the kitchen table and opened today's newspaper.

"The Sunday roast. As always," Paula dutifully replied.

"Pardon my ignorance. Any news?" He wasn't really interested; he just wanted to give his wife a chance to vent as he skimmed the paper in front of him. It was a lovely tradition.

"It depends on what you call newsworthy. The Jensen girl knows about Helena," Paula replied as she slowly stirred the sauce pot.

"Yes, I had heard something about that," Evans muttered, his eyes still fixed on the paper.

"She also knows about the baby."

Those words snapped Evans out of his reverie about the flooding in Germany. He removed his reading glasses and set them on the table as he looked up at Paula, hoping he had misheard her. How did Sara May know about the baby? It was one thing to know about Helena, but if she now knew of the bastard child, the situation had escalated from bad to utterly dire. That meant it was only a matter of time before she uncovered his most heinous crime. He remained calm. Paula was no beauty queen, if she had ever been one, but she was a loyal life partner. She had helped her husband craft the rumour that Helena had been nothing but a bedhopping tramp sleeping with married men—a lie that had proved so effective it eventually convinced people Helena had left town. Those who knew of her pregnancy naturally assumed she had taken the baby with her, and those aware of the truth had sworn secrecy. Nobody, not a single soul aside from Pastor Evans, knew the truth.

Chapter 47

The evening had fallen. The tension between Sara May and Maggie was reaching its breaking point, and Sara May left the house to see if Eric would pity her and take her in. Perhaps he had a spare room where she could stay. Or a large enough bed for both of them. She smiled at the naughty thought of their last sleepover, which had gone even better than she had hoped. All her worries about him not feeling the same way about her vanished at the first touch. Therefore, she wasn't nervous about asking him if she could stay. The bell above the Bread Box's main door announced her arrival to Bill and Laura as if she were the Queen of England. Bill looked up and smiled, putting away the red and white checkered cloth he had been using to wipe the counter.

"Hello, darling. What can I do for you today?" he asked in his usual cheerful tone.

"Is Eric around?"

"I'm afraid not. He's probably still helping Old Gilbert; he's usually there when he's not here."

"I really need to get a copy of his schedule," Sara May exhaled. Bill let out a laugh.

"I'm afraid it doesn't exist. The boy goes where he's needed."

Sara May thanked Bill and headed back out. She wasn't surprised to hear that Eric had turned out the way he had. He had always possessed the biggest heart, always willing to help those in need. There was no denying she had been the stronger character of the two, most likely because of how quickly she'd been forced to grow up. She'd always felt she had to be resilient and independent. She never needed anybody. Keeping people at arm's length was a defence mechanism to prevent her from experiencing the same pain she'd endured watching her father, the one man she trusted, abandon her. After that, she vowed never to let anyone in too close because, in her opinion, everyone could walk out of her life without notice. Maintaining distance from everyone was a form of self-protection. She'd convinced herself she didn't need anyone else. She was tough, as cold as ice. If nobody was important in her life, then nobody could hurt her.

Until now, the wall around her had served its purpose. Well, mostly. A few people had managed to slip through the cracks. Paige was one of them. And now Eric. But he hadn't just slipped quietly through; he shattered that wall and left her completely exposed and vulnerable. He'd gone deep, right to her heart, without any resistance, and she wasn't sure how to handle it. After walking for a while, she finally reached Old Gilbert's house. It would've been easy for those unfamiliar with the area to get lost, but luckily, her memory served her well. She'd been able to channel the young and feisty little girl inside her and let her lead the way. She knocked on the front door, and seconds later, a surprised Eric opened.

"Sara May? What are you doing here?"

"Mum and I had a falling out, and I was wondering if I could stay at your place tonight?"

"Yeah, sure. Hold on, I'll be out in a sec."

She waited patiently outside. She didn't want to intrude on the old man's house even though she knew she'd always held a special place in his heart. Life hadn't blessed him with children of his own, so instead, he opened his home and heart to all the children of

Northtown who sought his company. He'd taken a particular liking to the dynamic trio because most of their childhood escapades had ended in his kitchen, which, to them, had always been like a bakery, filled with all sorts of pastries that fuelled their energy and kept them going until their parents arrived. Old Gilbert enjoyed their company, so he spoiled them as if they were the children he never had. After a short while, Eric reappeared with a cheeky grin, sending tingling waves down her spine. He was so cute when he smiled like that.

"I've got a better idea. Come on," he said as he grabbed her hand.

She followed him to the large cement barn with the red tin roof that stood a few feet from the house. He led her inside, despite it being pitch-black and not much to see except the outlines of hay stacked high against the ceiling. She walked carefully behind Eric, making sure not to step on anything and trusting him completely. Old barns like these were known to be full of all kinds of junk that could easily cause injuries to those not paying attention. Suddenly, Eric stopped, making her almost bump into him from behind. He turned on the lights, revealing what had to be the most beautiful space she'd ever seen. She gasped. In the blink of an eye, the old, spooky barn had been transformed into an insanely romantic and dazzling fairytale. The walls were decorated with lanterns that cast a warm, soothing glow on the light-coloured hay, enchanting the barn. She turned halfway around and fell backwards onto the huge pile of hay. Eric chuckled. Ever since that sensual night at the Jensen house, he'd been unsure of his next move. One moment, he'd been convinced they were meant to be; the next, it was like she was pushing him away. Seeing her lying in the hay, so relaxed and happy, felt like confirmation of everything he'd ever dared to hope for.

"I thought you might like it," he said, his hands firmly placed in both pockets, a smile tugging at one side of his mouth.

Her teasing smirk invited him to lie beside her. As he did so, he turned to drape one arm over her torso, leaning over her. She looked stunning in this captivating lighting. Her hair shimmered, and a twinkle appeared in her eyes that he hadn't noticed before. At that moment, there was no need for words. The sexual tension between them had grown so intense that words would get in the way. He leaned in closer, searching for her lips. His heavy breathing indicated intense longing, sending waves of arousal through her body. Supporting himself with one hand, he studied her face while his fingers traced from her forehead to her lips, then pulled her closer and pressed his lips to hers. Their tongues danced playfully, and she allowed herself to feel the heat within, her nerves vibrating with erotic pleasure. She desired this man. She yearned for him. Seeing him barely contain himself, groaning with every touch, gave her a sexual confidence she hadn't felt in years. She was his addiction, and that was a pleasure on a whole other level. He bowed his head, guiding his lips to her neck and his hand to her feet, moving slowly at first, then faster until he reached the sweet spot, sending a thrilling jolt from her chest to her toes. Their breathing grew heavier, and as they surrendered to the pleasure and found their rhythm, a passionate moan could be heard from the old barn well into the night.

The moon had broken free from the clouds, casting a cold, teal-coloured light over Northtown. Inside the old cement barn, the heat had been turned up to a thousand degrees, causing the two naked, sweaty bodies to steam up the small windows near the ceiling. Sara May lay pressed against Eric's muscular body, running her fingers down his arm. She carefully examined his tribal tattoo from his shoulder to his upper arm, where it twisted into a snake that wrapped itself around his fingers. She'd never taken Eric for a bloke who liked tattoos, but it looked good on him. It made him appear somewhat dangerous, the sort of chap who considers hell a holiday spot. It low-key aroused her. She'd never felt so safe. Nothing could harm her as long as his solid arms were wrapped around her. His embrace was more potent than any wall she'd ever managed to build around herself, and she knew she wanted it to last forever. Eric gently brushed a wet lock of hair from her forehead, smiling softly as he admired her stunning beauty. There was no longer any doubt in his mind. He was deeply in love with this woman and had probably always been. Chris had been right, that son of a bitch. Lost in her thoughts, Sara May was quickly pulled back to reality as she suddenly felt something approaching them at an almost supernatural speed. She jumped, her body tensed up as if it were preparing for a fight. Eric laughed.

"Relax. It's just Max, don't worry."

"Who?" she asked, trembling slightly.

"Old Gilbert's trusted companion. Twelve years old, bless him, but as loyal as they come."

Max was a black and white Border collie who was well past his prime. He followed Old Gilbert like a shadow, but occasionally, he trotted behind Eric if he pleased. That night, the dog made sure his owner reached bed safely before checking why Eric hadn't returned from the barn.

"How long do you think he's been here?" Sara May asked, mortified they'd somehow shattered the poor creature's innocence. She pushed herself closer to Eric, who chortled.

"He's fathered about eighteen puppies, so I wouldn't worry too much," he replied sarcastically.

"Oh, God." Sara May buried her head in shame, prompting Eric to laugh.

"Come on. He won't need therapy, I promise you. Look."

He pointed at Max, who was busy pacing in circles, scratching the concrete floor, and brushing off the small patch of hay until it was all cleared away. He sniffed the floor thoroughly before taking a few more laps and then quietly lying down.

"What's he doing?" She'd never seen a dog act this way.

"He does this every time I come in here. I don't know why; he's done this ever since I started helping the old man on the farm and probably even longer. It's his favourite place."

Sara May watched for a while. He looked so peaceful, likely due to old age. Nobody can stay young and vibrant forever. She smiled and looked at Eric, who tightened his grip on her. The relaxation filled her with feelings of safety, sending her exhausted body and mind straight into a blissful sleep.

Chapter 48

"You goddamned slut! Why didn't you tell me about this bloody bastard?" the shadowy monster yelled.

"Stay away from me! You have no right to know!" Helena replied firmly, her fists clenched in apprehensive anger.

Sara May thrashed like a trapped animal, grunting with each movement. Sweat dripped from her face like tiny pearls, and her heart pounded like a honeybee's wings. She was caught in the nightmare that had enslaved her ever since she returned to Northtown. But this time, something was different. She wasn't standing outside, watching in. Without any sense of herself, she was right in the middle of the fight between Helena and the ghostly creature, which increasingly resembled a beastly version of the Grim Reaper. A faceless monster intent on killing. She sensed Helena's paralysing fear and the fury that consumed the violent monster of a man. But most of all, she felt her own helplessness. She watched the devilish man abuse Helena in a fit of rage until the poor woman slumped down, and she was powerless to stop him despite screaming at the top of her lungs. She felt tears stream down her face as she begged the beast to stop, though her plea remained silent. Not a sound escaped her mouth. The monster quickly turned his attention to her before dragging the lifeless body from the ground. It was then that Sara May realised the body did not belong to Helena, but to herself. The demon tightened his grip on her body, making her realise she was now his prisoner, completely at his mercy.

"Sara May! Sara May, wake up!" Eric called out and shook her tense body in a desperate attempt to reach her, causing her to leap up suddenly in sheer terror.

Someone snapped their fingers, jolting her back to reality. She quickly sat up and scanned the barn like a soldier surveying a battlefield, trying to gauge the passage of time and her surroundings. The barn had become dark again as the lanterns had been turned off, making everything colder and somehow much creepier. After a few attempts, Eric managed to lock eyes with the terrified woman who'd been so happy and relaxed in his arms just hours earlier. He'd never seen her mesmerising eyes so dreadfully dark and afraid. He quickly realised that she didn't recognise him, despite her eyes widening. She wasn't fully awake. Without warning, her head turned to where Max had lain earlier. The dog was nowhere to be seen. Instead, she saw Helena standing solidly in Max's spot, staring at her as if she was desperately trying to make her understand.

"I remember. I remember what happened," she cried out.

Sara May stared at her deceased aunt. It was as if an invisible chain had been tightly wrapped around the two women. Neither could look away. Sara May's eyes darkened, and the atmosphere grew heavy. Something was unfolding, and she didn't know how to break free from it. It was almost as though countless otherworldly creatures were weaving the threads, forcing her to confront the brutal reality of it all. The last piece of the puzzle had fallen into place, suddenly making everything so clear. She knew what had happened. Suddenly, she snapped out of her daze, scaring Eric, who felt trapped in a nightmare of his own.

"Who does this land belong to?" she shrieked. Eric looked confused.

"Old Gilbert."

"Who lived here before him? Who sold him this land?"

"It belonged to the church. Paula's family lived here, but Pastor Evans didn't want to live on a farm when he took over, so they sold it to Gilbert.

"What year did they sell it to him?"

"I don't know; you'll have to ask him. What's going on?"

"I have to know when he bought the place and who built this barn!"

She leapt up and ran the moment she uttered that last word. Eric called out for her, but to no avail. She sprinted out into the freezing night, barefoot and barely dressed, paying no attention to her surroundings. The icy winds cloaked her, but that didn't bother her. All she could think about was trying to make sense of the information she had been given. If interpreted correctly, it could turn her whole world upside down. She knocked loudly on Old Gilbert's front door, not stopping until he angrily tore it open.

"What the hell is going on here?" the old man growled, clearly annoyed about being forcefully woken up in the middle of the night.

"Can I come in?" Sara May pleaded breathlessly, trying to avoid Old Gilbert's death stare. Before he could answer, Eric came running.

"Sorry about that! She had a nightmare, and I couldn't stop her," he apologised. The old man huffed.

"Get in, both of you," he grunted, tipping his head to gesture them inside.

Usually, the elderly man was the sweetest and most soft-hearted old chap on Earth. But having his sleep disturbed could turn any saint into a sinner. Being a farmer was a tough job, especially for an ever-ageing geezer. Therefore, a good night's sleep was essential. Irritated, he marched to the living room, followed by Sara May and Eric. Once there, he invited them to sit before plopping into his favourite armchair with Max loyally trailing beside him. He seemed to be in a better mood than his owner, although he knew not to stand in his way at this ungodly hour. Too afraid to speak, the pair sat silently as Old Gilbert's patience stretched thinner with every ticking second.

"Well? Now would be a good time to explain why, in God's name, you brutally woke me up in the middle of the night like a couple of savages out for blood!" he growled.

"I'm so sorry. I didn't mean to disturb you this late," Sara May replied remorsefully, bowing her head.

"Then why the hell were you trying to break the door down? Making me think someone was out to murder me!"

"I've been looking into my aunt's disappearance, and I think I've just been given a vital piece of information," Sara May explained. Old Gilbert shrugged with annoyance.

And what does that have to do with me? Couldn't you just have told Eric? The boy certainly earned it. Don't think I didn't hear you out there!"

Stunned, the duo sat with crimson faces of embarrassment, unable to speak. Both had believed that only the dark winter night and piles of hay bore witness to their passion. Now, they were forced to face the reality that the old farmer, whom they'd assumed was half-deaf due to his age, had been subjected to an audio show he hadn't asked for.

Again, I'm truly sorry. But I have to ask you a few

questions if that's okay?" she pleaded. Old Gilbert thought about it briefly before exhaling and leaning back in his chair.

"Go ahead," he motioned with his left hand.

"Eric told me that you bought the land from Paula's family. What year was that?"

"In 1993," he replied.

"Around the time Pastor Evans returned from studying theology in the capital?" Suddenly, Eric's curiosity was awakened.

"I guess. Nobody knew why that God-forsaken son of a bitch suddenly decided to whitewash himself of all sins and become a pastor. His father-in-law paid for his studies and promised him the land if he graduated. But Evans had no interest in farming. When Paula's father died in February of '93, Evans was forced to come home because the people of Northtown couldn't be without a pastor."

"Why not? Is it that important?" Sara May asked.

"Seems so. I guess the poor, miserable souls around here didn't feel like continuing their sinful lifestyle without the possibility of an absolution."

"Was the barn here when you bought the place?"

"Yes, it was. But the floor needed redoing. Evans offered to help me with it. Probably the only good thing that rat-faced bastard has ever done for me."

Sara May suddenly found herself unable to move. Could it be? Everything pointed to Helena having left town because of Pastor Evans's despicable behaviour towards her. If her suspicion was right, she was close to uncovering Northtown's ugliest secret, which had been corrupting this rotten town for decades. She had to find out who knew what.

Chapter 49

Sheriff Decker zipped up his jacket and stuffed both hands firmly into his pockets. It was approaching Christmas, evident by the festive, multi-coloured lights flickering all over town. A flurry of snow covered the frozen ground, making each exhaled breath steam. The shadowy winter nights cast darkness, making the outlines of buildings barely visible. It was one of those quiet nights; the only sound was the echo of his footsteps in the fresh snow. The streets were dimly lit; the streetlights cast a dull glow on the pavement, just enough to attract rats hiding in every corner. Pests were best kept in the sewers. He had always loved this small town, but he couldn't deny it felt eerie, almost ghostly, on nights like these. That was probably true of most towns on this unforgiving yet mysterious island in the Atlantic Ocean. The otherworldly landscape did little to lessen people's belief that the nation shared the island with elves, trolls, ghosts, and other mythical creatures lurking behind every rock, ready to strike. No country could look like Iceland without being full of mythical beings hiding from human sight. He didn't want to run into such a creature, since most folklore considers them extremely dangerous if they are wronged. Darkness was their shield, so he wasn't keen on it, preferring to stay inside until daylight. But as the town's sheriff, staying indoors wasn't always possible. Tonight, he was a man on a mission. He quickened his pace until he saw the only care home in town appearing in the distance.

"Oh, hello, Sheriff Decker. Nice to see you here," Maggie greeted him, slightly surprised.

"Thank you, Maggie. It's nice to be inside; it's getting

a bit nippy out there."

"So I've heard. They say it's going to snow tonight. I hope it'll hold off until I get home"

"Let's hope so. No fun walking home in a blizzard."

"So, what brings you here in the middle of the night?" she asked, knowing the town's sheriff didn't just pop by to chat about the weather.

"I came to see Crow," he replied, his expression serious.

"I see. Well, this isn't the usual visiting hour. I'm not sure he's awake."

"I know my old mentor. I can assure you, he's up. If he ever went to sleep."

"Very well. He's in room 204."

Sheriff Decker nodded and muttered a quiet thank you. Walking down the seemingly endless corridor gave him the creeps. It felt so bare, so dull. The walls had been painted a faded salmon colour from the 1980s, and a few wall lights were evenly spaced along, casting a soft glow. Pictures of various landscapes had been hung between the lights to brighten up the otherwise boring hallway and cover up the fact that this was just a government-run institution and nothing more. Sheriff Decker hated how many ended up this way—old and tattered human remnants that no one cared about. That's how these care homes came to be. As the nation emerged from poverty and its economy improved, everyone became too busy fighting for a bigger share of the benefits. Generations of the same family had lived together under one roof for centuries, but when wealth and material gain became the main measures of success, the elderly were seen as outdated, as something to be discarded. So, care homes were built to house those who had sacrificed their health to make the country one of the richest in the world. They had paid for the party but weren't invited. The thought alone made Sheriff Decker's blood boil, and he vowed he would never become one of those people. He stopped in front of room 204 and knocked.

"Come in," a ragged male voice said from the room.

Sheriff Decker slowly opened the door. There was—Arthur Crow, Northtown's former sheriff and the father of Iceland's current prime minister. Once, Arthur had been a tall and somewhat intimidating man, towering over most people in town, a broad-shouldered beast who had the town under his control. People had mixed opinions about him. Some appreciated the security of having Arthur Crow on duty, patrolling the streets of Northtown. Others respected him. And some were genuinely afraid of him, and rightly so. Yet nobody ever dared to go against his word. What Arthur Crow decreed was regarded as law. But that was a long time ago. Now, there was little left of the former giant who once could have subdued the town's biggest gangbangers with one hand. Instead, what Sheriff Decker faced was a frail old man with messy, white hair, trying to solve a crossword puzzle with his thin, bony hands. It saddened him to see his old mentor reduced to such a state. Decker pulled out a chair and sat down beside Arthur's bed. He did not speak to him at first.

"You haven't changed. Sleeping during the day and staying awake most nights," Decker said to get Arthur's attention. It partly worked, despite the old man still not looking up from his puzzle.

"You should know. Men in our line of work are not permitted to close their eyes when night falls," Arthur replied, then giving Decker a serious stare. "That's when the rats crawl out of the sewers, you see. That's what makes or breaks us!"

Sheriff Decker smiled. It was almost comical how tightly Arthur clung to the old days, but it also served as a poignant reminder of how unforgiving life could be. The human spirit doesn't always align with the physical body it inhabits. It was hard to accept that the limitations of this fragile shell restricted the passion burning within everyone. In his mind, Arthur remained the mighty force of law and order, the hulking titan who strolled through the streets of Northtown, flaunting his power to scare locals into obedience. But time had moved on, just as it did for everyone else, like a cascading river that no one could halt. Eventually, it caught up with him. Sheriff Decker found it hard to watch his former mentor fade away and be unable to continue living his dream. His son was far too absorbed in his political career to bother visiting his elderly father, and the other three Crow children were so scattered across the world that none of them had the decency to drop by. Out of pity, Sheriff Decker paid Arthur regular visits, both as a gesture of gratitude for his wise guidance and partly because it brought the old man great satisfaction to act as the boss he once was. But this time, Decker faced a more urgent matter, and he needed Arthur's help.

"Why this hour, Decker? Did the broad finally kick you out?" Arthur grumbled, not taking his eyes off the crossword puzzle. Decker's brows drew closer together in annoyance.

"The broad is my loving wife, Martha. And she's just as beautiful as the day I met her, that much I can tell you." Arthur's grin widened.

"That's what they all say. So, why are you here?"

"I came to ask you about Helena Jensen. You remember her?"

"I guess," Arthur murmured. "What about her?"

"Why was her disappearance never investigated?"

"Huh! Some disappearance! The girl was running around with her knickers down, willingly lying with every married man in town! Why should we have noticed her skipping town to spread her legs in the capital?"

"Nobody ever saw or heard from her again after that. Don't you find that a bit odd?" Arthur frowned.

"No. She had a reputation she carved out for herself, so she ran. That was her choice."

"Reykjavik isn't a large city, Arthur. When a person goes missing, questions are asked." Decker was getting slightly irritated by the old man's lack of care.

"Maggie came to us, voicing some concerns. But if someone doesn't wanna be found, they have every right. She was already in the capital, so it was out of our hands, and the big boys down south had better things to do than look for a tarnished tramp."

Something about Arthur's brutal denial rubbed Sheriff Decker the wrong way. He knew the old-timer well enough to sense he was hiding something. But he didn't seem interested in further discussion, turning his attention back to the crossword puzzle. Sheriff Decker stood up and thanked Arthur for the chat. The old man exhaled with relief and waved him away, happy to see him go. On his way home, he wondered why Arthur had seemed so disinterested. It wasn't like him. Usually, he wouldn't shut up about old cases and how he seemingly resolved them all by himself, upholding the shining light of justice.

Something felt off. The weight of it all had thickened

the air between them, making it uncomfortable for both. Arthur knew more than he was revealing and was reluctant to share it with his former student and successor. He was fully aware of the nature of the job, and whatever he knew, he wanted to keep hidden. Sheriff Decker felt the frustration building. He didn't want to confirm Sara May's concerns, but when Marie arrived at the station, he had to admit that her worries were justified. And the fact that Arthur knew something about the case but chose to stay silent was more than disappointing.

Chapter 50

"Are you sure this is a good idea?" Chris asked, remembering how the last idea had panned out.

"No. "But I have to do this," Sara May replied, shaking slightly.

The day dragged on with little to report, and night eventually fell, bringing heavy snowfall and fierce gusts of wind that blew the snow in all directions as it tried to settle on the ground. Winter had arrived in full force. It hadn't been easy convincing Chris and Eric to follow her to Old Gilbert's barn, but as always, neither could resist her charm. They weren't sure if it was her beauty or the urge to protect her from the terrible situations she always seemed to find herself in. Old Gilbert had agreed to let them break up the concrete floor in the barn in exchange for their help fixing it afterwards. Max trotted around the trio, barking furiously to scare them away from his favourite resting spot, now at risk. Sara May had apologised to him repeatedly, but his understanding didn't extend beyond the destruction of his spot. She paced back and forth in the barn, desperately trying to convince herself that the nightmare hadn't just been her mind playing tricks. It was a vision. Every time she stopped on top of Max's spot, a jolt of electricity shot through her without warning or explanation. Something was down there. She was sure of it.

The concrete flooring had worn down after decades of use. Max's spot was worn from years of excessive scraping, making it easy for Eric to break up the floor with a sledgehammer. After a few swings, the floor was so shattered that it could be pushed aside, revealing the dirt underneath. Chris grabbed a shovel and started digging. Sara May watched nervously, her heart pounding faster each time Chris moved more dirt aside. She felt dizzy, like her head was about to explode, convinced that if Chris didn't find something soon, she would faint. She glanced at Helena, who stood motionless beside Eric. Something in her unmoving face sent shivers down Sara May's spine. It was almost as if she were waiting for the three of them to share the same shock she had experienced all those years ago. A shock hit her like a roaring wave in rough seas. She remembered every detail now. She knew who had so ruthlessly ended her life with brutal force. Suddenly, Chris stopped digging.

"What the hell is this?" he asked, stunned at what he had just discovered.

Sara May slowly opened her eyes. She was afraid to move closer to the edge of the hole Chris had dug, but her curiosity overpowered her. She took Eric's hand and carefully looked down to see what Chris saw. Something white lay at the bottom of the hole, covered in dirt. Chris started pulling it cautiously, and they began to realise what it was they were looking at. After a bit of dusting, Chris uncovered a broken skull. Horrified, he jumped out of the hole.

"Chris, call your dad. He's gonna want to see this!" Eric said, no less shocked than his friends.

Not needing to be told twice, Chris quickly pulled out his phone. Sara May stared into Helena's deep blue eyes with a sympathetic look.

"Is this you?" she asked. Helena nodded.

Eric chose to ignore the fact that the woman he loved was standing beside him, talking to herself. He wasn't sure if it was because of the blow to the head she'd suffered or if she truly possessed some supernatural talent to hear and see what others could not. He'd never dared question his grandmother's powers, but he always saw them as part of her peculiar personality. Sara May, however, had never shown any signs of being like Nana Lou. She was the complete opposite, which made her all the more captivating to him. He doubted he was man enough for a relationship with such a powerful woman. He was only half the man his grandfather had been; he stood firm by Nana Lou's side for decades without flinching, riding out the waves with her and loving her for all she was. How was he supposed to do that when he didn't even believe in all this mumbo jumbo?

Whether it was due to her head injury or some unexplained superpower, there was no denying that Sara May had uncovered a heap of bones beneath the poorly constructed floor on Old Gilbert's land. She had insisted they dig exactly here. He'd always prided himself on being rational, but this was ridiculous. There was no way she could have known about this, and it was impossible that she just guessed it. He decided to hold his questions for later. He needed to keep everyone calm under these insane circumstances until help arrived. A few moments later, Sheriff Decker arrived with Biggie Mac and two other officers. They had knocked on Old Gilbert's door and asked him to come with them to the barn. The old man wasn't too pleased about being pulled away from his dinner, but reluctantly agreed after a brief fuss. At the barn, they were met by the trio, who showed them the hole Chris had dug. Max ran around like mad, upset that his favourite spot was now the size of the Grand Canyon in his eyes. Sheriff Decker put on black gloves and climbed into the hole, careful not to disturb the bones. He attentively started brushing the rest of the soil away, pulling out what looked like a femur bone. Old Gilbert's eyes widened in disbelief.

"Well, I'll be damned," he muttered.

"Did you know about this?" Sheriff Decker asked, looking at the elderly man and secretly praying he wasn't a cold-blooded killer.

"I may be many things, but I'm not cracked! Don't you think I would have told you if I had?" he replied, slightly insulted by the insinuation. Sheriff Decker flashed a quick, relieved smile before adopting his serious expression.

"We need to send all of this to Reykjavik for further investigation. We need to find out who this is."

"I know who it is," Sara May replied sharply, her voice so cold the bystanders could almost feel it. All eyes were focused on her. "It's my Aunt Helena."

Silence settled over the group. No one knew how to respond. Sheriff Decker gazed at her intently without saying a word. Throughout his lengthy career as a sheriff, he had learned that silence was often the safest choice. There was no way Sara May could know who this poor soul was, but those past few days had shown him that nothing was as it seemed. He opted not to challenge her statement and instead cast a firm look at everyone present, witnessing this chaos unfold in real time.

What has been discovered here tonight will not leave this barn!" Not a word to anyone! Understood?" Sheriff Decker demanded. Everyone silently nodded in agreement.

"You're not gonna leave this here! The mutt will start yapping at it," Old Gilbert warned.

"We'll take the bones with us to the station. I'll get Biggie Mac to take them to forensics in Reykjavik.

Hopefully, they´ll be able to confirm whether Sara May is correct or not. Until then, everyone keeps their mouths shut! If I hear so much as a whisper from the town's twaddlers, heads will roll! Am I making myself clear?"

Nobody dared to object. Everyone present understood the significance of the situation. If news spread that human remains had been found on Old Gilbert's land, it would give whoever was responsible a head start. The chance that the guilty party was still in Northtown was slim, but as long as there was a possibility, everyone present had a moral duty to stay quiet. Biggie Mac helped Sheriff Decker out of the hole before being ordered to go down there himself and collect the bones in a black bag that Chris had insisted they bring. It wasn't very dignified, but the big man did his best to handle the remains as carefully as possible.

Sara May watched in silence. Helena had vanished again, leaving her niece with a flood of emotions she didn't know how to manage. She was happy that her aunt's remains had finally been found, but at the same time, she was trapped in an endless pit of sorrow over her tragic end. She had been so innocent, caring, and loving towards her new baby before a merciless monster took her life, destroying her future. The thought of her aunt's horrifying last moments on Earth, the injustice she faced at the hands of the people of Northtown, and the grim realisation that she had been forgotten filled Sara May with more anger than she had ever known before. It was then that she decided to set aside all her grief and self-pity and instead channel this hate-filled anger to seek justice for Helena once and for all.

Chapter 51

Maggie paced nervously in the living room, feeling uneasy without knowing why. Sara May had grown closer to Eric over the past few days, so it was no surprise that she decided to spend the night at his place. It didn't bother her. Eric was a good man from a good family. She was confident he would be kind to Sara May, provided she had the good sense not to chase him away with her fluctuating temper and quirks. The mother-daughter duo had never seen eye to eye, but those last few days had been exceptionally frosty. It had reached a point where they couldn't even be in the same room without tensions boiling over, and any attempt to talk ended in a fierce argument that only deepened the rift between them.

But it wasn't just the strained relationship with Sara May that troubled her. Something was in the air, wrapping itself around her shivering body. The storm clouds were gathering above Northtown, and she didn't know where to turn. Her mind raced with countless thoughts she couldn't contain, driving her mad. Since Sara May learned about Helena and her baby, life had felt heavier and more dreadful. It was as if she were in shackles, forced to walk around, dragging the heavy chains wherever she went. She couldn't tell Sara May the whole truth; that would be like throwing a nuclear bomb into a closet and expecting it to stay intact after the blast! And she couldn't tell a single soul about the thoughts that were slowly sinking her sanity into a bottomless pit of darkness. She had to keep her composure; she couldn't step out of character now. The show had to go on. But for how much longer? She slumped onto her sofa, finished the last of the lukewarm wine, and let out an exasperated sigh. She feared how long she would be able to keep this up. Cracking under this tremendous pressure was not an option!

No one knew that Margarete Rachel Jensen had never stopped thinking about her baby sister Helena, the tiny little bundle born so puny and fragile. She remembered how happy she felt to become a big sister and no longer be the youngest sibling, whom Marie had made into a personal assistant. Now, she had her own assistant she could boss around. But as soon as she looked at that tiny, adorable little creature, so innocent and sweet, all her plans to be a dictator vanished. From the very beginning, Helena had her completely under her spell. She felt a strong urge to protect her from all the dangers a little sister might face. They had been close despite the age gap, and it had hurt her deeply when Helena rebelled and appeared to lose control of her life. It had nearly broken their God-fearing mother's heart when rumours started spreading that Helena was nothing but a cheap slut who was having carefree sex with married men all over town. Northtown had always been small, but it resembled a village in those days. Gossip like that spread quickly.

Housewives became hysterical with fear that their husbands were involved with an infamous whore, and at least three marriages were believed to have ended because of Helena's behaviour. The hatred towards her, coupled with a flood of threats, eventually became overwhelming, prompting the youngest Jensen sister to flee to the capital city to start anew, leaving her newborn behind. The child was regarded as a bastard, a result of infidelity and betrayal, despite no one knowing who the father was. The rumours had a profound impact on the Jensen women, but with the birth of the baby, all hell broke loose. That virtuous little infant was turned into the main character of the worst horror story ever written through no fault of its own. The grandmother had suffered a nervous breakdown, refusing to have anything to do with the child since it reminded her too much of her daughter's destructive behaviour. She'd been angry at Helena for bringing such shame to the Jensen name by having liaisons around the town, but an illegitimate pregnancy was more than the poor woman could bear. Marie had sided with their mother, and together, they vowed never to mention Helena's name again. She should be forgotten; that would be her punishment for abandoning her child.

Maggie had always tried to be on their side. She had carved herself a mask and mastered pretending she was just as angry at her sister as everyone else. She publicly denounced her and snapped at anyone brave enough to mention her name, as well as forbade anyone to speak of the child. But the truth was that Maggie had never been able to forget the beautiful little bundle of joy she once cared so much for. Deep down, she had always doubted the truthfulness of those nasty rumours, and after Helena had left town, she was plagued with guilt for believing them. Not a day went by that she didn't feel remorse. She missed her little sister tremendously, and the anger had long since given way to pain over how brazenly Helena had severed their contact. Not a single word for over thirty years. Oh, if she could only talk to her for five minutes so she could apologise to her for not being there when she needed her the most.

Suddenly, the living room felt colder than the Arctic, and the fire in the fireplace flickered wildly. Despite the windows being tightly shut, the delicate silk curtains swayed gently from side to side. Her heart slowed as she sat on the sofa, frozen with fear. Sitting alone in the dark, lit only by the glow of the fire, she lost her ability to think clearly. All at once, every sound became frightening. Her breathing grew heavier, and she felt the cold enveloping her. It was almost like someone was hugging her. But she saw no one. Whatever it was, it brought her a strange sense of calm. Her body, once stiff with fear, relaxed as she embraced this odd sensation. There was something so familiar about this feeling, this hug. She quickly stood up and shook her head. Was she losing her mind? She hurried into the kitchen to make herself a cup of tea. Once again, she had allowed her mind to play tricks on her; the coal-black winter nights had been the cause of many nightmares that had haunted the island nation over the centuries. She always considered herself a rational woman who didn't believe in anything beyond what her senses could perceive. But tonight, she couldn't shake the feeling that she wasn't alone.

"I'm here. I know you can hear me. Oh, dear sister, if you could only see me," Helena pleaded."

As Maggie was about to take the first sip of the warm, delicious tea, she felt a tingling sensation beside her right ear, as if someone was calling her name from a distance. She turned around, but no one was there. She had to be on the verge of madness! Her boss had warned her that too many consecutive night shifts could have that effect. She put her cup down and went back to the living room. She needed to get some sleep. Not long after she lay down, her eyelids grew too heavy to keep open.

"Sleep tight, dear sister. "I'll be with you," Helena whispered, receiving a smile from Maggie, who was half-asleep.

"I know," she replied.

Chapter 52

Sara May turned onto her other side for the eleventh time that night. Nana Lou had had to leave town for a few days and asked Eric and Sara May to look after her birds during her absence. In return, they were allowed to stay in the house until she returned, which they happily agreed to. Over the past few nights, they had enjoyed having the whole house to themselves, using the cover of darkness to hide their passionate lovemaking and to be somewhere that kept them safe from the curious eyes and ears of the locals. They were aware of the gossip about their supposed relationship, although no one had bothered to confirm whether or not it was true. It seemed as if the interest in Simon's death had faded quickly once rumours started swirling about the Jensen girl and the Bread Box boy's supposed hookup. It was impossible to know what would catch the town's gossipmongers' attention each time, but both Sara May and Eric had agreed to lay low for as long as possible. Neither of them wanted to give the town's chatterboxes more material than they already had.

Sara May turned again, facing Eric, who was sound asleep. She studied his face intently. She never, in a million years, thought things would turn out this way. They'd known each other since childhood; she had always considered him a friend. But this wasn't the innocent little blond boy who had followed her every step and obeyed her every command. This was someone entirely different — a strong, muscular man, his arms and half of his back covered in sinful tattoos, and his scruffy beard matched his dark, tattered hair. His broad shoulders supported his large frame, his jaw so sharp it could cut through glass, and his trim nose was perfectly positioned between the two darkest-blue and most mysterious eyes. He was like some devilish version of perfection. A dangerous temptation she couldn't resist. How he had gone from a scrawny little weirdo to this stunning mix of attractiveness and a heartthrob was beyond her understanding. After turning for the thirteenth time, she gave up trying to sleep. She got up, careful not to wake Eric, and tiptoed to the kitchen.

The night sky blessed her with a billion stars, the moon casting its beams through the kitchen window. This was a welcome break from the gloomily grey clouds that had covered the sky above Northtown for days. She opened the fridge and poured herself a glass of ice-cold milk. She paused for a moment and gazed out at the dazzling scene. With the moonlight illuminating the nearby surroundings, everything appeared calm and silent. Yet she didn't feel at ease. She half-expected a group of dead people to suddenly appear out of nowhere and rush towards her, hoping to catch her attention as Helena had done. Despite the soothing glow of the night outside, Sara May was on edge. Just to be safe, she moved away from the window.

"What are you doing up at this hour?" Eric asked sleepily, making her jump.

"God, you scared me! Don't do that!" she hissed, trying to calm her rapidly beating heart.

"Sorry, but when the woman I fall asleep next to isn't in my arms when I wake up, I go look for her," Eric replied defensively, placing his hands firmly on each side. Sara May sighed. Could he be any sweeter?

"I couldn't sleep."

"Any particular reason why?"

"I was just thinking about Helena and all the stuff that's been going on lately." Eric let out a loud exhale and sat down by the kitchen table.

"How did you know there were human remains underneath the flooring of Old Gilbert's barn?" he asked, his voice sounding even more serious.

"She led me there. Those nightmares I've been having. It was her, showing me what happened to her."

Eric didn't say a word. There was no logical explanation for how Sara May could have known about the bones, but he was unwilling to accept her ridiculous story. The idea that the spirit of a deceased woman had somehow appeared in her dreams to lead her to her remains was so absurd it bordered on insanity.

"You don't believe me, do you?" she asked without taking her eyes off the kitchen window.

"It's not that I don't want to; it's just that... you have to admit that this isn't something that would stand up in court." She turned around, crossing her arms as she did so.

"And why not?"

"Because it's crazy! Telling people that a ghost came to you in a dream and told you where she was buried? It's ludicrous!"

"What do you want me to say? That I've always known about the bones and just decided to keep my mouth shut until now?" she asked, louder than she intended, escalating the argument. Eric quickly stood up, facing Sara May.

"You're trying to blame this on the pastor! That's like dragging God to court!" he yelled, louder than necessary, with her standing inches away from him.

"Only if you believe in him!"

"You are so bloody stubborn! Why can't you just leave it?"

"Why don't you want her to have the justice she deserves?" Sara May asked, her voice trembling.

"You don't even know if it's her or not!"

Just as she was about to lash out at the impossibly thick-headed moron in front of her, a loud crashing noise snapped both of them out of their fierce argument. A rock was hurled through the kitchen window, shattering the glass into countless pieces all over the floor and the kitchen counter. Sara May screamed as Eric instantly pulled her to safety. In his peripheral vision, he saw a dark-clad figure run away from the house, hoping not to be seen. He swiftly ran to the front door and flung it open, only to be met with the empty, moonlit street and no sign of the culprit. Sara May bent down to pick up the rock that had smashed Nana Lou's kitchen window. Around it, someone had wrapped a piece of paper with a rubber band. She carefully removed the crumpled paper. The large, black letters stood out from the creamy white paper.

Leave!

Her hands trembled. She hadn't allowed herself to think about the danger of delving into people's personal lives and secrets, many of which needed to remain hidden. She knew she was playing with fire but buried the potential consequences deep down. A furious Eric, still seething from their intense argument, stormed into the kitchen, angry at himself for letting the felon escape. After checking that Sara May was unharmed, he looked at the paper she handed him. Who would want to hurt her? Was this threat aimed at her or Nana Lou? Northtown had always been a quiet little place where nothing truly exciting ever happened. Now, it seemed as though it had been thrown into a hurricane overnight, as if some malevolent deities had been awakened and ordered to take over, destroying everything in their wake, sparing neither people nor property.

"Are you going to?" he asked, referring to the threatening note.

"No. I'm doing this for Helena, and I will take this all the way, whether people like it or not!" Sara May replied, confidence mixed with anger.

Eric stared at her so intensely that she wasn't sure whether he was going to shout at her or make mad, passionate love to her. From the start, he had opposed this whole thing because he knew digging too deep would stir up trouble that could endanger her. But his strong feelings for her had become more dominant than his frustration. This message was a clear threat, and he had to decide. Was he going to keep pushing back against what he considered complete nonsense, or stand by the woman he clearly loved, despite being horrified by all this ghost talk? He lowered his hands to his sides, shook his head, and stepped away from her.

"Fine. If you're gonna keep being stubborn, I won't stop you."

"Is this your way of saying you're going to believe me?" she huffed, not impressed with this response.

"No. But despite you being impossibly dogged and incredibly irritating, I'm in love with you, so I would rather be on your team than against you."

Sara May offered a coy smile. This was the first time she had heard Eric admit to his feelings, and somehow, that made him even more irresistible than ever before. She slowly approached him, as enticingly as she could.

Pressing her body against his, she gently ran her fingers from his belly button to his neck, caressing his sharp, bearded jaw as she stared into his deep blue eyes. This was an invitation filled with temptation, one he would never be able to resist. He threw his arms around her waist, pulling her in for a lustful kiss before swooping her up to carry her back into the bedroom.

Chapter 53

Sheriff Decker looked at the phone in front of him. He had a job to do, a task he desperately wanted to avoid at all costs, but he knew he couldn't delay it much longer. Biggie Mac had managed to get the bones undetected to Decker's friend, a forensic anthropologist who had worked tirelessly for days trying to identify who they belonged to. Sheriff Decker had taken a considerable risk by going behind Chief Chase's back, but he didn't trust him. Chase had been too eager to dismiss Simon's death as a suicide. It was like he wanted the case closed so he could sweep it under the rug without further investigation; to Sheriff Decker, that seemed very suspicious. Therefore, he ordered confidentiality from his entire staff and entrusted Biggie Mac to deliver the bones to Mike Miller, the on-call forensic anthropologist.

The process took two weeks. Time dragged slowly, and it didn't help that Sara May was glued to the doorstep of his office, bombarding him with questions about the case. Finally, the results landed on his desk and confirmed his fears. Although he couldn't identify exactly whose remains they were, Mike managed to estimate that it was a young woman in her mid-twenties and that the bones had probably been buried for over thirty years. Sheriff Decker sat by his desk, staring at his office phone, pondering his next move. It wasn't often that he found himself at a loss for words and ideas, but suddenly, all options seemed closed. He rubbed his eyelids and let his hands slide down his face sluggishly before resting on the desk. Damn it. The Jensen girl was right. But he couldn't bring himself to pick up the phone to tell her. It bothered him, not knowing how she had discovered the bones or how she knew they belonged to Helena. She couldn't have just stumbled upon the exact spot by chance; that was impossible. Something must have led her there. Sheriff Decker had always been sceptical; anything that reality couldn't verify was simply a trick of a tired mind. He resented talk of the supernatural and despised those who claimed to have powers enabling them to communicate with ghosts and mythical beings. He was a man of science, as he had always been. But no matter how hard he tried, he couldn't find an explanation for how Sara May knew what she knew.

Suddenly, he felt as though the temperature in the office had dropped below freezing, and a cold gust of wind swept through it at lightning speed. How could this be possible? The window was closed, and the A/C had had the same setting since September. The lightbulb above his head began flickering as he caught his breath and steadied his rapidly pounding heart. He cursed his laziness for delaying the bulb change despite its signs of failure. He had barely finished the last silent curse when the desk phone's receiver popped off, landing by his left hand. Startled, he jumped and quickly stepped back from the desk. He pressed his back against the wall and swiftly scanned the room with his eyes, wiping sweat from his forehead. His breathing was heavy, and his heart pounded faster than horses in a race. This couldn't be happening. He refused to let some silly ghost story get the better of him, composing himself as he desperately searched for a logical explanation. However, the suddenly eerie atmosphere offered little room for clear thoughts. Sheriff Decker slapped himself on both sides, causing his entire body to shake.

"Get a grip, man!" he threatened himself, annoyed that

he had allowed his fears to undermine his sense of reason.

If Sheriff Decker had given in to his imagination, even for a moment, he would have opened his mind to the idea that something was beyond his common sense, and it wouldn't have surprised him that Helena was now standing beside him. It wouldn't have fazed him that she had used all her energy to throw that receiver his way, lower the temperature, and mess with the broken light bulb. After making sure there were no witnesses to his sudden outburst of character, Sheriff Decker summoned the courage to pick up the phone and call the one person he did not want to speak to.

"Sara May? Hi, it's Sheriff Decker. Can you come to my office? I need to speak to you."

She didn't need to be told twice. She'd been waiting for that dreaded phone call for what felt like an eternity, repeatedly having to assure Eric that she was fine and nothing was wrong. It was only half-true, but that didn't matter. Everything she'd worked towards over the last few weeks depended on the outcome of this one phone call. She knew that Pastor Evans was a cold-blooded killer, a liar, and a lowlife. Helena had not only shown her his heinous crime, but she'd been able to describe it in detail after her bones were found. It was a bittersweet victory. Sara May felt guilty for forcing her to relive the trauma that her merciful death had taken away from her to ease her suffering. She felt terrible for pushing her aunt to recall all those painful memories, but there was no turning back now. Justice had to prevail. Sheriff Decker leaned forward, his hands clasped as he prepared to deliver the news to Sara May, who sat across from him on the other side of the desk.

"Alright, I'm just gonna get straight to it. "How did you know about those bones?" he asked in a firm tone, one he'd perfected after years on the force.

"It's Helena. Isn't it?" Sara May replied with a straight face. Decker's demanding tone and emotionless expressions did not affect her.

"That's not important right now."

"That's what this is all about! Was I right or not?" She was growing increasingly agitated. After trying to throw her off with a stern stare and failing, Sheriff Decker let out a loud exhale as he leaned back in his chair.

"Yes. You were right," he finally acknowledged.

Sara May sat quietly. She had known for some time. Everything that had transpired had brought her to this point. But hearing it aloud that her suspicions were correct was not as fulfilling as she had imagined. Without warning, a wave of profound sorrow swept over her, and she could feel the ball in her throat swell, threatening to unleash a flood of tears. She shook herself and straightened up. No! This was not the moment to break. She had to keep face; she had to carry on! Sheriff Decker, still with his palms firmly pressed together, stared at her intently, waiting for a logical explanation despite knowing the chances of that were slim to none.

"How did you know it was Helena, and how did you know she was there? This doesn't make any sense."

"She showed me. And she told me what happened," Sara May replied, knowing Decker wouldn't believe her.

"She told you?" he sceptically replied, raising his eyebrows a wee bit.

"Yes. Ever since I returned to Northtown, she's been appearing in my nightmares.

"And I assume you talk to her as well."

"Yeah. I wouldn't have found her otherwise." Sheriff Decker sighed heavily.

"You must hear how crazy this sounds, right?"

"Do you prefer any other explanation?"

"Any explanations that make more sense would be greatly appreciated! I suppose you'll tell me Pastor Evans is behind all this."

"He is!" Decker buried his face in his hands, resisting the urge to scream. After calming down, he moved his hands, revealing his frustrated face.

"And why do you say that?" he asked as gently as he could.

"Helena was found on Old Gilbert's land. He bought it from Paula's father after his son-in-law, Evans, refused it despite it being owned by the church. When Old Gilbert needed to fix the barn flooring, Evans offered to do it for him. If Helena had been there before he started fixing the floor...."

"He would've found her."

"Exactly."

Sheriff Decker had to summon all his strength to maintain his professional composure as a respected police chief. He couldn't risk being perceived as an unstable lunatic, especially with the stakes so high. However, his inability to find a logical explanation tested his patience and nerves. Sara May had been right about Helena, so there was no reason she shouldn't be right about Pastor Evans. For a long time, he had suspected the holy fool to be more sinister than anyone dared imagine. Since childhood, he'd disliked Evans, but because he'd also been friends with the now prime minister, Crow, he had pretended to be amiable towards him. The thought of the pastor committing one of the most heinous crimes known to man made his skin crawl, and he could feel his stomach knotting. If Sara May was correct, it would turn all assumptions about the disappearance of the youngest Jensen sister upside down. Sheriff Decker leaned in toward Sara May, who sat silently, more determined than ever.

"Very well. I'll look into this. But until I figure something out, I want you to keep this to yourself."

"What? You know I can't do that!" Sara May protested.

"That's an order, Sara May. I need time to work this out."

"What am I supposed to tell Mum and Aunt Marie?"

"Nothing. They still think Helena is alive, living in the capital. Let them think that until we have something concrete to work with."

Sara May rolled her eyes and slumped back in her chair. The excitement of finally finding her aunt's remains was completely gone. Nana Lou had warned her to brace for the worst once it surfaced, but she couldn't have known how brutally she was paying the price. Her blood boiled. The thought that Sheriff Decker wasn't as eager as she was to tackle this head-on filled her with more fury than she believed she had. He had belittled her. He had completely ignored the fact that she'd handed him this case on a silver platter, and in return, he'd tied her hands behind her back by ordering her to keep quiet until he'd investigated it in his own time, as he thought best. She could feel her veins, which pulsed like scars, and her blood boiling like lava deep within the Earth's core. How dare he? But what could she do? She was only one woman. All her efforts to bring attention to this case had fallen into his hands—a sheriff who had now taken control without her consent, ensuring that the silly little girl didn't interfere with his big, manly job. She wasn't going to let him get away with this.

Chapter 54

Paula, the pastor's wife, stood in her elegant dining room, adding the finishing touches to the renowned afternoon tea party she hosted at her home each month. To outsiders, it appeared to be the most lavish buffet of delectable treats she had effortlessly prepared. She enjoyed inviting the other socialites of Northtown and listening to them praise her culinary skills, as she loved basking in the compliments she received. In a way, it had become somewhat of a game. Being a practical housewife and keeping a home that was always pristine reflected well on any respectable woman with polished homemaking skills. It was something likely to garner admiration and envy from other women — the most coveted prize in town. One mistake, however, could cost her everything, turning their respect into spite, making her the subject of gossip, and causing a swift fall from the top of the social hierarchy. That thought chilled Paula to her core. As she placed the final apple pie on the large dining table, she removed the apron snugly tied around her waist and gazed with pride at the beautifully decorated table, smiling at her performance, which was once again exemplary.

The doorbell rang, and Paula hurried to answer it. Her lively little minions had arrived, all dressed in their finest and eager to critique every detail. After numerous kisses, insincere compliments, and fake flattery, the women moved to the dining room to praise the feast. As usual, not a single piece of negative criticism could be heard. The elegantly dressed gossipers agreed that such a lavish banquet hadn't been seen since the Last Supper. It was all very superficial, like a well-rehearsed play, but to stay in the good graces of the woman who controlled the town and its people behind the scenes, they had to sacrifice their dignity. After flooding Paula with a standing ovation and false praise, the women sat down and prepared to exchange news over delicious pies and a cup of tea.

"I heard that Mitchell, Athena's boy, has finally settled down!" one minion gleefully announced.

"About time!" another scoffed as she took a dainty sip of Earl Grey from the hand-painted china cup, pinkie finger raised.

"Is she from around here?" the third one asked.

"No, she's an out-of-towner, I heard. From the city." The whole lot gasped in collective shock.

"Well, I never! Poor Athena, having to endure such crude barbarism in her own home! I bet you she can't even cook!" the fourth minion hissed.

"Nothing but vulgar savages crawling from city sewers!" The other women nodded in agreement.

"You got that right! I mean, look at that pitiful Jensen girl! So uncouth! And now she's got her filthy paws all over the Baker boy! He's such a fine young man; it's just tragic!

"The Baker Boy isn't the only thing she has her hands on." I heard she's knee-deep in Helena's disappearance. She's relentless, and it's driving poor Maggie absolutely mad!"

As usual, Paula sat quietly at the end of the table, listening intently and weighing each rumour like a ruthless judge. Hearing those two names mentioned in the same sentence sent shivers down her spine, causing the hairs on the back of her neck to stand in unison. She had always believed that the rumour she had started over thirty years ago was enough to make people sigh with relief that the hyper-sexual homewrecker had finally left town. No self-respecting woman cared for having such a nasty whore sniffing around her husband, regardless of how good the marriage was. It had made it much easier for Paula to convince people that Helena had left of her own free will and that she would never return. That settled the matter. Evans could finally get her out of his mind and begin directing all his love and attention towards the woman he'd married and pledged to remain faithful to.

But three decades later, the dust stirred up again, swirling into a formidable sandstorm. Pastor's wife Paula never thought she needed to worry about Sara May. She had never shown any interest in her family history, being too eager to leave town at the first chance she got. When she turned eighteen, she packed her bags and kept her promise, prompting Paula to celebrate triumphantly. Her plan had worked. Helena had disappeared, and Sara May had left. There were no loose ends. She never imagined the girl would return with an unexplained interest in her family's darkest secrets. However, three decades of lies and deceit had transformed the respectable pastor's wife into a professional. She could almost make a large dining table buckle under the weight of a generous buffet, and she could easily hide her emotions and malevolent thoughts behind the well-polished mask she had crafted. Nobody dared to mess with the fierce vixen that was Paula, the pastor's wife.

Later that night, when the grandiose yentas had gone, full of pies, tea, and new gossip that would last until next month, Paula sat by her desk, powdering her nose before going to bed. Being a religious woman, she always believed that it was every woman's duty to look her very best at all times, especially before going to sleep, just in case the Almighty Father might suddenly end her life in the middle of the night. No woman should ever want to meet her Maker looking like a common street hoe. She was about done combing her hair when Pastor Evans entered and went straight to bed, exhausted after a busy day. It was difficult to uphold Christian values and ensure that people behaved accordingly. Paula continued combing her hair without acknowledging her husband, giving it a rounded, puffy appearance. Her makeup was flawless, and so was her hair.

"There was much talk at today's meeting," she announced, admiring herself in the mirror.

"Anything good?" he asked, showing no interest at all. He'd never been one to follow the latest gossip, but he learned a long time ago that it was worth at least pretending to listen.

"The Jensen girl is up to her elbows in her family history, they tell me." Pastor Evans looked up from his book. Paula had caught his attention. "You know what that means?" she calmly continued.

He didn't reply. He had always known it would come back to haunt him, having failed to tie up all the loose ends when he had the chance. He silently cursed himself for being so reckless. Thinking the problem had been resolved when Sara May willingly moved away was a foolish assumption. He had always counted on her refusal to return, given how eager she'd been to leave in the first place. When Maggie told him Sara May had left town, it was like a divine intervention in a sequence of events he was about to lose control of.

"Don't worry, darling," he said after a long pause. "I'll handle this."

"You better. We've spent too much time building our reputation around here, and I don't want to repeat the previous fiasco to fix it!" Paula sternly reminded her husband.

That said, she gracefully rose from the desk and slipped into bed, turning her back to him before closing her eyes. Pastor Evans watched her as she fell asleep, wide awake himself. Paula was a good woman. Had circumstances been different, he probably could have loved her the way a husband is meant to love his wife. She had been a faithful companion all these years and a valuable asset to his reputation as the noblest man in Northtown. She had looked the other way each time he was overcome by a sexual itch that prompted him to betray his vows. She overlooked many of his character flaws and quickly dismissed any rumours that might have landed him in hot water. She fiercely defended him, mainly to protect her own reputation, and for that, he was forever grateful. Therefore, he could tolerate the fact that she had shown him virtually no romantic affection since they married. Their marriage had always been more for show than anything else.

Not feeling remotely tired, he got out of bed and walked to the kitchen. Something didn't seem right. A storm was approaching, and if nothing were done, the house of cards would collapse faster than he could handle. He needed to act quickly. He thought of all the connections he'd built over the years that could now benefit him. His ace had to be Prime Minister Crow, who not only knew about his most heinous misdeed but had also helped him cover it up all these years. Having a friend who held the highest office in the land was about to pay off. Crow could use his influence as the most powerful man in the country to quash any rumours that might start to circulate. Chief Chase was also a valuable asset. He'd always been under Crow's thumb, and in return, Crow had granted Chase more freedom to bend the rules as police chief, even going as far as breaking the law without a second thought. That sort of leverage would be helpful.

All of a sudden, the temperature in the house plummeted below zero with the flick of a finger. The darkness became so thick he could almost reach out and touch it, and the cold was so fierce he could see his own breath. The kitchen had turned into a walk-in freezer. His feet felt frozen to the floor, and he was unable to move a muscle. He sensed someone beside him. Then, behind him. And again, beside him. But he saw no one. Terror overwhelmed all his senses, causing his palms to become clammy and his whole body to tremble like a leaf.

"Who's there?" he managed to yell into the empty void. No reply. "Show yourself!" he shouted again, his voice trembling with fear. Still no reply.

Was he losing his mind? Despite portraying the perfect servant of God who believed in all things holy, he was, deep down, a sceptic—so much so that he thought those who truly believed were laughable at best. But at this very moment, he felt as if his inky black conscience had summoned a devilish figure that now held him hostage. The intense fear had stripped him of all reason, and the only thing he could think of to fend off this hellish creature was flailing his arms around like a lunatic. It seemed to work. An eerie silence followed, so profound that it increased the cold that enveloped him. He looked around without turning. Hell was waiting for him in every corner, and for a moment, without warning, Helena

Jensen's angry face appeared before him, scaring the last nerve out of his body and sending him running out of the front door into the pitch-black night, screaming in panic.

Paula was awakened by her husband's frantic shouting and came running down the stairs, seeing only the pastor's receding back. She sighed. It wasn't unusual for him to have terrifying nightmares that affected his mental health. Often, they had been so real and ghastly that they made him bolt out of the bedroom, overwhelmed with hysteria. She was used to it, but it still worried her. He had never run out of the house before; he usually stopped at the foot of the stairs. The nightmares had to be worsening. Despite her many attempts, he had never been willing to tell her what they were about, let alone discuss them to understand. But she suspected that the events from thirty-one years ago played a part. If that were the case, she could expect his already fragile temperament to deteriorate further in the days and weeks ahead.

Chapter 55

Maggie sat silently by the kitchen table, staring at her half-empty cup of tea. It had been nearly two weeks since she last spoke to her daughter, and it weighed heavily on her. She wanted to be angry at Eric for supporting this ridiculous behaviour, but he couldn't help how insanely tenacious Sara May was. Naturally, he would always stand by her now that he finally had her. The man had loved her for years, and now that she'd finally noticed him, he would never let a mother-daughter row come between them. She groaned as she clutched her cup more tightly. She knew this wasn't Eric's fault; she just had an urge to blame someone else to ease her guilt towards her daughter. She'd raised a headstrong mule and needed to approach her accordingly.

Finally, she stood up from the table and poured the remaining cold tea into the sink. From there, she walked into the living room and slumped on the sofa, both physically and mentally drained. She glanced at the bookcase next to the fireplace for a moment. It was where she kept all the family albums since John packed his bags and left the sinking ship. She reached for one, and before she knew it, she was walking down the yellow brick road of memories. The album was filled with baby pictures of Sara May. She'd been such a beautiful child. Maggie's tear ducts tightened. She felt like such a hypocrite. None of this would have happened if she'd just been honest with her from the beginning. She had a right to know the ugly truth that her mother had let spread like cancer ravaging a sickly body. After browsing for a bit, she put the album away and got up. She needed to find Sara May. She had allowed this to continue for too long, and Pastor

Evans's attempts to extinguish the flames hadn't worked. She wrapped her dark blue coat around herself, determined to make things right. As she pulled open the front door, she was startled to see Pastor Evans standing outside, about to knock.

"Jesus, you scared me!" she gasped as she put one hand on her chest, her heart beating like a drum.

"Pardon me, I didn't mean to startle you, my dear," the pastor calmly replied.

"No, that's fine. What can I do for you, pastor?"

"I need to talk to you about Sara May." Maggie took a step back.

"Is everything okay? Did something happen?" she quickly asked, fearing the worst.

"No, no. Everything is fine. I've just been thinking about her sudden interest in her family history, and I wanted to stop by to see how you're doing. Is she here, perhaps?" Maggie shook her head.

"I haven't seen her in days. I was just on my way out to go find her and hopefully have a talk about all this." Pastor Evans's sinister grin quickly turned to a frown.

"I don't think that's the best idea, my dear."

"Oh? Why not?"

"It's been so long, and I'm afraid it will just upset her even further if she hears the truth after all this time. It might even push her further away from you. Is that what you want?"

"No, of course not. But what can I do? She's asking all these questions."

"Try to distract her; have her think about something else. Think of the consequences if she were to find out," the pastor warned.

As he turned to walk away, Maggie was left with more

questions than answers. What on earth was that? She decided to heed the pastor's warning and went back inside. This called for another cuppa! Moments later, she was back where she started — sitting alone at the kitchen table with a cup of tea that would turn cold before she could finish it. Pastor Evans's cautionary words echoed in her mind, and the more she thought about it, the more convinced she was that he was right. Sara May knew bits and pieces of Helena's story, but she deliberately kept things from her out of fear of pushing them further apart. Pastor Evans reminded her that there was a reason why she and John demanded silence from everyone who knew anything about the day Helena left.

She was pulled out of her thoughts by a faint thumping sound coming from the living room, as something had fallen on the floor. She hurried to check and discovered the album she had been browsing lying in front of the bookcase. She cursed at not putting it back in its place and bent down to pick it up, only to see a photograph lying next to the album—one she thought she had thrown away years ago. Wide-eyed, she picked up the picture and examined it closely. In the photo, Helena was standing beside the large oak tree just outside of town, a tree that the sisters all loved. In the picture, she was smiling from ear to ear, looking nothing like the troubled young woman she later became. Suddenly, Maggie's composure broke, and tears streamed down her cheeks. She didn't understand why the album had fallen open right where this particular photo had been put, but nothing felt like a coincidence anymore. She put the album away again and sat on the sofa, still clutching the photo. She should have known that bringing Sara May back to Northtown was a bad idea. Ever since they pulled into the driveway, everything had started to go downhill. She felt as though she was strapped onto a roller coaster she was forced to ride, with no sign of slowing down. Oh, if only Sara May could find it in her heart to return her mother's phone calls. Then she could tell her about this strange feeling she had been experiencing for a while—the sensation that her dead sister had returned. She was constantly around her. It was she who pushed the album; it was she who whispered in her ear. Was she trying to get her to speak to Sara May in person? Was she trying to tell her the opposite of what Pastor Evans had said? How was she supposed to decide whom to listen to? Her dead sister or the town's pastor?

She sighed heavily. Life had suddenly become so complicated and cruel. She'd known for a while that Helena was dead but had been too afraid to ask what had happened. Who was she going to ask anyway? The other Jensen women didn't want to hear her name mentioned, and nobody in town seemed interested in remembering anything about her. So, none of them seemed likely to know what had happened. Not even Laura, Helena's best friend, had spoken a word for years, and Maggie never dared to ask. She knew how Laura felt about the Jensen women after the way they'd treated Helena, so she wasn't likely to speak. Sara May was the only person who seemed somewhat interested in knowing the whole story. Maggie felt more alone than ever. This was a heavy burden to bear, but it was damn near impossible without any help. She couldn't talk to the church because Pastor Evans was the figurehead who ruled that institution with an iron fist, and he'd already made his feelings on the matter quite clear. Sara May wasn't allowed to know anything. Nothing should be said; nothing should be done. Maggie sank further into the sofa. She looked outside the living room window and saw a beautiful white bird sitting on her front garden fence, staring straight at her. Her heart leapt. Was this a sign? Of course it was! She fished her phone out of her left pocket and quickly dialled.

"Nana Lou? Hi, it's Maggie Jensen. Did I catch you at a bad time?"

Chapter 56

While Maggie went to speak with Nana Lou, Prime Minister Crow had just finished an important call with his childhood friend back in Northtown, prompting him to sit in his leather armchair and carefully consider his next move. Pastor Evans had informed him that there was a real threat that the events thirty-one years ago might resurface due to a young woman's persistent questioning. Her relentless digging into the matter jeopardised everything they had built over the past three decades, and that was something Prime Minister Crow wouldn't tolerate. He'd made one foolish mistake as a young man, and now that was coming back to haunt him, threatening to destroy his entire life. He should have known. Such things could never remain hidden forever.

With his hands securely in his pockets, Crow stood up and walked towards the giant floor-to-ceiling window in his office. Pastor Evans had financed his early political career and continued to do so whenever he needed Crow to be present at the right place and time. This support had enabled Crow to climb the bloodstained social ladder, which ultimately earned him the title of Prime Minister— the most powerful position in the country. With this newfound power came the privilege of decision-making. Some were made very publicly to boost Crow's image as someone elected by the people, for the people. But then there were the deals made discreetly, three pints in after a few rounds of golf. He was eternally grateful to Pastor Evans, but couldn't help but think he would have been better off getting the money from someone else. He had, without thinking, helped Evans bury Helena Jensen's body beneath the concrete flooring at Old Gilbert's barn simply because he believed he was assisting a friend in desperate need.

But Evans had never shown so much as an ounce of remorse. He simply went on with his life as if nothing had happened. He even chose to study theology to reduce the likelihood that anyone would connect him to Helena's disappearance, because nobody would suspect a pastor, God's most sacred servant, of anything criminal. For years, Crow had held onto the hope that Evans would regret his actions, but he never did. Instead, he confided in Crow that he had killed again, this time a poor, innocent chap from Northtown. Simon had simply been in the wrong place at the wrong time when he accidentally saw the duo bury Helena. He'd kept that secret over the pastor's head for years and paid for it with his life. Now, Crow faced a serious dilemma. He was no stranger to it, but this time, it was different. Should he drive to Northtown to warn this young woman that her snooping was endangering her, or should he keep his mouth shut and, by doing so, secure his place as the most powerful man in the land? A position he had no interest in giving up; it was too comfortable. It was true he hadn't earned this role by acting on his conscience; he had repeatedly had to push it aside to justify his numerous wrongful actions over the years. Gradually, he stepped back from the window, grabbing a half-full glass of whisky on his way to his desk. He drained it in one gulp, then placed the glass down and shook his head slightly. He had made a decision. He had worked too hard for his place in society to give it up for some dim-witted girl in a lousy farmer's town nobody cared about.

"Celia. Could you contact Chief Chase and ask him to meet me at my office as soon as possible? Thank you."

Crow ordered through the desk intercom.

His assistant, Celia, did as she was told, and within half an hour, Police Chief Chase was sitting opposite Crow, separated by a large, dark-brown mahogany desk. The Prime Minister flashed a grin. It had its advantages, being an authority figure who could make people drop everything and rush to kiss the ring whenever he wished. Chase had been appointed chief of police when Crow was Minister of Justice years earlier. The man had always remained loyal to Crow's political party, proving he could be trusted to look the other way when necessary. Therefore, Crow didn't hesitate to let him in on what had happened to Simon, keeping Chase well-informed about the situation. His lucrative career was largely supported by members of his party, and he was well aware of the responsibilities that came with it. Crow cleared his throat, fixing his gaze on Chase.

"Evans called me earlier. He informed me that some woman up north has started snooping around things she shouldn't."

"Is that something we need to worry about?" Chase asked.

"Perhaps. If there is even the slightest chance of anything leaking out, I can almost guarantee that jobs and reputations are at stake. That goes for both of us." Chase wriggled in his seat.

"With all due respect, Crow, I had nothing to do with the burial of this Jensen woman."

Crow lowered his brows, making his face so severe that even the hardened capital city police chief felt a sense of discomfort. "If this gets out, the media will learn about the police chief who was aware of the crime and chose to ignore it. We wouldn't want to exclude anyone now, would we?" Crow subtly threatened with a broad, malevolent smile. Chase shook his head and sighed, recognising he was in an impossible situation.

"What do you want me to do?"

"Make sure that Sheriff Decker stays on top of this. At all times."

Chase smiled as he stood up and shook Crow's hand, promising to take care of this little mess. The lack of morality never troubled him; it let him handle things his way without guilt. Throughout his career, he had earned the respect of the elite simply by obeying their every command without question. Kissing the ring had never been an issue for Chief Garret Chase, as long as it benefited him. And it had. While the public was outraged by his often brutal methods of maintaining law and order, the aristocracy turned a blind eye and pretended not to notice. The public condemned his corruption; the elite relished it. Bringing Sheriff Decker to his knees wouldn't be a problem. After the deal was sealed, Chief Chase straightened his back and walked confidently out of Crow's office, knowing he had just strengthened his position.

Celia had been standing outside the door, listening in. Something didn't sit right with her. She's worked as the Prime Minister's personal assistant since he was Minister of Justice, so this wasn't unfamiliar; organising his meetings with high-profile individuals was routine, and Chief Chase was no exception. But something about the meeting she'd been asked to arrange on such short notice had unsettled her. Knowing what was at stake, she straightened her posture and strode confidently into her boss's office.

"Was there anything else you needed, sir?" she asked.

Crow looked up from the pile of paperwork he was currently working on.

"No, thank you," he replied, returning to the paperwork.

"Okay. I'll be heading home then, sir."

Crow waved her away, clearly annoyed by the interaction. Celia stepped backwards towards the door before closing it behind her. With one hand full of work-related folders, she retrieved her phone from her back pocket and called her boyfriend, Mike, who had previously worked on identifying the origins of the bones found in Northtown.

"Mike? Hi, it's me. Listen, you have to call Decker. You'll never believe what I just heard!"

Chapter 57

Sheriff Decker thanked his friend Mike for informing him and hung up. The war had begun. However, Decker believed he still had the upper hand because Chief Chase and Prime Minister Crow didn't know about the bones. It was more crucial than ever to keep that a secret. Weighed down by the sudden heaviness of life, he exhaled deeply as he looked outside his living room window. From there, he had a clear view of the valley where Northtown was located. The Deckers had decided to build their future home on a small hill overlooking the town so nothing could block this beautiful view. As the town expanded, town officials ensured that no skyscrapers could spoil the view for those who had chosen to build a bit further south. Sheriff Decker smiled just a little. This town held so many memories. He remembered his childhood when he had run around with Evans and Crow like wild animals, carefree and happy, innocent and naive. He remembered the old warrior games they'd played for hours on end. They'd fought hard with carved-out wooden swords and wooden shields painted with every colour of the rainbow. It was every man for himself, and the battles sometimes lasted for days, taking place all over Northtown.

This childhood memory now felt uncomfortably relevant. He'd never been close with Evans, only tolerated him for Crow's sake. And although he still cared for Crow, he'd drifted away from him years ago because of his extreme political views and the ruthless methods he used to climb the ranks. To think that Crow also had a hand in this horrific crime shattered all the rules they had ever set during their relentless childhood battles. He'd never been this corrupt, and Sheriff Deker believed he hadn't become so dishonest until his political career began. He had to act the part. That was the only way he could justify his friendship with someone like Crow because being friends with someone capable of such heinous acts was too much to bear. It was increasingly clear that Sara May had been right all along. The Pastor's hands were stained with blood, and the Prime Minister's conscience was disturbingly ruddy. If the media uncovered the truth, it would turn the nation upside down overnight. Sheriff Deker was pulled back to reality by the vibrating phone in his back pocket.

"Decker."

"Hi, it's Chief Chase here. Listen, I just got off the phone with our good friend Crow, and he seems to be worried about some rumours that might be going around in that little town of yours. Have you heard anything about that?"

"Why does he think that?" Sheriff Decker replied, trying to stay calm so as not to raise any suspicions.

"You tell me," was the ice-cold answer on the other line. Damn it. The stoic tone didn't work.

"I don't think he has anything to worry about. Life is as dull as ever around here. Nothing exciting to report."

"I'm glad to hear that. I won't bother you then; I'm sure you're pretty busy with all that boredom. Just remember, Decker, there is no tenure in our line of work."

"Is that a threat?"

"Make of it what you will."

There was a click before Sheriff Decker could reply, and everything went silent. He threw his phone onto the sofa and cursed the situation. He should have known it wasn't safe to poke a sleeping bear. This confirmed his fears. Chief Chase was as corrupt as they come and had chosen to play the Devil's game. He was acting on behalf of those who controlled this country, and it wouldn't be easy dodging their attempts to shut this thing down. He needed to act quickly. He knew roughly who was on his team, but paranoia infiltrated every thought. Could he really trust them? He thought about Sara May, whom he hadn't heard from since he forbade her from sharing her information. He wasn't sure if she'd obeyed him or not. That woman danced to the beat of her own drum, and trying to get her to comply was as tough as taming a zebra. A wild-born creature would always stay true to its nature despite the shackles.

After a while, he decided to take a walk to clear his mind. Martha was still at work. She was a cashier at the town's only bank, so she had little time to show any sympathy for her husband. He buttoned up his dark grey cashmere coat, put on his matching cap, and headed out into the harsh November cold. On his way through town, he passed many familiar faces. He nodded and gave occasional greetings with a smile. But he couldn't help but feel some were not keen on returning his gestures. He felt malice, as if someone was watching his every move. Was he succumbing to some mental disorder? He couldn't walk around letting people think the sheriff in town was nothing but a bloody crackpot. He looked around for Sara May but didn't spot her anywhere. He passed Nana Lou's house, where he saw Eric fixing her kitchen window.

"Hello there, mate!" he called out. Eric turned around.

"Hello, Sheriff. What's up?"

"Not much, I'm afraid. Say, you don't happen to know where I can find Sara May, would you?" Eric shook his head.

"No, I'm sorry. She hasn't spoken to me in a couple of days." With his hands placed firmly at his sides, Sheriff Decker sighed deeply and shook his head disapprovingly.

"What the hell did you do now, boy?"

"Me? She's the one running around telling people she's seeing dead people!"

"And you don't believe her?"

"Do you?" Eric asked, as if it were the stupidest question he'd ever heard.

"It's not a matter of believing as much as supporting."

"I can't be a bloody cheerleader for this kind of bullshit. I told her that a ghost's testimony would never fly in court. We had a big fight, and she walked out on me. I haven't seen her since."

Sheriff Decker thanked Eric for his time and moved on. He deliberately kept his worries to himself, knowing it was useless to try to get information about a woman from a man who was angry with her. Not knowing her location or her mental state unsettled him. If she believed everyone was against her, she was far more likely to catch the first bus out of town. She could easily blend into the crowded capital; she would ensure no one could find her. A burnt child fears the fire; if that was true, this was now a race against time.

Eric watched as the sheriff walked away. He was too upset to continue fixing the window, so he put his tools away. There was no point in carrying on if all he could think about was his own misery. He'd started the repair to distract himself from Sara May, but now the sheriff had forcefully reminded him of their latest quarrel, stripping him of the little peace he'd managed to find recently. He entered the empty house, only to be greeted by the occasional loud tweets of birds. Nana Lou had been at

Maggie Jensen's home for the last two days, so she was completely unaware of the latest developments between the two lovers. He slumped onto the sofa, frustrated with the situation, but most of all, he was angry at himself. He knew it was his duty to support Sara May in any way she needed. That was part of committing to another human being. But at the same time, he felt that in doing so, he would be denying her the help she so desperately needed.

And if that wasn't enough salt in a fresh wound, he knew exactly how this fight would end. She would eventually storm up to him and shout at him for a short while, and he would shout back even louder, then they would end up having sex — so lustful and animalistic it was like they loved to hate each other. They'd become addicted to this viciously passionate cycle, so much so that they'd lost all desire to break free from it. As much as he wished for a healthy relationship with a normal person, he knew very well he was in love with a very unusual woman. Sara May had always been one of a kind, which initially attracted him to her. He finally sat up and stared into the empty nothingness. How could he be so foolish? He was in love with a fierce warrior who showed all signs of being as rare as a unicorn. Loving her in the conventional sense would never work. He was supposed to support all this ghost nonsense because the relationship demanded it. He was supposed to accept this woman because Sara May's unusual traits demanded it. He had to love her for everything she was, not for what he wished she could be.

Chapter 58

The snowy blizzard howled outside, bringing a wave of tension as the stormy winds swept through. Sara May turned onto her other side. This bed was so uncomfortable that she considered walking out into the storm and sleeping on a snow-covered rock. Northtown had never been known as a luxurious stop for memorable nobles and movie stars, but this was ridiculous. This was the only motel in town, and it definitely needed a freshen-up. After tossing and turning and growing increasingly frustrated, she turned onto her back and stared at the ceiling. It had been painted a dark brown, somehow matching the floral wallpaper that covered most of the walls, only peeling in a few places. The wooden floor was sticky, and the old tube television sitting in the corner of the desk across from the bed hadn't been updated since the 90s. The room smelled of cigarettes and sweat, a deadly combination for anyone hoping for a good night's sleep.

As she gazed at the ceiling, she couldn't help but feel like the main character in a low-budget horror film, about to be murdered by a desperate drug addict on acid. But this was her only option. She couldn't go home to her Mum; that was out of the question. The rift between them had grown wider than the entire continent of Asia recently; every conversation turned into a full-blown argument. She couldn't go home to Eric; she knew how that would end, and she wasn't about to fall into that trap again. The man seemed to possess some sort of superpower. All he had to do was look deeply into her eyes, and her willpower snapped like twigs. How was she supposed to win a fight with an impossibly handsome man who played dirty like that? Because of this, she had decided to stay away until they had both calmed down. Although she wasn't at all sure she had done anything wrong.

The problem was that no one believed her. Everyone just assumed she didn't realise how crazy this was or how insane she sounded. All her life, she had to listen to lectures about how she didn't understand her own feelings, and how what she felt was somehow invalid. She was constantly told she was making a big fuss about nothing and was just being overly dramatic. She ought to stop whining, wipe away those tears, and hold her head high. As a result, she'd always been ashamed when feeling down, so she trained herself not to feel that way—she would talk herself out of any negative emotions. She'd never been free to let those feelings flow. It was almost as if only positive feelings were allowed because everything else was depressing, and nobody wanted to deal with that. Now, she was a grown woman who didn't know how to deal with anything negative, despite it being such an intergrated part of human existence. Some days, she was a sobbing mess. Some days sucked. But she always felt she was doing something wrong if she expressed herself properly. Stop being such a baby! Toughen up! It was a mantra she had grown up with. These feelings were in her way, tripping her at every turn, and she didn't know how to handle any of them. The humiliation of having to listen to people lecture her on how ghosts weren't real, even though she saw them as clearly as living humans, was the ultimate punch in the gut. She'd never felt so alone, just when she needed her closest people the most. They had failed her. Instead of listening to what she had to say, they blamed the accident for her sudden craziness. They had no trouble listening when everything was sunshine and rainbows, but ran away like rats in the rain when life hit back. Nana Lou was the only person to offer any support, but she'd spent the last few days with Maggie, so she was no help.

Again, Sara May turned to her side, fighting back tears. *"You don't know what true love is; you're not a mother"* was another thing she'd been told quite regularly. *"What do you have to be proud of? Not like you're doing anything with your life"*, Paige's friends had once said on a night out she'd stupidly agreed to. Then they laughed. *"Come on, Sara May, be real. You think you have a chance against the big shots in the city? The real authors? Those people are professionals!"* Paige had repeated again and again. The cruel fact was that Sara May had nothing to offer except her feelings and conviction. And when that was marked as being overly dramatic, she started to doubt herself and the justification of those feelings. It was hard moving forward when the resistance had the mighty force of a hurricane that knocked her down repeatedly.

After attempting to fall asleep on all sides, she finally gave up and sat upright, feeling every bone in her body ache with pain. She looked around. She was alone. Alone in this room, alone in a lonely struggle. At this moment, she made a decision. It was time to stop allowing people to bring her down when they couldn't even stay by her side when she needed them most. This was her life, her feelings. She had lived with them for over three decades; she knew them better than anyone. She wouldn't allow anyone to call her dramatic, sensitive, or overly emotional ever again. No one would be allowed to tell her how to feel or think. She might not be a highly educated CEO or the mother of many children, but she knew who she was and what she saw. She was a single, emotional, fierce woman who saw ghosts. And right now, one in particular needed her help, whether others chose to believe it or not. She smiled, confident in her newfound strength. So what if people thought she was odd? She had no use for them anyway.

Not even a blizzard or powerful ocean waves could stop her now. She wrapped her light brown coat around herself and hurried out into the howling snowstorm outside. Oh, how she despised this never-ending Nordic winter. It was just endless snow and wind, chillingly cloaked in the coal-black darkness until it turned into a greyish slush. Usually, she would have stayed indoors on nights like these. But not this time. Thinking of Helena, she marched through the growing mounds of powdery snow, heading straight for Sheriff Decker's house. She was determined to put him in his place and regain control of her aunt's case. Halfway to the Decker's home, she suddenly glanced to her left and saw a light shining through the kitchen window of the Lewis's house. That was odd; Suzy usually went to bed early. Seeing this, the wind swept all her plans away. She turned and walked over to the house. As she approached, she saw Suzy leaning on her kitchen table, a half-empty vodka bottle in one hand and a cigarette in the other. She looked rough.

She sighed before carefully knocking on the door and stepping inside. It was common in Northtown for people not to lock their doors. She didn't know the house's layout very well, but Suzy's heart-wrenching sob from the kitchen was hard to ignore. As she rounded the corner, her heart missed a beat. There she was, the poor widow, all alone, her soul empty and cold. Her sunken eyes had dark circles around them, her skin was dry and colourless, and her cheeks were so hollow they resembled a skull of someone recently deceased. Her untidy hair was a mess, her clothes were stained, and she reeked of cigarettes and alcohol. Suzy hadn't been seen by anyone since Simon's funeral. She had withdrawn from life, becoming nothing more than a shell of her former self, and it seemed nearly impossible to bring her back.

The latest gossip was that the poor woman had gone mad with grief. She spent her days alone, behind closed curtains, with the lights off and the TV on. The only people unfortunate enough to encounter her were the ill-fated workers at the liquor store whenever she needed a refill. Jack and Jake avoided their mother like the plague, Jake because he couldn't stand being around drunks for too long, and Jack because he felt his mother's behaviour was a stain on his otherwise flawless reputation. He wasn't about to let her addiction, which was rooted in grief and loneliness, harm his chances of a burgeoning political career. In a way, the twins had lost both parents the day Simon's body was discovered. Sara May edged herself closer to Suzy, who didn't seem to notice her at first.

"Suzy? Hi, it's me. Sara May," she whispered carefully, coaxing Suzy to look at her, so wasted and grubby she could barely hold her head up.

"What the hell do you want?" she growled before taking another gulp of the vodka.

"I just stopped by to see how you're doing."

"Huh! Like you care! Nobody gives a damn! Except for my Simon." Suzy stared down at the empty glass.

"You truly loved him, didn't you?" Sara May sympathised with the grieving woman.

"He was mine! Always mine!" Suzy howled, her voice cracking, wiping her dripping nose with her dirty sleeve.

"The service was beautiful. Pastor Evans did a good job."

"Hah! That pathetic prick! That miserable waste of air! He's nothing but a demonic murderer!" Suzy shouted and slammed her clenched fist on the table so forcefully that the vodka bottle nearly fell over, almost rolling off before Sara May caught it and put it back.

"What do you mean?" she asked, steadying the half-empty bottle.

"Simon knew what he did," Suzy mumbled. "That's why he killed him! That holy clown murdered my husband!"

Sara May's eyes widened. "What did Simon know?" she asked, knowing the chances of getting a solid answer from a severely drunk and slightly hysterical woman were slim.

"He saw Evans and Crow bury Helena under Gilbert's barn. So, Evans bought his silence," Suzy slurred. "How do you think the Brewer managed to stay open in this dump all these years? The pastor was paying!" Sara May couldn't believe what she was hearing.

"But if he chose to pay, then why did he kill Simon all these years later?" Suzy let out a chuckle as Sara May assisted her with pouring the last of the vodka into the glass.

"Because Simon found out the twins were not his. I got knocked up the only time I ever lay under Evans. Ain't that a bitch? Simon went berserk and threatened to snitch. Evans couldn't allow that."

Sara May sat opposite Suzy, completely numb. It was easy to dismiss this as crazy talk from a woman so intoxicated it would shame even the town's drunks. Suzy had drunk herself halfway to hell; people often lost their credibility after too many drinks. Of course, the trauma she'd endured and the grief that followed might have eventually driven her to madness, so it was best to take her words at face value. But if what she said was true, it could be a vital testimony. If she managed to persuade Suzy to speak with Sheriff Decker and tell him everything, it would likely be enough evidence to arrest Pastor Evans and make him confess to Helena Jensen's murder. Suddenly, she felt overwhelmed, unsure of her next move. The pastor of Northtown, the town's most revered man, had committed two murders thirty years apart without anyone suspecting a thing. And before her sat a woman so distraught with anguish that she was willing to sacrifice what little she had left—booze, the only thing that seemed to bring her even a hint of peace. She felt deeply sorry for Suzy. Her only crime was willingly sleeping with a venomous predator and bearing his two children. And for that, she had paid the ultimate price—losing the love of her life, her sons, and her dignity—gaining only crippling pain and sorrow.

Sara May slowly rose from the kitchen table and said farewell to Suzy. There was nothing she could do for her, but plenty she could do for Simon. As she left, she made up her mind. This was not just about seeking justice for Helena and granting her the long-overdue peace of mind she deserved. It was also about ensuring Simon's name was cleared for Suzy's deteriorating mental health. She'd given her vital information, and Sara May chose to believe her despite her fragile mental state. She'd claimed that Pastor Evans had killed Simon because he threatened to expose him. But that didn't explain why he killed Helena. What had she known?

Chapter 59

"Helena? Are you here?" Sara May called out to the empty hotel room.

"I'm here," Helena's soft voice whispered behind her, making her jump.

"Stop doing that! Can't you ever manifest in front of me?" Helena smiled.

"And miss this reaction?" she chuckled. Sara May was in no mood to echo her laughter, not even sparing a smile.

"We know that Pastor Evans murdered you. We know he's the evil man, right?" Helena's coy smirk faded.

"Yes. he's the evil man. You saw what he did."

"There is a Sunday service tomorrow at the church. I'll be there."

She didn't need to explain herself any further. Helena understood. Her smile widened more than ever as she nodded in agreement and vanished into thin air. Sara May lay down on the hard bed and began devising a plan in her mind. Her phone buzzed every few seconds with messages from her mother, Sheriff Decker, Chris, and Eric, all desperately trying to find her. Frustrated by the constant interruptions, she quickly turned her phone off. She didn't intend to ghost them forever, but if she was to succeed, she had to ignore them for now.

Sunday arrived bright and beautiful, which was unusual for Northtown in mid-November. The fresh snow sparkled where it hadn't been touched and lay like a white, duck-feather duvet over everything in sight. She knew the service was scheduled to start at noon. Pastor Evans had begun preaching early a few years back so the churchgoers could use the rest of this holy day to relax. At least, that was the public reasoning. The atheists in town, however, believed it was so the pastor could hurry home and enjoy his whisky and cigar, exhausted after a few hours of work. Sara May kept her distance at first, watching the faithful herd flock into the small, timbered church. It soon filled up. Slowly but surely, she made her way inside, taking a seat on the bench nearest to the door on the right. Nobody acknowledged her; everyone's eyes were fixed on God's holiest servant by the altar. Pastor Evans stood like a towering mountain, dressed in his black vestment, holding an open Bible in one hand and using the other to emphasise his words, much like a choir conductor.

"Our Lord in Heaven, forgive all those who ask. Be kind to one another, tender-hearted, and forgiving, as God in Christ forgave you. Judge not, and thou wilt not be judged. Condemn not, and thou wilt not be condemned. Forgive, and thou will be forgiven." As those last words left the Pastor's mouth, Sara May quickly stood up, seething with fury.

"Is my family supposed to forgive you? Or is God the only one who can do that?" she asked confidently. She didn't flinch despite all eyes suddenly resting on her. Pastor Evans remained calm.

"What do you mean, my dear?"

"You know damn well what I mean!" she shouted, the flock gasping at the cursing in Lord's house. "You preach that if we confess our sins, God, being ever so merciful and righteous, will forgive us and grant us absolution. But what about us? What about Suzy and the boys? Where's our justice? Are we just supposed to forgive you for what you did?" she continued, clenching her fists, fighting the fire within.

"May I remind you, Ms Jensen, that you're in God's

house," Pastor Evans ominously warned, becoming increasingly angry with how the situation unfolding. He hated losing control, and no one had ever challenged his authority in church.

"You're a murderer!" Sara May hissed through clenched teeth. Her entire body shook with a mix of adrenaline and pure hatred. She didn't give a damn anymore. She had entered this battle armed with heavy weapons, ready to fight to the last drop of blood.

The congregation gasped in collective shock. Some were appalled by the blatant accusations, and others were astonished that this young woman dared to be so bold in the house of their Lord! Seconds later, the Sunday service descended into utter chaos. Aunt Marie, who sat on the left in the front row, hurried down the aisle, dragging her niece outside, while Maggie attended to Grandma Gladys, who had nearly fainted with shame. Paula's face was contorted with outrage as her husband tried unsuccessfully to regain control of the crowd. Aunt Marie managed to push Sara May out of the church. Furious with rage, she forcefully shoved her niece onto the muddy ground.

"What the hell is wrong with you?" she shouted, consumed by blinding rage over this latest humiliation. Sara May half-rose, only managing to get on her knees after the brutal fall.

"People need to know who he is!" she yelled, her voice trembling.

"Have you completely lost your mind? I've spent too many years clearing our names in this town after Helena's bullshit; if you think you can just come in here and…."

"He killed her!" Sara May interrupted. Her vision was

growing blurry, and her voice had taken on a high-pitched, screeching tone.

"Are you mentally ill? Helena left town!"

"Helena's dead! Pastor Evans murdered her!"

She couldn't hold back her tears any longer. They spilt down her cold cheeks, mingling with snot all over her pinkish nose. It didn't matter what she said; nobody would ever believe her. Before Aunt Marie had the chance to bury her alive, the crowd stormed out of the church with Maggie and Grandma Gladys leading the way. Sara May had never feared for her life as much as she did at that very moment. Her grandmother strode towards her, cane in hand, her face flushed with embarrassment, and Maggie trailing behind, ready to stop her mother from committing whatever crime she was hellbent on carrying out without a second thought. Seeing her sniffling granddaughter, nearly crippled with fear in the mud, shivering and alone, didn't seem to affect Gladys Jensen in the slightest. Her bony hand tightened its grip on the cane. She was angrier than ever before.

Sara May, I have lived a long life. I've seen and heard many things. But I've never been as humiliated as I am today! This family has been through enough! The Jensen name was mercilessly dragged through the mud, and it has taken over thirty years to restore it to its rightful glory! And now, here you are, bound and determined to shatter it to pieces once again! How dare you?" Grandma Gladys preached, her fragile old body trembling with anger and disgust.

"Grandma, you have to believe me, I...."

"Enough! I don't wanna see you, I don't wanna hear from you, I don't wanna know you. You are no longer part of this family."

After passing her judgment, the old lady turned and walked back towards the church, where the stunned crowd stood silently, witnessing this public execution. Sara May was left behind, tears in her eyes, trying to save face as best she could. Grandma Gladys had never treated her like a grandchild anyway; why should she deserve those tears now? Aunt Marie cast her niece one last disapproving look before catching up with her mother, leaving Maggie to handle the sobbing mess on the ground. Caught between a rock and a hard place, Maggie sympathised with her daughter, who'd just hammered the final nail into her coffin. She would probably never be able to show her face in Northtown again.

"Mum. They found some bones…" Before she could finish the sentence, Sheriff Decker stepped in, placing himself between the mother and daughter.

"I'll handle this, Maggie, don't worry. Sara May, if you would follow me, please," he suggested.

"I'm not going anywhere with you!" she protested, stepping away from him.

"I am the Sheriff in town. I'm not asking again. Either you come with me, or I'll be forced to use the cuffs," he replied sternly, waving the handcuffs in front of her.

Chapter 60

Sara May sat in Sheriff Decker's office, her hands clasped and her eyes refusing to meet his. The silence was so tense it could cut glass. With every passing second, she half-expected him to drop a bombshell. There was no chance in hell he'd let her get away with this. The Sheriff was furiously pacing behind his desk, trying to devise a plan to salvage what was left. The two viewed this case from two different angles. Sara May knew Pastor Evans was the twins' father, a fact that had sparked the fight between Simon and Suzy. The pastor had killed Simon, just as he had killed Helena years earlier. But what motivated him to murder her remained a mystery she hadn't managed to solve. Therefore, it was crucial to force the pastor to confess as soon as possible. In her view, calling him out in front of everyone had been necessary. Sheriff Decker, however, had wanted to take a different approach. He had taken a huge risk, jeopardising his entire career by going behind Chief Chase's back when the bones were discovered. The longer he kept it all secret, the better his chances of making sense of it and hopefully solving the case. But now, Sara May had blown everything apart without a second thought. He ran his right hand through his messy, greying hair. Two twisted strands fell onto his forehead, hiding the wrinkles above his lowered brows. His eyes flashed with anger as he fought to regain his composure.

"Would you mind telling me what the hell you were thinking back there?" he shouted, slamming both hands on his desk. A tactic he'd seldom used on the town's lawbreakers but which always proved very effective.

"Does it matter? You're gonna yell at me either way,"

Sara May replied calmly, rolling her eyes as she snapped the sheriff's last nerves in half.

"You were screaming like a lunatic, accusing the town's pastor of being a murderer! In a church!"

"I didn't scream; I yelled. There's a difference. And he is." Sheriff Decker sighed as he sat down, burying his face in his hands. Why was this woman so bloody difficult?

"This had to happen. Somebody had to say it," she continued.

"No. Nobody had to say it! And especially not right there! Now the whole town is talking, and I've lost all control damn it!"

"Everybody's talking about me and my psychotic meltdown. Nobody's thinking of Pastor Evans. You still got time."

Sheriff Decker lowered his hands from his face as he leaned back in his chair. He was about to give up. He had no control over this case or Sara May, so there was no point in trying. This infuriatingly headstrong fighter across from him didn't listen to any reasoning or suggestions. She answered to no one. This was like picking a fight with a tiger and hoping not to get mauled to death. Sheriff Decker had thrown in the towel for the first time in his long career as a police officer in Northtown.

"Why did you decide to do this? Why do you think that Evans is a murderer?" he asked, his facial expression indicating exhaustion.

"Suzy told me everything," Sara May replied without hesitation. At this point, she didn't care if the Sheriff didn't believe her.

"Suzy Lewis?

"Yeah. I met her last night."

"She's nothing but a darn drunk! You can't possibly think you can build a solid case based on her yakking!" Those words lit Sara May's heart and soul on fire.

"She's not a damn drunk, Decker! She's a very broken woman in pain who lost her footing when her husband was murdered, and this is how she deals with it! She doesn't have to make excuses for how she's repairing what Pastor Evans broke!"

Sheriff Decker raised his brows as he clenched his fists in shock. Hearing those words startled him. Until now, he'd been convinced that no one knew what really happened to Simon. He'd asked Mike to stay quiet, mainly to buy himself time to process the fact that his friend of many years had endured such a terrible fate. If Suzy knew more than she was revealing, she needed to be questioned immediately, regardless of her credibility. Sara May crossed her arms again. She could tell by the look on the Sheriff's face that this had caught him off guard. The tables had turned once again, and a smile played on her lips over her small but significant victory. Standing firm and refusing to back down had paid off.

"I'll tell you what I know and how I know it if you promise to listen and believe me," she negotiated.

Lowering his brows once more, Sheriff Decker stared deeply into her eyes. Those eyes reflected a bold, dynamic woman with a fiery soul and a fighting spirit. She was a warrior who showed no mercy. Nobody had ever put him in his place like this. Giving him an ultimatum was out of the question; that's how he had worked to become the town's sheriff. He didn't like this latest power move. She had pinned him to a wall, and he had no choice but to comply if he wanted any chance of a countermeasure.

"I can only promise to do my best," he muttered, against his better judgment.

"That will do," she replied, lowering her weapons.

While Sara May poured out every piece of information she had gathered, a wave of shock and confusion swept over Northtown. Her meltdown at the church was all anyone could talk about, and every venomous gossip in town scrambled to come up with reasons for her sudden psychotic episode. What caused it? Why had she accused the town's holiest man of being a murderer? Those had been some heavy words, coated in sin, spoken in the house of God, creeping into every crack and smearing the church with blood. People were horrified; some even felt physically sick. Others hurried out of the church, fearing the Lord's looming wrath. Whatever caused this unexpected outburst, it was clear that it stemmed from somewhere. A sane person wouldn't throw around baseless accusations, especially accusing a clergyman of being a ruthless killer. Something must have triggered it. Northtown was turned upside down. This was the main topic of conversation in every home and workplace.

"The Jensen home must be on fire right now," could be heard from one house.

"I just can't imagine Gladys will stand for this!" echoed from another.

"Some nerves that girl has! Coming back here after all this time and straight away callously attacking that sweet, innocent man!" was heard at one out of two hair salons in town.

Not a corner could be found where this juicy conversation wasn't being dissected. The town's gossip factory had been supplied with enough material to keep it running smoothly into next year. But some had no interest in it being aired publicly, let alone discussed. In at least three houses in Northtown, emergency meetings were held. The old rotary phone at the pastor's manor was about to catch fire from Paula's excessive use, emitting a loud screech to whoever answered on the other end. Her role was to regain control of the chaos, and she did so by trying to convince people that Sara May's outburst could be blamed on her accident weeks earlier. She had suffered a severe blow to the head before returning to Northtown, which caused her to hallucinate. While Paula used her position as a respected woman of high status to influence local opinion, her husband sat at his desk in the office, waiting patiently. He relied on his wife's detailed lies to persuade others and to protect his reputation from further damage. He had spent years shaping a favourable image of himself, and now that was being tested. He knew he had some loyal followers who would never believe anything negative about him, even if the evidence was shoved down their throats. But that wasn't enough. Paula had to convince every man, woman, and child in town that Sara May was just a wacky screwball who was mentally impaired after the accident.

The Jensen house was also convening a crisis meeting. Grandma Gladys and Aunt Marie spun around in circles, furious and utterly speechless, aside from a few carefully chosen curse words. It cut deep that one of their own had dared to pull out the dagger and force it into an open wound. It was more than the two could handle. Sara May had no respect for the relentless effort they had put into repairing their reputation and cleaning the dirt off the Jensen name after Helena's shameless behaviour. Maggie had, however, spent an evening at Nana Lou's house earlier that week and gained insight into parts of Sara

May's complicated character, parts that Maggie had never known about. That had affected her perspective so profoundly that she could no longer align herself with her mother and sister. Shouting and crying could be heard from the Jensen house, prompting passersby to stop and listen, quickly realising that the conflict stemmed from a fractured family with a shattered reputation.

Bill and Laura also arranged a meeting at the Bakers' home. Nana Lou had contacted her son and convinced him to host the gathering because their house was larger and could accommodate more people. Her guides in the spirit realm had warned her that if nothing was done, more people would suffer the consequences than she realised. When Maggie unexpectedly arrived at her door on a chilly Wednesday evening, Nana Lou knew it was time. She welcomed her inside and spent the next few hours revealing to her Sara May's colourful yet intricate reality, which was connected to a different realm hidden from most. The war had begun. Time was running out, and Nana Lou needed to rally her troops and give instructions like a five-star general. Those troops were now huddled in the Bakers' living room, ready to gear up for a fight.

Chapter 61

The harsh Nordic winter had arrived with all its tyrannical might. Occasional blizzards, combined with freezing temperatures, formed a relentless alliance. Icy pavements and heavy snow replaced blooming flowerbeds, and instead of the uplifting sounds of chirping birds, the ghostly howling wind battered everything in its path. Sara May strolled along Northtown's High Street. She wrapped her light-brown coat more tightly around her shivering frame and pulled her hat just below her eyebrows, tilting her head down to avoid awkward eye contact. That was wishful thinking. She felt the spiteful stares of the locals burn holes in her with every step she took. Some pointed, others whispered, and the occasional few turned away, revolted by her very presence. Every thought was filled with hate; every nerve stretched to its limits with boundless wrath. It was clear she was no longer anyone's favourite. Some felt sorry for her, recognising she had brutally lost her mind after the accident. But most wanted nothing to do with her. They preferred to feast on the gossip she had thrown their way with her unprecedented behaviour at the church.

She wasn't delusional. She knew what she faced. Very few were willing to show understanding or goodwill. But it still hurt. It crushed her to hear Grandma Gladys condemn her so openly in front of everyone without giving her a chance to explain her side. It shouldn't have surprised her, though. Grandma Gladys had long sought an excuse to cut ties with her. She'd never understood why the old lady hated her so much, her only granddaughter, but over time, she learned to accept it. It had been a bigger blow to see her aunt turn against her. In a moment of madness, she thought Aunt Marie might still have a bit of kindness left. But that was clearly just a pipe dream. The larger-than-life socialite had always been the centre of attention, the sun revolving around her. Still, from time to time, she genuinely cared about her niece, even watching out for her like a dutiful aunt. All that was now behind her. Sara May wiped away a sneaky tear and quickened her pace. She just wanted to reach the filthy motel, crawl under the duvet, and forget the world for a little while. She had used her last money to pay for a few nights' stay; soon enough, she'd be rummaging through rubbish bins for food. It was odd how she knew so many people in one town but was practically homeless. There was no sanctuary anywhere, only a cold, dark place. Tragic was the tale of Mary and Joseph.

When Sara May reached the motel, she suddenly saw a striking figure walking towards her. It was a lady everyone noticed as she stormed down the street with her head held high, dressed in a thick, brown fur coat that kept out the bitter cold but made her look like a giant yeti. Sara May prepared to step aside to let the boastful pastor's wife pass, but instead of ignoring her, the grandiose madam stopped right in front of her, foaming with violent fury.

"How dare you show your face around here? After everything you've done!" Paula hissed through her tightly clenched teeth.

"I don't wanna argue with you, Paula," Sara May replied, trying not to let her see how terrified she was.

Nobody wants you here! Get the hell out of town, and don't even think about ever coming back! We lived in perfect peace and harmony before you came back, and we would like to continue doing so!"

Before Sara May could fight back, Paula hurried past her, deliberately bumping into her so hard she nearly fell onto the snowy street. At that moment, something inside her broke. Trembling and humiliated, she looked around to see that a group had gathered to witness this unexpected duel. The look on their faces showed they all agreed with Paula. It would be best for everyone if Sara May left town as soon as possible. They won. At last, she didn't hold back the tears, allowing them to flow freely and mix with the freezing snow battering her face. She turned around and ran. Away from the motel, away from everyone. She didn't care about her belongings in the room; it no longer mattered. A little while later, she arrived at a small café that also served as a bus station for those needing to catch the coach, which came twice a week. Suddenly, Helena appeared before her.

"Where are you going?" she asked, her expression perplexed.

"Leave me alone! I'm done with this shit!" Sara May shouted, her voice trembling, her breath heavy.

"What do you mean?"

None of this matters! I haven't had any breakthrough, and everyone around here thinks I'm just a delusional psycho who needs to be kicked out of town!

"Then don't prove them right!" Helena pleaded.

"I can't do this anymore," Sara May replied, her chin trembling. "I'm going back to Reykjavik."

"Sara May. Everyone here thinks that's what I did. That I just gave up and ran away. Please don't make them think the same thing about you. Please. One of us has to win."

Sara May knelt over, sobbing uncontrollably. No one had her back. No one stood up for her. She had exposed Pastor Evans as a savage murderer, but that backfired, and she was branded as a hysterical lunatic who had gone crazy after a blow to the head. She led Sheriff Decker to the human remains, but he muzzled her and forbade her from speaking of it. She had given Eric all her love and affection, but he rejected it. She was a one-woman army sent by the ghost of a dead person to fight a horde of monsters in the hope of long-overdue justice. But her soul was severely bruised. She was so exhausted and hurt that she barely had the strength to stand up.

"Helena, I can't do this! I'm done! Do you hear me? I'm done!" she shouted so loudly that it startled nearby passers-by. But she didn't care.

"Sara May, do you need help?" she suddenly heard behind her. She turned around to see Chris standing a few feet away.

"Why would I need help?" she yelled, still enraged.

"Because you're standing out in a snowstorm, shouting at no one."

She looked around. There was no shortage of judging faces that had already formed an opinion of her odd behaviour. Whoever was to blame, the Jensen girl had completely lost her mind, and those who chose to believe her over the compassionate and generous Pastor Evans were no better. Chris approached his friend slowly until he was close enough to put his arms around her and pull her into temporary safety. She buried her face in his chest, allowing the tears to flow like a river.

"Come on. I'll open the Brewer." We can't have you standing out here in this weather; you're freezing," Chris said as he took off his jacket and wrapped it around her, rubbing her shoulders to generate some warmth.

Without saying a word, she obeyed and walked, pressed against Chris's left side, enjoying the protective comfort of his arm over her shoulders. Amidst the chaos, she had forgotten how good a friend he was. She had become lost in her love for Eric; the rosy-coloured glasses had blinded her and prevented her from seeing how kind and attentive Chris was. She genuinely cared for him and regretted not turning to him sooner as her problems started to mount. As they walked, he pulled her close, shielding her and allowing her to carry on without worrying about the judgmental locals all around. He shot dagger-like glances at anyone daring to stare, turning them away in shame. He hated how she had been treated, and his warning death stare made that very clear to anyone passing by. After what felt like forever, the two friends finally reached the Brewer. Chris opened the door and told Sara May to sit while he locked the doors behind them.

"Wait here. I'll go and find something for you to dry off. I think there's a blanket and some staff clothing in the back that should fit you."

She thanked him as he disappeared behind the bar. For a moment, there was silence. A strange atmosphere filled this old, empty pub, which had once thrived with activity. The emptiness eerily reflected what had once been. She felt Simon's spirit drift around, leaving its mark on every table and chair. He had fostered a rough culture in town, according to those who considered themselves too proud to engage in such blasphemy. Nonetheless, there were hardly anyone who hadn't at some point sat down at the Brewer for a pint. Chris had bought the pub shortly after Simon's death in a bid to expand his business empire. To his surprise, Suzy directed him to Pastor Evans, who eventually agreed that Chris could take over, provided he demonstrated better management skills than his predecessor. The fact that Pastor Evans had been the main financier of the Brewer was unsettling and made Chris doubt his motives. What had Simon been involved in? When Sara May stood up in church and accused the pastor of being responsible for the deaths of both Helena Jensen and Simon, that unsettling feeling returned. He had discussed it with Eric, whose main concern was that he hadn't been able to contact Sara May, given her seemingly rapid mental decline.

It had taken Chris some time to persuade Eric that she wasn't crazy and might genuinely be onto something. He was devising a plan that involved Eric's support because Sara May needed him more than ever. He'd been hesitant at first, but as he approached her now, all doubt vanished from his mind. He was in the right place at the right time. Sara May backed away when she noticed him slowly walking towards her. What kind of ambush was this? Her body immediately shifted into defence mode, and her eyes searched the pub for a quick escape. But Eric's fiercely determined stare held her in place. He moved closer, taking each step slowly. If he went too quickly, she'd run. Time seemed to stand still, and life was on hold. Their surroundings blurred; at that very moment, only the two of them remained on the planet. Eric kept his eyes on her, and within seconds, he was standing so close she could feel his heartbeat. He slowly raised his left arm, gently caressing her cheek, then softly moved his hand up through her damp hair. He placed his right arm around her back, drawing her nearer. For a split second, they were as one. Her trembling body invited him in as her lips desperately searched for his, but he teasingly moved away with a coy smile, kissing her nose, cheeks, and neck instead. Their breathing grew heavier, their vulnerable bodies losing the fight to the uncontrollable passion they always failed to resist.

"I'm so sorry," Eric whispered in her ear.

"You've been such an ass!" she replied without pulling away from him.

"I know."

"Promise me you'll stop being so difficult."

"I promise," he replied, continuing to place lustful kisses on her neck.

Nothing prepared an unprotected heart for love. Life could adapt to ever-changing times, but a loved-up heart remained unchanged. She was mad at him, so she fought hard against the urge to forgive him. She wanted to be mad at him forever, but at the same time, she wished he'd never loosen the hold he had on her. His embrace assured her that from this moment on, she'd never have to fight her battles alone. Suddenly, she heard a commotion behind him, snapping her out of her daze. Eric turned around, revealing a group of people marching from behind the bar. Her eyes widened in surprise, and her hands released their grip on Eric's shoulders. He smiled as if to confirm that he was behind this unexpected ambush.

Chapter 62

"What are you all doing here?" Sara May asked, dumbfounded.

"You can't do this alone, dear. You need all the help you can get," Nana Lou replied, placing her soft hand on Sara May's cheek.

Those words, along with the feeling of Nana Lou's warm, reassuring touch, sent a shockwave through her body, nearly causing her to collapse. Her vision had become so blurred that she could barely distinguish who was standing before her. She saw Nana Lou and Old Gilbert. Between Bill and Laura stood Eric; to the left, she saw Sheriff Decker and his wife Martha; to the right stood Chris, then Biggie Mac and his wife Mary, who, along with Jake, supported Suzy Lewis between them. Overall, twelve people had turned up to support her.

"We've been talking, and we all agree that something is off with Pastor Evans," said Laura.

"And that has nothing to do with us not liking the church," Bill added with a cheeky grin.

"I spoke to Martha, and she assured me it wasn't just you and me who had information about Helena's case. She urged me to go speak to more people," Sheriff Decker admitted, receiving a smile from his wife.

"And after your mother came to see me, I thought it was time for people to stop this nonsense and band together," Nana Lou announced firmly.

"We're stronger together," Chris reminded the group.

"And we all hate Pastor Evans," Jake added, prompting a protest as nobody wanted to use such a heavy word.

There was a strong sense of unity within the group.

Everyone had kept a secret they never thought worth sharing publicly. But now, it was like a powerful yet mysterious energy had been released. Everyone felt an overwhelming urge to talk about what they had kept to themselves for so long. Some secrets had been buried deep within their souls for years, poisoning their mental health like a nasty infection. Others were more recent and needed to be shared. Chris rang the Pizza-Lot and arranged for the staff to prepare boxes of pizzas to feed the group but asked the delivery driver to come through the back door of the Brewer to avoid being seen. This was a highly confidential meeting that required discretion.

After the food had been served and eaten, it was time to talk. Everybody agreed that Pastor Evans was not as he appeared, and that had probably been the case for years. Mary, Martha, and Laura all admitted to being victims of sexual harassment—two of them while working for the church in their twenties, and one after a Christmas Day service five years ago. That had been their last time attending church. The fear of rumours spreading and eventually excluding them from society had been the main reason for their silence rather than pressing charges. Martha and Laura had seen what happened to Helena Jensen, and neither fancied the same fate. Jake recounted how his twin brother Jack had been lured to hell by the devil disguised in a vestment. He offered him a pot of gold if he pledged his loyalty to him. The pastor had exploited Jack's selfishness, but Jake never knew exactly what the pastor needed his brother for.

Sheriff Decker had previously informed the group about the human remains, indicating that all evidence pointed to it being Helena. Suzy then confirmed what she had told Sara May—that Simon had seen Pastor Evans and Prime Minister Crow bury Helena's body—and that was how Simon had been able to get the pastor to fund the Brewer and Jack's ambitious political plans. All in exchange for his silence. Laura corroborated what everyone had suspected: that Evans had always been enamoured with Helena and had forced her beyond all boundaries. But she wasn't ready to admit that Helena's rejection had ultimately cost her her life, as that seemed too far-fetched. Each person contributed a piece of the puzzle that would eventually complete the entire picture. It was clear that events from thirty-one years ago had triggered a domino effect that had led them to this point. Pastor Evans and Prime Minister Crow appeared to have troubled pasts that had spared no one.

Listening intently, Sara May was able to piece together a timeline of events in her mind. Evans and Crow had been childhood friends. Decker had initially gone along with things but eventually drifted away from this increasingly dubious company, focusing all his attention on his new love, Martha. Evans had captivated Suzy, but he didn't want anything to do with her, which drove her into the arms of Simon, who had recently moved to town with his parents. Maggie and her sister, Marie, had been friends with Evans and Crow for some time, but Helena preferred the company of Laura Baker, who did her best to defend her from Evans's unwanted attention. He finally gave up and agreed to marry Paula, who, up to that point, had shown him no interest whatsoever. People suspected that Paula's father had arranged the whole thing. At some point, Evans became a drunken, sexually starved man in a loveless marriage who took advantage of Suzy's affection one night, resulting in the birth of twin boys whom Suzy was forced to claim were Simon's to protect the reputation of the holy clergyman, who was, after all, a faithfully married man and the embodiment of Christian values. For thirty-one years, Suzy managed to maintain the facade. But it was not to last. Simon discovered the truth and threatened Evans with exposing what he knew to the public. The foundation of his silence was broken, so nothing was stopping him from revealing everything he'd witnessed that fateful night when Helena was killed. That decisive outburst sealed his fate.

As Sara May pieced the clues together in her mind, Sheriff Decker revealed that Simon's death had not been accidental, nearly causing poor Suzy to faint. She knew deep down, but wasn't ready to accept it so plainly. Jake decided to take his mother home since he had already revealed everything he knew about the event, including when he saw the pastor leave his house in the middle of the night. The mother-son duo needed time to process this latest development without Jack. After they had left, the group continued for a while before it was time to go home. But Sara May still needed one more puzzle piece to complete the big picture.

"All this explains why he killed Simon...."

"Allegedly," Sheriff Decker quickly reminded everyone.

"But it doesn't explain why he killed Helena. Laura, you're not ready to admit he just went completely off the deep end when he couldn't win her over, right? Laura shifted uncomfortably in her seat.

"I mean, it's obvious he's absolutely bat shit crazy. But to kill her? It just sounds so barbaric."

"Didn't she give birth to a baby?" asked Martha. Laura hung her head.

"Yes. She gave birth at home about a month before she

disappeared. I assisted her with the birth; she wanted to keep it quiet," she admitted.

"So, isn't it just as likely that Evans fathered that kid as well?" Bill asked, remembering how the pastor had knocked Suzy up without anyone knowing.

"Who was the father?" Mary asked, facing Laura.

"I don't know. That was the only thing I could never get out of her."

"Helena would never have slept with Evans," Martha objected, repulsed by the notion.

"Not willingly, no," Sheriff Decker replied.

Suddenly, every lightbulb in Sara May's mind flashed like a giant roadwork sign! Of course! How could she have been so blind? Pastor Evans was known for his sleazy, womanising ways. Was it so far-fetched that he gave up waiting and decided to take what he believed was rightly his? Sara May slowly turned around. In one corner of the pub stood Helena. She'd been listening in, pleasantly surprised to see how many people were willing to defend her. All these recollections hit her like a tsunami, leaving her soaking wet and abandoned, trapped in a state of limbo. Their eyes met, creating a misty fog around them. No words were needed. The sorrow poured from Helena's broken face, her entire demeanour shifting to a dull grey. She'd lost the glowing spark she once possessed.

"He raped her," Sara May muttered without thinking.

"What are you talking about?" asked Eric, concerned that her mental state was once again taking a nosedive.

"Pastor Evans. He's the father of Helena's baby. He raped her, and she became pregnant. That's why she never wanted to reveal the father's identity. He's the evil man."

"Sweetie, what do you mean, the evil man?" Laura

asked.

"My dear, are you sure you're up for this? If not, we can save this conversation for another time," Nana Lou gently pleaded. But Sara May didn't budge. She turned to face the old lady.

"I'm ready. We've all been sharing our stories here tonight. I don't see why I should be exempt from that."

With everyone fixated on her, Sara May stood up confidently and prepared to reveal her own secret. An awkward silence fell over the group as they braced themselves to listen to a woman who, by all accounts, had completely lost all touch with reality.

"You've all heard the rumour," Sara May continued. "That the accident left me mentally challenged and unable to distinguish between reality and fiction. That may very well be. I was in a coma for two weeks; that kind of thing can permanently ruin a person. But the fact is that when I woke up, I could see dead people. Ghosts, if you prefer. I can hear them, and I can talk to them. I know how crazy this sounds. So, I thought I'd show you a little something. Does anybody have a pen?"

Puzzled, Sheriff Decker reached into his button-down shirt pocket and handed her a blue pen he always carried, just in case. She carefully placed it on the round table in front of her and took two steps back to make sure no one could accuse her of fabrication. Doubts turned into curiosity, and the group leaned in closer. Sara May looked at Helena, who understood the assignment. A collective gasp escaped from the Brewers as those present witnessed Sheriff Decker's blue pen spin rapidly before shooting upwards, where it briefly floated in the air. Curiosity gave way to a mixture of shrieks and confused stares, causing utter chaos. The idea of invisible attendees troubled some, but others felt ashamed for not believing Sara May from the start. Eric was among them, looking at the woman he loved, deeply embarrassed.

"I'm sorry. I should have believed you," he quietly admitted.

"You do now. That's all that matters," she replied.

"Are you telling me Helena is here with us? Right now?" Biggie Mac asked, his voice trembling slightly. Seeing this tall, strong giant afraid was a side of him that few people ever saw.

"Yes. That's what I'm telling you," Sara May replied with conviction.

"So, it was she who led you to her bones?" Sheriff Decker asked.

"Yeah. She also showed me what happened to her. She told me about the evil man. I always thought she was telling me she'd been in a bad relationship. I didn't realise until later that she was showing me her death."

"Then we just need to find out what happened to her baby," said Chris.

"Pff, that has to be the worst-kept secret of them all," Old Gilbert muttered, having remained silent until now. The group glared at him, some reprimanding him and warning him to stay quiet.

As Sara May was about to ask the old man what he meant, startled by people's reactions, there was a knock on the door, and the group fell silent. Nobody wanted to open it, fearing who was on the other side. Eventually, Biggie Mac stood up to see who had decided to join this highly classified meeting. He was voted the most likely to handle any crazed criminal who dared to crash the party. Slowly but steadily, he opened the creaking wooden door. Outside stood Maggie Jensen. Biggie Mac moved aside to let her in. The tension in the pub was so thick it was almost hard to breathe. Nobody knew what to do or say. When Sara May saw her mother standing by the door, she felt a huge black hole suddenly form and swallow her whole. No! It couldn't be!

Chapter 63

"Please. Tell me it's not true," she pleaded. Everyone at the pub felt her agony.

"I'm so sorry, baby. I should have told you," Maggie admitted in a trembling tone.

"Then why didn't you?" Sara May yelled out.

"Because I knew it would break you, and I couldn't bring myself to do it after everything you've been through."

"And you all knew?" Sara May questioned, spinning around to see people's faces.

Nobody said a word; most wished they could vanish into thin air and escape this highly uncomfortable situation. Northtown's worst-kept secret had finally been revealed, crashing into the pub like an unstoppable tsunami. Chris and Eric seemed to be the only ones who had no idea about any of this, as neither of them belonged to the relevant generation. Sara May's whole body shook with anger and disgust. Her life had been violently ripped apart in seconds, leaving her unable to focus. Everything had been a lie. The foundation upon which she'd built her entire existence had come crashing down. How could she believe anything any more? Agitated, she turned back to Maggie, her lips pressed tightly together, as she tried to form words into a sentence through her gritted teeth.

"What happened? I want to know every detail, and don't you dare leave anything out!" she demanded, seething with rage. Maggie looked visibly uncomfortable.

"I think it's best we talk this through, just the two of us," she replied.

"Is that why you came here?"

"No, I came here to show my support. Because I know

my sister is dead! I've known for a while, and if there's any chance I can help figure out what happened to her, I want to do so!" Sara May looked at her with a defeated expression.

"Helena isn't my aunt. Is she?"

Maggie stayed silent. Since Sara May found out about Helena, she had been preparing for this conversation. It had taken a long time, many arguments, and a lot of inner struggle, but she finally felt strong enough to face it. She would have preferred to discuss this with Sara May privately, but it was probably wiser to have witnesses present, just in case things went wrong. She took a deep breath and looked her daughter in the eyes as she sighed.

"No. She isn't," she replied, shaking her head slightly.

Sara May felt paralysed. Her body had gone into a state of shock. Every muscle was stretched to its limit, and every nerve vibrated with intense anger that threatened to consume her. Millions of thoughts raced through her mind, becoming tangled like a fisherman's net. She was transported back to the high street outside, where she was being judged by the crazed mob wanting to burn her at the stake. Her throat closed, her fingers went numb, and her breathing grew so heavy she felt faint. When she finally managed to steady herself, she stormed outside, rushing past Biggie Mac and bumping shoulders with Maggie, who didn't say a word; she was too busy trying not to cry in front of everyone.

"Sara May!" Eric called out and hurried after her.

She didn't get very far. He'd always been quicker than her. At this difficult period in their relationship, he threw everything away just in time to catch her as she collapsed in despair. He'd never had to hold someone so tightly before. She fought like a trapped animal, her agonising wails drowning out his every attempt to calm her down. After what felt like an eternity, he could feel her body go limp from exhaustion. He didn't release her, pulling her closer while stroking her hair. Her distressing cries overwhelmed her. It was like every painful experience she'd ever endured was building up inside her. The group at the Brewer had decided to stay put. Hearing Sara May's heart-wrenching screams in the street was agonising. All they could do was wait. After a while, she had no more tears left, leaving behind nothing but an emotionally drained shadow of a woman in Eric's arms. He flung her left arm around his neck as he lifted her and carried her back into the Brewer.

The morning after, Sara May woke up in her old bed at Maggie's house for the first time in three weeks. The events of the previous night were hazy; she remembered very little after Eric had taken her back into the pub. Maggie had left the Brewers shortly afterwards, asking Chris and Eric to look after her and bring her home when they thought suitable. Sara May sat up in her bed. She'd suffered a nervous breakdown, which had caused her both physical pain and memory loss. She recalled Nana Lou telling her she needed to sit down with Maggie and try to see things from her perspective. She tried to protest and point out that Maggie had never wanted to see things from anyone else's perspective. But Nana Lou wouldn't hear of it, and she was reminded that Maggie had chosen to see things through her daughter's eyes, which kept her silent all this time. And now it was Sara May's turn to do the same. To put herself in Maggie's shoes, listen to her, and try to find common ground so they could confront the issue directly—Pastor Evans's criminal behaviour and how to seek justice for Helena and Simon. In great pain,

Sara May managed to get out of bed and stagger to the kitchen.

Maggie sat at the kitchen table with a cup of tea in her hand. She'd been forming a plan while waiting for Sara May to wake up. She was still unsure about how to proceed. Her closely guarded secret, which she'd deliberately kept from her daughter for over thirty years, was no longer a secret. It had surfaced differently than she preferred, but now it was out in the open, so she had to adapt. She had no idea what to say or do. She'd never allowed herself to think this far ahead, semi-hoping it would stay hidden forever. Nana Lou had advised her as best she could and told her to just roll with it. Sara May would have to handle this her own way, in her own time. She was a vital part of solving this case, so Maggie needed to make sure her daughter's feelings about the whole situation were considered. She swallowed her pride as she asked Sara May to sit down. At first, there was only silence between them.

"Is there anything you'd like to say?" Maggie finally asked.

"It's not me who needs to talk," she shrugged, remembering Nana Lou's words about not making this about her.

"You must have a million questions." Sara May sat silent for a moment.

"What happened?" she asked after careful consideration. Maggie sighed and put her cup down.

"The 6th of December 1994 was a Tuesday. Your dad and I were watching telly when we heard a knock on the door. John went to answer it and was greeted by Pastor Evans, who was holding what looked to be a twine-woven basket. And there you were. Wrapped in a pink blanket, so tiny and fragile. You were about a month old, I would guess. Pastor Evans handed John the basket and told him that Helena had left you on his doorstep with a note saying she didn't trust herself to raise you and she wanted God to take care of you."

"Then why didn't he raise me? He and Paula?"

"He believed it was in your best interest that your family members raised you. He'd never admit to being your family. Then he just left, as if nothing had happened, but our lives were forever changed. I knew Helena had given birth, Laura told me. I truly believed she'd be a great mum. And then all of a sudden, I was just supposed to believe that she abandoned you, the baby she'd given birth to and loved with her whole heart. It didn't make sense."

Sara May listened intently. Hours earlier, she was overwhelmed with anger, feeling the world was against her. She hadn't realised how big this had been for the young couple, John and Maggie. They must have had their own dreams and hopes for the future, which were cruelly shattered when a newborn was suddenly thrust upon them — a baby they neither wanted nor asked for. Yet despite everything, they accepted the responsibility. Sara May was beginning to understand what Nana Lou meant by seeing things from Maggie's perspective.

"Did you believe it? That Helena had abandoned me?" Maggie sighed.

"I don't know. I guess I did at first. But it never sat right with me just how gone she was. No letters, no phone calls, nothing. That wasn't the sister I'd known and loved. Besides, she would never have left you like that."

"You reported her missing."

"I mentioned it to Sheriff Decker. I told him how I felt

about this, and he promised to do everything possible to figure out what happened. I saw a small announcement in The Morning Paper once. It was like a little ad, but that was it. It was brushed under the carpet, and we heard nothing about it afterwards."

"Did nobody find this odd?"

"There was no social media back then. What was reported in the papers was all you needed to know. Everyone around here was convinced she'd just run away from all the nasty rumours, and nobody thought to question it. I suppose she didn't matter enough to anyone for it to go any further."

"What about Grandma Gladys and Aunt Marie?"

"They've always been so consumed by hatred and humiliation, there really was no way to reason with them. After John left, I had to take on additional work to support us. If I'd gone against my mother and sister, I wouldn't have had any help."

Sara May said nothing. She was struggling with overwhelming guilt towards Maggie. All this time, she'd believed that her mother was merely selfish, deliberately hiding crucial information because it suited her. It was as if Sara May was discovering a side of Maggie she had never known—one deeper than she had ever imagined. The woman sitting across from her was deeply broken after years of life's relentless attacks, but still stood tall with her head held high. Margarete Rachel Jensen had been caught in a vicious storm for decades, quietly fighting her battles behind closed doors, abandoned and alone, yet still proud. She'd navigated life with clenched fists and had never given up, even when the fights often became bigger than she could bear. She'd even driven herself home after Sheriff Decker told her it was indeed her baby sister who'd been found beneath the flooring at Old Gilbert's barn.

"So I guess this is why you and I have never gotten along," Sara May said after a long silence.

"I guess so. You take after Helena more than me. You remind me so much of her every single day," Maggie replied, prompting them to chuckle before continuing. "I want you to know that this doesn't change anything, as far as I am concerned. I'll always be here for you, and I'll always love you, regardless of the decision you make. Whether you continue to call me 'mum' is entirely up to you."

"You'll always be my mum. I mean, you took me in, and you raised me. You didn't have to, but you did."

Maggie was taken aback. Her eyes filled with tears, and two finally found their way down each cheek. For years, she'd feared Sara May's reaction when she discovered the truth, and her meltdown the night before hadn't filled her with much hope. As she wiped away the tears, she could feel a cold wind swirl around her and a tiny gust brushing through her hair. Her cheeks tingled, almost as if someone was gently caressing them, trying to soothe her pain.

"Is Helena here with us?" she asked.

Sara May nodded and smiled as she watched Maggie place her hand against her right cheek, trying to feel her sister's hand against hers. That was all it took. The dam burst, and moments later, Maggie sat at the kitchen table, sobbing. She'd been carrying this heavy burden all by herself ever since Sara May entered her life so unexpectedly, and now she finally felt like she'd been freed from the shackles. Sara May stood up and hugged her mum. The long-overdue hug confirmed her decision not to hold her own frustration over Maggie's head any longer. She hadn't done anything to deserve it. On the contrary, she'd shown incredible strength, surviving all she'd gone through without a scratch. She owed her life to this woman and was sure Nana Lou had been right. It'd been necessary to see things from Maggie's perspective. The last puzzle piece had been put into place, completing the bigger picture as clearly as possible. Sara May was more determined than ever before. She now knew she had to be the one to take down Pastor Evans. She was of his flesh and blood. She was the daughter he'd denounced, and that had cost Helena her life. For that, he would have to suffer. This was her fight and hers alone.

Chapter 64

"Are you absolutely sure?"

I saw her run out of the Brewer like a maniac. Eric ran after her. And they weren't the only ones at the pub. Yesterday, I went to grab a pizza at the Pizza-Lot, and my mate Brian was working. He said they'd made at least five pizzas to be sent to the Brewer after opening hours. He was asked to deliver them out back.

"Did he see anyone there?" Pastor Evans asked nervously.

"No, all the curtains were closed. Something fishy was going on for sure."

"Alright, thank you, Jack," said the pastor and hung up the phone.

The boy was as daft as a doorknob but could be useful sometimes. Being a spy suited him well, given his insatiable nosiness. But even he had his limits. He hadn't been able to tell who had attended the Brewer meeting, even though Evans had a pretty good idea who the traitors were. He felt the fire beneath his feet, the flames immersing his legs, making him more nervous by the minute. He knew he could count on his most loyal supporters, but if that was enough, then why was he so anxious? Was this fear? What did he have to be afraid of? He controlled this town. Or, at least, that's what he'd always convinced himself of. But what if that wasn't as concrete as he thought?

He stood up from his leather chair, not bothering to turn on the lights to brighten the dim office, and looked outside. He hadn't been able to shake this constant chill he'd been feeling for weeks. He was always cold, and he couldn't understand why. A man of his size was rarely affected by the cold air. He was sleep-deprived after weeks of virtually no sleep, and on the nights he managed to drift off, he was violently awakened by a vicious nightmare, drenched in sweat and on the verge of a heart attack. Paula had eventually ordered him to see a doctor, who hadn't done much else than prescribe some sleeping pills that did fuck all. He couldn't have known that his rapid mental decline was the work of demonic shadow figures who desired the blackened pastor's soul. It was so rotten and dark after years of misuse that Hell's most monstrous creatures had started draining what little life was left in it a long time ago, causing the pastor to feel like the shell of his former self. But he wasn't ready to admit it to anyone, least of all himself.

Prime Minister Crow was battling the same uneasy feeling in the capital city. He'd dealt with it by dismissing it and burying himself in work. Being a Prime Minister was no easy task, but he'd turned it into a comfortable, cushy job over the years. Countless holidays abroad and frequent golf tournaments had significantly eased the stress. He'd become numb to the opposition's constant attacks on his obvious character flaws, which, in their view, were the selfish acts of a highly corrupt Prime Minister. He usually didn't care. But this time, the situation was serious. Since word had started spreading that a young woman had accused a pastor up north of being a murderer, the heat had been turned up, and Crow was feeling the slow burn. The holidays abroad and the frequent golf tournaments no longer soothed his troubled conscience as they once did. His mind constantly wandered, obsessing over this young woman. Who was she, and how much did she know? He hoped the locals of Northtown had just written her off as a psychopath. But, even if they had, he knew better, and that was unsettling him. He feared this would escalate, and eventually, everyone would uncover his deepest, darkest secret. That would mean the end of his political career and possibly his life. Nobody would remember all his good deeds; they would simply see him as the man who helped a murderer hide a body. How could he have been so stupid? There was no way people would see this as *boys just being boys*.

Crow's mind had been in Northtown ever since the first article about Sara May's erratic outburst was published online in the town's local paper. He'd tried wearing a fake smile and pretending everything was fine by burying himself in paperwork. He asked his assistant, Celia, to answer all his calls so he could avoid speaking to any journalist or reporter demanding more answers on behalf of the nation if the situation worsened. He'd contacted Chief Chase and asked him to stay alert, giving him full permission to take action if anything seemed out of the ordinary, which Chase had gladly agreed to. He also requested that he stay in regular contact with Pastor Evans. However, that hadn't had the calming effect he'd hoped for, because the pastor was so deeply paranoid that he was halfway to La-La Land by now. Evans had become so delusional that he was barely functioning. He spoke of shadow figures and hell on Earth, sounding completely out of touch with reality. As a result, Crow had limited their contact. If Evans wouldn't offer logical solutions to their little problem, Crow had no use for him. He should have known better than to think that a man who believed in heavenly intervention was capable of logical thinking.

All those years in politics had dulled Crow's

conscience to almost nothing. He'd never felt accountable for anything other than his own ideas. He wasn't responsible for how the media twisted his words. He wasn't liable for how the media presented his ideas to the crowd, and he certainly wasn't accountable for the protests that often erupted. Those plebs were never happy! He refused to take responsibility for the oversensitive, bloodthirsty mob that he could never please anyway. His loyalty was to his investors and, occasionally, his voters. The investors gave him the financial stability he needed to sell as many lies as his loyal voters could stomach.

But he couldn't lie to himself. This agonising pain that tore him apart from the inside was entirely new to him, and he didn't know how to deal with it. He couldn't tell anyone about it because that would lead to questions like "Why are you feeling this way?" To which he had no answer. He could fake it, but that would only increase his stress and add to his anxiety. Besides, he couldn't take any chances. If he said too much, he risked going to hell or, worse, jail. The worst part was that he didn't know if the pain was rooted in some guilt over his actions thirty-one years ago or the fear that it might all be exposed. He'd never been religious, so he wasn't afraid of what awaited him beyond his mortal life. No matter how he'd behaved. That was his soul's sentence he would only accept once that day arrived. But the same couldn't be said about the consequences of his actions in Northtown all those years ago. That terrified him more than anything! That woman knew something, and he had to find out what it was. Who had been talking? Simon was dead and buried, so he was hardly gossiping from the grave! Shaking, Crow picked up the phone and called his good friend, Police Commissioner Harold Gibson.

"Gibson," a baritone-sounding voice could be heard on the other end of the line.

"Hello, this is Prime Minister Crow."

"Hello, sir, what can I do for you?"

"Didn't you owe me a favour for appointing you Police Commissioner three years ago?" At first, there was silence. Then, the baritone voice spoke.

"What do you need?"

Chapter 65

Sheriff Decker sat at his desk, contemplating his next move. He didn't remember the last time he had been this angry. Even Biggie Mac had kept his distance after informing his boss about a message from the shark tank down south. The news didn't surprise Decker. It was only a matter of time before the big boys back at the capital realised what was happening in the tiny town in the north, and with many powerful nitwits invested in the matter, they needed to extinguish the problem immediately. Now, all he could do was wait for the inevitable. He wished things had gone differently, but there was nothing he could do now. Suddenly, Maggie and Sara May burst into his office.

"We came as soon as we could. What happened?" Maggie asked nervously.

"I was fired," Sheriff Decker replied, calm despite his fury.

"What? What do you mean? Aren't you the boss around here? Who can fire you?" a dumbfounded Sara May asked, staring wide-eyed at Decker.

The National Police Commissioner oversees all hiring, firing, and replacement of Police Chiefs and Sheriffs nationwide. With the authority from the Ministry of Justice."

"Who did you piss off at the Ministry of Justice?" Sara May was more confused than ever.

"No one that I'm aware of. But Prime Minister Crow isn't exactly my biggest fan at the moment.

"What authority does he have? That's not his ministry!" Maggie rightfully pointed out, now more enraged than baffled.

"He's the chairman of the party that holds that ministry. They were handed it on a silver platter after the last elections. Crow made sure to put his men in charge so he could call on them when he needed them to do his dirty work."

"Is there nothing we can do?" Sara May asked. Decker sympathised with her.

"Don't quit. Nothing has changed on our end. We still have the same suspects in the two cases. You guys need to find solid evidence."

"What difference would that make? If everything is so rotten and corrupt in the capital, isn't it just as likely that Crow and his people will appoint a new Sheriff?" Maggie asked rather discouragingly.

Sheriff Decker leaned silently back in his chair, plagued with worries despite his best efforts to appear calm and composed. Maggie was right; this latest move had left them in a very tight spot. The letter informing him of his immediate dismissal stated that a new Sheriff would be appointed to prevent lawlessness in Northtown. Decker knew the snakes in the Ministry of Justice couldn't care less about a lousy little town in the countryside; placing one of their loyalists in the role to keep the flames under control was a political move no less. They had wrapped the rope so tightly that Decker and his team couldn't make a move. Corruption seeped into every part of the country like radioactive waste, making it almost impossible to find someone unwilling to sell their soul to the powerful, in the hope of a few crumbs. The prospect of the pendulum swinging in their favour was fading. Just as Decker was about to give up, Biggie Mac entered his office with his head held high. Behind him was the entire police force on duty that day.

"We heard the news, boss, and we just want you to know that you have our full support!" he proudly stated. Decker pressed his lips together and smiled as he gave them a solid nod.

"Thank you, all of you. But unfortunately, my sheriff's authority is rather limited at the moment."

"Don't worry about it, boss! We'll figure something out!" a man named Joe Parker promised, making Decker nearly tear up.

After the group had left the office, Decker turned his attention back to the two women standing opposite him. Sara May tried her hardest to summon Helena but to no avail. She'd been absent for a while, and it was beginning to get on her nerves. She was doing all this for her; the least she could do was show up and lend a hand.

"What do you want us to do?" Maggie asked.

"I want you to go out there and do whatever you can. Gather the troops, spread the word, anything. The sharks in the south have smelled the fear and tasted the blood, so nothing is safe anymore. The most effective thing would be to turn the public's opinion against them."

"Can we contact the Chief of Police in Reykjavik? Get him to help us out?" Sara May asked rather sheepishly.

"No. Chief Chase is under Crow's thumb. He knew Helena was missing, but he dismissed the case." Maggie was startled.

"Why would he do that?"

Because Crow is linked to her disappearance, and Chief Chase's career depends on Crow remaining the most powerful man in the country. When you asked that Helena's disappearance be investigated, Pastor Evans found out. He contacted Crow, who called Chase and asked him to handle it. Chase was newly appointed then;

Helena's case was his ticket into the glittering abyss of the elite.

Stunned, Maggie sat down, completely immobilised. She'd long suspected that something more was behind her sister's disappearance, but she never dared to imagine something like this. It was like someone had lit a bonfire deep inside her gut, a fire that now spread through her veins as if fuelled with gasoline, causing uncontrollable rage to consume her completely. That someone had dared to do something so inconceivable was more than she could handle! Her family had been ridiculed with nasty rumours that turned out to be nothing but filthy lies all along. For over thirty years, the Jensen women had endured humiliation and gossip from vulgar curtain twitchers, all due to a web of lies carefully spun by a few sick-minded individuals hoping to cover their horrifically twisted acts. They'd managed to conceal their trail, but all their secrets were about to be dragged into the daylight. Blind with fury, Maggie finally stood up again, her body trembling. She was done playing nice.

Sara May, I want you and Eric to write an email and send it to all the country's major media outlets. Notify them of the bones that were found. Let Martha and Laura handle Paula's vicious minions, and have Chris and Jake monitor Jack. Nana Lou needs to look after my mother, so she doesn't find out about any of this because it could kill her. Decker, you and the rest of the group make sure that the rats in this rubbish pile don't make a move. Understood?"

"Yes, ma'am!" Sheriff Decker agreed, impressed with Maggie's sudden burst of confidence.

"What are you gonna do, Mum?"

I'm gonna talk to my sister and have her take care of

Prime Minister Crow. Chief Chase is mine!"

Sara May and Sheriff Decker exchanged looks, bewildered, without saying a word. Maggie's unexpected enthusiasm had caught them off guard, but neither dared to object. It was clear that fiery lava was bubbling beneath her usually calm surface and now threatened to erupt. The burden Maggie had borne for over three decades due to other people's selfish acts was now fuelling her determination to fight like hell and ensure those responsible paid a hefty price for what they'd done.

Chapter 66

Everyone who attended the Brewer meeting had been notified and agreed to participate. Nana Lou warned that the opponents knew more than they were letting on, so everyone needed to be careful not to say anything. Jack had leaked every word to Pastor Evans, who had alerted Prime Minister Crow. In response, he activated all his powerful connections, hoping to minimise the damage. Part of that plan was to invite his friend the Minister of Justice, Arnold Price, and his wife, Carol, to dinner one Sunday evening. The booze flowed freely, and the misty cigar smoke filled every corner of the living room. That was how Crow liked to conduct business. In his opinion, formal discussions often made things more complicated. That Sunday evening proved fruitful. The women discussed real estate and interior decorating, while the men finalised a deal concerning key changes within the Northtown police force. When the last drop of whiskey had been enjoyed, both men agreed that a certain sheriff had to go. He was only a few years from retirement anyway.

Things changed rapidly after that fateful evening. A few hours after Price had contacted the Police Commissioner, Sheriff Decker received a call informing him that Richard Bennett, the former Police Chief of Iceland's North-West district, would be taking over his position. Bennett had long been a boot-licker, which eventually paid off. He was granted a generous retirement package in recognition of his loyalty to the party, enabling him to spend his golden years in Spain with his devoted wife. But when the big guns within the party called, it didn't matter if he was in the middle of a golf game; his political party needed his support! Crow had informed Pastor Evans about what was happening, so it was no surprise that Paula's followers weren't spreading rumours about a new Sheriff in town. She kept them at bay. But what no one had expected was that the entire Northtown police force walked out of the station the moment the new, pot-bellied Sheriff squeezed himself into Decker's old chair. On his first day in office, Bennett walked into an empty police station. Humiliated and eager to prevent the locals from discovering that the town had no police force, he immediately picked up the phone on Decker's desk and called Chief Chase.

"Chase," a gruff-sounding voice said on the other end of the line.

"What the hell is going on?" Bennett furiously howled. Being well aware of the bloody game of chess they were playing against the other side, Chase had a sinking feeling.

"What's happening?" he asked, more stern than confused.

"I was told I was supposed to be appointed a sheriff here in Northtown, but when I arrived, the whole goddamned station was empty!"

Chase's hands trembled. "What do you mean empty?"

"They all walked out! The whole lot! I got no manpower!"

"Shit!" Chase snapped a fist on his desk and ran his other hand through his grey hair, which was becoming sticky with sweat. Two locks of hair slid down to his dripping forehead.

"I don't know what the hell is going on here, but I ain't dealing with this bullshit! I ain't sacrificing a golf tournament in Greece for this crap!" Bennett yelled.

"Calm down; I'll fix this! Let me call Crow and see what he says."

"You better because I'm about fifteen seconds away from losing my goddamn shit here!"

Bennett had said his piece. The way he slammed the phone down was a power move, enraging Chase beyond belief. He felt trapped. He was caught up in some fiery shitshow he had no involvement in, yet had no way of escaping. He'd sealed his fate when he, along with the former Police Commissioner, decided to obey the orders of the then Minister of Justice, Stephen Crow, and sweep the disappearance of a young woman from Northtown under the rug. He'd long suspected there was more going on, but throughout his long and prosperous career, he'd learned not to ask questions, as that could cost him dearly. Now, he was up to his elbows in mud, completely unable to move. He picked up the phone again, but when he was halfway through typing Crow's number, a stranger burst loudly into his office, demanding his attention. That had happened a time or two during his career and had never upset him. But, something about this invasion sent a cold shiver down his spine. The chill intensified rapidly when he realised who the furious woman was.

"You! You're the reason my sister was never granted the justice she deserved!" Maggie screamed so loudly her voice shook just as much as her finger pointed at Chase, who stared at her wide-eyed with fear.

"Can….can I help you?" he stammered.

"Don't pretend you don't know! Helena Jensen was my sister! The woman you were supposed to find, but you were more interested in your big fat paycheck than her life!"

Chase felt his skin turn cold and the lump in his throat

swell so much he struggled to breathe. He knew the timing of this attack was no accident. It was almost like the vanished woman was hovering above him, ready to strike at any moment.

"I...." I don't know what you're talking about," he stuttered nervously, but Maggie was having none of it. She slammed her fists on his desk, prompting him to jolt upwards in his seat.

"You know damn well what I'm talking about! Don't play dumb with me, mister! I asked that you investigate my sister's disappearance back in '94. And what did you do? One shitty little announcement in the paper! That was it! My sister was missing, and her life meant nothing to you! One announcement was all she was worth to you!" Chase stood up from his chair, preparing for a counterstrike.

"Listen..." But he didn't get a chance to finish his sentence. Maggie pushed him back down in his chair, prompting a stunned reaction from Chase.

"No, you listen! You may think you'll get away with this! But mark my words: as long as I'm breathing, none of you will rest so much as a second! I will find you and hose you out of the sewer like the dirty rats you are! While your hearts beat, I'll make damn sure you won't ever have a moment of peace!"

"Is that a threat?" he asked, trying to sound intimidating in a desperate attempt to regain his confidence. Maggie stared into his eyes, then leaned forward so she towered over the shivering coward.

"That's a promise," she threatened, crushing all that was left of his conviction.

After menacing the Police Chief of the capital city, Maggie turned around and stormed out of the office, unbowed, slamming the door behind her. She'd never felt so powerful in her life. She sensed Helena in the office with her, encouraging her, which gave her a superhuman strength she never believed she had. She trembled with anger but couldn't help but smile at what that anger had achieved. She was done hiding, and she was certainly done sitting idly by while others tyrannised her life. She left the capital city police station with her head held high, ready for the battle ahead.

Inside his office, Chase sat astonished. His nerves were rattled like never before. He wasn't used to being spoken to in that manner, and quite frankly, he didn't know how to handle it. He hadn't always had the public's best interests at heart; he preferred if his decision-making benefitted him personally. He'd never allowed himself to think about the domino effect it might have. After a while, he gathered himself and phoned Crow to alert him that the Northtown troops were gearing up and then some!

Chapter 67

After Maggie returned to Northtown from her heroic journey to the capital, she sat down with her sister Marie for hours into the night. She knocked on Marie's mansion door and demanded that she listen. First, she needed to lay all her cards on the table and tell her sister everything that had been going on. Then, she had to give her time to comprehend that their baby sister was truly gone and that her death had not been an accident. She hadn't just become fed up with life in Northtown and run away to find herself in Reykjavik. Two men, whom Marie had considered her two best friends for years, had murdered her little sister. That was a lot to take in. She'd sat in her high, pink armchair, which she always thought of as her throne, and listened intensely to every word from Maggie's mouth. Marie had always suspected that something had happened to Helena because she'd never heard a word from her after she left town. But hearing that she'd been met with such a gruesome fate was almost too much to bear. Maggie had begged her to push the sorrow aside so they could focus on getting justice for their sister and holding the responsible ones accountable. The anger would have to be their driving force; that was their only chance to uproot the tightly spun web of corruption and lies that lay like a crisp wintry fog over the country. It was time for the two of them to face the fact that greed and ruthless addiction to power had cost their baby sister her life.

"You think Crow has something to do with this?" Marie cautiously asked, almost like she was afraid of the answer.

"I know he is," Maggie replied.

"And what do you want me to do? Just knock on his door and ask him if he murdered my sister?"

"He didn't kill her. He helped Evans hide her body, and when he started gaining influence as a politician, he started making powerful connections to make sure his filthy little secret was kept hidden. That must mean something; we're talking about Helena here!"

"I know that, Maggie, I just....I find all of this so hard to believe."

"What about Simon? You told Decker that you heard Evans and Crow talk."

"They could have been talking about anything!"

"Marie, come on. All I'm asking you to do is go and speak to Crow. I know you guys are friends, but Helena needs us. Plus, if you got him to confess, can you imagine what that would do to his wife's reputation?"

That last sentence brought a devious smile to Marie's face. She had always hated the condescending braggart Crow had married. A woman with a more extended middle finger than a rebellious teenager, her nose so sharply pointed that it was a wonder how she managed to breathe. A woman too good for anything but the most expensive things, she looked down on those who couldn't afford to parade around with the most exquisite luxury items. Marie had always despised how poorly Mrs Crow treated those considered lower in class. She was hated by almost all shop employees in the capital city for her downright rude behaviour towards them. Some shop owners had been known to close their shops swiftly when they saw the fashionable she-devil approach, dressed in her finest mink coat and ready to claw their eyes out for not kowtowing to her or catering to her every whim. Known for her signature red lipstick, high heels, and capricious whims, she reminded most people of Disney's Cruella De Vil with a devilish twist. She was the woman Marie had looked at when shaping her own aristocratic image, so she could take notes on what to avoid. She was herself a very wealthy woman, but she had no interest in competing with Mrs Crow or anybody, for that matter. She preferred dancing barefoot in the rain on the streets of Rome rather than pretentiously eating French macarons and sipping champagne at fancy cocktail parties that would no doubt land her in a social column titled *Who was where*.

"Just tell me what I need to do," Marie finally said, with a giant smirk.

After hours of discussion and planning, Marie slept for a few hours, then got up early in the morning and drove to the capital city. It was a four-hour drive, giving her ample time to channel the fury Maggie had repeatedly urged her to focus on. She did this by recalling all the times she'd been shunned for refusing to play by the rules of the hierarchy. She certainly flaunted her wealth and disliked how Reykjavik tried to imitate metropolitan cities like Milan and New York. But she had always crafted her own morals, which she lived by. She made sure never to step on anyone society deemed beneath her and befriended people from all walks of life, one of the biggest sins you could commit if you wanted to be taken seriously among the rich and powerful. Besides, she hadn't become wealthy through hard work; she possessed the acumen of marrying well and securing herself a share of everything in every divorce.

Keeping all this in mind fuelled the fire Maggie had started. But the guilt towards Helena was overwhelming. Why had she been so proud? Why had she chosen to believe all those nasty rumours instead of supporting her sister through the storm she had been forced to endure, vulnerable and alone? Why did the public's opinion seem more important than her sister's well-being? Marie felt sorrow overpower her anger, and before she knew it, tears blurred her vision, forcing her to pull over on the side of the road. Three decades of lies and shame flooded her mind in seconds, compelling her to confront herself amid sobs. Then she felt a presence beside her. She lowered her hands from her face and looked out the front window, terrified to glance at the empty passenger seat beside her.

"Helena?" she whispered.

"Don't cry, Sister. It's gonna be alright," Helena whispered back.

The tears dried up instantly, replaced by fierce determination. Marie gave herself a good shake, tightened her grip on the steering wheel, and let out her loudest scream in years. Every feeling burst out of her like a gushing waterfall, releasing thirty years of constant fighting and heaviness. She restarted her car and drove the rest of the way to Reykjavik. Once there, she pondered her next move. She couldn't call Crow because he would never agree to meet her if things had gotten as bad as Maggie described. She had to surprise him. She checked the time. It was almost one o'clock on a Tuesday. He was most likely at a meeting or at lunch. She had to hope he'd decided to eat at his desk. Because of their well-known friendship, nobody batted an eye as she walked confidently towards Crow's office. His assistant warned her he was swamped but did not try to stop her in any other way. Crow jumped back when he saw her storm into his office unannounced. He knew the stakes, but he had half-expected it to be Maggie who would bombard him when he least expected it. He could handle her better than the fearsome beast he knew his friend to be.

"Marie! How nice to see you. Have a seat," he said, pretending her sudden appearance didn't faze him.

"Thank you, Stephen. But this isn't a courtesy visit, I'm afraid."

"I'm sorry to hear that. Has something happened?" he asked, acting all innocent.

"Cut the crap. You know why I'm here."

"No, I'm afraid I don't."

"Stephen, you're not talking to a reporter. Cut the bullshit and talk to me." Crow stared at her, then let out a loud exhale.

"Very well. What do you want to talk about?" He leaned against his mahogany desk and crossed his arms, hoping to intimidate her. It didn't work.

"Is it true that I'm hearing? About Evans and Helena?"

Crow said nothing at first. He had often found himself in situations requiring carefully chosen words to prevent unnecessary chaos in the country and dodge nasty tabloid headlines. He was well-practised in tackling his political opponents, who seized every opportunity to throw shade at him, often armed with sharp pens. But nothing, not even years in politics, could have prepared him for having to own up to his deepest, darkest mistake from thirty years ago. And the fact that his good friend would eventually force him to accept responsibility was something he hadn't anticipated.

"Marie, you're talking about something that happened over three decades ago. We were just kids. Young and stupid."

"Are you telling me the rumours are true?"

"No, I'm telling you it's been so long; who can tell the

403

truth from fiction?"

"Apparently, you and Evans can. At least, that's what I'm hearing."

"Come on, Marie. You know how people are in that shithole. Munching on every darn bit of garbage they can sink their teeth into, not caring if it's a lie or not."

Then, wouldn't it be wise to knock some sense into them by telling the truth? It can't be that difficult," Marie calmly replied, almost like she was trying to freak him out. She was engaging in a mental war, and it appeared to be working. Crow had started pacing nervously back and forth.

"Why are you doing this?" he asked, irritated that he was losing control.

"Because I want you to tell me the truth!" she shouted. "This is my sister we're talking about!"

"A sister, you haven't given a damn about in thirty years! You've never cared for what happened to her! Why now?"

Crow had hit her with a heavy blow. She had no answers for his surprise attack. He was right. She had chosen to believe the rumours instead of supporting her baby sister, and that was a burden she was doomed to carry for the rest of her life. But this was not the time or the place to make it about her, and she'd be damned if she handed Crow that weapon! For the first time, Marie didn't feel the need to be the centre of attention.

"This isn't about me, Stephen. This is about Helena. I know she was murdered. And I know it was Evans who killed her. He couldn't have her, so he forced himself on her and got her pregnant, but instead of stepping up and owning up to it, he butchered Helena so she wouldn't talk. I want to know your part in all this."

"You really think I would tell you if he were a cold-blooded murderer? I am the Prime Minister of this country! I have a reputation to uphold and an honour to protect!"

"So, you're worried that your involvement in this will cost you your cushy job and fat paycheck? Is that more important to you than Helena?" Crow began trembling with fear, his eyes wide with terror as he stared at the steadfast woman before him.

"You don't know what you're talking about! I'm not afraid of you! You can't judge me!" he shouted, deranged and consumed with paranoia.

"You're right, Stephen. Only God can do that. You'll have your judgment day like the rest of us. That's the terrifying truth you should fear the most," she calmly reminded him.

Marie stood up and sauntered out of the office without looking back, leaving Crow alone with his thoughts. He was confused and frightened beyond reason. His heart was pounding dangerously fast, and his palms were disgustingly clammy. If Marie had turned against him, he might as well throw in the towel. Up until now, he believed it was enough to fire Decker, thinking that would automatically settle everything. But then, Chief Chase phoned him, saying that the entire Northtown police force had resigned in protest of Decker's dismissal. It was now clear to him that the opponents had started to growl. This was indeed a bloody game of chess. Every move had to be carefully calculated. He couldn't talk to Evans; he had become so neurotic with despair that he had stopped making sense long ago. He slumped into his chair and devised a new plan. Who could he call? What was the best strategy here?

Chapter 68

Stormy clouds had begun to gather over Northtown once more. Bill and Laura Baker were in a unique position. They could transform their bakery into a kind of alternative news outlet by listening in on every conversation at the Bread Box. Even customers stopping in for their morning pastries received fresh updates on the rumours circulating about Pastor Evans and his followers. Bill and Laura made it their mission to ensure everyone knew that their cherished pastor was nothing but a monstrous murderer who had killed an innocent young girl thirty-one years ago. Their tactic had started to create a divide among the locals. On one side were those who weren't surprised that the pastor had a shady past, though they could never have guessed just how dark his conscience really was. On the other side were those who dismissed the rumours as nothing more than careless gossip from people who hated their beloved religious leader and wished to see him gone. Before long, the rumours reached Paula, who was shocked and appalled by the chaos engulfing the town and turning it into a dystopian nightmare.

She'd kept the locals on a leash for years, skillfully managing every rumour that originated in Northtown. She was the one who controlled the topics of discussion and always guided public opinion in whatever way best served her and her community. She'd surrounded herself with loyal watchdogs who loved nothing more than to smear their neighbours, regardless of whether their words were true or a vicious lie. But now, something had shifted. There had been a seismic change, and suddenly, she felt she had lost all control, powerless to stop the spreading chatter in every corner. It was everywhere—in every home, café, and workplace. It was gut-wrenching to witness. Running between houses, correcting the misconception that her husband was a ruthless killer, was maddening. She had to choose her next move with care, just like everyone else caught up in this war of psychological games. Voicing her worries to her husband didn't make much difference, as he had secluded himself in his office for almost two weeks and refused to speak to anyone unless it was Jack Lewis, who kept him updated. Which was just as well because Paula didn't dare deliver bad news. She avoided her husband's office as if it were cursed.

But something had to be done. So, one day, she dressed in her finest and headed out of the house. She'd heard that the Bread Box had become the latest gossip hotspot. She had to go and check it out. As Paula strutted, puffed up, down Northtown's high street, she could feel the public's sharp opinions carve themselves like markings on her body. The poisonous tongues whispered from all directions despite the elegant pastor's wife pretending not to notice. She still had her pride, if nothing else. When she entered the Bread Box, the usual chatter fell silent instantly. Nobody had expected to see her.

"Hello, Paula. What can we do for you?" Laura asked, her spite expertly disguised as professionalism.

"I just came to buy coffee and some freshly baked bread buns, thank you," Paula lied without flinching.

"You're in luck; the coffee's still hot, and we got plenty of buns," Bill replied, hiding his distaste for the vixen behind his experienced smile.

"I hear you got plenty of other things as well," Paula huffed as she looked around the bakery, giving other customers a disgusted look.

"What's that supposed to mean?" Laura swiftly asked, feeling her well-polished mask slipping. Oh, how she hated that woman.

"A little birdie told me you could get all the latest gossip in town here at the Bread Box. One barely has to read the newspaper nowadays."

"It's always been that way, my dear. It would do you good to get out and chat with us measly peasants more often," a regular named Hugh snarkily replied, receiving smiles and a few chuckles from the other customers. Paula's face went bright red.

"I'll have you all know there's nothing to those smears and whispers that are going around about my husband, and I must say, I'm thoroughly disappointed in you all for spreading such obvious and downright disgusting lies!" she snapped.

"That's rich, coming from you!" a woman named Mandy clapped back.

When Paula was about to craft a clever comeback, an elderly man named Lawrence Mitchell rose from his table at the back of the Bread Box, leaning on his cane. The crowd fell silent as he slowly made his way towards Paula, who dared not utter a word. Mr. Mitchell was one of the town's elders, respected for his age and admired for his unmatched wisdom and sharp mind, which could outshine even the most esteemed intellects. When he spoke, everyone listened. And Paula knew better than to argue with this grey-haired, wrinkled figure who was slowly approaching like an intimidating version of Yoda.

"You listen to me, Paula Evans. Those who play with the devil's toys will eventually be brought to wield his sword. Mark my words."

Paula felt her veins bulge with fierce rage. How dare he? That menacing warning had silenced the crowd, who nodded in agreement and stared at her with intense judgment. She knew what was coming. Without saying another word, she spun around so swiftly her fur coat swung with her as she stormed out of the bakery. She slammed the door behind her, blocking out the cheers erupting in the Bread Box, along with laughter and applause. Bill and Laura high-fived each other. They had won this battle with the support of their loyal customers and, most importantly, the cherished Mr. Mitchell, who was celebrated as a hero that day.

Meanwhile, Marie had asked Eric and Sara May to look after her mansion while she drove south to the capital city to confront Prime Minister Crow. It was late into the evening, and the large marble coffee table was cluttered with too many cups of tea, coffee, and occasional empty energy drink cans. None of it had helped them in the slightest. The email they'd been asked to write still wasn't captivating enough to capture the attention of the journalists and reporters they had chosen to send it to.

"How about just telling it like it is?" an exhausted Eric suggested.

"Then they'll want proof, which we don't have," an equally tired Sara May replied.

"Then, can't we just tell them to call Pastor Evans?"

"He'd never answer them." Eric groaned with frustration.

"Fine. What do you wanna do?"

"I think it's best just to tip them off. Tell them that human remains were found under the flooring of an old farmer's barn up north, and there are rumours in town that the pastor in town and the nation's Prime Minister are involved."

"You think those pompous capital reporters give a damn about some old pastor in a shitty cesspool up north?"

"That's why we have to mention Crow. They might not give a shit about Evans and Northtown, but as soon as we mention human remains and the Prime Minister in the same sentence, they'll pay attention." Eric sighed as he ran his hand through his hair.

"Fine. Do what you have to do."

Sara May smiled. It was comforting to know that not only did he believe her now, but he also trusted her. She'd been foolish to think she could handle this on her own. The enormity of the case called for cooperation from everyone involved, so having an ally in every corner was vital. Bill and Laura had done a great job of engaging the locals by turning their bakery into the Gossip Inc. Headquarters, where people got the latest news while enjoying their morning pastries. Nana Lou had taken Grandma Gladys under her wing and calmly and rationally explained all that was happening, giving the elder Jensen woman time and space to process the news of her daughter's tragic death. Old Gilbert occasionally dropped by, transforming Nana Lou's place into a lively senior citizens' centre. Their companionship did them good. In strong solidarity, Biggie Mac and the rest of the police force refused to work with Sheriff Bennett. Chris and the Bakers' family had made sure no one went unpaid, securing temporary jobs at the Pizza-Lot, the Bread Box, and the Brewer. Martha and Mary looked after Suzy, keeping her informed, while Jake kept a close eye on his brother, reporting to Decker whenever he could. Maggie tore Chief Chase apart, and Aunt Marie confronted Crow with fierce threats. Sara May couldn't help but tear up with gratitude for all this incredible support, but she didn't cry. Now was not the time to show too much emotion. She had to stay focused.

"How are you feeling?" Eric suddenly asked.

"What do you mean?"

"About all this. Maggie and Helena."

"You mean about Helena being my real mother and not my aunt? About Pastor Evans possibly being my real father and that I'm the unfortunate result of horrific rape and abuse that led to my father murdering my mother?"

"Yeah. That," Eric replied, instantly regretting he even asked. Sara May sighed.

"I don't know, honestly. I haven't allowed myself to think about it. And I won't. Not until this is all over."

The truth was, she didn't want to think about it. Hearing it from Maggie at the Brewer had been such a gut punch; she wasn't sure she'd be able to handle the thought of how this all came about. Suppose she had been the baby in the nightmare, the unwanted result of Pastor Evans forcing himself on Helena and raping her brutally. That fact weighed more on her than a ton of bricks and threatened to shatter her already fragile ego. She couldn't afford to give in to her emotions right now. She had worked too hard to solve this case. If she were to have any hope of justice for Helena, she needed to keep her head above water. But no matter how hard she tried, she couldn't shake off the tangled web of mixed emotions this had stirred up.

"You were never unwanted," she heard Helena whisper as Sara May wiped away a single tear that slid down her cheek.

Chapter 69

After he and Sara May had spent around eight hours crafting the perfect email, Eric sent it out. They carefully selected a few recipients they knew would be interested in the matter and likely to pursue it further. Sara May believed deep down that they'd be successful if they mentioned human remains and Prime Minister Crow in the caption, so that's exactly what Eric had done. After he pressed send, she rang Chris and Sheriff Decker, asking them to spread the word. The case was now out of her hands. It was up to the general public to do what they did best. Exhausted, she quickly fell asleep, secure in Eric's muscular arms. He, however, had not been as fortunate.

As she drifted to sleep, he eased his hold and shifted to the side for a better view. She was stunningly beautiful, yet her dainty face was a porcelain mask, shattered after life's relentless blows. Much had happened since she ran away at eighteen, but his feelings for her had never faltered. He had to learn to love a deeply complex woman, someone who gave more of herself than she had in store. Could he love someone marked with the blood of a murderer? A woman who was the product of the Devil himself? He sensed Sara May hadn't fully realised how twisted this was. Watching her sleep, he traced his finger along her cheek, gently brushing away a stray lock of hair. He knew he had a big task ahead of him that required all the mental strength he could muster. Sara May was unique. She saw things others didn't, which was a power she would hold for the rest of her life. Therefore, he had a choice. He could easily walk away from it all. The rules changed the moment her true identity was revealed. But if he decided to love her despite all that, he would have to accept that her complexity could consume him like fiery flames from hell, and he would have to love and embrace every crackle and spark. She didn't need his help or his protection. She needed a sanctuary amid battles, and he was willing to provide that. He moved closer, wrapped his arms around her once more, and drew her closer. He had made the choice to love her. From this moment forward, with all that it entailed.

Sara May's phone vibrated on the nightstand beside her, waking her up. Half-asleep, she reached for it and pressed the green answer button seconds before Chris became fed up with waiting for a reply. What he had to say woke her up more abruptly than if she'd been slapped in the face. She thanked him, hung up, threw her duvet aside, and sprang out of bed. Eric mumbled in annoyance, being so rudely awakened.

"What the hell is going on with you?" he asked, dazed, his eyes still closed.

"It's everywhere!" she frantically yelled.

"What is? What are you talking about?" He sat up and rubbed his face.

"Our email! It's on every news website in the country! Chris just called; he says it's blowing up the internet!"

That woke Eric up. Quick thinking early in the morning had never been his strong suit, but committing to a racehorse that sprang out of bed without warning didn't leave him much of a choice. She paced back and forth in the bedroom, distressed and agitated.

"Calm down! Why are you so nervous?" Eric asked.

"I can't calm down, Eric! Chris said there is chaos everywhere! We have to do something!"

Eric quickly recognised this as one of those moments when he needed to step up. He swiftly got out of bed and confidently approached the neurotic firecracker he'd chosen to love. He pulled her into his arms and held her tightly until she stopped fighting him and calmed down. He kissed her on the forehead, making sure she was okay.

"There's nothing we can do. This is what we wanted, remember? This is why we sent that email. Now, we'll just have to wait and see what happens."

This seemed to knock some sense into her. Her heart was pounding, and she wanted to run through Northtown's streets to check on everyone and see if Eric was right. But she knew staying at Aunt Marie's place was probably the smartest thing to do for now. Despite hating it there, Aunt Marie had decided to extend her stay in the capital to monitor the rapidly unfolding situation and report any updates. Crow had tried to get hold of her for days, but after the email turned into a major news event, her phone had gone silent. She smiled, knowing that the opposite side had suffered a major blow and was now in crisis mode, holding meetings all over the city.

"Is it true what I'm reading, Crow?" the vice-chairman of his party had asked.

"What the hell, Crow? We´re days away from elections! This will ruin us!" the Minister of Justice had harshly warned, sounding his state of panic.

"Get this under control, Crow! Otherwise, we'll have to hand our jobs over to latte-drinking liberals with some damn hippie agendas!" the Minister of Finance loudly cautioned.

Chief Chase had switched off his phone, making it impossible to reach him. All his calls went unanswered, and he smoothly avoided talking to anyone outside his trusted inner circle. In his humble opinion, he hadn't done anything wrong, so it was highly unjust that his good name was being dragged through the mud like this.

His only offence was helping Prime Minister Crow resolve this minor issue. He'd simply helped a good friend in need; he had just done him a favour. A favour that had, since then, repeatedly benefited him throughout his lucrative career as police chief. There was nothing wrong with that. The snowflakes, now outraged and feeling betrayed and unfairly treated, were being overly sensitive. They obviously had never helped a friend in need.

While Crow cursed Chase for not answering his calls, he desperately tried to extinguish the raging fires across the country. Feeling like a multitasking octopus, he had sent his loyalists to minimise the damage caused by the email. But it was becoming increasingly clear that the public wasn't settling for hazy, nonsensical answers. They demanded the truth, and Crow felt like had been thrown naked onto the battlefield. There was no way to reach Evans; that psychotic peacock had been mentally offline for weeks. As the day went on, the Establishment began to feel the effects of the shake-up in the financial markets, and the reactions from those involved did little to ease the situation. The numbers were in free fall, causing the wealthiest one per cent to check their pulses constantly. The media frenzy fed the public's insatiable appetite for updates, with news websites refreshed every five minutes. Society was in uproar, prompting Prime Minister Crow and his party members to break into a sweat. Some had already begun to sever ties with their beloved chairman to save their own skin. Others had decided to weather the storm, but Crow's repeated lies in office had created a cry-wolf scenario, making it difficult to convince the furious public that he was now telling the truth.

Mrs Crow had reached out to Paula, who was fighting her own battle with battered credibility and no husband to lean on. She advised Mrs Crow that her best chance was to spread the lie that the woman who sent the infamous email was a mentally unstable individual who had it out for Pastor Evans because of her hatred of Christianity. She told Mrs Crow about Sara May's accident, suggesting she use it as proof that she wasn't to be taken seriously. Mrs Crow clung to every word and quickly sent out her own email to every news outlet in the country, hoping it would turn things around. The situation had become so volatile that foreign news outlets had started to pick up the story, further increasing the nation's outrage and calls for action. Nobody, not even his voters, could bear the thought of their Prime Minister being involved in such a horrific crime—helping a country pastor conceal the body of a young woman he'd killed, then using his influence as a powerful politician to cover it up. The police chief had been aware but deliberately kept it quiet to secure his position as an MP's puppet.

"They're trying to paint you as crazy. That you shouldn't be taken seriously," Sheriff Decker had cautioned Sara May.

"That was predictable," Jake muttered under his breath.

"They're becoming desperate," said Biggie Mac proudly.

"Let them talk. The media isn't dropping this anytime soon. This will be investigated down to the last drop of blood spilt until they discover the truth," Eric stated, infuriated that his girlfriend's name was being dragged through the mud.

Sara May sat quietly in the corner of the Brewer, listening in. She felt the storm raging all around her. She knew she was being called insane and an attention-seeking whore, among other things. Some blamed the blow to her head; others said that her unstable home life growing up was the cause of her vicious attack on the Prime Minister, turning her into a shameless anarchist who rejected the laws of society. All this had caused her to withdraw. She needed to build her strength and not let the public's opinion of her tear her down. She had to shut down her insecurity and focus on her final goal. It wasn't enough that the media was ripping Evans, Crow and Chase to shreds. It wasn't enough that the very foundations of society were crumbling. No. This was more personal. She knew what she had to do. And she was the one who had to do it.

Chapter 70

After an eventful day, night was quickly falling. The elite was in an uproar, the government teetered on the edge of collapse, and anyone with ties to the now-tainted Prime Minister was frantically running in circles like headless chickens. The rats deserted the sinking ship in abundance, leaving few willing to show loyalty to Crow. Every news outlet in the country was on high alert, sending their best reporters to dig up any detail they could find about this mysterious case that had turned the nation on its head. Was it simply someone making a mountain out of a molehill, just a crazy woman obsessed with the church? Or was it a disturbing truth that the nation had to confront—that their own Prime Minister was indeed caught up in the most scandalous incident to shake the government in modern times? People often had to bow and kiss the ring in the hopes of being awarded a few bread slices from those in charge but, more often than not, had to settle for nothing but measly crumbs. Everyone knew corruption flowed more freely in the country than champagne at a wealthy person's party, with little resistance from the public. But this was a much bigger problem than the suppressed nation was used to. It was a disaster of epic proportions, so heavy that it nearly overwhelmed the country's moral sense.

The public demanded that Prime Minister Crow resign. He, however, had decided to do the same as his friend in Northtown and lock himself in his office, hoping the situation would soon blow over. Most of his party members had already turned their backs on him, aside from a few sycophants who had decided to stick by him, hoping he would somehow steer the ship to shore and continue the financially lucrative feast they had all grown accustomed to. The government had been in back-to-back meetings all day, trying to stabilise the financial markets and establish an independent committee to investigate police procedures internally. Chief Chase had been placed on sabbatical while the investigation was underway, and officials in Northtown had been told to expect a visit from government officials to assess the town's situation. In the eye of the storm stood Sara May, with her clenched fists and her head held high. She had only one goal. After pushing Jack against a wall to force him to reveal what he knew, she discovered Pastor Evans was now hiding in the church. Of course, he was. Damn coward.

She marched towards the church, more determined than ever. It was quite a long walk, but she didn't mind. Nothing mattered anymore except justice for Helena and Simon. She was angry, which made her feel invisible. She was furious, which made her feel unstoppable. As she stomped down the old country road, the darkness of night shrouded her surroundings, giving them a ghostly, terrifying feel. It didn't affect her. She had deliberately kept her destination secret to protect others. This was a matter between her and Pastor Evans. It was a battle between the two. She'd been warned not to approach the pastor, but she wasn't afraid of him. Helena walked confidently beside her, giving her strength. She wasn't scared because she had the truth on her side. As she neared the church, she saw light shining from its windows. It was unusual because the church had been closed since the pastor's mental health had started to decline rapidly. Many locals blamed Sara May for this. They accused her of being responsible for their beloved pastor's condition, claiming it was her fault he hadn't led a Sunday service for weeks. Such sacrilege was bound to throw the town's moral compass into disarray. Some even accused her of being the Devil's tool, sent to destroy the Christian faith in Northtown. None of that bothered her anymore.

She had been physically and mentally strengthening herself for days. Chris and Eric had pulled her into the gym, teaching her some much-needed self-defence techniques and helping her lift weights to better prepare her for anything that might happen. Nana Lou had taught her prayers and sat with her through guided meditation, overseeing her progress as a person with a supernatural gift. She called on those who had assigned her this task, asking them to guide Sara May with her newfound powers. As a result, she now stood in front of the church's closed doors, fully prepared to face whatever awaited her. What she saw was both beautiful and horrifying at the same time. Pastor Evans had lit hundreds of candles of all sizes scattered across the wooden church, raising the temperature to match that in Hell. The light was surprisingly gentle, but the eerie silence it brought reminded Sara May of an open grave. At the end of the aisle, in front of the altar, Pastor Evans sat on a creaky old chair with a half-empty vodka bottle in one hand and a sharp dagger in the other. He was dressed in his clerical vestments, his grey hair looked messy and unwashed, like a mad scientist, and his beard hadn't been trimmed in days. He stared at the floor with a hellish smirk, eyes wide and crazed. It was as if some demonic creature had taken over his body because nothing about this person reminded Sara May of the pastor who once stood at that altar and preached about love and kindness for all. He suddenly let out a bizarre chuckle, and once again, she could see the dark, misty smoke surrounding him. With two fingers pressed together, he coaxed her closer to him.

"Come here, Sara May Jensen," he said, continuing to grin from ear to ear.

She stood her ground but was helpless against the fear that now bound her with shackles and grounded her feet. Then, she felt warmth envelop her. Unseen forces reminded her that nothing could harm her here—the church belonged to God. And He stood for nothing but kindness and positive force. This was the holy temple of love; evil wouldn't thrive on sacred ground. With that in mind, she closed her eyes briefly and took a deep breath before opening them again and walking confidently towards Pastor Evans. She stopped only a few feet from him. She didn't recognise the person who stared so blankly into her soul. His eyes were darkened with hatred that fizzled within him. But he recognised hers. They were the eyes of Helena Jensen.

"I knew you'd come. So predictable," he laughed.

"It's over, Evans. Everybody knows what you did," she warned him.

"Do they now?" he sarcastically asked as he slowly stood up. "I guess I'm not as good a liar as I thought."

"Why did you do this?" Sara May asked, somewhat surprised at how brazen she was, given the seriousness of the situation. Again, Evans laughed. He turned away from her and slowly walked up to the altar. Deranged with blinding rage, he suddenly threw the vodka bottle at the altarpiece, loudly smashing it into pieces.

"Because that filthy whore didn't want me! She thought she was too good for me!" he yelled, facing Sara

May, who didn't step back. That stunt of his had enraged her even more.

"So, you went after Paula instead? Because she was financially well off and suited your agenda? Was it she who told everyone that Helena was sleeping with married men?" Pastor Evans smirked, showing his yellowish teeth, causing Sara May to gag.

"The flesh is weak. Paula wouldn't allow me to touch her before the wedding. I was young and horny, so I took what belonged to me! What I was entitled to! She fought me, but she was too young to understand that I was simply loving her. Nine months later, I found out the bitch had given birth to a bloody bastard!"

"Is that why you killed her? Because of me? Then why didn't you kill Suzy?"

"Because she could blame her crotch goblins on Simon. No one questioned that."

"You killed Helena because she was single?" Evans chuckled.

"I couldn't be the main character of my own deception, Sara May. But I made a mistake. I spared you."

"You murdered my mother. You think you'll be shown mercy just because you allowed me to live?"

"That's up to God, I guess." Pastor Evans shrugged.

"You don't believe in God! You never have! That's another one of your damn lies because who's going to believe that God's servant is actually the Devil's puppet?" Sara May yelled back, her blood boiling with uncontrollable anger, which deepened as she looked at Evans's infuriating grin.

"Well, if that's the case, then my actions truly don't matter now, do they? I spared you! But you're not a baby anymore, Sara May. So, now I must do what I should have done thirty-one years ago!"

Before she could react, Pastor Evans let out a demonic roar as he lunged towards her, wielding the dagger. Helena was a step ahead and positioned herself in front of her daughter, trying to prevent her from sharing the same fate. But, no longer made of flesh and blood, there was little she could do. Instead, she hurried out of the church, trying to find a way to alert Chris and Eric, who were among those frantically searching for Sara May. After discovering she was missing, Sheriff Decker alerted the group, convinced her life was in grave danger, and she needed to be found immediately. Helena then focused her energy on Nana Lou. The old lady was receptive enough to receive her message telepathically. Nana Lou rushed to find Sheriff Decker, telling him that Sara May was with the pastor at the church. Deker assembled the crowd, sending a stream of cars racing along the country road, breaking all possible speed limits. That was a matter for later. When they finally arrived at the church, Chris and Eric jumped out of the car and hurried to break open the door.

What they faced as they entered sent a shockwave of terror and fury through their bodies. Pastor Evans had thrown the dagger away and was now sitting on top of Sara May's lifeless body, his hands griping her neck tightly. His forehead was dripping with sweat, and his whole body shook with the intense rage of a man who had completely lost all touch with reality. Both men charged at him and tackled him to the ground, just as the rest of the group burst into the candle-lit church that now looked more like Satan's secret lair. After Chris had thrown a few punches at the pastor, Sheriff Decker pulled his son away. Eric hurried to Sara May's side, administering mouth-to-mouth resuscitation and a few gentle slaps on her cheek, but to no effect. As he desperately tried to wake her, he felt his body go numb with disbelief. He wasn't ready to lose her. He couldn't bear to lose her. Sobbing uncontrollably and shouting at her to wake up, he was dragged back by Biggie Mac, who was strong enough to hold him, while the women tended to Sara May, who was still unconscious on the floor. Chaos erupted. Bill and Sheriff Decker held Pastor Evans down while Decker called the rest of the police force in Northtown. Laura and Martha struggled to wake Sara May, while Nana Lou and Mary comforted Maggie, who was inconsolable by this point, crying hysterically and calling her daughter's name. Nothing worked. Sara May's soul was far away.

Chapter 71

Sara May slowly opened her eyes, looking around in a daze. At first, everything was foggy. When her eyes adjusted, she could see the outlines of tall buildings around her. This was all too familiar. She'd been here before. Except then, everything had been white as snow, completely drained of all colour. But now, the buildings and their surroundings displayed every colour of the rainbow, so bright and beautiful it was like the sun shone from within each item she could see. She'd never seen anything like it; the colours were somehow brighter and more prismatic than she had ever known, almost psychedelic. One building displayed a mixture of silky sapphire and vibrant lilac, while the one beside it had a perfect blend of ruby-red and gold. The buildings still stood neatly next to each other, just as they had before. In front of them were the smoothest pavements Sara May had ever seen; they looked like marble, decorated with multi-coloured trees and benches. Last time, she had only seen white trams running back and forth, seemingly without purpose, and a handful of people all dressed in white. Now, the street was filled with life. The trams were painted in various hues and packed with happy people. The pavements were busy as well. Those who had been dressed in white robes before were now wearing colourful clothing, each more mesmerising than the last. Sara May could feel the love and happiness radiate from them. Everyone had something to be cheerful about. It was so unbelievably beautiful and loving.

She turned around. Was she dreaming? It didn't feel like a dream. Yet she didn't feel awake either. It was all so strange. Despite her best efforts, she couldn't work out where she was. She didn't feel pain. She wasn't hungry. She didn't feel anything at all except that odd weightlessness. All of a sudden, she noticed a woman approaching her. She recognised her. The same woman had given her that enormous task the last time she was in this bizarre city. The same warm, angelic light surrounded her as before. Her smile made Sara May tingle. What a strange sensation this was. In the blink of an eye, the woman stood before her in all her glory, smiling from ear to ear.

"You've done good, Sara May. Helena is very grateful, and so are we."

"Did I help her?"

"You sure did," the woman replied with a motherly tone.

"What about Simon? Where is he?"

"Don't worry about him. He is being well taken care of." Sara May sighed with relief.

"Is this Heaven? Can I stay here?" The woman let out a chuckle.

"This is your version of Heaven. But no, you can't stay here. It's not your time yet."

The woman extended her hand. Sara May hesitated, reluctant to return. She had never felt so loved and at peace as she did at that moment. Yet deep down, she knew it wasn't up to her. Reluctantly, she grasped the woman's hand, and in a flash, she was back. She opened her eyes and gasped. That was when she realised she was in a hospital bed, connected to all kinds of wires and monitors. Maggie and Paige sat on the right side of her bed. On the left side sat Eric. As she gasped, all three hurried to her side, fighting back tears of joy that she had finally woken. She was still dazed and confused about what had happened, but she recognised her loved ones immediately. They were the reason she had been sent back; she needed to be with them. Later that day, after the doctors completed various tests to ensure no lasting damage, she was allowed a much-needed conversation with the trio in her room.

Maggie explained that she had been airlifted to hospital and rushed into surgery. The doctors had just about managed to save her life. She had been kept in a medically induced coma for just over a week to prevent any possible brain damage and to give her body a chance to heal from the horrific ordeal in the church. When she was unconscious, her name became known to every man, woman, and child in the country. She was recognised as the woman who blew up the government and held the Prime Minister, the Chief of Police, and a pastor accountable for their despicable actions. She was hailed as a hero by those who had fought against a broken system and demanded their voice be heard. Putting herself in harm's way to seek justice for a victim of sexual abuse inspired many other victims to fight even harder against a rigged system that had oppressed them for too long and refused to believe them.

Protests erupted as people demanded an investigation into the upper echelons of society and a re-examination of the country's rules and laws. Paula and Mrs Crow had gone into hiding, and Sara May had gained many powerful enemies. But she had the nation's support, so it would be a cause for celebration when the media reported that she was awake. Pastor Evans was arrested on the night of the attack. He was now in custody, along with the former Prime Minister Crow, who had been stripped of his titles and shamefully expelled from the party he once led. Chief Chase was also dismissed and was now under intense surveillance. The events of the past week had shaken society's pillars so violently that decades of corruption now threatened to engulf all those who had so greedily benefited from it.

Sara May didn't care about her new hero status or the admiration. She was pleased to hear that the toxic trio was being held by the firm arm of the Lady of Justice, who never discriminated. It was nice to know that the truth had prevailed. It was a relief to know she wasn't being viewed as a mentally ill psychopath with ill intentions. Of course, there were still those who firmly believed that she hated religion and linked this directly to the decline of Christianity in Iceland. None of this mattered to her. She only cared that Helena had received her long-overdue justice and her honour had been restored. She looked around but couldn't see her anywhere.

A few days later, she was cleared by the doctors and allowed to return home. It was an unusually sunny winter day. The grey clouds had dispersed, letting the sun's rays shine brightly and illuminate everything they touched. It made the freshly fallen snow sparkle, and the cool, crisp air made each breath feel invigorating. The bare, delicate tree branches bowed under the weight of the snow, giving the whole scene an enchanted feel. Sara May stood outside her childhood home, admiring the colourful Christmas lights that reflected off the snow in front of the house. She felt good. The worries and anxiety that had troubled her for weeks had completely disappeared, leaving only pure happiness. It was as if she was floating on a soft cloud of total calm. Everything suddenly felt so magical that she struggled to put it into words. For the first time in a long while, she welcomed the silence. Maggie stepped out of the house, and together they sat in her car and drove to Aunt Marie's mansion to pick up her and Grandma Gladys, who had been living with her oldest daughter since everything came to light.

The car ride was silent. Predictable, Sara May thought to herself. Despite the case being solved, there were still many things left for the Jensen women to deal with. Thirty-one years of anger, humiliation, and frustration wouldn't disappear overnight. This marked the beginning of their healing journey; each would have to navigate it at their own pace. It would undoubtedly be helpful to sit down and discuss the events of the past few weeks, but she chose not to push it. It would happen when the time was right. She thought of Grandma Gladys, who sat in the passenger seat and gazed out the front window—that poor old lady. Sara May felt a wave of guilt towards her. She was so old and fragile. The fact that her whole life had been shattered without warning must have been quite a shock to her. She had to re-evaluate everything she had ever believed to be true and reconsider her stance on her youngest daughter, whom she'd always thought of as nothing but a damned troublemaker.

After what seemed like an eternity, Aunt Maggie's car finally stopped. She opened the boot and took out a large, green bag. The remaining Jensen women had decided that Helena's bones should be buried again, just as they would have been if everything were normal. They also chose not to accept the church's help in burying the bones in a cemetery because they all felt the church had completely failed them. Despite Pastor Evans being dismissed from his position and expelled from Northtown for good, many still regarded him as a man of God. Because he was at the root of this whole affair, the Jensen women couldn't bear the thought of the church being involved in their healing in any way. This was their recovery, the beginning of their journey toward a better future, and that, in Grandma Gladys's words, wasn't any of their Goddamn business! Given the circumstances, they requested that Helena's remains be exempt from burial in sacred ground as the law specified. Their request was granted, and Maggie asked Chris and Eric to dig a grave beneath the big oak tree that had stood a mile out of town for as long as anyone could remember. It had been the sisters' favourite play spot when they were children. It felt like the perfect place.

It was a therapeutic moment for all of them. The sun shone down on them, enveloping them like a mother's comforting arms, and made the snow glisten so beautifully that it appeared almost as if it were covered with a million tiny stars. Aunt Marie lowered the green bag containing her sister's bones into the open grave and was then assisted by Maggie in filling it with soil and dirt. Sara May stood beside her grandmother, offering her support. Unexpectedly, the old lady grasped her hand and squeezed it tightly. Sara May could feel her cold hand trembling. It was an emotional moment. Grandma Gladys then approached the grave and placed two red roses on top. Eric had promised her he would make a cross, an offer she had gladly accepted. Now, she was kneeling beside her youngest daughter's grave, sobbing uncontrollably, causing Sara May's heart to ache for her. It was traumatic to watch this frail elderly woman realise for the first time that her child was truly gone. That she had slipped through her fingers and endured all this pain and hurt alone.

"I'm so sorry, my baby! I failed you! I should have been there for you! I should have listened!" she wailed.

All of a sudden, their surroundings illuminated as if someone had turned the sun to its highest setting. The women had to turn away to protect their eyes, feeling overwhelmed by the brightness. When they managed to look again, they couldn't believe what was before them. Next to her grave stood Helena. Smiling, she placed her hand on her mother's shoulder. Grandma Gladys rose without taking her eyes off this beautiful creature of light that had once been her daughter.

"Mother. You did nothing wrong," Helena reminded her in a soft tone.

Stunned, none of them spoke a word. Maggie finally understood how Sara May had managed to uncover all those well-hidden secrets that had plagued Northtown for so long. It had seemed so unbelievable, but now everything was falling into place. Standing before her baby sister, seeing her shine brighter than the sun itself, didn't feel weird. Helena slowly approached Sara May, who was just as amazed as the other women. She'd never seen Helena look like this. She caressed her cheek and brushed a lock of her hair away from her face, evoking the same warmth she had felt as a baby in her arms.

"My daughter," she said, smiling as she proudly studied Sara May's face. "Thank you for everything. I can go home now." Two single tears rolled down Sara May's cheeks. "Don't cry for me. You did good," Helena reassured her as she wiped away the tears.

"You sacrificed yourself for me. I'm gonna miss you so much," Sara May wept in grief.

"I'll always be with you, my baby girl. Always."

Sara May looked over Helena's shoulder and

recognised a familiar face. It was the mysterious woman from her dreams—the nurse who had fluffed her pillow at the hospital after her accident. The being of light that had given her this significant task, and then congratulated her on a job well done. She smiled as Helena walked towards her. As she took her place beside the angelic woman, she cast one last loving glance at the women in her family, sending them a reassuring sign of love and promising never to be far away. After confirming they would be okay, she took the angelic woman's hand, and together, they vanished into a bright ball of light that disappeared just as quickly as it had appeared.

"Bye, Mum," Sara May whispered, allowing the tears to flow freely.

Chapter 72

Sara May sat by the living room table in her new flat, gazing out the window. The sun was shining once more, brightening everything in its path. The navy-blue sky had cleared away the rainy clouds, allowing the yellow sun to embrace the world with warmth and kindness. It was almost like being on another planet. Suddenly, Sara May sensed movement behind her. She turned round and saw Helena sitting in a light brown leather chair, dressed in a beautiful rosy-red dress and matching slippers, similar to those of a ballerina. Her light, wavy hair shimmered, and her smile looked so lovely that it seemed to be made of pure gold. Sara May smiled back, then walked over to a large bookcase, pulled out a manuscript, and handed it to Helena.

"I'm writing a book, Mum," she proudly announced.

Helena looked through the pages, still radiating a maternal smile that made Sara May melt with feelings of love and security. She had found her mum. She was home. After a moment, Helena looked up from the book, closed it, and handed it back to Sara May.

"It's good. It's excellent."

"I'm so glad. Your opinion means the world to me. You're my supernatural editor," said Sara May, pleased with her mother's response.

As she let go of those words, she woke up. She had fallen asleep without realising it. After gathering her thoughts, she looked around. She had often fallen asleep like this, but when she woke up, she was so disoriented she didn't even know which planet she was on. But not this time. She felt at ease, knowing that her mum had visited her and approved of her book, reassuring her that this was the story she was meant to tell the world. She had risked everything to solve her mother's case and help her cross over. That had garnered widespread attention, and the nation craved more details. Sara May hadn't realised it until suddenly it became so clear. Helena's story was the story she was meant to write about, to tell the world. She was destined for great things in this life. She was meant to help lost souls find their way home by sharing their stories because they were the nation's stories. They had once been part of a society that had forgotten them. Their stories were the forgotten tombstones that nobody cared for anymore. Their stories were the rocks and hills that held more secrets than anyone could ever know. Helena had been one of those people. A young and innocent woman was about to start her life when she fell victim to pure evil, but now her honour was restored. Her story had to be told. As Sara May began writing, Helena visited her daughter through her dreams more than once.

"Mum, I'm going to write a book!" she had told her, beaming with pride.

"I know, darling," Helena had replied, radiating happiness and affection.

Sara May wrote the last few words, closed the laptop, and looked at the living room. Sitting in front of the TV, discussing the latest development in their favourite TV show, were her new flatmate, Eric, and her two best friends, Chris and Paige, who had unexpectedly found love amidst all this chaos. She smiled. The sun was shining, just like in her dream. She didn't know why but felt it had started doing that more often than before, given that it was still January. Her whole outlook on life had changed. The entire atmosphere had shifted for the better.

The people of Northtown had been freed from the crippling burden of secrets and lies, the guilty party was in prison, and Helena and Simon were being looked after on the other side. Everything was as it was meant to be. Aunt Marie had even promised her niece that the book would be published; she would make sure of it.

"What good is it to have all these connections if I can't use them to my advantage?" she had gleefully boasted.

The relationship between Maggie and Sara May had likewise never been better. Sara May had decided that the latest revelation didn't change anything. Maggie hadn't done anything wrong. She had done everything right. Her life had been turned upside down one fateful evening when she was just a young girl in her late twenties. For thirty-one years, she had carried the heavy cross of knowing that it could all come crashing down one day. It had destroyed her marriage and put her life on hold for over three decades while she navigated motherhood, caring for a demanding and challenging girl whom she had not asked for. But she had never complained. Instead, she had tackled it like a pro, mostly on her own. Sara May felt she owed it to her to show her understanding.

Grandma Gladys also deserved forgiveness. From her perspective, despite many objections, it was easy to sympathise with her. She had been led to believe that her youngest daughter was a sex-obsessed tramp who had run around, sleeping with married men and bringing shame to her family, before ultimately fleeing. To Grandma Gladys, Helena had abandoned her newborn, and by doing so, she not only ran from her responsibilities as a mother but also failed to take accountability for her dreadful actions. This shaped Grandma Gladys's outlook on life, making her angry and hostile towards everyone and everything that reminded her of that painful time, including Sara May. Seeing things this way, she overcame most of the hurt caused by her grandmother's aggressive behaviour. She simply didn't know any better and behaved according to the information she had been given for the past thirty-one years, which wasn't her fault. But now, times had changed, bringing a whole new and better understanding and appreciation of life. Sara May stood up from the living room table. The coffee had gone cold.

THE END

About the Author

Kat K is an Icelandic author based in the UK who has been writing stories since childhood. She graduated with a Bachelor's degree in media and communication at the age of 29, and went on to work as a journalist in Iceland before moving to the UK in 2017 to study scriptwriting at Bournemouth University.

After obtaining a master's degree from BU, Kat wrote her first novel, *The Skeleton Sisters,* followed by its sequel, *The Skeleton Sisters II: The Road Back to Ridgefield.* Since then, Kat has written several scripts, attended writing festivals and literature lectures. *The Day She Died* is her third book, published by Blossom Spring Publishing.

www.blossomspringpublishing.com

www.ingramcontent.com/pod-product-compliance
Lightning Source LLC
Chambersburg PA
CBHW020829030726
47496CB00001B/158